A MADMAN'S DEFENSE

A MADMAN'S DEFENSE

(*Le plaidoyer d'un fou*)

by August Strindberg

Translation Based on Ellie Schleussner's
Version, *The Confession of a Fool*
Revised and Edited by
Evert Sprinchorn

ANCHOR BOOKS
DOUBLEDAY & COMPANY, INC.
GARDEN CITY, NEW YORK
1967

A NOTE ON THIS TRANSLATION

Le plaidoyer d'un fou was originally published in France by Albert Langen in 1895. The book first appeared in English in 1912 under the title *The Confession of a Fool*, translated by Ellie Schleussner and published by Stephen Swift and Co., London. This was reprinted in 1913 by Methuen in London, in the same year by Small, Maynard & Co. in Boston, and again in 1925 by Viking Press, Inc., New York. Schleussner apparently based her translation on the German *Die Beichte eines Toren*, translated by Emil Schering (Munich: Georg Müller, 1909), as part of the German edition of Strindberg's collected works. Unfortunately, Schering took many liberties with Strindberg's text and these are repeated by Schleussner.

The version printed here is based on the Schleussner translation, but it has been thoroughly revised by comparing it with the French *Le plaidoyer* and with two Swedish translations: that prepared by John Landquist and Erik Staaff (Stockholm: Albert Bonniers Förlag, 1925) and that of Tage Aurell (Stockholm: Albert Bonniers Förlag, 1962).

The original French *Le plaidoyer* was reissued in Paris by Mercure de France, 1964.

Material based on the Ellie Schleussner translation of *The Confession of a Fool* is reprinted by permission of Methuen & Co., Ltd.

The Anchor Books edition is the first publication of Evert Sprinchorn's new translation of *A Madman's Defense*

Anchor Books edition: 1967

CONTENTS

CONTENTS

INTRODUCTION

TRUTH AND POETRY

Strindberg called his *Madman's Defense* a terrible book; readers are more likely to find it exasperating. Strindberg was not trying to write a book that would produce one of the conventional artistic effects, such as those associated with tragedy, melodrama, comedy, sentimental stories, horror tales, and so on. A novel by Zola, for instance, calls for a different reader attitude than a story by Poe, and what Strindberg gives us is, in a sense, Zola and Poe simultaneously. Consequently, the reader does not know whether he should identify with Strindberg's hero and be gripped by his mental collapse or stand comparatively aloof from the action, observing it with the detached curiosity of a scientist or a reporter. Not that Strindberg was trying to mix styles, but he was deliberately violating certain artistic conventions. He wanted to create a kind of novel more realistic than Flaubert's and more scientific or "experimental" than Zola's. Having learned from them in the past, Strindberg now wanted to improve on them. The French realists and naturalists constructed their novels by consulting newspaper reports, police files, medical journals, and seed catalogues; and the most crucial moments in their stories—those of suicide, murder, and rape, for example—were based on nothing more than educated guesses, or simply made out of whole cloth by a powerful imagination. The Swedish author wanted to bring literature and life into closer correspondence. If literature were to have any utilitarian value, there should be less guesswork in it. Therefore, one should write about the life that one knows most about, one's own. It was this line of reasoning that led Strindberg to begin writing his autobiography in 1886 when he was still only in his thirties.

By July 27 he had finished three volumes, which carried the story of his life from the circumstances of his birth in 1849 to that "fateful stroke of fortune" that sent him in 1875 to Number 12 Northgate Street in Stockholm, where he met the woman who was to become his wife. While still at work on the third volume, Strindberg wrote to his publisher Bonnier to discuss plans for the next volume:

> What volume 4 should contain is not quite settled. The proper thing would be to march right ahead and include this unusual and highly dramatic story [of my marriage] as part of my evolutionary history, but, unfortunately, one does not possess exclusive proprietary rights over one's experiences, and the peace and happiness of many people would be at stake if I followed that course. However, there are other important considerations, and the question is whether the personal interests of a few individuals should prevent a whole life story, truthfully told, from seeing the light of day for once. I have sacrificed all my peace and privacy and given myself completely to my flock; why shouldn't others also give a little of themselves for a good and worthy cause? As you can see, my autobiography is no *Ehrenrettung* or whitewash; it is an analysis of the soul, psychological anatomy.
>
> My wife and I have often thought that for our own sakes and that of our children we should publish, anonymously and without mentioning any names, our correspondence during the crucial year 1876 under the title *He and She*. Reading over these remarkable documents that fill a whole volume, I found them so interesting in themselves, so well written, in part so beautiful, and reflecting so much credit on all those concerned, that they could very well be read by the public not as an attempt at a whitewash but as

a novel with human interest, and not fictionalized or prearranged but actually lived and experienced. If I were to go back to constructing a novel now, it would be colored by new points of view and would be untruthful. (Letter to Bonnier, June 21, 1886.)

When he sent the *He and She* letters to his publisher, Strindberg argued that they would make a better work than a novel, since "a novel would always look like a self-defense and would provide the occasion for denials and misinterpretations, and would not be in style with the great and unique work I have so far carried out" in the first three volumes of the autobiography. He then went on to add:

It disgusts me to be nothing but an artist. My intelligence has evolved from daydreaming to thinking. The deliberate summoning up of hallucinations at the writing desk seems like masturbation to me. The novel and the theater are about right for the ladies; let them take charge of these entertainments.

It is this battle against my calling that is undermining my health. I have seen through the shams of fiction writing, and I have no illusions about it. That's why I cannot work in that vein any more. (Letter to Bonnier, August 9, 1886.)

The proposed volume was to tell the story of Strindberg's affair with Siri von Wrangel (née Essen) and would consist of the letters that had passed between them. Since Siri wrote these letters while she was still married to Baron Wrangel, who was himself romantically involved with another woman, the correspondence contained highly inflammable material that could not be rendered safe simply by replacing the names with three asterisks, as Strindberg suggested. Having been prosecuted two years previously, albeit unsuccessfully, for transmitting to the reading public a blasphemous remark in one of Strindberg's stories, the publisher Bonnier, once burned and twice shy, immediately rejected Strindberg's proposal. Strindberg then

wrote *The Author*, which dealt with the intellectual background of his works during the period 1877 to 1887. This
replaced *He and She* as the fourth volume in "The Story
of the Evolution of a Human Being." However, Bonnier
also rejected this manuscript on the ground that Strindberg had exercised no restraint in attacking the younger
generation of writers.

Well over a year after Bonnier refused to print *He and
She*, Strindberg's attitude toward the novel as a genre was
the same. The novel is "false," he said.

> We really know only fragments of the lives of others,
> and the only novels we can write are those about our
> own lives. That is why *The Son of a Servant* repre-
> sented the literature of the future; it pictured a certain
> human being and a certain epoch. . . . I have to
> write for those who understand me and according to
> my own thoughts, even at the risk of going unpub-
> lished. Since the ephemeral political and social ques-
> tions, so-called, no longer hold any attraction for me,
> I'm hoping to bring about an artistic-psychological
> series of works, which should be capable of interesting
> both me and my public.

This letter was written on December 22, 1887, when he
had finished perhaps a third or more of *A Madman's Defense*, though he is referring primarily to other works
that were in the planning stage. The autobiographical
novel was finished three months later, in March 1888.
Knowing that this slightly disguised story of his marriage
had no chance of being published in Sweden as long as
the chief participants were still alive; aware that by pur-
suing his own aims in literature he was alienating himself from the Swedish public; and probably deliberately
challenging comparison with the psychological novels of
Zola, Bourget and the Goncourt brothers, Strindberg had
written it in French and called it first *Histoire de mon
mariage* and later *Le plaidoyer d'un fou*.

This fifth volume in his autobiography differs from the

earlier ones in three seemingly superficial but quite significant respects. Not only is it written in French instead of Swedish, but Strindberg's alter ego has changed his name from John to Axel: a different persona has been adopted. Furthermore, the book is devoted to a single subject, love and jealousy, whereas the previous volumes pictured the hero as passing through several stages of life and as the focal point of a number of environmental and hereditary forces. These superficial differences suggest a major change of intention and method from those of *The Son of a Servant*. The tone of the latter is dry and unemotional, the prose is flat and economical. The tone of the *Defense* is supercharged with emotion of one kind or another, and its prose is overrich. The words are not weighed but spewed forth. In *The Son of a Servant* the reader is asked to respond to a rather sober presentation of events and facts. In *A Madman's Defense* the reader is compelled to respond to an emotional hurricane of growing intensity in which facts are uprooted and dispassion overwhelmed.

What brought about the change? And how could Strindberg justify to himself the fact that he had (apparently) abandoned his former position on the truthfulness of the novel and had reworked the material pertaining to his marriage into that despised form? There are two answers. The first has to do with Strindberg's economic situation, and the other with the way in which a writer like Strindberg makes his life into an artwork.

I am not saying that Strindberg wrote the *Defense* to make money. From his letters it is clear that by the time he had finished writing it he did not even want it to be published. But his steadily worsening financial condition, his failure to sell his works put him in the proper frame of mind for writing this bitter novel. Very little money had come Strindberg's way after he stood trial in 1884 for the "blasphemous" remarks in *Married,* a volume of short stories. Though he was acquitted, publishers were disinclined to print what he wrote, and, in turn, his work became more immoderate in tone as he felt increasingly persecuted by women (who instigated the trial), by publishers (who were parasites living off authors), by other writers (who were deluded feminists and Ibsenites), and by the public (who were sheep without minds of their own). Like Rousseau, whom he resembles in many respects, Strindberg had a persecution complex. Perhaps he had more cause: he saw enemies all around him because they were all around him. "That you as an author," wrote his publisher Bonnier, "are suffering an unfortunate unpopularity, an unpopularity without parallel, is a fact that cannot be unfamiliar to you, although, living far from home [Strindberg had left Sweden in 1883 and had been living in France and Switzerland], you cannot possibly imagine how terrible the situation really is." (Letter of July 25, 1887.)

And the situation was indeed terrible. In March 1887 John Personne, a doctor of divinity, had published a pamphlet, *The Strindberg Literature and Immorality Among Our School Children*, which attacked Strindberg for trying to "provide for himself and his family by publicly smearing his wife," and which accused Strindberg's publisher Bonnier of being no better than "a brothelkeeper and a fence." On top of that had come, in April, the stormy meeting of the Swedish Association of Publishers at which the chairman, Albert Bonnier, was harshly criticized for issuing Strindberg's works. A great number of the members had walked out of the meeting in protest against Bonnier, and formed their own association.

In the meantime, Strindberg's marriage to Siri was breaking up, a process that began about the time of his trial for blasphemy in 1884. Although in the spring of 1887 he could describe his life as idyllic, on August 5 he began a long letter to a close friend by saying, "So the comedy of my marriage is over after ten years of delights and annoyances." (Letter to Pehr Staaff) The rest of the letter sets the stage for *A Madman's Defense*. The suspicion that Siri is hiding something from him, the certainty that others know what the husband is always the last to know, the willingness to put the worst construction on trivial incidents, such as his wife's going to Dr. Forssberg for a massage, and the insistence on knowing that his wife has been unfaithful in order that he may have peace of mind—all is there. The whole letter is like a chapter from the novel.

A week later Strindberg sent an application for divorce to Stockholm; but nothing came of this since the parties were not residing in Sweden. (In the back of his mind did not Strindberg know what answer he would get? Almost certainly.) About a month later Strindberg began to write *A Madman's Defense*.

AN ACTOR CREATES

If we consider Strindberg only as a husband, it seems clear that he wrote the book because his marriage was on the rocks and he saw no way to save it. However, if we consider Strindberg the creative artist, who deplored mere fiction-making and admired the scientist's laboratory methods, in which the scientist must sometimes serve as his own guinea pig, then we must ask ourselves a disturbing and fascinating question: Was Strindberg's marriage going on the rocks because the artist-scientist was conducting an experiment with himself as guinea pig to be inoculated with the germs of sexual jealousy and the virus of insanity? Was Strindberg deliberately letting the ship be dashed to pieces because he wanted to discover—to quote from his own introduction—"some elements in the physiology of love, some clues to the pathology of the soul, and, into the bargain, a curious fragment from the philosophy of crime"?

A mad genius, paranoid and Oedipal, is driven by some compulsion to set down the experiences he believes he has had—such is the usual view of the *Defense*. It seems an extraordinarily naïve view that ignores the evidence offered by Strindberg's letters and takes no account of his avowed principles as an artist. A far more sensible view is that Strindberg created his experiences in order to write about them. Interested in exploring the frontier where jealousy encroaches on madness, he set up a model of the terrain in his own home. That is the scientific method. It is also a method not unfamiliar to actors. But Strindberg could not step out of his role without being called a fraud. He had to play the game for real even if it meant injuring himself and others. When he compared himself to Hercules who lights his own funeral pyre, he was not joking.

To some the suggestion I have offered here may seem absurd. To those who know Strindberg the question is not: Is it true? but How true is it? Certain it is that Strindberg wrote best when he identified himself with a role. We know that when at work he took fiction for reality, just as an actor takes the stage for a real room. We also know that in the summer of 1887 he was looking for a good serious subject to write about and that he had never entirely abandoned the story of his marriage as a subject. We know, too, that in 1887 his plays were not being staged, his books were not being printed, and that he had "seven unpublished manuscripts lying around" (letter of June 13 to his brother Axel). And, as a noted Strindberg authority has convincingly argued, Strindberg's marital happiness stood in direct relation to his economic situation.*

As far as his career was concerned, the only encouraging signs came from Copenhagen, where there had been a growing interest in his work since 1879. The Danish capital began to look more and more like the only place where

---

* Harry Jacobsen, *Strindberg och hans första hustru* (Stockholm, 1946), p. 160. This is an excellent study of the relationship between *A Madman's Defense* and the ascertainable facts of Strindberg's marriage.

Strindberg might redeem his fortunes. If he succeeded there, he could return in triumph to Sweden, from which he had felt virtually ostracized during the last three or four years. A Danish actor named Hunderup, who had recently acquired the management of a theater customarily devoted to farces and musicals, had decided to raise its artistic level by producing Strindberg's *The Father*—with a comic afterpiece lest the regular customers be offended. Hunderup was, of course, counting on the considerable notoriety that surrounded the play and its author. Within a short time Strindberg's fame was such that he was represented in the local wax museum. The published version of the play received mixed reviews that called attention to its controversial nature. The author was described as being on the brink of insanity; he was known to be seeking a divorce; and the play itself was presumed to be a direct transcription of the author's married life. Moreover, the radical element in Copenhagen, led by Georg and Edvard Brandes, were using the play to assail their opponents by pointing out that the stage of the Royal Theater was denied to controversial writers like Strindberg. Georg Brandes himself directed the play, and its premiere was set for November 14, the birthday of Denmark's great romantic poet Oehlenschläger.

The effect of all this on Strindberg was twofold. On the one hand he saw that *The Father* might presage a happier phase in his career and bring about an improvement in his finances, which were now so desperate that when he and his family arrived in Copenhagen from Bavaria in the first week of November, he had to go first to a pawnbroker to raise money to claim his baggage. On the other hand, *The Father* revived in him the mood that produced that masterpiece, giving rise simultaneously to anguish in the husband and creative excitement in the artist. As we have seen, Strindberg had started to put the story of his marriage on paper in September. In August, when we may presume that the novel was being planned in his mind, he had sent strange letters to faithful friends inquiring about the unfaithfulness of his wife. In October a new factor entered the picture. At that time Axel Lundegård, who had been hired to translate *The Father* into Danish, first wrote him about the play. On October 17 Strindberg replied with a letter that might have been written by Bernard Shaw. He advised that the role of the Captain be entrusted to

> an actor of a generally happy temperament who with the somewhat scornful, self-ironic, slightly cynical air of a man of the world goes in tolerably good spirits to meet his fate, wrapping himself as he dies in these spiders' webs that he cannot, because of natural laws, tear asunder.
>
> A cuckold is a comic figure in the eyes of the world, and especially in the eyes of a theater audience. He must indicate that he knows this, and that he too would laugh if only someone else were the cuckold.

Yet on the very next day, on October 18, Strindberg wrote an extraordinary five-page letter to a judge in Sweden in which he accused his own wife of being a whore and a lesbian and of attempting to have him locked up in an insane asylum. It is this last idea, that of his wife trying to destroy him by driving him insane, that is now added for the first time to the story of his marriage as it takes shape in his mind; and, clearly, he got it from *The Father*. In that play he had produced a masterpiece; why not try the same theme again?

And now the actor in him takes charge. To write this story he must become the husband being driven mad. He doesn't consult books, visit the local sanitarium, or talk to his doctor. He submerges himself in the role, just as he did when he wrote *The Father*. That play was supposed to have been completely true to life—his life—when he wrote it; but now in the letter to the Swedish judge Strindberg can say that he wrote *The Father* only to "find out something" about his wife Siri; he can even venture the opinion that Siri got the idea of driving him mad with lies from reading *The Father!*

By November 12, the day before the dress rehearsal of the play, Strindberg has invested himself so completely with the mood and qualities of the role that he is contemplating suicide, and writes to Lundegård a letter in the form of a testament. He concludes it with the oft-quoted lines:

> It seems as if I am walking in my sleep, as if fiction and reality were mixed together. I don't know if *The Father* is a fiction or if my life has been a fiction; but I have the feeling that in a moment not far off I shall find out which is which, and then I'll crumble into dust either through insanity and a sick conscience or through suicide.

The "sick conscience" betrays Strindberg's technique. For if it were true that Siri was driving him mad of her own volition, then *she* should have the sick conscience, not he. But if he is deliberately destroying his marriage and the happiness of his wife in order to experience sexual jealousy and insanity and to create a work of art, then and only then would *he* suffer from a sick conscience. And once he has had his experience and once fiction and reality have separated from one another and drawn back to their distinct spheres, what could he with his tender conscience do but kill himself or go mad—unless some part of the fiction turned out to be true. What irony! The more he can prove that he has been deceived, cuckolded, and driven mad, the more will his conscience be assuaged. But these considerations could not be allowed to interfere with the actual writing of a book. In his preface Strindberg could say that he bitterly regretted having written the book. But the preface is dated 1887, while the book was not completed until March 1888. Nothing better demonstrates Strindberg's complete awareness of what he was doing while he was doing it.

Madness and the battle of the brains were among

Strindberg's constant preoccupations. In the spring of
1887, a few months after writing *The Father*, he had returned to the subject of madness and delusions in an es-
say, "Soul Murder." Now, after another respite of a few
months, during which he wrote the comic novel *The Natives of Hemsö*, he once again took up the theme of sexual
jealousy and the madness it can inspire. *Othello* was the
classic treatment of the theme. Shakespeare had improved
on the countless Renaissance plays that dealt with the
subject by building his plot on a fabrication, a lie invented by Iago. In *Othello* there was no adultery, no love
triangle; there was only a mind being poisoned by a
villain. In *The Father* and *A Madman's Defense* Strindberg further refined this plot idea by making the villain
(villainess) into a mere flickering shadow projected by
the fire in the hero's mind. Strindberg poisons his own
mind, and the question of whether his wife Siri is or is not
guilty of the crimes he charges her with is irrelevant.

The artfulness of *A Madman's Defense* must be apparent to everyone who reads it carefully. Strindberg, like
Dante, writes in the first person but gives us two points
of view: that of the omniscient author and that of the
hero experiencing hell for the first time. The hero Axel
is continually astonished and horrified at what is happening to him, while the author Strindberg is carefully arranging matters to suggest Axel's growing madness and
eventual mental collapse.*

Since he was not permitted to use the documentary approach—letting the correspondence speak for itself—or the
fairly objective approach of the first autobiographical volumes, Strindberg seems to have determined to write up the

---

* Sven Rinman, "En dåres försvarstal," *Svensk Litteraturtidskrift*, 1965, pp. 63–75, is an excellent discussion of the nar-
rative techniques Strindberg employs. The Swedish dramatist
Lars Forsell has also written on the same subject in a piece
which I have not seen: "Försvarstal för en dåre," *Dagens
Nyheter* (Stockholm), September 7, 1955.

affair in the manner of a sensational French novel: frank, scabrous, naturalistic. His immediate objective seems to be to defame Siri, and she is given no chance to defend herself as she would have had in the letters. But in order not to appear a complete cad, Strindberg must convince the reader that he is Siri's victim. By building the novel to show his mounting suspicions and his growing madness, he creates a strange ambiguity. He cannot be trusted to tell the truth because he is going mad; but if he is going mad, then there may well be some truth in his accusation that his wife is deliberately driving him mad. He must hate her for what she is doing to him, but only a great love can lie behind that hate if his jealousy and his suspicions of her can drive him to the brink of insanity.

This ambiguity produces a unique kind of love story, feverish but cool, intense yet ironic, passionate but unsentimental, and above all terribly true in a way that art seldom is. Strindberg could honestly say that the book was "true" and "corresponded to actual conditions" (letter to Hansson, February 20, 1891), while his wife could with equal honesty exclaim, "There is scarcely an incident in it that doesn't have *some* foundation in fact—only everything is so horribly twisted and distorted."* For the entire method of the novel is to make use of distortion in precisely the same way that any great work of art does, only here the method is applied where it has a double relevance—as art and as insanity. I leave it to the reader to equate the two if he wishes.

Let me give just two instances that may serve to illustrate Strindberg's general method. In the novel there is a description of a rather wild party that turns into an orgy of sorts and fills Axel with disgust, especially for his wife's lesbian girlfriend. (Part Four, Chapter 3, pp. 267 ff.) Now there actually was at least one such party in November

* Karin Smirnoff, *Så var det i verkligheten* (Stockholm, 1956), p. 205. Karin was the oldest child in the Strindberg-Siri marriage.

1885, when Strindberg was living in Grèz, France, and not long after it was over Strindberg wrote an altogether different description of it to his friend Heidenstam.

> Life is very sociable here. Old friends from Paris come out on Saturdays, and last Saturday we had ourselves a fair orgy that went on for two days, with singing, guitar, tambourine, flute, and wild *joie de vivre;* a variety show (my own), dancing, billiards, midnight snack, pickled herring and breakfast at the Danish girls' [Sofie Holten and Marie David, the lesbians of the novel], dinner with our own *café chantant,* and dancing at the Chevillons' pension. Almost Decameronesque . . . and everyone who had any talent had contributed some verses (I wrote a French chansonnette) or whatever. Nordström is a merry old soul(!) who sings, and sculptor Vallgren (with his wife) is a great ballad singer. We had everything you and I had written about (except naked women!). Fun and games and *joie de vivre.* And all because my very existence has never been so imperiled as now. One dances with the noose around one's neck and thinks: better make the most of it; tomorrow nothing but herring and potatoes. It's really a terrible crisis (evolution) that's going on, and the crash will soon come. And when I think of all the dinner parties and supés I've got to make up for from my pious theist period!

One can see that in the novel, written some two years later, Strindberg has not invented a new episode; he has merely chosen to view the event through a dark and distorting lens that would make the weekend party harmonize with the mood his book required.

The second illustration is even more enlightening. At one point in the novel Axel takes the long trip from Switzerland to Copenhagen to check on his wife's fidelity. He questions everyone who might possibly know the truth. But he is told nothing. Discussing his wife's possible unfaithfulness was "like beating my head against a stone wall. . . . No information was given me." (Part Four, Chapter 9, p. 285.) Strindberg's letters tell us what actually happened on this trip. He went to Copenhagen on business—to confer with publishers and peddle his manuscripts. But he had no luck. "In Copenhagen I ran into a solid wall. My publisher, with whom I have a five-year contract, didn't want to talk business with me. Everywhere No!" (Letter to his brother Axel, June 13, 1887.)[*]

What Strindberg, the perfect histrionic personality, is doing instinctively here every actor learns to do at some point in his training. Stanislavsky calls this element of his "system" emotional memory, by which he means the ability to feel and express an emotion in a particular scene by evoking a personal experience that involved the same emotion but under different circumstances.

Of course there is a crucial difference between an actor and an author. Strindberg is not simply enacting somebody else's scenes; he is creating his own. In this process he allows his present mood to play a major part. Consequently, since Strindberg was a man of many moods, he usually had more than one iron in the fire so that he could switch from one to the other to accommodate his moods. This is part of the secret of his amazing productivity. While he was completing his comic novel about the fisher folk of the Stockholm skerries, the idea for *A Madman's Defense* was already festering in his brain; and while writing *A Madman's Defense* he was simultaneously reworking his comedy *Comrades* and writing a volume of essays. And shortly after he had finished the *Defense*, he set to work on a series of stories about the people in the Stockholm skerries, darker in mood this time. After that came "Tschandala," another battle-of-brains story based on his experience with the overseer of a dilapidated Danish country estate on which Strindberg was living with his family. Once that was out of the way he wrote *Miss Julie*, the perfectly balanced summing-up of the love affair be-

[*] I owe this illustration to Jacobsen, *op. cit.*, p. 130.

tween Siri and Strindberg, the baroness and the son of a
servant. He finished that on August 10, and then turned to
write *Creditors,* the tragicomic treatment of what occurs in
the first part of *A Madman's Defense.*

One of the most interesting features of the series of
works inspired by his marriage is the order in which they
were written. In *The Father,* the first of the series, the
husband is driven mad and dies. In *A Madman's Defense*
the battle between the husband and wife is not resolved;
it ends where the last act of *The Father* begins. *Miss Julie,*
the next work in the series, is nothing but a long seduction
scene, the distillation of the first part of *A Madman's Defense,* only now it is the woman who is the neurotic one
and who is driven to destruction. Finally comes *Creditors*
in which Strindberg ties up the beginning and end of the
series by introducing the first husband of the woman and
having him come back to destroy the happy couple. As a
demonstration of the skill with which a genius manipulates
his material there is nothing more dazzling in dramatic
literature than this series of works (unless it be the works
Strindberg wrote a decade later). And few authors have
let us examine so closely the creative process itself—the
process by which "real experiences" are subjected to the
pattern-making genius of the artist to produce different
versions of the truth.

How the Defense Got Published

Strindberg finished *A Madman's Defense* in a frenetic
burst of energy, writing about sixteen pages a day. The
last neatly-written page was filed away about March 20.
He was of two minds as to what to do with the manuscript.
On March 12 in a letter he had offered it to Hans Österling,
publisher of *The Father;* but on March 15 he had written
Edvard Brandes that this story of his marriage would
never be printed. Then, after the book was definitely finished, he wrote long letters to his cousin J. O. Strindberg

and to his old friend Rudolf Wall, who had been his employer in the days when Strindberg was a newspaper reporter. These letters, dated March 23, April 10, and April 11, have exactly the same import as the ones he sent out six months before inquiring about Siri's unfaithfulness and sexual immorality. Just as he had to whip himself into a jealous state of mind in order to start work on the novel, so now that it was completed he had to justify to himself what he had done. The pangs of conscience he mentioned in his letter to Lundegård were making themselves felt.

However, now that the poison was out of his system and he was no longer deeply involved in the work, he could ease his conscience by the simple expediency of not publishing it. Instead he deposited it with his cousin.

Thoughts of publishing it were revived in 1891 after divorce proceedings had gotten under way. Strindberg and his wife were then living apart from one another in the environs of Stockholm. The church council that had charge of the divorce awarded the three children to their mother. Being deprived of them was a great blow to Strindberg, and he was unable to reconcile himself to their loss. He felt, too, that, living with Siri, they would turn against him. Two months before the church council issued an interlocutory divorce decree, Siri's good friend Marie David moved in with her. Strindberg now tried to convince the church council that the children should not be entrusted to an alcoholic mother living with an alcoholic lesbian. The council, however, saw no reason to alter its decision. This, combined with his literary failures, served to embitter Strindberg against Siri and against the council, which he felt was part of the compact majority that opposed him in the church, in the publishing houses, in the theaters, in the daily press, and in the universities. By February 1891 he had decided to publish the *Defense* outside Sweden. "Why should I feel obligated to let myself be assassinated without having the right to scream?" (Letter to Hansson, February 20.) At the suggestion of a fellow writer, Ola Hansson, who also felt ostracized, Strindberg sent it first to Joseph Kürschner in Germany, who rejected it on the ground that it lacked general interest. On May 12 (the day after part of his library was sold at auction to pay his debts) Strindberg wrote to Hansson that, on the one hand, he himself had entertained the same doubts, "since the book seems to have been written in self-defense; but on the other hand, don't the larger questions, the vital questions about paternity, about the battle of the sexes, about desexualization, etc. have a general interest?"

Later in the year the French publisher Albert Savine expressed an interest in the manuscript, and the book was actually in the press when Savine went bankrupt in 1893.

By that time, however, Strindberg had sold the manuscript to a German firm, the Bibliographisches Büro, which issued it in May 1893 under the title *Die Beichte eines Thoren*. It did not sell well, and to stimulate interest, Frida Uhl, Strindberg's second wife, and another woman teamed up with the German translator in a little conspiracy to promote sales. They took a copy of the book, underlined the more daring passages, and sent it to the public prosecutor, urging that something be done to protect German women and children from this kind of filth.*

The book was confiscated in September, under the so-called Lex Heinze, which dealt with the spreading of obscene writings and had already been used against Tolstoy and Hauptmann. It stipulated that the offender could be subject to a fine of not more than 300 marks or to a maximum six months in prison. And, of course, the plates of the book were to be destroyed. According to the phrasing of the law, it was possible for the plates to be destroyed if judged obscene by "objective" standards while the author of the material was cleared because he was not aware of any obscenity. When Strindberg's case came up for hearing in March 1894, his lawyer sought to establish

---

* Adolf Paul, *Min Strindbergsbok* (Stockholm, 1930), p. 142. Paul repeats the story as Strindberg told it to him; and it is partially confirmed by Frida Uhl herself: *Strindberg och hans andra hustru* (Stockholm, 1933–34), vol. II, pp. 132–33.

that Strindberg had not intentionally violated the law. Under questioning, Strindberg said that he wrote the book to free himself from the oppressive memories of the past; and introduced as evidence was the letter Strindberg had written to his cousin J. O. Strindberg on March 20, 1888, asking that the manuscript be "deposited in the family archives" and not opened or read without Strindberg's permission. After two more hearings, the book was cleared.

The original French version of *Le plaidoyer d'un fou*—strictly speaking it may be incorrect to refer to this as the original version, since Strindberg's manuscript* was revised by Georges Loiseau—did not appear until January 1895. Strindberg asked the publisher Albert Langen that there be as little publicity as possible. This was consistent with his reluctance to give the book to the world, but it may also have been due to the German obscenity trial. At any rate, the book was not widely reviewed in the Paris press. The longest and warmest review, an eight-column piece in the *Revue Encyclopédique*, was written by Julien Leclercq, a close friend of Gauguin. Enraptured, Leclercq praised Strindberg's novel at the expense of Musset's *Confessions d'un enfant du siècle* and Ernest Feydeau's *Fanny*, and found the two Frenchmen sentimental striplings compared to the mature Strindberg.† Of this French edition, an anonymous British reviewer had this to say:

> . . . Of Strindberg's talent, however, there is no question, and in these days of the false idolatry of woman, and general namby-pamby flattering of the sex, it is curious to meet with one writer who rages against the eternal feminine like a medieval monk, the more so because his denunciatory wrath but thinly veils his admiring preoccupation. . . . —Unsigned review in *The Saturday Review* (London), April 27, 1895, p. 556.

* Strindberg sold his holograph manuscript in May 1896, and it has not since come to light.

† Stellan Ahlström, *Strindbergs erövring av Paris* (Stockholm, 1956), pp. 270–71.

When the novel was republished in Paris at the end of 1964 the French critics hailed it as a modern masterpiece and assigned it a permanent place in world literature. They said it was:*

A book that prefigures Freud and existentialism. Schizophrenia, the disease of our own century, is here. Here, too, is the modern game of ambiguity: who is lying? who is mad? who is wrong? which one the executioner, and which one the victim? —Roger Grenier, *Nouvel Observateur*, December 17, 1964.

One of the masterpieces of world literature. . . . A prophetic book that contains in embryonic form the power of all the present-day conflicts of love and of alienation. You must read Strindberg: he is still our contemporary, and, sad to say, more *present* among us than a great number of our "living" writers. —Alain Jouffroy, *L'Express*, December 28, 1964.

A Madman's Defense does not command our attention as a treatise on schizophrenia, but rather as a testament to the truth as schizophrenics see it. For what speaks here, what interprets, what hurls insults, what storms and raves is love—true love; and Strindberg knows it when he goes on to speak lucidly of the Beloved. . . . Strindberg belongs to the twentieth century. —Robert Kanters, *Figaro littéraire*, January 13, 1965.

The good reviews meant little to Strindberg in 1895. Several years before he had abandoned literature for science. When he returned to creative writing, he would again venture into the borderland of insanity—not the insanity that begins with sexual jealousy and points to the madhouse, however, but the insanity that begins with a sick conscience and leads to the church.

Evert Sprinchorn

* These notices are cited by Sven Rinman, "En dåres försvarstal," *Svensk Litteraturtidskrift*, 1965, p. 75.

A MADMAN'S DEFENSE

PREFACE

This is a terrible book. I admit that without any reservations, and I bitterly regret having written it.

What brought it about?

The obvious necessity of washing my corpse before it is sealed up forever in my coffin.

I remember—it was four years ago—that one of my literary friends, the sworn enemy of all forms of indiscretions (in others), let slip the following words one day when the conversation touched on my marriage: "You know, that's a perfect subject for a novel. It's made to order for my pen!"

From that moment on I resolved to put my own order in, since I was virtually certain that my friend would take a liking to it.

But, dear friend, don't get the wrong idea and think that as first possessor I am claiming proprietary rights!

And I also remember—this time, sixteen years ago—that the mother of my wife-to-be, then a baroness and separated from her husband, said to me as I watched her daughter flirting with a group of young men: "She'd make a good subject for a novel, now wouldn't she?"

"What would you call it?"

"*A Woman of Fire*," she answered.

Lucky mother, who departed this earth in good time, your wishes are fulfilled. The novel is written. Now I myself can die.

The Author

1887

A NEW PREFACE

Just the other day I met the hero of this novel. I reproached him vigorously for having beguiled me into publishing the story of his first marriage. Now that he is married a second time and the father of a sweet little girl, he looks ten years younger than he did ten years ago.

When he heard me complaining, he replied, "Dear friend, the sympathy that the heroine of the book has won since its publication acquits me in my own eyes. You can judge for yourself how incredibly deep my love for her must have been if it could survive so much cruelty and even be passed on to the reader. Not that that prevented a certain French academician* from branding my undying devotion as a weakness, my steadfast loyalty to my family, children included, as a sign of inferiority compared to the woman's brutality, fickleness, and faithlessness. Would that man be willing to consider the insignificant Caserio as superior to the high and mighty Carnot simply because the former stuck a knife in the living flesh of the latter?†

"Besides, in this book that you wanted to write, love is only a thread, only the woof in a rich pattern whose com-

---

* A reference to Victor Cherbuliez, permanent secretary of the French Academy, who published under his pen name, G. Valbert, a review article, "M. Auguste Strindberg et 'la Confession d'un fou,'" in *Revues des Deux Mondes*, November 1, 1893. —ED.

† Sadi Carnot, president of the Third Republic of France, was assassinated by Caserio, an Italian anarchist, in June 1894. Because of certain political and social scandals that had come to light, the general public felt more sympathy with the assassin and with the anarchists than usual.—ED.

plexity only my countrymen appreciate, those of them who have followed my literary career as it developed parallel to disappointments in my love affairs but without being disrupted by them. I could have fled from the field of battle. But I remained at my post. I fought the enemy at home and in bed. Doesn't that take courage, if I may ask?

"That 'poor, defenseless woman' had all of Scandinavia on her side, where she has nothing but friends, all fighting against a sick man who was alone and in dire need and whom they wanted to lock up in a madhouse because his superior intelligence rebelled against the glorification of women, that penultimate superstition of the free-thinkers.

"Those well-wishers who hide their shabby revenge under the pretentious label 'Heavenly Justice' have condemned my *Defense* in the name of their *Nemesis Divina* and argued, on false grounds, that I deceived and betrayed the husband in my wife's first marriage. Let them read that scene in which you show how that husband got rid of his wife by throwing her into my arms—I whose hands were clean when I confessed to him my innocent love for his abandoned wife! And may they remind themselves—this little detail is not without its significance—of those pages where I took upon my young shoulders the whole burden of this mistake in order to protect the officer's position and the future of the children, and then let them explain what sort of retribution it is whose logic consists in punishing an act of self-sacrifice.

"One must have been young and stupid to act as rashly as I did—I admit that. But it shall never happen again, I assure you. . . . No . . . Let's not say anything more about it. . . . And besides . . . No, no . . . Goodby!"

He turned and quickly disappeared. But he left behind him an impression of absolute sincerity.

I no longer regret having written this novel about a type of idealist now vanished from life and literature. And I

shall always refrain from carrying out a decision I once
made to write *A Madwoman's Defense*, for it now strikes
me as contrary to all good sense to let the criminal woman
testify against her victim.

The Author

Paris-Passy, October 1894

INTRODUCTION

Seated at my writing table, pen in hand, I fainted. A sudden fever prostrated me. I had not been seriously ill for fifteen years, and this sudden attack, coming at such an inopportune time, distressed me deeply. Not that I was afraid of dying—it would take more than that to frighten me—but as I was only thirty-eight years old, with a stormy career behind me, my last word still unsaid, the promises of my youth only partly fulfilled, pregnant with plans for the future, I could scarcely be delighted by the prospect of a sudden end. For the last four years I had lived with my family in half-voluntary exile, buried in a Bavarian village, worn out—recently forced to stand trial, my work confiscated—ostracized, pilloried—and when I collapsed on my bed I was possessed by one feeling only, that of revenge. A conflict raged within me, although I had not the strength left to call for help—weakened as I was by the fever that shook me as one shakes a pillow, that grabbed me by the throat, and put its knee on my chest. My ears burned, and my eyes felt as if they would start from their sockets. I was alone with Death, who had crept into my attic room by stealth and was attacking me.

But I didn't want to die! As I resisted, the battle became ferocious. My nerves relaxed, the blood coursed through my veins. My brain twitched like a polyp in vinegar. All at once I realized that I had to succumb in this dance of death. I relinquished my hold, fell on my back, and submitted to the horrible embrace of the dread monster.

Immediately an indescribable calm came over me, a

voluptuous apathy spread through my limbs, a supernatural peace soothed body and soul, which had been deprived during so many years of toil of any kind of relaxation.

I fervently desired that it really should be the end. Slowly all will to live ebbed away. I ceased to observe, to feel, to think. I lost consciousness and only a dim awareness of the blessed Nothing filled the void that opened up when the nameless pains, the confused thoughts, and the inadmissible anguish disappeared.

When I awoke, I found my wife sitting by my bedside and gazing at me with a worried look.

"What is it, dear?" she asked. "What's the matter?"

"Nothing. I'm sick," I replied, "and it's good to be sick."

"What does that mean? . . . You're joking."

"No, it's the end. Anyhow, I hope it is."

"Lord help us, you can't leave us like this without a cent," she exclaimed. "What's to become of us, in a strange country, no friends, no money?"

"There's my life insurance," I said, attempting to console her. "I know it isn't much, but it's enough to get you home."

She had not thought of the insurance money. Looking a little less anxious, she continued, "But you can't lie here like this! Let me call the doctor."

"No, I don't want any doctor!"

"Why not?"

"Because—I don't."

The glances we exchanged were like a long freight train filled with unspoken thoughts.

"I want to die," I said finally. "Life disgusts me. The past is all snarled up and I haven't the strength to unravel it. Let the shadows fill my eyes. Let the curtain come down."

My bold and dauntless words didn't move her a bit.

"Your old suspicions—do you still have them?" she wondered.

"Yes, I still have them! Drive the specter away! So far you're the only one who could chase it away."

Gently laying her soft hand on my forehead, she began playing mama.

"Does that feel good?"

"Good, very good . . ."

It was true enough. The mere touch of that light hand, which had weighed so heavily on my life, had the power of exorcising the evil spirits, forcing back the secret anxieties. But soon the fever came again, more violent this time. My wife rose to make me a broth from elder leaves, supposedly good for fever.

Left by myself, I sat up in bed and looked out through the window opposite. It was a large window, divided like a triptych, and framed by bright green vines through which I could see a part of the landscape. In the foreground the beautiful scarlet fruit of a quince tree rocked gently among the dark green foliage; apple trees, a little farther off, studded the green grass; the steeple of a small church, a blue streak—the Boden See—and far in the background the Tyrol Alps.

It was the height of summer, and, illuminated by the slanting rays of the afternoon sun, the whole scene formed a charming picture.

From below rose the twittering of the starlings that sat on the vine props of the vineyards, the chirping of the young chickens in the yard, the strident note of the crickets, the crystal-clear tinkling of cowbells; and mingling in this happy concert of nature was the voice of my wife, giving orders and talking to the gardener's wife about my illness.

Then the lust for life returned and the fear of annihilation gripped me. No, no, I did not want to die! I had too many duties to perform, too many debts to pay. Tortured by the pangs of conscience, I felt an overpowering need to confess myself, to ask all men's forgiveness for the wrongs I had committed, to humiliate myself before someone, anyone. I felt guilty, stricken with remorse, I did not know for what secret crime. I was burning with the desire to relieve my conscience by a full confession of my imagined guilt.

During this moment of weakness, which stemmed from my inborn timidity, my wife returned carrying the tea in a bowl, and alluding to my persecution complex, of which I formerly had a slight touch, she tasted the liquid before offering it to me. "You can drink it," she said smilingly, "it's not poisoned."

I felt ashamed. I didn't know what to say. And to please her I emptied the cup in one long swallow.

The somniferous elder tea, the fragrance of which stirred up memories of my native land, where the mystic elder tree is venerated by the country folk, made me feel so sentimental that I had to let a stream of self-reproaches gush forth.

"Listen to me carefully, darling. I think my days are numbered. I confess that I have always lived a life of utter selfishness. I have sacrificed your theatrical career for the sake of my literary fame. . . . I'll tell you everything now . . . only forgive me. . . ."

And when I saw she was trying to find some way of consoling me, I interrupted her and continued. "In compliance with your wishes we married under the dotal system. In spite of it, however, I have wasted your dowry to cover money I had thoughtlessly gone bond for. But what hurts me most now is the fact that you have no rights in the proceeds of my works. Send for a notary at once so that I can settle on you all my property, whatever value it might have. . . . One thing more: promise that you'll return to the stage, which you gave up to please me."

She refused to listen to me, treated my confession as a joke, advised me to go to sleep and rest, told me that everything would come out right, and assured me that I was not on the point of death. I seized her hand, exhausted. I begged her to sit with me until I had fallen asleep. Grasping her little hand more firmly, I again implored her to forgive me for all the wrong I had done her. A delicious drowsiness stole over me and closed my tired eyelids. Under the irradiance of her shining eyes, full of infinite tenderness, I felt as if I were melting away like ice in the rays of the sun. Her cool lips, touching my forehead, seemed to set a cool seal on it, and I plunged into the depths of ineffable bliss.

It was broad daylight when I awoke from my stupor. The rays of the sun were flaming across the Land of Cockaigne naïvely painted on the roller curtains. To judge from the morning sounds that rose from below, it must have been about five o'clock. I had slept soundly during the whole night without dreaming or waking up. On the little table by my bedside stood the bowl for the tea; the stool on which my wife had been sitting when I fell asleep was still in place. But now I was wrapped in her cloak, and the soft hairs of the fox skins lining it tickled my chin.

I thought I had never really slept before in the past ten years, so rested and refreshed did my overtired brain feel. My thoughts, which had been rushing hither and thither in wild disorder, now fell into rank and file, and with this powerful, well-drilled, and disciplined army I prepared to meet my attacks of morbid remorse, a symptom of constitutional weakness found in degenerate types.

Soon those two black spots in my life began to plague me, those two things I had revealed to my wife while I was making what I thought was my last confession, the two black spots that had tortured me for so many years, even up to the last extremity.

I resolved to re-examine them at once, to analyze those two confessions, which up to now had burdened my conscience but had never been looked at too closely. I had a vague presentiment that in the form I had presented them there was something not quite right.

"Let me see," I said to myself. "What have I done that

I should look upon myself as a selfish coward who sacrificed the artistic career of his wife to his ambition? Let
me see what really happened. . . ."

At the time of our betrothal she was playing very small
parts. Her position as an actress was a very modest one;
her second appearance in public, a deplorable performance, had revealed her lack of talent, character, and
originality. She lacked everything the stage demanded.
On the day before our wedding she was playing the insignificant part of a society lady in an equally insignificant
play; she had all of two words to speak.

And yet how many tears, how many disappointments,
were all due to our getting married—if one was to believe
her. It robbed the actress of all her charm, she who had
been so fascinating as baroness, she who had left her husband out of love for her art.

Now it was true, I was to blame for her debacle on
stage, which came when the management flatly refused to
renew her contract—this after two years' weeping over
steadily shrinking parts.

At the time her contract was up for renewal, I scored
a success as a novelist, an undoubted success. I had already had a few short and unimportant plays produced.
Now my first concern was to write a popular play, I mean
a commercial type of play, written especially for my wife
so that she could get that renewal of contract she so earnestly wished for. It was a repugnant task, for one of my
most cherished dreams was the reform of the drama. But
I wrote the play and for the moment sacrificed my literary
convictions. I meant to force my wife on a hostile public,
make her a success by using all the tricks of the trade,
move heaven and earth to make her popular. But it was
no good.

The play was a failure. The crowd in the orchestra
would have none of the divorced wife who had married a

second time; the manager hastened to cancel an unprofitable contract.

"Now, was that my fault?" I asked myself, stretching myself in the bed, well satisfied with the result of this first self-examination. "Ah, there's nothing like a good conscience!"

With a lighter heart I continued my musing.

A miserable year passed, washed away in tears, despite the happiness it brought us in the birth of a little girl.

And all of a sudden my wife had another attack of stage mania, more violent than the previous one. We besieged the agencies, stormed the managerial offices, advertised ourselves extravagantly—but everywhere we were turned out, turned down, and always advised to give it up.

Disillusioned by the failure of my play just as I was on the point of making a nice career for myself in literature, I had sworn never again to write a commissioned play for an actress, more especially as that sort of work had no attraction for me, and not being inclined to break up our home merely to satisfy one of my wife's whims, I limited myself to bearing my share of the inevitable complaints.

But after a time I found these beyond my strength to bear. I made use of my connections with a theater in Finland, and, thanks to my efforts, my wife was signed up for a number of performances.

I had made a rod for my own back. For a whole month I was a widower, bachelor, head of the family, housekeeper; and by way of compensation my wife brought back with her to our marriage bower two large packing cases full of wreaths and bouquets.

But she was so happy, so young, and so charming that I couldn't help sending out inquiries for a fresh engagement for her.

Think about it! I was willing to give up my country, my friends, my position, my publisher—and for what? For a woman's whim. . . . But that's how it is. Either a man is in love or he isn't.

Fortunately for me, the theater producer had no room in his company for an actress without a repertoire.

Was that my fault? At the thought of it I literally rolled over in my bed with pleasure. What a good thing an occasional little self-examination is! It lightens the heart . . . I felt rejuvenated—instantaneously.

But to continue. Children were born to us at short intervals. One—two—three. We believe in sowing tightly.

But again and again her mania for the stage returned. One ought to persevere! A new rival theater had just been opened. How simple, how very simple! Why not offer the manager a new play with a good female part, a sensational play, one that dealt with the "woman question," since that was what everybody was talking about. No sooner thought than done. For, as I have already said, either a man is in love or he isn't.

The play was produced. Splendid part for the leading actress, magnificent dresses (at the request of the theater, of course), a cradle, much moonshine, a villain for a bright daub of color, an abject husband in love with his wife, timid, cowardly (myself), a pregnant woman on the stage (that was something new), the interior of a convent—and so on.

A colossal success for the actress. For the author a failure, an awful failure . . . alas!

She was saved. I was lost, ruined. But in spite of everything, in spite of the supper that we gave to the manager at a hundred crowns per head; in spite of a fine of fifty crowns which we had to pay for illegal cheering late at night before the director's house—in spite of all this, not the whiff of a contract came her way.

Now, certainly that wasn't my fault. But nevertheless I was the martyr, the victim. In the eyes of all respectable ladies, I was a cad who had ruined his wife's career. And for years I've suffered pangs of conscience that robbed my nights of peace.

And how often hasn't the bitter accusation been pub-

licly flung in my face! And it was always I who was guilty!
. . . That things really happened in quite a different way,
who cared? . . . One career had been cut short, that's
true. I admit it. . . . But which one, and by whom?

A cruel sort of joke crossed my mind, but the irony in
it disappeared when I realized that posterity might blame
me for this ruined career, unless I had an advocate who
could present the matter in a true light.

There remained the squandering of her dowry.

I remember I once had been made the subject of a
newspaper item entitled "Squanderer of His Wife's Fortune." I also remember, on another occasion, having been
charged with living on my wife's income. Nice words,
which had made me put six cartridges into my revolver.

Let us examine this charge also, since it is felt that an
investigation is desirable, and let us judge, since it is felt
that it is proper to judge.

My wife brought to our little nest ten thousand crowns
in doubtful shares; I had raised a loan on these shares for
50 percent of their face value. Like a bolt from the blue
the general crash came. The shares were hardly worth
the paper they were printed on, something we already
knew since we had neglected to sell them at the right
moment. I was consequently compelled to pay the full
amount of my loan: 50 percent of the face value. Later on,
my wife received 25 percent of her claim, this being the
proportion that the creditors received after the bank's
failure.

Here's a problem for a mathematician: "How much
could I have squandered, honestly, now?"

Not one penny, in my poor opinion. Shares you can't
sell aren't worth very much, but by giving my personal
guarantee I had given them an effective value of 25 percent.

In truth, I was as innocent of this accusation as of the
other.

But the remorse, the despair, the suicide attempts so often planned! And the suspicions, the old distrust, the cruel doubts that constantly rose up to torture me afresh. I nearly went out of my mind when I thought how close I had come to dying thinking I was a wretch. Worn out with care, overwhelmed with work, I had never had time to pay much attention to the dark innuendoes, the veiled allusions, the nasty taunts. And while I, completely absorbed in my daily toil, lived unsuspectingly from day to day, a false legend took shape and form, grounded on nothing but the talk of the envious and the rumormongering of the café crowd. And I, idiot that I was, believed everybody except myself. Ah! . . .

Could it be possible that I had never been crazy, never sick, never a degenerate? Maybe I had simply been the victim of an adored temptress whose little embroidery scissors had cut off Samson's locks when he laid his weary head on the pillow, worn out by hard work, exhausted by care and anxiety on her account and the children's? Trustful, unsuspicious, I had lost my honor during my ten years' sleep in the arms of the sorceress—and my manhood, my will to live, my intellect, my five senses, and still more, God help me!

Was it possible—the thought filled me with shame—that a crime had been committed in that dense fog in which I had passed a phantom-like existence for years? Just a little crime, premeditated, springing from a very hazy, undefined wish for power, from a gnawing itch in the female to get the better of the male in that duel called marriage?

Without a doubt, I was the one who had been taken in! Seduced by a married woman; compelled to marry her to explain her pregnancy and thus save her theatrical career; married under the dotal system and the condition that each should contribute half of the expenses, I was ruined after ten years, plundered, stripped bare; for wasn't it I, when all is said and done, who had to bear the financial burden of our union all alone?

At this very moment when my wife shrugs me off as a good-for-nothing, incapable of providing the necessities of life, and pictures me as the squanderer of her imaginary fortune—at this very moment it is she who owes me forty thousand crowns, her share of the expenses, according to the verbal agreement made on our wedding day. It is she who is my debtor!

Determined to know the whole truth, I jumped out of bed like a man who, having dreamt he was lame, flings away the crutches he had in his dream. I dressed quickly and went downstairs to confront my wife.

Through the half-open door my enraptured gaze met a charming spectacle.

She lay stretched out at full length on her tumbled bed, her lovely little head buried in the pillow over which her hair, the color of wheat in the sun, waved and curled. Her nightgown had slipped off her shoulders, and her virginal bosom peeped through the lace. The soft, red-and-white striped coverlet betrayed the swelling curves of her graceful, fragile body, leaving her bare feet uncovered—tiny arched feet with rosy toes and transparent flawless nails. A genuine work of art, perfect, fashioned in flesh after the model of an antique marble statue: that was how my wife appeared to me. Lighthearted and smiling, with an expression of chaste maternity, she watched her three little ones as they climbed and tumbled about among the flowered down pillows, as if on a heap of newly mown flowers.

The delightful spectacle disarmed me. But a voice within me said, "Beware of the she-panther playing with her cubs."

Awed by the majesty of motherhood, I entered her room with uncertain steps, shy as a schoolboy.

"Ah, my big boy's up already!" she greeted me, surprised, but not as pleased as one might have expected.

I stammered a confused reply, smothered by the chil-

dren who had climbed on my back when I stooped to kiss
their mother.

Was it possible? She a criminal? I pondered the question as I went away, subdued by her chaste beauty, the
candid smile of those lips that could surely never have
been tainted by a lie. No, a thousand times no! . . .

I stole away, persuaded to the contrary.

But, alas, a cruel sense of disquiet followed in my footsteps.

Why had my unexpected recovery left her so cool? Why
hadn't she asked me how my fever was? Why hadn't she
asked me how I had slept? How to explain that almost
disappointed look on her face, that somewhat surly expression when she saw I was my old self again? . . . And
that haughty, condescending laugh of hers! . . . Had she
been entertaining the hope of finding me dead one fine
day, of being rid of the crazy man who kept making life
unbearable? Was she hoping to cash in my life insurance
and start a new life? No, a thousand times no! . . .

But still the doubts remained with me, doubts about
everything—my wife's chastity, the legitimacy of the children, doubts about my mental faculties, doubts that constantly attacked me and left me no peace, no quiet, no
rest.

No matter how one looked at it, it was time to make an
end, to arrest the flood of sterile thoughts. I had to find
some ground of certainty or else die. A crime had been
committed in secret or else I was mad! I must know the
truth!

To be a deceived husband, a cuckold—what did I care,
as long as I knew it! The important thing was that I must
be the first to laugh at it. Was there a single man in the
world who could be absolutely certain that he was his
wife's only lover? . . .

When I let pass in review all the friends of my youth,
all those that were married, I could not pick out one who
was not, to some extent, hoodwinked. Lucky men whom

no doubts tortured! It was silly to be small-minded of course. Whether two shared the wife, or whether one was alone, what did it matter! But not to know, that makes one ridiculous. The main thing is to know. One has to know. Yet if a husband lived for a hundred years he would still never know anything about his wife's true existence. He might know everything in the world, the whole infinite universe, but he would never have a clear idea of the woman whose life is bound up with his own. That is why the story of poor Monsieur Bovary lives in the happy memories of all fortunate husbands.

As far as I was concerned I wanted the truth! I had to know! . . . For the sake of revenge? What nonsense! Revenge on whom? On my favored rivals? They were only making use of their prerogative as males! On my wife? Did I not say one ought not to be small-minded? And to hurt the mother of my little angels? What do you think I am?

What I insisted on was absolute certainty. And to achieve that I determined to examine my life, carefully, discreetly, scientifically. With the aid of all the resources of modern psychology, relying on hypnotic suggestion, mind-reading, mental torture, and not neglecting the good old methods of theft, interception of letters, lies, forged signatures, I would find out everything, everything. Is that monomania, the rage of a lunatic? It is not for me to say.

May the enlightened reader serve as the court of last appeal, after he has carefully read this honest book, written in good faith. Perhaps he will find in it some elements in the physiology of love, some clues to the pathology of the soul, and, into the bargain, a curious fragment from the philosophy of crime.

PART ONE

1

It was the thirteenth of May 1875, in Stockholm.

I can still see myself in the Royal Library, which takes up a whole wing of the Castle. I was in the main reading room, with its beechen wainscoting brown with age like the meerschaum of a well-smoked pipe. This enormous room, with its rococo beadings, garlands, chains, and armorial bearings, around which, at the height of the second floor, ran a gallery railed in by small Tuscan columns, was yawning like a great chasm beneath my feet. With its hundred thousand volumes it resembled a gigantic brain, the thoughts of long-forgotten generations neatly arranged on shelves.

An aisle running lengthwise divided the hall into two principal parts, the walls of which were completely hidden by shelves nine feet high. The golden rays of the spring sun were falling through the twelve windows, illuminating the volumes from the Renaissance, bound in white and gold parchment, the black morocco silver-mounted bindings from the seventeenth century, the red-edged, calf-bound volumes from the eighteenth century, the green leather bindings that were the fashion under the Empire, and the cheap paper covers of our own time. Here theologians hobnobbed with apostles of magic, philosophers hobnobbed with naturalists, poets and historians dwelt in peace side by side. It reminded one of a geological deposit of unfathomable depth where, as in a pudding stone, layer was piled upon layer, marking the successive stages arrived at by human folly or human genius.

I can see myself now. I had climbed onto the encircling gallery and was engaged in arranging a collection of old books that a well-known and prudent collector had just presented to the library. He had been clever enough to ensure his own immortality by endowing each volume with his ex libris bearing the motto "*Speravit infestis.*"

Since I was as superstitious as an atheist, this motto, meeting my gaze day after day whenever I happened to open a volume, had made an undeniable impression on me. He was a lucky fellow, this brave man, for even in misfortune he never abandoned hope. . . . But for me all hope was dead. There seemed to be no chance whatever that my play in five acts, and six sets, with three set changes taking place on the open stage, would ever see the footlights. Seven men stood between me and promotion to the post of librarian—seven men, all in perfect health, and four with private incomes. A man of twenty-eight, earning a monthly salary of twenty crowns, with a drama in five acts stowed away in a drawer in his attic, is only too inclined to embrace the modern form of pessimism, the latest flowering of skepticism, so comforting to all failures. It compensates them for unobtainable dinners, and enables them to argue freely and brilliantly, which pleasure often has to make up for the loss of an overcoat, pawned before the end of the winter.

Notwithstanding the fact that I was a member of a learned bohemia that had succeeded an older, artistic bohemia, a contributor to important newspapers and excellent but badly paying magazines, a partner in a society founded for the purpose of translating Hartmann's *Philosophy of the Unconscious,* a member of a secret federation for the promotion of free and paid love, the bearer of the empty title of "Royal Secretary," and the author of two one-act plays that had been performed at the Royal Theater, I was having the greatest difficulty in making ends meet. I hated life, although the thought of relinquishing it had never crossed my mind; on the contrary, I had always done my best to continue not only my own existence but also that of the race. It cannot be denied that pessimism, misinterpreted by the multitude and generally confused with hypochondria, is really a quite serene and even comforting philosophy of life. Since Everything is, relatively speaking, Nothing, why make so much ado, particularly as truth itself is here today and gone tomorrow. Are we not constantly discovering that the truth of yesterday is the folly of tomorrow? Why, then, waste strength and youth in discovering fresh fallacies? The only proven fact is that die we must. Let us live, then! But why? And for whom? . . . Oh, well . . .

All the old junk that had been thrown out at the end of the previous century was brought back in upon the enthronement of Bernadotte, that disillusioned Jacobin. The generation of 1860, to which I belong, had seen all its hopes collapse after the parliamentary reforms of 1864, which had been introduced with so much hoopla. The two chambers that replaced the four estates were found to consist mainly of peasants, and these had transformed parliament into a parish board in which each member fell into the habit of occupying himself with his own small affairs, not concerning himself with vital issues or general progress. After that, politics seemed to us to be a compromise between communal and private interests, with the result that the remnants of what we used to call the Ideal disappeared in bitter quarreling. Add to this the religious reaction that set in after the death of Charles XV, when Sophia of Nassau became queen,* and there are reasons other than purely personal ones for justifying the emergence of an enlightened pessimism. . . .

* Queen Sophie was largely responsible for the bringing of charges in 1884 against Strindberg's publisher for blasphemous expressions in Strindberg's collection of short stories *Married.* —ED.

The dust stirred up in rearranging the books was choking me. I opened a window on the Court of Lions side to catch a breath of fresh air and a glimpse of the green landscape.

A balsamic breeze fanned my face, a breeze laden with the scent of lilac and the rising sap of the poplars. The latticework was completely hidden behind the green tapestry woven by the honeysuckle and wild vine. The acacias and plane trees, well acquainted with the fatal whims of a northern May, were still holding back. It was spring, though the skeletons of the shrubs and trees were still plainly visible underneath the tender young foliage. Beyond the parapet with the Delft vases bearing the mark of Charles XII, rose the masts of the anchored steamers gaily decorated with flags in honor of the Mayday festival. Behind them glittered the bottle-green line of the bay, and from its wooded shores on either side the trees mounted higher and higher, gradually, like steps, evergreens on one side and deciduous trees on the other. All the boats lying at anchor were flying their national colors, more or less symbolic of the different nations: England's red as roast beef, Spain's striped red and yellow like the Venetian blinds of a Moorish balcony, the United States' striped like a bedspread, the gay tricolor of France alongside the gloomy German flag with its sinister iron cross close to the flagstaff, ever reminiscent of mourning; the jerkinet of Denmark; the veiled tricolor of Russia. They were all there, side by side with outspread wings under the blue cover of the northern sky. The noise of carriages, whistles, bells, and cranes lent animation to the picture. The combined odors of oil, leather, salt herring, and groceries mingled with the scent of the lilac. An easterly wind blowing from the open sea and cooled by the drift ice of the Baltic freshened the atmosphere. I forgot my books as soon as I turned my back on them and leaned out of the window, all my senses taking a delicious bath, while below the guards filed past to the strains of the march from

Faust. I was so intoxicated with the music, the flags, the blue sky, the flowers, that I had not noticed the porter entering my office in the meantime with the mail. He touched my shoulder, handed me a letter, and disappeared.

Hm! . . . A letter from a lady.

I hastily opened the envelope, scenting some delightful adventure. It was!

> Meet me punctually at five o'clock this afternoon in front of No. 65 Government Street. Be there! You will know me by the roll of music in my hand.

A short time ago a little vixen had made a fool of me, and I had sworn to take advantage of every favorable opportunity that presented itself. I was going to grab whatever I could lay my hands on. Only one thing jarred on me: the commanding, dictatorial tone of the note offended my manly dignity. What gave this unknown correspondent the idea of ambushing me this way? What the hell were they thinking of, these women with their low opinion of masculine virtue? No question of asking for permission; they issue orders to their conquests!

As it happened, I had planned a trip to the country with some of my friends for this very afternoon. Moreover, the thought of a flirtation in the middle of the day in one of the principal streets of the town was not very alluring. At two o'clock, however, I went into the chemical laboratory, where we picnickers had agreed to meet.

They were already crowding the anteroom: doctors and candidates of philosophy and medicine, all of them anxious to learn the entertainment program for the night. I had changed my mind in the meantime, and with many apologies refused to be one of the party. They all demanded to know why I wouldn't participate in the evening's orgy. I produced my letter and handed it to a zoologist who was looked upon as an expert in all matters pertaining to love. He shook his head while perusing it.

"No good, that . . . ," he muttered disconnectedly; "wants to be married not bought . . . family girl, my dear old chap . . . straight and narrow . . . but do what you like. You'll find us in the Deer Park later on, if the spirit moves you to join us, and if the lady doesn't fit my horoscope."

At the hour indicated I took up my position near the house mentioned and awaited the appearance of the unknown beauty.

That roll of music in her hand, what was it but an invitation to domesticity? It differed in no way from the announcements on the fourth page of certain newspapers. I suddenly felt uneasy. Too late—the lady had arrived and we stood looking at each other.

My first impression—something I attached great importance to—was quite vague. She was of indeterminate age, between twenty-nine and forty-two, in a daring dress. What was she? Artist or bluestocking? A family girl or a hussy? Emancipated or a cocotte?

She introduced herself as the fiancée of an old friend of mine, an opera singer, and said that he wanted me to look after her while she was staying in town. A lie, as I found out later.

She belonged to the little-bird class of women who twitter incessantly. After she had talked for half an hour I knew all about her; I knew all her emotions, all her thoughts. But I was only half-interested, and asked her if I could do anything for her.

"You want me to escort you?" I exclaimed, after she had explained what she wanted. "Don't you know that I am the devil incarnate?"

"You only think you are," she replied; "but I know all about you. You're unhappy, that's all. You need someone to lift you out of the dumps."

"You know me, hm? To the bottom of my soul, I suppose. All you know about me is the already antiquated opinion your fiancé may *possibly* have."

It was no use protesting; my "charming friend" had all the answers. She knew how to read a man's heart, even from a distance. She was one of those sticky, slimy creatures, eager to conquer by worming their way into the hidden depths of men's souls. She kept up a large correspondence, bombarded prominent people with boring letters, gave advice and warning to young people, and believed she was called upon to direct and guide the destinies of men. Greedy for power, head of a business for ensuring the salvation of one's soul (highly recommended!), patroness of all the world, she now felt called upon to save me!

In a word, a schemer of the purest water, with little intelligence but a great deal of female impudence.

I began to tease her by making fun of everything—the world, men, God. She told me my ideas were decadent and old-fashioned.

"Decadent! How can you say that? On the contrary, they're as fresh as today. But what about yours? Relics of the past, commonplaces of my boyhood, bottom of the rubbish pile. You think you're offering me fresh goods, but it's nothing but old preserves in leaky cans. And it's beginning to stink, if you know what I mean."

Furious, unable to control herself, she left me without a word of goodby.

Finished with her, I went to join my friends in the Park, and spent the evening with them.

My head was still cloudy the following morning when I received a letter from her, a letter filled with feminine vainglory in which she overwhelmed me with reproaches, largely tempered by forbearance and compassion; she said she was praying for my spiritual health, and concluded by arranging a second meeting. We ought to pay a visit, said she, to her fiancé's aged mother.

Having been brought up to behave politely, I resigned myself to facing another shower of words; but, determined to get off as cheaply as possible, I made up my mind to appear perfectly indifferent to all questions relating to religion, the world, and everything else.

But—miracle of miracles!—the lady, dressed in a tightly fitting cloth dress, trimmed with fur, and wearing a Rembrandt hat, greeted me most cordially; she was full of the tender solicitude of an older sister, avoided all dangerous ground, and was altogether so charming that our souls, thanks to a mutual desire to please, met in friendly talk, and before we parted a feeling of genuine sympathy had sprung up between us.

After having paid our call we took advantage of the lovely spring evening and went for a stroll.

I am not sure whether it was from an imperative desire to get even with her or whether I felt annoyed at having been made to play the part of a confidant; whatever it was, the iniquitous idea occurred to me to tell her, in strict confidence, that I was practically engaged to be married. This was only half a lie, for I was really going rather steady with a certain lady.

Her manner changed immediately. She talked to me like a grandmother, began to pity the girl, questioned me about her character, her looks, her social status, her circumstances. I painted a portrait well calculated to excite her jealousy. Our eager conversation languished. My guardian angel's interest in me waned when she suspected a rival who might possibly be equally anxious to save my soul. We parted, still feeling the chill that had imperceptibly arisen between us.

When we met on the following day we talked exclusively of love and my supposed fiancée.

But after we had visited theaters and concerts for a week and taken numerous walks together, she had gained her object. Seeing her every day had become a habit which I felt unable to break. Conversation with an unusual woman is an art. There is an almost sensual pleasure in the rubbing together of the souls, the spiritual embrace, the emotional hide-and-seek.

One day, on meeting her as usual, I found her almost beside herself. She was full of news that she had just received. Her fiancé was furiously jealous. She accused herself of having been indiscreet. He was recommending her to observe the utmost reserve in her association with me: my opera singer seemed to have a presentiment that the matter would end badly.

"I can't understand such detestable jealousy," she said, looking distressed.

"Because you don't have the faintest idea what love is," I answered.

"Not that sort of love!"

"That sort of love, my dear lady, is the highest form of possession. Jealousy is only the fear of losing what one possesses."

"Possession! Disgusting!"

"Mutual possession, don't you see, since each possesses the other."

But she refused to understand love in that sense. Love to her was something unselfish, exalted, chaste, inexplicable.

Of course she did not love her fiancé, but he was head over heels in love with her, and I proved this to her.

She lost her temper and then blurted out that she had never loved him.

"And yet you contemplate marrying him?"

"Naturally. He would be lost if I didn't."

"Always trying to save souls!"

She grew more and more angry. She insisted she was not, and never had been, really engaged to him.

So we had both been lying! What a coincidence!

There remained nothing for me to do but to make a clean breast of it, and take back my previous statement that I was "as good as engaged." Now we were at liberty to make use of our freedom.

As she had now no longer any cause for jealousy, the game began afresh, and this time we played it in deadly earnest. I confessed my love to her—in writing. She forwarded the letter to her fiancé, who lost no time in heaping insults on my head—by post.

I told her that she must choose between him and me. But she carefully refrained from doing so, for her object was to have me and him and as many more as she could get, kneeling at her feet and adoring her.

She was a flirt, a man-eater, a chaste polyandrist.

Nevertheless, perhaps for want of someone better, I had fallen in love with her, for I loathed one-night love affairs, and the solitude of my attic bored me.

Towards the end of her stay in town I invited her to pay me a visit at the library. I wanted to dazzle her, show myself to her in impressive surroundings that would overawe this arrogant little brain.

I dragged her from gallery to gallery, exhibiting all my bibliographical knowledge. I compelled her to admire the miniatures of the Middle Ages, the autographs of famous men. I evoked the great historical memories held captive in old manuscripts and incunabula. In the end her insignificance came home to her and she became embarrassed at her inferiority vis-à-vis me.

"But you are a very learned man!" she exclaimed.

"Of course."

"Oh, my poor old actor!" she murmured, alluding to my friend, her so-called fiancé.

That was the end of him once and for all, I thought. How wrong I was!

He threatened—by post—to shoot me. He accused me of having robbed him of his future bride—*whom he had entrusted to me!* I proved to him that he could not have been robbed, for the simple reason that he had not possessed anything. After that, our correspondence ceased and gave way to a menacing silence.

Her stay in town was drawing to an end. On the eve of her departure I received a jubilant letter from her, telling me of an unexpected piece of good luck. She had read my play to some prominent people who had influence in the theater. The play had made such an impression on them that they were anxious to make my acquaintance. She would tell me all the details in the afternoon.

At the appointed hour I met her and accompanied her on a shopping expedition to make a few last purchases. She was talking of nothing but the sensation my play had created, and when I explained to her that I hated patronage of any sort, she did her utmost to convert me to her point of view. I paid little attention to her and went on grumbling.

"It disgusts me. Ringing doorbells, meeting strangers, and talking to them of everything except what's important, whining like a beggar for favors."

I was fighting as hard as I could when suddenly she stopped before a young lady, very well, even elegantly dressed, with a pleasing figure and a distinguished appearance. The lady, whom she introduced as Baroness X, said a few words to me which the noise of the crowd rendered all but inaudible. I stammered a reply, annoyed at having been caught in a trap set for me by a wily little schemer. It was obviously prearranged.

A few seconds more and the Baroness had gone, but not without having personally repeated the invitation that my companion had already brought me a little earlier in the afternoon.

The girlish appearance and baby face of the Baroness, who must have been at least twenty-five years of age, surprised me. She looked like a schoolgirl. Her little face was framed by roguish curls, golden as a cornfield. She had the shoulders of a princess and a supple, willowy figure. The way she bowed her head expressed at the same time candor, respect, and superiority. And this delicious little girl of a mother was still hale and hearty after having read my tragedy! How fortunate!

Married to a captain of the Guards, the mother of a little girl of three, she took a passionate interest in the theater, without, however, having the slightest prospect of ever being able to enter the profession herself; a sacrifice demanded from her by the rank and position not only of her husband but also of her father-in-law, who had recently received the appointment of a gentleman-in-waiting.

This was the state of affairs when my love dream melted away. A steamer was bearing my lady love into the presence of her actor. He would vindicate his rights now and take delight in making fun of my letters to her: just retribution for my having laughed at his letters in the company of his inamorata while she was staying here.

On the dock, at the very moment of our affectionate farewell, she made me promise to call on the Baroness without delay. These were the last words we exchanged.

The innocent daydreams, so different from the coarse orgies of learned bohemia, left a void in my heart that had to be filled. The friendly, seemingly harmless company of a gentlewoman, this exchange between two people of opposite sexes, had been sweet to me after my long solitude, for I had quarreled with my family and was very lonely. The love of home life, which my bohemian existence had deadened for a while, was reawakened by my relations with a very ordinary but respectable member of the other sex. At any rate, one evening at six o'clock I found myself at the entrance gate of a house in Northgate Street.

Fate is strange. It was the same old apartment in which my father had lived, the house in which I had spent the most miserable years of my childhood, where I had fought through the troubles and storms of puberty and confirmation, where I had seen my mother die and replaced by a stepmother. I suddenly felt ill at ease, and my first impulse was to turn back. I was afraid to stir up the memories of the misery of my youth. There was the courtyard with its tall ash trees; how impatiently I used to wait for the tender young green leaves at the return of spring. There was the gloomy house, built against a sand quarry, the unavoidable and steady collapse of which had lowered the rents.

But in spite of the feeling of depression caused by so many melancholy memories, I pulled myself together, entered, walked upstairs, and rang the bell.

As I stood listening to the echoing sound of the bell, I could not help thinking that my father himself would come and open the door to me. But a servant appeared and disappeared again to announce me. A few seconds afterwards I stood face to face with the Baron, who gave me a hearty welcome. He was a man of about thirty, tall, rather corpulent, with a noble carriage and the perfect manners of a man of the world. His strong, slightly puffy face was animated by a pair of intensely sad blue eyes. The smile on his lips was forever giving way to an expression of surprising bitterness, which spoke of disappointments, miscarried plans, lost illusions.

The drawing room—once upon a time our dining room —was not furnished in any particular style. The Baron, who bore the name of a famous general, a Turenne or Condé of our country, had filled it with the portraits of his ancestors, dating back to the Thirty Years' War; heroes in white cuirasses with Louis XIV wigs. Among them hung landscapes of the Düsseldorf school of painting. Pieces of old furniture, restored and gilded, stood next to straight chairs and easy chairs of a more modern date. The whole room seemed to breathe an atmosphere of peace and domestic love.

Presently the Baroness joined us—enchanting, as cordial as her husband, direct and pleasant. Yet there was a certain stiffness in her manner, a trace of embarrassment that chilled me until I discovered a reason for it in the sound of voices coming from an adjacent room. I concluded that she had other visitors and apologized for having called at an inconvenient time. They were playing whist in the next room, and I was forthwith introduced to four members of the family: the gentleman-in-waiting, a retired captain, and the Baroness' mother and aunt. As soon as the old people had sat down again to play, we younger ones be-

gan to talk. The Baron mentioned his great love of painting. A scholarship, granted him by the late King Charles
XV, had enabled him to pursue his studies at Düsseldorf.
This fact constituted a point of contact between us, for I
had had a scholarship from the same king, only in my case
it had been granted for literary purposes. We discussed
painting, the theater, the personality of our patron. But
gradually the flow of conversation ceased, largely checked
by the whist players, who joined in every now and then,
laying rude fingers on sensitive spots, tearing open scarcely
healed wounds. I began to feel ill at ease in this hetero-
geneous company. I got to my feet to say goodby. The
Baron and his wife accompanied me to the door and
dropped their constrained manner as soon as they were
out of earshot of the old people. They asked me to have
dinner with them, just the three of us, on the following
Saturday, and after a little chat on the landing we parted
as old friends.

2

At three o'clock on the following Saturday I started for
the house on Northgate Street. I was greeted like an old
and trusted friend and unhesitatingly admitted to the intimacies of the house. Dinner was seasoned with mutual
confidences. The Baron, who had developed a distaste for
his work, belonged to the malcontents under the new regime, their dissatisfaction with things having arisen upon
King Oscar's coming to the throne. Jealous of the great
popularity of his deceased brother, the new ruler attempted to thwart all the plans and projects his predecessor had sponsored. Consequently, the friends of the old
regime, who recalled those happy days, the tolerant out-
look, the dreams of progress, quietly got together and
formed an opposition group representing common sense,

but without any intention of involving themselves in the petty wranglings of the political parties.

As we revived our memories of the good old days, we drew closer and closer together. The last of the prejudices that I as a *petit bourgeois* formerly held against the upper nobility, which was in retreat after the constitutional reforms of 1865, vanished to make room for sympathy with the fallen giants. The Baroness, who was of Finnish birth and had not been in the country long, was not initiated into the situation in Sweden and could not take part in our talk. As soon as dinner was over, she went to the piano and began to entertain us with some songs, and after that the Baron and I discovered that we possessed a hitherto unsuspected talent for Wennerberg's duets.* The hours passed rapidly. Finally we amused ourselves by casting the parts and reading a short play that had just been performed at the Royal Theater.

But suddenly our spirits flagged and the inevitable pause ensued, that awkward pause certain to occur after one has tried so hard to appear at one's best. Again the memories of the past oppressed me and I grew silent.

"What's the matter?" asked the Baroness.

"There are ghosts in this house," I replied, trying to account for my silence. "Ages ago I lived here—yes, ages ago. That's how old I feel."

"Can't we drive away those ghosts?" she asked, looking at me with a charming expression, full of motherly tenderness.

"I'm afraid we can't; that's the privilege of someone else," laughed the Baron. "She alone can banish the gloomy thoughts. Come now, aren't you engaged to Miss X?"

* Gunnar Wennerberg composed the words and music for a number of songs for two singers, called *Gluntarne* (1847–50), which picture student life in Uppsala in the 1840s and have remained perennially popular.—ED.

"No, Baron, it was all a mistake; it was love's labors lost."

"What! Is she someone else's?" asked the Baroness, scrutinizing my face.

"What a question!"

"Oh, I am sorry! That girl's a treasure. And I'm certain she's fond of you."

I lashed out at the poor actor. Then all three of us began to rail against the unfortunate singer, accusing him of attempting to compel a woman to marry him against her will. The Baroness tried to comfort me by insisting that things were bound to come out right in the end, and promised to intercede for me on her next trip to Finland, which was to take place very shortly.

"No one shall succeed," she assured me, with an angry flash in her eyes, "in forcing that dear girl into a marriage her heart doesn't approve of."

It was seven o'clock as I rose to go. But they pressed me so eagerly to spend the evening with them that I almost suspected they were bored in each other's company, although they had only been married for three years, and heaven had blessed their union with a dear little girl. They told me that they were expecting a cousin and were anxious for me to meet her that I might tell them what I thought of her.

While we were still talking, a letter was handed to the Baron. He tore it open, read it hastily, and, with a muttered exclamation, handed it to his wife.

"That's incredible!" she exclaimed after glancing at the contents. She cast a questioning look at her husband, who nodded. Then she turned to confide in me as if I were a close friend.

"It's from my cousin. Can you imagine, my aunt and uncle forbid their daughter to stay here, with the excuse that there's been talk about her and my husband."

"It's preposterous!" said the Baron. "A mere child, pretty, innocent, unhappy at home—she likes to be with us.

We're young, newly married, close relatives. . . . But people have to gossip!"

Did a skeptical smile betray me? His remark was followed by a dead silence, a certain confusion, badly concealed under an invitation to take a walk in the garden.

I left after supper, about ten o'clock, and no sooner had I crossed the threshold than I began to ponder on the happenings of that eventful day.

I felt convinced, in spite of every appearance of happiness, and notwithstanding their evident affection, that my friends harbored a very formidable skeleton in their closet. Their wistful eyes, their fits of absent-mindedness, something unspoken but felt, pointed to a hidden grief, to secrets, which I dreaded to discover.

Why in the world, I asked myself, do they live so quietly, voluntary exiles in a wretched section of town? They were like two shipwrecked people in their eagerness to pour out their hearts to the first comer.

The Baroness in particular perplexed me. I tried to call up her picture, but was confused by the wealth of contradictory characteristics I had discovered in her and from which I had to choose. Kindhearted, amiable, brusque, enthusiastic, communicative, reserved, cold, excitable, she seemed to be subject to melancholy moods and brooding over ambitious dreams. Though she was neither commonplace nor clever, she impressed people. Of Byzantine slenderness, which allowed her dress to fall in simple, noble folds, like the dress of a St. Cecilia, her body was of bewitching proportions, her wrists and ankles exquisitely beautiful. Every now and then the pale, somewhat rigid features of her small face warmed into life and sparkled with infectious gaiety. It was difficult to say who was master in the house. He, the soldier, accustomed to command but burdened with ill health, seemed submissive—more, I thought, from an innate indolence than lack of will. They were certainly on friendly terms, but there was none of the ecstasy of young love. When I made their acquaintance they were delighted to rejuvenate themselves by calling up the memories of the past before a third person. In studying them more closely, I became convinced that they lived on souvenirs of the past and bored each other. Why else did they invite me so frequently after my first call?

On the eve of the Baroness' departure for Finland I called on her to say goodby. It was a lovely evening in June. The moment I entered the courtyard I caught sight of her behind the trellis; she was standing in a shrubbery of aristolochias, and the transcendent beauty of her appearance came upon me almost with a shock. She was dressed in a white piqué dress, richly embroidered, the masterpiece of some Russian serf girl. Her chain, brooches, and bangles of alabaster seemed to throw a soft light over her, like lamplight falling through an opalescent globe. The broad green leaves threw deathlike hues on her pale face with its shining coal-black eyes.

I was shaken, utterly confused, as if I were gazing at a vision. The need to worship, latent in my heart, awoke, and with it the desire to proclaim my adoration. The void left behind when religion was cast out was now filled again; the yearning to adore had reappeared in a new form. God was deposed, Woman took his place. But woman as both virgin and mother, for when I looked at the little girl by her side, I could not understand how that birth had been possible. The relationship between her and her husband seemed to put all sexual intercourse out of the question, so incorporeal did their relationship appear. Henceforth this woman represented to me a soul incarnate, a soul pure and unapproachable, clothed with one of those radiant bodies with which the Holy Scriptures endow the souls of the dead. I worshiped her—I worshiped her against my will. I adored her just as she was, as she appeared to me at that moment, as mother and wife; wife of this husband, mother of this child. For me to worship her to my satisfaction, there had to be a husband. If she had no husband, I said to myself, she would be a widow, and could I be certain I would worship her then? Maybe if she were mine . . . my very own . . . ? No! I could not conceive such a desecrating thought. Moreover if she were married to me, she would no longer be the wife of this particular man, the mother of this particular child, the mistress of this particular house. Such as she was I adored her, I would not have her otherwise.

Whether it was the melancholy childhood memories that exerted an influence on me, or whether it was my lower-class instincts, my admiration for a superior race, the pure blood—a feeling that would vanish the instant she no longer stood so high—I do not know. At any rate, the adoration that I had conceived for her resembled in every point the religion from which I had just emancipated myself. I wanted to adore, to sacrifice myself, to suffer without hope of any other reward but the ecstasies of worship, self-sacrifice, and suffering.

I appointed myself her guardian angel. I wanted to watch over her lest the power of my love should sweep her off her feet and engulf her. I carefully avoided being alone with her so that no familiarity her husband might resent would intrude between us.

But today, on the eve of her departure, when I found her in the summer arbor, she was alone. We exchanged a few commonplaces. But soon my excitement rose to such a pitch that it communicated itself to her. Gazing at her with burning eyes, I saw the desire to confide in me forming itself in her heart. She told me that the thought of a separation from her husband and child, however short, made her miserable. She implored me to spend as much of my leisure with them as I could and not to forget her while she was looking after my interests in Finland.

"You love her very much—with all your heart, don't you?" she asked, looking at me steadfastly.

"Can you ask?" I replied, oppressed by the painful lie.

For I had no longer any doubt that my May dream had been nothing more than a fancy, a whim, a mere pastime.

Afraid of tainting her with my passion, fearful of entangling her against my will in the net of my emotions, intending to protect her against myself, I dropped the dangerous subject and asked after her husband. She made a face, evidently interpreting my somewhat strange behavior quite correctly. Perhaps also—the suspicion rose in my mind much later—she found pleasure in the thought that her beauty confused me. Or maybe she was conscious at that moment of the terrible power she had acquired over me, a Joseph whose coldness was only assumed, whose chastity was forced upon him.

"I'm boring you," she said smilingly. "I'd better call for reinforcements."

And with a clear voice she called to her husband, who was in his room upstairs.

The window was thrown open and the Baron appeared, a friendly smile on his open countenance. A few minutes later he joined us in the garden. He was wearing the handsome uniform of the Guards and looked very distinguished. With his dark-blue tunic, embroidered in yellow and silver, his tall, powerful figure, he was a worthy pendant to the image, alabaster against white, that I admired at his side. They were really a strikingly handsome couple; the charms of the one served but to heighten those of the other. The sight of them was an artistic treat, a brilliant spectacle.

After dinner the Baron proposed that we should accompany his wife on the steamer as far as the last customs station. This proposal, to which I gladly agreed, seemed to give the Baroness a great deal of pleasure; she was delighted with the prospect of admiring the Stockholm skerries from the deck of a steamer on a beautiful summer night. . . .

At ten o'clock on the following evening we met on board the steamer a short time before the hour of sailing. It was a clear night; the sky was a blaze of brilliant orange; the sea lay before us, calm and blue. The wooded shores passed by bathed in a light that was neither that of day or night, but left the viewer wavering between two vague sensations, sunrise and sunset.

After midnight our enthusiasm, which had been kept alive by the constantly changing panorama and the memories which it called up, cooled a little. We were fighting against an overwhelming desire to sleep. The early dawn found us with pallid faces, shivering in the morning breeze. We suddenly became sentimental. We swore eternal friendship. It was fate that had thrown us together, and already we felt that fatal chain that was to shackle our lives together. Having not yet regained my strength after an attack of ague, I still looked haggard and I was treated like an ailing child. The Baroness wrapped her rug around me and made me drink some wine, all the while babbling to me like a tender mother. I let her have her way. I was so tired I was past caring. My heart, which I had thought was closed forever, opened up. Weaned long ago from womanly tenderness, the secret of which none but a motherly woman knows, I deluged her with words of respectful adoration. My brain, feverish from lack of sleep, teemed with poetic dreams.

All the half-formed dreams of that lost night began to take shape, a vague, mysterious, insubstantial shape. All the pent-up need of a suffocating poetic talent to express itself found release in airy visions. I spoke for hours, without interruption, drawing inspiration from two pairs of eyes, which gazed at me fascinated. I felt as if my weak body was being consumed by the burning fire of my imagination. I gradually lost all sense of my physical existence.

Suddenly the sun rose, the myriads of islets that seemed to be swimming in the bay appeared enveloped in flames. The branches of the fir trees glowed like copper, their slender needles yellow as sulphur. The windowpanes of the cottages, dotted along the shore, sparkled like golden mirrors. The columns of smoke rising from the chimneys indicated that breakfasts were being cooked. The fishing boats were setting out to the bays to bring in their nets. The seagulls, scenting the small herring underneath the dark green waves, were screaming themselves hoarse.

But on the steamer absolute silence reigned. The travelers were still fast asleep in their cabins; we alone were on deck. The captain, heavy with sleep, was watching us from the bridge, wondering, no doubt, what we could be talking about.

At three o'clock in the morning the pilot cutter appeared from behind a neck of land, and parting was imminent.

Only a few of the larger islands now separated us from the open sea. The swell of the ocean was already distinctly discernible. We could hear the roar of the huge breakers on the steep cliffs at the extreme end of the land.

The time to say goodby had arrived. They kissed one another, he and she, with heartbreaking tenderness. She took my hand in hers and pressed it passionately, her eyes full of tears. She begged her husband to take care of me, and implored me to bring him some comfort during his two weeks as a widower.

I bowed, I kissed her hand without considering whether it was quite proper or whether I might be betraying to her my inmost feelings. The engines stopped, the steamer slowed down, the pilot took up his position in the wheelhouse. Two steps toward the accommodation ladder—I descended, and found myself at the side of the Baron in the pilot cutter.

The steamer towered above our heads. Leaning against the rail, the Baroness looked down upon us with a sad smile, her innocent eyes brimming over with tears. The propeller slowly began to move, the giant got under way again, her Russian flag fluttering in the breeze. We were tossing on the rolling waves, waving our handkerchiefs wet with tears. The little face grew smaller and smaller, the delicate features were blotted out, two great eyes only remained gazing at us fixedly, and presently they too were

swallowed up like the rest. Another moment and only a
fluttering bluish veil, attached to a Japanese straw hat,
was visible, and a waving white handkerchief; then only
a white spot, a tiny white dot; now nothing but the shape-
less mass, wrapped in dirty gray smoke. . . .

We went ashore at the Pilots and Customs Station,
which was also a popular summer resort. The village was
still asleep. Not a soul was on the pier, and we turned
and watched the steamer altering her course to starboard
and disappearing behind the rocky island that formed the
last bulwark against the sea.

As the steamer disappeared the Baron leaned against
my shoulder, shaking with the effort of stifling his sobs. We
stood for a while without speaking a word. Were these
tears caused by lack of sleep, by the nervous exhaustion
following a sleepless night? Had he a presentiment of misfortune, or was it merely the pain of parting with his wife?
At that moment I couldn't say.

We went to the village, depressed and taciturn, in the
hope of getting some breakfast. But the inn was not yet
open. We strolled through the town and looked at the
closed doors, the drawn blinds. Beyond the village we
came upon an isolated spot near a small strait. The water
was clear and transparent, and tempted us to bathe our
eyes. I produced a little case and took from it a clean
handkerchief, a toothbrush, a piece of soap, and a bottle
of eau de Cologne. The Baron laughed at my fastidious-
ness but nevertheless availed himself gratefully of the
chance of a hasty toilet, borrowing from me the necessary
implements. On returning to the village I noticed coal
smoke sifting through the leaves of the alder trees down
by the shore. I implied by a gesture that this was a last
farewell greeting brought by the wind from the steamer.
But the Baron pretended not to understand my meaning.

He was a distressing sight at breakfast, with his big,
sleepy head sunk on his breast, and his swollen features.
Both of us suffered from self-consciousness; he was in a

sullen mood and maintained an obstinate silence. Once he seized my hand and apologized for his absent-mindedness, but almost directly afterwards impolitely relapsed into his reveries. I made every effort to rouse him but in vain. We were out of harmony, the tie between us was broken. An expression of coarseness and vulgarity had stolen into his face, usually so frank and pleasant. The reflection of the charm, the living grace of his beloved wife had vanished. The uncultivated man reappeared.

I didn't know what he was thinking. Did he suspect my feelings? To judge from his behavior, he must have been a prey to very conflicting emotions, for at one minute he would press my hand, calling me his best, his only friend; at the next he would turn his back on me.

I discovered, with a feeling of dismay, that we only lived in Her and for Her. Since our sun had set we seemed dull and lusterless.

I determined to shake him off as soon as we got back to town, but he held on to me, entreating me for God's sake to accompany him to his house.

When we entered the deserted home, we felt as if we had entered a morgue. We were seized by another crying attack. Full of confusion and embarrassment, I did not know what to do. I finally decided to laugh at it all.

"It's too absurd," I said. "Here are a captain of the Guards and a royal secretary whimpering like—"

"It's a relief," he interrupted me.

He sent for his little girl, but her presence only aggravated the bitter feeling of regret at our loss.

It was now nine o'clock in the morning. Tired out, he invited me to take a nap on the sofa while he went to lie down on his bed. He put a cushion under my head, covered me with his military cloak, and wished me a sound sleep, thanking me cordially for having taken compassion on his loneliness. His brotherly kindness was like an echo of his wife's tenderness; she seemed to fill his thoughts completely. I sank into a deep sleep, dimly aware, at the moment before losing consciousness, of his huge form stealing to my improvised bed, asking me once again whether I was quite comfortable.

It was noon when I awoke. He was already up. He was afraid of being alone and proposed that we should breakfast together in the Deer Park. No sooner said than done. We spent the day together, talking about all sorts of things, but every subject led us back to her on whose life our own lives seemed to have been grafted.

3

I spent the two following days alone, looking for solitude in my library, the cellars of which, once the sculpture rooms of the museum, suited my mood. The large room, built in the rococo style and looking on to the Lion's court, contained the manuscripts. I spent a great deal of time there, reading at haphazard anything that seemed old enough to draw my attention from recent events. But the more I read, the more the present melted into the past, and Queen Christine's letters, yellow with age, whispered into my ears words of love from the Baroness. To avoid the company of inquisitive friends, I shunned my usual restaurant. I would at no cost sully my tongue by confessing my new faith before those scoffers; they should never know. I was jealous of my own personality, which was henceforth consecrated to her alone. As I walked through the streets, I had a vision of acolytes walking before me, their tinkling bells announcing to the passers-by the approach of the Holy of Holies enshrined in the monstrance of my heart. I imagined myself in mourning, deep mourning for a queen, and longed to bid the crowd bare their heads at the passing of my stillborn love, which had no chance of ever being resurrected.

On the third day I was roused from my lethargy by the rolling of drums and the mournful strains of Chopin's

"Funeral March." I rushed to the window and noticed the captain marching by at the head of his Guards. He looked up at my window and acknowledged my presence with a nod and a smile. The band was playing his wife's favorite piece, at his orders, and the unsuspecting musicians had no inkling that they played it in her honor for him and for me, and before an even more unsuspecting crowd of onlookers.

Half an hour later the Baron called for me at the library. I took him through the passages in the basement, overcrowded with cupboards and shelves, into the manuscript room. He looked cheerful and at once communicated to me the contents of a letter he had received from his wife. All was going well. She had enclosed a note for me. I devoured it with my eyes, trying hard to hide my excitement. She thanked me frankly and graciously for having looked after "her old man"; she said she had felt flattered by my evident grief at parting, and added that she was staying with my "guardian angel," to whom she was getting more and more attached. She expressed great admiration for her character, and in conclusion held out hopes of a happy ending. That was all.

So she was in love with me, this "guardian angel" of mine! This monster! The very thought of her nauseated me. I was compelled to act the part of a lover against my will; I was condemned to play an abominable farce, perhaps one without an end. The truth of the old adage about playing with fire suddenly hit me. Caught in my own trap, furious, I pictured to myself the detestable creature who had forced herself on me: Mongolian-eyed, sallow-faced, red-armed. With infernal satisfaction I recalled her seductive tricks, her suspicious behavior, which had set my friends to asking snidely, "Who's that wench you take out to pasture in the clover fields on the edge of town?"

Remembering her tricks, her attentions, her flattering tongue gave me a kind of vicious pleasure. I remembered the way she took her watch out of the bosom of her dress in order to reveal a bit of dainty underclothing. I remembered a certain Sunday in the Park. We were strolling along the broad avenues when she all at once proposed that we should walk among the trees. I was amazed at her, for a walk in those woods could give anyone a bad reputation. But she answered all my objections with a short "Bother propriety!"

Saying she wanted to gather anemones under the hazel bushes, she left me standing in the avenue and disappeared behind the shrubs. I followed, embarrassed. She sat down in a sheltered spot under a buckthorn bush, spreading out her skirts and showing off her feet, small but disfigured by the bunions of frost bite. An uncomfortable silence fell between us. I thought of the old maids of Corinth who would rage in fury if they weren't raped on schedule. She looked up at me with a stupid expression on her face. I swear the only thing that saved her virtue that time was her extraordinary homeliness and my dislike of easy conquests.

Every one of these details, which I had always put away from me as odious, came into my mind and oppressed me, now that there seemed a prospect of winning her. I prayed fervently for the opera singer's success. In the meantime I had to be patient and hide my feelings.

As I was reading his wife's note, the Baron sat down at the table, which was littered with old books and documents. He was playing with his carved ivory baton, absent-mindedly, as if he were conscious of his inferiority in literary matters. He defeated all my attempts to interest him in my work with an indifferent, "Yes, yes, very interesting!"

Abashed by the evidence of his rank, his neckpiece, the sash, the whole brilliant uniform, I endeavored to readjust the balance by showing off my knowledge. But I only succeeded in making him feel uncomfortable.

The sword versus the pen! The aristocrat on his way down, the commoner on his way up! Perhaps the woman unconsciously, but clairvoyantly, saw into the future when she chose the father of her children from the aristocracy of intelligence.

In spite of his constant efforts to treat me as his equal, the Baron, without admitting it even to himself, was always constrained in my presence. At times he paid due deference to my superior knowledge, tacitly acknowledging his inferiority to me in certain respects. At other times he would ride the high horse; then a hint from the Baroness was sufficient to take him off it. In his wife's eyes the inherited coat of arms counted for very little, and the dusty coat of the man of letters completely eclipsed the full-dress uniform of the captain. Had he himself not been aware of this when he donned a painter's blouse and entered the studio at Düsseldorf as the least of all the pupils? In all probability he had, but still there always remained a certain refinement, an inherited tradition, and he was by no means free from the jealous hatred that exists between students and officers. For the moment I was necessary to him, since I shared his sorrow, and therefore he invited me to dine with him.

After the coffee he suggested that we should both write to the Baroness. He brought me paper and pen and compelled me to write whether I wanted to or not. I racked my brain for platitudes under which to hide the thoughts of my heart.

When I had finished my letter I handed it to the Baron and asked him to read it.

"I never read other people's letters," he answered, with hypocritical pride.

"And I never write to another man's wife unless the man reads what I write."

He glanced at my letter and, with an enigmatical smile, enclosed it in his own.

I saw nothing of him during the rest of the week until I met him one evening at a street corner. He seemed very pleased to see me and we went immediately to a café, where I had to listen to his inescapable confidences.

He had just returned from the country, where he had spent a few days with his wife's cousin. Without ever having met that charming person, I was easily able to draw a mental picture of her from the traces of her influence on the Baron's character. He had lost his haughtiness and his melancholy. His face looked as if it were made up to suggest gay sensuality. His vocabulary had been enriched by slang expressions of doubtful taste. Even the tone of his voice was altered.

"A weak mind," I said to myself, "susceptible to every influence; a *tabula rasa* on which the lightest woman's hand can write, according to her sweet will, either the most stupid of her thoughts or the best bits of her embryonic genius."

He behaved like an operetta hero who joked, told off-color stories, and made a spectacle of himself. His charm was gone with his uniform; and when after supper, slightly intoxicated, he suggested that we should go looking for girls, I thought him positively repulsive. All that was left of the man I had known was the neckpiece, the sash, and the collar of his uniform.

He got more and more drunk and finally wanted to confide to me the intimate secrets of his bedroom. I interrupted him curtly and indignantly started to leave, but he assured me that his wife had given him absolute freedom to amuse himself in any way whatever while he was a grass widower. At first I thought this very understanding, but on further thought it confirmed me in my opinion of the Baroness' naturally frigid temperament. We parted very early, and I returned to my room perplexed and disturbed by the indiscreet disclosures to which I had been forced to listen.

This woman, although apparently in love with her husband, after a union of three years permitted him every freedom without claiming the same right for herself. It was strange, as unnatural as love without jealousy, light without shade. It was impossible; there must be more to it. He had told me the Baroness was naturally cold. That, too, was an anomaly. Perhaps she really was the embodiment of the virgin mother, such as I had already divined. And was not chastity a characteristic, an attribute of a superior race? Was it not a purity of soul intended to correct the mores of the upper class? This was exactly as I had imagined it in my youthful meditations when a young girl roused my admiration without in the least exciting my senses. Childish dreams! Charming ignorance of woman, a problem more complex than a bachelor imagines!

At last the Baroness returned, radiant with health, rejuvenated by the many memories she had experienced in meeting her childhood friends again.

"Here is the dove with the olive branch," she said, handing me a letter from my so-called sweetheart.

I waded through the presumptuous twaddle, the effusions of a heartless bluestocking anxious to win independence by marriage—any marriage.

I began to read with pretended enjoyment, but before I had finished I had made up my mind to put an end to the idiotic affair.

"Can you tell me for certain," I asked the Baroness, "whether the lady is engaged to the singer or not?"

"Yes and no."

"Has she given him her word?"

"No."

"Does she want to marry him?"

"No."

"Do her parents wish it?"

"No."

"Why is she so determined to marry him, then?"

"Because . . . I don't know."

"Is she in love with me?"

"Perhaps."

"Then she's simply husband-shopping. She has only one

thought, to make a bargain with the highest bidder. She doesn't know what love is."

"What about you? What do you think love is?"

"A passion stronger than all others, a force of nature absolutely irresistible, something like thunder, rising floods, waterfalls, storms—"

She gazed into my eyes, forgetting the reproaches which, in the interest of her friend, had risen to the tip of her tongue.

"And is your love for her a force like that?" she asked.

I had a strong impulse to tell her everything. But suppose I did? . . . The bond between us would be broken, and without the lie that protected me from my illicit passion I would be lost.

Afraid of committing myself, I asked her to drop the subject. I said that my cruel sweetheart was dead as far as I was concerned and that all that remained for me to do was to forget her.

The Baroness did her utmost to comfort me, but she did not cloak the fact that I had a dangerous rival in the singer, who was on the spot and in personal contact with his ladylove.

The Baron, evidently bored by our conversation, interrupted us peevishly, telling us that we would get our fingers burned.

"Meddling with other people's love affairs is utter folly!" he exclaimed, almost rudely. The Baroness' face flushed with indignation. I hastily changed the subject to avoid a scene.

4

The stone had been set rolling.

The lie, originally a mere whim, took shape and form. Full of apprehension and shame, I told myself fairy tales that I ended in believing. In them I played the part of the

ill-starred lover, a part that came easy enough, for with
the exception of the object of my tenderness, the fairy
tales agreed in every detail with reality.

I was indeed caught in my own net. One day, on returning home, I found a visiting card from a Mr. X, an
official at the customs house and none other than the father
of my "little monster." I returned his call at once. He was a
little old man, unpleasantly like his daughter, the caricature of a caricature. He treated me in every way as if I
were his prospective son-in-law. He inquired about my
family, my income, my prospects: a regular cross-
examination. The matter threatened to become serious.

What was I to do? Hoping to divert his attention
from me, I made myself as insignificant as possible in his
eyes. The reason for his visit to Stockholm was obvious.
Either he wanted to shake off the singer, whom he disliked, or the lady had made up her mind to honor me with
her hand if an expert should approve of her bargain. I
showed my most unpleasant side, avoided every opportunity of meeting him, refused even an invitation to dinner
from the Baroness. I wore out my unlucky would-be
father-in-law by giving him the slip again and again,
pleading urgent duty at the library, until I had gained my
purpose, and he departed earlier than he had planned.

Did my operatic rival ever guess whom he was indebted
to for his matrimonial misery when he married his madonna? No doubt he never did, and proudly imagined that
he had ousted me.

An incident that to some extent affected our destiny was
the sudden departure of the Baroness and her little
daughter to the country. It was in the beginning of August.
For reasons of health she had chosen Mariafred, a small
village on Lake Mälaren, where the Baroness' cousin happened to be staying at the moment.

This hurried departure so soon after her homecoming
struck me as very extraordinary, but as it was none of my
business I made no comment. Three days passed; then the

Baron wrote asking me to call. He was restless, nervous, strange. He told me that the Baroness would be back almost immediately.

"Indeed!" I exclaimed, more astonished than I cared to show.

"Yes! . . . Her nerves are upset, the climate doesn't suit her. She's written me an unintelligible letter which frightens me. I've never been able to understand her whims. She gets all sorts of fantastic ideas into her head. Right now she imagines that you're angry with her!"

What a test for my powers of self-control!

"It's too absurd!" he continued, "but I beg you not to take any notice of it when she returns. She's ashamed of her moods. She's proud, and if she ever thought you disapproved of her, she'd do something stupid."

"This is going all wrong," I said to myself. And from that moment my thoughts were bent on flight, for I had no desire to figure as the hero of a romantic drama in which the catastrophe was imminent.

I refused the next invitation, making excuses which were badly invented and completely misunderstood. The result was a call from the Baron, asking me what I meant by my unfriendly conduct. I did not know what explanation to give, and he took advantage of my embarrassment and exacted a promise from me to join them in an excursion into the country.

I found the Baroness looking ill and worn out; only the black eyes in the livid face seemed alive, shining with unnatural brilliancy. I was very reserved, spoke in indifferent tones, and said as little as possible. After a short trip by steamer we went to a famous hotel where the Baron had arranged to meet his uncle. The supper, which was served in the open, was anything but gay. Before us spread the sinister lake, shut in by gloomy mountains and framed by the blackened trunks of centuries-old lime trees.

The conversation dragged as we tried one dry, boring

subject after another. I sensed the after-effects of a quarrel between my hosts that had not yet been patched up and was on the verge of a fresh outbreak. I ardently desired to avoid the storm, but unfortunately uncle and nephew left the table to discuss business matters.

Now the mine would explode!

As soon as we were alone the Baroness leaned towards me and said brusquely, "Do you know that Gustav was angry with me, really terribly angry for coming back unexpectedly?"

"I knew nothing about it."

"Then you don't know that he'd been counting on meeting my seductive little cousin on his free Sundays?"

"My dear Baroness," I interrupted her, "if you want to bring charges against your husband, hadn't you better do it in his presence?"

Great God, what had I done? It was brutal, this harsh, uncompromising rebuke flung into the face of a disloyal wife in defense of a member of my own sex.

"How dare you!" she cried, amazed, changing color. "You're insulting me!"

"Yes, my dear Baroness, I am insulting you."

All was over between us. Forever!

As soon as her husband returned she hastened toward him as if she were seeking protection from an enemy. The Baron understood something was wrong, although he didn't know what emotions were involved.

I left them at the dock, pretending that I had to pay a visit at one of the neighboring villas. I don't know how I got back to town. My legs seemed to carry a lifeless body; the vital node was cut. I was like a corpse walking in its own funeral procession.

Alone! I was alone again, without friends, without a family, and without anything to worship. It was impossible for me to recreate God. The statue of the Madonna had fallen down. Woman had shown herself behind the beautiful image, treacherous, faithless, her sharp claws unsheathed. When she attempted to make me her confidant, she was taking the first step toward breaking her marriage vows; at that moment hatred of her sex rose in me. She had insulted me as a human being and as a man, and I took the part of her husband against her. Not that I flattered myself with being a virtuous man. In love affairs man is never a thief; he only takes what is given to him. It is woman who steals and sells herself. The only time when she gives unselfishly is when she betrays her husband. The young girl sells herself, the bride sells herself; only the faithless wife gives to her lover—whatever she stole from her husband.

But I had not desired this woman in any other way than as a friend. Protected from me by her child, I had always seen her invested with the insignia of motherhood. Always seeing her at the side of her husband, I had never felt the slightest temptation to share with her those essentially unclean pleasures that are ennobled only by entire and exclusive possession.

I returned to my room annihilated, tired to death—and more lonely than ever, for I had dropped my bohemian friends from the very outset of my relations with the Baroness.

5

I occupied in those days a fairly large attic with two windows that looked on Newbridge harbor, the bay, and the rocky heights of the southern suburbs. In the window recesses on the roof I had managed to create a tiny garden. Bengal roses, azaleas, and geraniums provided me in their turn with bowers for my secret cult of Madonna and child. It had become a daily habit with me to pull down the blinds toward evening, arrange my flowerpots in a semicircle, and place in the center a picture of the Baroness with the lamplight full on it. She was represented in this portrait as a young mother with somewhat severe but deliciously pure features, her delicate head crowned with a wealth of golden hair. She wore a light dress that reached up to her chin and was finished off with a pleated frill. Her little daughter, dressed in white, was standing on a table by the side of her, gazing at the beholder with pensive eyes. How many letters to "My dear Friends" had I not written before this portrait and sent off on the following morning addressed to the Baron! These letters were at that time the only channel into which I could pour my literary talent. I put the best part of me into them.

To open a career for the repressed, artistic soul of the Baroness, I had warmly encouraged her to seek an outlet for her poetic imagination in literary work. I had provided her with the masterpieces of all literatures, had taught her the first principles of literary composition by furnishing endless summaries, commentaries, and analyses, to which I added advice and practical illustrations. She had been only moderately interested and from the first expressed doubts about her literary talent. I told her that every educated person had the ability to write at least a letter, and was therefore a poet or author *in petto,* whatever the degree of accomplishment. But it was all in vain; the passion for the stage had taken too firm a hold of her obstinate brain. She insisted that she was a born elocutionist, and because her rank prevented her from following her inclination and going on the stage (the only thing she dreamed of), she acted like a martyr, heedless of the consequences. Her husband sympathized with my benevolent efforts, undertaken in the secret hope of saving their marriage from shipwreck. He was grateful, although he had not the courage to take an active and personal interest in the matter. The Baroness' opposition notwithstanding, I had continued my efforts and urged her in every letter to cut out this tumor that was only doing her harm, and to express herself in a poem, a drama, or a novel.

I said to her in one of my letters, "Why not make use of

your own experience?" And, quoting from Börne, I added, "Take paper and pen and be candid above all, and you are bound to become a writer."

"It's too painful to live an unhappy life all over again," she had replied. "I want to find forgetfulness in Art; I want to make myself over into characters different from me."

I had never asked myself what it was that she wanted to forget. I knew nothing of her past life. Did she shrink from allowing me to solve the riddle? Was she afraid of handing me the key to her character? Was she anxious to hide her true self behind the personalities of stage heroines, or did she hope to magnify herself by taking on roles that were really beyond her?

When I had come to the end of my arguments, I suggested that she should make a start by translating the works of foreign authors; I told her this would help to form her style and make her known to publishers.

"Is a translator well paid?" she asked.

"Fairly well," I replied, "if she knows her business."

"Perhaps you will think me mercenary," she continued, "but work for its own sake doesn't attract me."

Like so many women of our time, she was seized with the mania of earning her own living. The Baron made a grimace plainly indicative of the fact that he would far rather see her taking an active interest in the management of her house and servants than contributing a few pennies toward the expenses of a neglected home.

Since that day she had given me no peace, begging me to find her a good book and a publisher.

I had done my utmost and had succeeded in procuring for her two quite short articles, destined for one of the illustrated magazines, which did not, however, remunerate its contributors. For a whole week I heard nothing of the work, which could easily have been accomplished in a couple of hours. She lost her temper when the Baron teasingly called her a sluggard. In fact, she was so angry that I saw he had touched a very sore spot. After that I let her alone. I had no desire to become an apple of discord between them.

This was how matters stood at the time of my rupture with her.

. . . I sat in my attic with her letters before me on the table. As I reread them, one after the other, my heart ached for her. She was a soul in torment, a talent wasted, a voice unable to make itself heard, just like myself. This was the secret of our mutual sympathy. I suffered through her as if she were an organ grafted on my sick soul that had become too atrophied and dull to enjoy by itself the cruel pleasure of pain and misery.

And what had she done that I should deprive her of my sympathy? In a moment of jealousy she had complained to me of her unhappy marriage. And I had repulsed her, I had spoken harshly to her, when I ought to have reasoned with her. That should have been quite easy, for hadn't her husband told me that she allowed him every license?

I was seized with an immense compassion for her and suffered from the knowledge that her physical and psychic development had been perverted. I was certain she was concealing some frightening secrets. It seemed to me that I should be guilty of a terrible wrong if I abandoned her. Desolated and depressed, I began a letter to her, asking her to forgive me. I begged her to forget what had happened and tried to explain the painful incident as a misunderstanding on my part. But the words would not come, my pen refused to obey me. Worn out, I threw myself on my bed.

The following morning was warm and cloudy, a typical August morning. At eight o'clock I went to the library, melancholy and exhausted. As I had a key, I was able to let myself in and spend three hours in perfect solitude before the general public began to arrive. I wandered through the passages between rows of books on either side in that exquisite solitude which is not loneliness, in close communion with the great thinkers of all times.

Taking out a volume here and there, I tried to fix my mind on some definite subject in order to forget the painful scene of yesterday. But I could not banish the desecrated image of the fallen Madonna from my mind. When I raised my eyes from the pages, which I had read without understanding a word, I seemed to see her as in a vision coming down the spiral staircase, which I could dimly make out far down the endless perspective of the low gallery. As she climbed down, she lifted the straight folds of her blue dress, showing her perfect feet and slender ankles, looking at me furtively with a sidelong glance, tempting me to the betrayal of her husband, soliciting me with that treacherous, that voluptuous smile I had seen yesterday for the first time. The apparition awakened all the sensuality that had lain dormant in me for the last three months, for the pure atmosphere that surrounded her had kept all my thoughts chaste, proof that all my ardent desires had begun to fix themselves on a single object. Of course I desired her. Suddenly I imagined her naked by letting the soft lines of her clinging dress, lines which I knew by heart, be transferred to a white body. And when my thoughts had reached this point, I hunted up a work on art which contained illustrations of all the famous sculptures in the Italian museums. I intended to discover this woman's formula by systematic scientific research. I wanted to find out the species and genus to which she belonged. I had plenty to choose from.

Was she Venus, with firm breasts and powerful hips, the normal woman who awaits her lover sure of her triumphant beauty?

No.

Juno? The fertile mother with her child, the woman who gives birth, who lies stretched out on the birthbed displaying all those parts of her magnificent body that propriety demands be concealed?

No, not her either.

Minerva, the bluestocking, the old maid, who hides her flat bosom under a coat of mail?

On no account!

Diana, then! The pale goddess of night, shy and afraid of the clear light of day, cruel in her enforced chastity, solely the result of a defective physical constitution, too much of the boy, too little of the girl, modest of necessity, and so made furious by Actaeon, who surprised her bathing? Was she Diana? The genus, perhaps, but not the species!

The future will speak the last word. Still, with that delicate body, those exquisite limbs, that sweet face, that proud smile, that modestly veiled bosom must be burning with secret passions, passions that could well rise to such intensity that only the sight of blood could appease them. Ah, Diana, of course! Yes, unmistakably Diana!

I continued my research. I looked through a number of publications on art stored up in this incomparable treasure-house of the state. I wanted to drive this chaste goddess out of my mind. I compared, I verified my conclusions like a scientist, rushing from one end of the huge building to the other to find the volumes to which I was being referred until the striking of a clock recalled me from the world of my dreams. My colleagues were beginning to arrive, and I had to begin my daily duties.

6

I decided to spend the evening at the club with my friends. On entering the laboratory, I was greeted with deafening acclamations, which helped raise my spirits. The center of the room was occupied by a table dressed like an altar, in the middle of which stood a skull and a large bottle of cyanide of potassium. An open Bible, stained with spots of liquor, lay beside the skull. Surgical bougies served as bookmarkers.

A number of punch glasses were arranged in a circle all around. Instead of a ladle, a retort was used for filling the glasses. My friends were on the verge of intoxication. One of them offered me a glass bowl containing half a liter, and I emptied it without catching my breath. All the members yelled out in unison the oath of the club, "To hell with everything!"—to which I replied by intoning "the song of the prodigal sons":

> *S'enivrir*
> *S'accoupler*
> *C'est le vrai but de la vie.*

After this prelude an unholy noise broke out, and amid shouts of applause I began to recite my familiar blasphemies. In rhyming verses and with explicit anatomical references I glorified woman as the personification of man's inability to gratify himself solely by the means *at hand*. Intoxicated with the coarse suggestions, the vulgar profanation, I surpassed myself in heaping insults on the head of my Madonna. It was the morbid result of my unsatisfied longing. My hatred for the treacherous idol broke out with such virulence that it afforded me a sort of bitter comfort. My comrades, poor devils, who had experienced love only in brothels, listened eagerly to my wild defamations of elegant ladies, who were utterly beyond their reach.

The drunkenness increased. The sound of men's voices delighted my ears after I had passed three months amid sentimental whining, mock modesty, and hypocritical innocence. I felt as if I had torn off the mask, thrown back the veil under which Tartuffe concealed his cupidity. In imagination I saw the adored woman indulging every whim and caprice merely to chase away the boredom of a dull existence. To her, the Absent One, I directed all my insults and obscenities, all the scorn, all the vomit I threw up in my insane and impotent anger, furious with myself for not being able to possess her because of some power within me that stopped me on the verge of committing the crime.

At this moment the laboratory appeared to my overexcited brain as the temple of monstrous orgies in which all the senses participated. The bottles on the shelves gleamed with all the colors of the rainbow: the deep purple of red lead, the orange of potash, the yellow of sulphur, the green of verdigris, the blue of vitriol. The atmosphere was thick with tobacco smoke. The smell of the lemons used in brewing the punch called up visions of happier countries. The piano, carefully put out of tune and then retuned in a strange key, groaned Beethoven's march in a manner that made it unrecognizable except for the rhythm. The pallid faces of the revelers seesawed in the blue-black smoke that rose from the pipes. The lieutenant's sash, the black beard of the doctor of philosophy, the physician's embroidered shirt front, the skull with its empty sockets, the noise, the disorder, the abominable discords, the lewd images evoked, bewildered and confused my maddened brain, when suddenly there arose a call to arms, shouted unrhythmically by a chorus of disjointed voices:

"To the women, bucks, cocks, rams, bulls!"

The whole chorus broke into the exit song:

> *S'enivrir*
> *S'accoupler*
> *C'est le vrai but de la vie.*

Hats and overcoats flew on, and the horde trooped out. Half an hour later we stormed into a brothel. Stout was ordered. Soon the flames crackled and leaped up in the tile stove as my comrades initiated the saturnalias of the night with *tableaux vivants*. . . .

7

When I awoke on the following morning in my own bed in broad daylight, I was surprised to find that I had regained complete mastery over myself. Every trace of unhealthy sentimentality had disappeared; the cult of the Madonna had been forgotten in the excesses of the night. I looked upon my fantastic love as a weakness of the spirit or the flesh, which at the moment appeared to me to be one and the same thing.

After I had had a cold bath and eaten some breakfast, I returned to my daily duties, content that the whole matter was at an end. I plunged into my work, and the hours passed rapidly.

It was half-past twelve when the porter announced the Baron.

"Is it possible?" I said to myself. "And I had thought the incident was closed!"

I prepared myself for a scene.

The Baron, radiant with mirth and happiness, squeezed my hand affectionately. He had come to ask me to join in another excursion by steamer to see the amateur theatricals at Södertälje, a small watering place.

I declined politely, pleading urgent business.

"My wife," he recommenced, "would be very pleased if you could manage to come. . . . Moreover, Bébé will be one of the party. . . ." Bébé, the notorious cousin . . .

He went on urging me in a manner at once irresistible and pathetic, looking at me with eyes so full of sadness that I felt myself weakening. But instead of frankly accepting his invitation, I replied with a question:

"The Baroness is quite well?"

"She wasn't very well yesterday; in fact, she was really ill, but she felt better this morning. My dear fellow," he added after a slight pause, "what the devil happened between you two the night before last at Nacka? My wife says that you had a misunderstanding and that you're angry with her without any reason."

"Really," I answered, a little taken aback, "I don't know myself. Perhaps I had a little too much to drink. I probably said something stupid."

"Then let's forget all about it. Right?" he replied briskly. "And let us be friends as before. Women are often strangely touchy, I don't have to tell you that. It's all right, then; you'll come, won't you? Today at four. Remember, we're counting on you. . . ."

I had consented!

Unfathomable enigma! A misunderstanding! . . . But she had been ill! . . . Ill with fear . . . with anger . . . with . . . ?

The fact that the little unknown cousin was about to appear upon the scene added a new interest, and with a beating heart I went on board the steamer at four o'clock as had been arranged.

The Baroness greeted me with sisterly kindness.

"You're not angry with me because of my unkind words?" she began. "I forget myself so easily—"

"Don't let's speak about it," I replied, trying to find her a seat behind the bridge.

"Axel . . . Miss Bébé."

The Baron was introducing us. I was looking at a girl of about eighteen; the soubrette type, exactly what I had imagined. She was small, rather common-looking, dressed simply but with a certain striving after elegance.

But the Baroness! Pale as death and with hollow cheeks, she looked more fragile than ever. Her bangles jingled at her wrists. Her slender neck rose from her collar, plainly showing the blue arteries winding toward the ears, which, owing to the careless way in which she had arranged her hair, stood out from her head more than usual. She was badly dressed, too. The colors of her frock were garish and did not go together. She was downright plain. As I looked at her, my heart was filled with compassion, and I cursed my recent conduct toward her. This woman a coquette? She was a saint, a martyr, bearing undeserved sorrow.

The steamer started. The lovely August evening on the Lake of Mälaren tempted one to peaceful dreams.

Was it accidental or intended? The little cousin and the Baron were sitting side by side far enough away to prevent our overhearing each other. Leaning toward her, he talked and laughed incessantly, looking young and happy, as if he had just gotten engaged.

From time to time he looked at us, slyly, and we nodded and smiled back.

"A jolly girl, the little one, isn't she?" remarked the Baroness.

"It seems so," I answered, uncertain how to take her remark.

"She understands exactly how to cheer up my melancholy husband. I'm afraid I don't possess that gift," she added, with a frank and kindly smile at the couple.

And as she spoke, the lines of her face betrayed a hidden sorrow, suppressed tears, superhuman resignation. Across her features glided, cloudlike, those incomprehensible reflections of kindness, resignation, and self-denial common to pregnant women and young mothers.

Ashamed of my misinterpretation of her character, tortured by remorse, nervous, I suppressed with difficulty the tears I felt rising to my eyes. I had to find something to talk about, no matter what.

"But aren't you jealous?" I asked.

"Not at all," she answered, quite sincerely and without a trace of malice. "Perhaps you'll think it strange, but it's true. I love my husband; he's very kind-hearted. And I adore my little cousin, she's such a sweet creature. And it's all really so innocent. Jealousy is disgusting. It makes you look ugly. And at my age I have to be careful."

And, indeed, she looked so plain at that moment that

it wrung my heart. Acting thoughtlessly, on impulse, I advised her with fatherly solicitude to put a shawl around her shoulders, pretending that I was afraid of her catching cold. She let me arrange the fleecy fabric around her face, framing it and transforming her into a sweet little beauty.

How pretty she was when she thanked me smilingly! A look of perfect happiness had come into her face. She was grateful, like a child begging for caresses.

"My poor husband! How glad I am to see him a little more cheerful. He's got his troubles. If you only knew!"

"If I'm not indiscreet," I ventured, "then, for heaven's sake, tell me what it is that makes you so unhappy. I feel there's a great sorrow in your life. I have nothing to offer you but advice, but if I can be of any help I entreat you to make use of my friendship."

My poor friends were in financial difficulties: the phantom of ruin was threatening them. Up to now the Baron's inadequate income had been supplemented by his wife's dowry. But they had recently discovered that the dowry existed on paper only, since it was invested in worthless shares. The Baron was on the point of resigning and getting a position as a cashier in a bank.

"That's the reason," she concluded, "why I want to make use of my talents. I could contribute my share to the necessary household expenses. It's all my fault, don't you see? I'm to blame for the difficulties he's in; I'm the one who ruined his career. . . ."

What could I say or do in such a serious case, one that went far beyond my power of assistance? I attempted to smooth away her difficulties, to deceive myself about them.

I assured her that things would turn out all right, and in order to allay her fears I painted for her the picture of a future without cares, full of bright prospects. I quoted the statistics of national economy to prove that better times were coming in which her shares would improve. I invented the most extraordinary remedies; I even conjured

up a reorganization of the army that would result in an unexpected promotion for her husband.

It was all pure invention, but thanks to my power of
imagination, courage and hope returned to her and her
spirits rose.

After landing, and while we were waiting for the play
to start, we went for a walk in the park. I had not as yet
exchanged one word with the cousin. The Baron never
left her side. He carried her cloak, devoured her with his
eyes, bathed her in a flood of words, warmed her with his
breath all the while she remained callous and self-
possessed, with vacant eyes and expressionless features.
From time to time she seemed to say things to which the
Baron replied with roars of laughter while she didn't move
a muscle in her face. Judging from his animated face, she
must have been indulging pretty freely in repartee, innuendoes, and *double-entendres*. At last the doors opened,
and we went in to take our seats, which had not been reserved.

The curtain rose. The Baroness was blissfully happy to
see the stage and smell the mingled odors of powder and
paint, sizing and sweat.

They played Musset's *A Caprice*. A sudden indisposi-
tion seized me, the result of the distressing memories of
my vain efforts to conquer the stage as a playwright, and
also, perhaps, the consequence of the excesses of the
previous night. When the act curtain fell, I left my seat
and made my way to the restaurant, where I refreshed
myself with a double absinthe, which I made last until
the performance was over.

My friends met me after the play, and we went to have
supper together. They seemed tired and unable to hide
their annoyance at my flight. Nobody spoke a word while
the table was being laid. A desultory conversation was
started with the greatest difficulty. The cousin remained
mute, haughty, reserved.

We discussed the menu. After consulting with me, the

Baroness ordered *smörgåsbord*. Roughly—too roughly for my unstrung nerves—the Baron countermanded the order. Lost in gloomy thoughts, I pretended not to hear him and called out "*Smörgåsbord* for two!"—for her and for me—since that was what she said she wanted.

The Baron turned pale with anger. There was thunder in the air, but not a word was spoken.

The Baroness inwardly admired my courage in answering a rudeness with an insult, which in a more civilized country would have drawn a demand that I explain myself. The Baroness, encouraged by the way in which I had stood up for her, began teasing me in order to make me laugh. But in vain. Conversation was impossible; nobody had anything to say, and the Baron and I exchanged angry glances. In the end my opponent whispered a remark in his neighbor's ear. In reply she made a grimace, nodded, pronounced a few syllables without moving her lips, and regarded me scornfully.

I felt the blood rising to my head, and the storm would have burst there and then if an unexpected incident had not served as a lightning rod.

In an adjacent room a boisterous party had been pounding on the piano for the last half-hour. Now they began singing an indecent song, with the door standing wide open.

The Baron turned to the waiter: "Shut that door," he said curtly.

The door had hardly been closed when it again burst open. The singers repeated the chorus and challenged us with impertinent remarks.

It was as good a moment as any for me to explode.

I jumped up from my chair. With two strides I was at the door and banged it in the faces of the noisy crew. Fire in a powder barrel could not have had a more rousing effect than my determined stand against the enemy. A short struggle ensued, during which I kept hold of the door handle. But the door yielded to the vigorous pull from the other side, and I was dragged toward the howling mob, who threw themselves upon me, eager for a hand-to-hand tussle. At that moment I felt someone touching my shoulder and heard an indignant voice asking these gentlemen whether they had "no sense of honor, ganging up like that on a single opponent?"

It was the Baroness who, under the stress of a strong emotion, forgetting the dictates of convention and good manners, betrayed warmer feelings than she probably was aware of.

The fight was over. The Baroness regarded me with searching eyes.

"You're a brave little hero," she said. "I was trembling for you."

The Baron called for the bill, asked to see the *maître d'* and requested him to send for the mayor of the community.

After this incident perfect harmony reigned among us. We vied in expressions of indignation about the rudeness of the natives. All the suppressed wrath of jealousy and wounded vanity was poured on the heads of those vulgar barbarians. And later on, as we sat drinking punch in one of our own rooms, our old friendship burst into fresh flames. We forgot all about the mayor, who had failed to put in an appearance.

On the following morning we met in the coffee room, full of high spirits, and in our inmost hearts glad to have done with a disagreeable business, the consequences of which it would have been difficult to foretell.

After the first breakfast we went for a walk on the banks of the canal, still in couples and with a respectable distance between us. When we had arrived at a lock where the canal made a strong curve, the Baron waited and turned to his wife with an affectionate, almost amorous smile.

"D'you remember this place, Marie?" he asked.

"Yes, yes, my dear, I remember," she answered, with a mingled expression of passion and sadness.

"It was here where he first told me of his love," she explained to me. "One evening, under this very birch tree, a shooting star just as he spoke to me made a brilliant arc across the sky . . ."

"That was three years ago," I said, filling in her thoughts, "and you are reviving old memories already. You live in the past because the present doesn't satisfy you."

"Oh, stop!" she exclaimed. "You're all wrong. . . . I loathe the past, and I am grateful to my husband for having delivered me from a vain, tyrannical mother who was driving me to desperation. I adore Gustav. He's a loyal friend to me. . . ."

"As you like, Baroness. I'll agree with anything to please you."

At the stated hour we went on board to return to town, and after a delightful passage across the blue sea, with its thousands of green islands, we arrived in Stockholm, where we parted.

I had made up my mind to return to work, determined to cut out of my heart this growth that took the form of a woman. But I soon found that I had reckoned without forces much stronger than myself. The day after our excursion I received an invitation to dinner from the Baroness; it was her wedding anniversary. I could not think of a plausible excuse, and although I was afraid of straining our friendship, I accepted the invitation. To my great disappointment, I found the house turned upside down, undergoing the process of a general cleaning. The Baron was in a bad temper, and the Baroness sent her apologies for the delayed dinner. I walked up and down the garden with her irritable, hungry husband, who seemed unable to control his impatience. After half an hour's strenuous effort, my powers of entertaining him were exhausted, and conversation ceased. He took me into the dining room.

Dinner was laid and the appetizers had been put on the table, but the mistress of the house was still invisible.

"If we took a snack standing," said the Baron, "we should be able to wait."

Afraid of offending the Baroness, I did my utmost to dissuade him. But he remained obstinate, and, caught between two fires, I was compelled to acquiesce in his proposal.

At last the Baroness entered: radiant, young, pretty, dressed in a diaphanous silk frock, yellow, like ripe corn, with a mauve stripe reminiscent of pansies, her favorite combination of colors. The well-cut dress suited her girlish figure to perfection and emphasized the beautiful contour of her shoulders and the curve of her exquisitely modeled arms. I handed her my bouquet of roses, wished her many happy returns of the day, and eagerly cast all the blame for our rude impatience on the Baron.

When her eyes fell on the disordered table, she pursed her lips and addressed to her husband a remark more stinging than humorous. He was not slow to reply to the undeserved rebuke. I threw myself into the breach by recalling incidents of the previous day that I had already discussed with the Baron.

"And what do you think of my cousin?" asked the Baroness.

"Absolutely charming," I replied.

"Don't you agree with me, my dear fellow, that the child is a perfect treasure?" exclaimed the Baron in a voice that expressed parental solicitude, sincere devotion, and pity for this imp of Satan, supposed to be martyred by imaginary tyrants.

But in spite of the stress laid by her husband on the word "child," the Baroness continued mercilessly.

"Just look how that dear Bébé has changed the way my husband combs his hair!"

The part that the Baron had been accustomed to wear had indeed disappeared. Instead, his hair was combed in the manner of the young students, his mustache waxed—a style that did not suit him. Through an association of ideas, my attention was drawn to the fact—which, however, I kept to myself—that the Baroness, too, had adopted from the charming cousin certain details of dressing her hair, of wearing her clothes, even of manner. It made me think of the elective affinities of chemistry, in this case acting on living beings.

The dinner dragged on, slowly and wearily, like a cart that has lost its fourth wheel and heavily lumbers along on three. But the cousin, the indispensable fourth in our quartet, which was beginning to be out of tune without her, was expected to come later on and take coffee with us. At dessert I proposed a toast to the married couple in conventional terms and without spirit or wit, as flat as old champagne.

Animated by the memories of the past, husband and wife kissed tenderly, and in mimicking their former fond ways, became affectionate, amorous even, just as an actor will feel genuinely depressed when he has been feigning tears. Or was it that the fire was still smoldering beneath the ashes, ready to burst into fresh flames if fanned by a skillful hand? It was impossible to guess how matters stood.

After dinner we went into the garden and sat in the summerhouse, the window of which looked onto the street. Digestive drowsiness did not encourage conversation. The Baron stood at the window, absent-mindedly watching the street in the hope of catching a glimpse of the cousin. Suddenly he darted off like an arrow, evidently with the intention of going to meet the expected guest.

Left alone with the Baroness, I at once became embarrassed—not out of shyness but because she had a queer way of looking at me and paying me compliments on certain details of my appearance. After a long, almost painful silence, she burst out laughing, and pointing in the direction in which the Baron had disappeared, she exclaimed, "Dear old Gustav, he is head over heels in love!"

"It looks like it," I replied. "And you're really not jealous?"

"I couldn't be," she said. "I'm in love myself with the pretty little cat. And you?"

"Oh, I'm all right. I don't want to be rude, but I shall never feel the slightest sympathy with your cousin."

And this was true. From the first moment I had taken a dislike to this young woman who, like myself, was of middle-class origin. She saw in me the intruding witness, or rather the dangerous rival, hunting in the preserves she had reserved for herself and through which she hoped to make her way into society. Her piercing eyes, her small pearl-gray eyes had at once recognized in me a mere acquaintance of whom she could make no use; her plebeian instinct scented an adventurer in me. And up to a certain point she was right, for I had entered the Baron's house in the hope of finding a patron for my unfortunate play. Unluckily, the contacts between my friends and the stage were nonexistent, a mere fabrication of my friend from Finland, and with the exception of a few banal compliments, my play had never been mentioned.

It was also undeniable that there was a marked difference in the Baron's manner whenever his charmer was present. He was fickle, easily impressed and was evidently beginning to regard me through the eyes of the sorceress.

We had not long to wait. The pair appeared at the garden gate, merrily talking and laughing.

The girl was brimming over with fun and merriment. In a slovenly, careless way, she swore with absolute nonchalance, made ambiguous remarks with utter innocence, and seemed to be quite unconscious of her *double-entendres*. She smoked and drank without forgetting for one single moment that she was a woman, and, what is more, a young woman. There was nothing masculine about her, nothing of the emancipated woman, nor was she in the least prudish. She was certainly amusing, and time passed quickly.

But what surprised me most and ought to have been a warning to me was the excessive mirth with which the Baroness greeted any doubtful remark that fell from the girl's lips. Then she would laugh wildly and a frankly salacious expression would flit over her face, showing she was deeply versed in the secrets of sensual excess.

While we were thus amusing ourselves, the Baron's uncle joined our little party. A retired captain, a widower of many years' standing, very chivalrous, of pleasing manners, a little daring in his old-fashioned gallantry, he was, thanks to his connection with the family, the declared favorite of these ladies, whose affections he had succeeded in winning.

He looked upon it as his right to fondle them, kiss their hands, pat their cheeks. As he came in, both of them fell on his neck with little exclamations of pleasure.

"Take care, my little ones! Two at a time is too much for an old fellow like me. Careful, or you'll burn yourselves! Quick, take your little paws off me, or I won't be responsible for the consequences."

The Baroness held her cigarette, poised between her lips, towards him.

"A little fire, please, Uncle!"

"Fire? I'm sorry I can't oblige you, child, but my fire went out five years ago," he answered roguishly.

"Not really?"

She boxed his ears playfully with her fingertips. The old man seized her arm, held it between his hands, and massaged it all the way up to her shoulder.

"You're not as thin as you look, my darling," he said, stroking her soft flesh through her sleeve.

The Baroness did not object. The compliment seemed to please her. With a loud and sensual laugh, she pushed up her sleeve, exposing a beautiful arm, daintily rounded and white as milk. Almost immediately, however, she remembered my presence and hastily pulled it down again; but not before I had seen a spark of the consuming fire that burned in her eyes, the same expression that comes into the face of the embraced woman at the climactic moment of love. The burning match I held between my fingers with the intention of lighting my cigarette accidentally dropped between my coat and waistcoat. With a scream the Baroness rushed at me and tried to extinguish the flame between her fingers.

"Fire! Fire!" she shrieked, her cheeks flushed with excitement.

Completely confused, I started back and pressed her hand against my breast as if to smother the smoldering fire. Then shamefacedly releasing her hand and pretending that I had escaped a very real danger, I thanked the Baroness warmly, over and over again.

We talked and joked valiantly till suppertime. The sun had set, and the moon rose behind the cupola of the Observatory, illuminating the apple trees in the orchard. We amused ourselves by trying to differentiate between the apples suspended from the branches and half-hidden by the leaves, which looked sedge-green in the pale moonlight. The ordinary blood-red Calville seemed but a yellow spot; the grayish Astrachan apple had turned green, the Rennet a dark, brownish red, and the others had changed color in like degree. The same thing had happened with the flowers. The dahlias presented to our eyes unknown tints, the stocks shone in the colors of another planet, the hues of the Chinese asters were indefinable.

"There, you see, Baroness," I said, commenting on the phenomenon, "how everything in the world is imaginary. Color does not exist in the abstract; everything depends on the nature of the light. Everything is illusion."

"Everything?" she said softly, remaining standing before me and gazing at me with eyes magnified by the darkness.

"Everything, Baroness!" I lied, confused by this living apparition of flesh and blood, which at the moment terrified me by its unearthly loveliness.

The disheveled golden hair formed a luminous aureole round her pale, moonlit face. Her exquisitely proportioned figure rose by my side, tall and straight and more slender than ever in the striped dress, the colors of which had changed to black and white.

The stocks breathed their aphrodisiac perfumes, the crickets chirped in the dewy grass, a gentle breeze rustled in the trees, twilight wrapped us round with its soft mantle. Everything invited to love. Nothing but the cowardice of respectability kept back the avowal that trembled on my lips.

Suddenly an apple dropped from a wind-shaken bough and fell at our feet. The Baroness stooped, picked it up, and gave it to me with a significant gesture.

"Forbidden fruit!" I murmured. "No, thank you."

And to efface the impression of this blunder, which I had committed against my will, I hastened to improvise a satisfactory explanation of my words, hinting at the niggardliness of the owner. "What would he say if he saw me?"

"That you are at least a knight above reproach," she replied as if to reproach me with cowardice, and she glanced at the shrubbery that effectively screened the Baron and her cousin from indiscreet observers.

The maid appeared to announce supper. When we rose from the table the Baron proposed that we should accompany "the dear child" home. At the front door he offered her his arm, and then turned to me.

"Look after my wife, old man," he said, "and prove to her that you really are the perfect cavalier I know you to be." He spoke to me like a father.

I feared the worst. As the evening was warm, the Baroness, leaning lightly on me, was carrying her scarf in her hand, and from her arm, the graceful outline of which was plainly perceptible through the thin silk, emanated a magnetic current that excited in me an extraordinary sensitiveness. I imagined that I could detect at the height of my deltoid muscle the exact spot where the sleeve of her undergarment ended. My sensitiveness was intensified to such a degree that I could have traced the whole anatomy of that adorable arm. Her biceps, the great elevator that plays the principal part when two people embrace each other, pressed mine, flesh against flesh, in supple rhythms. As I walked by her side I could distinguish the curve of her hips through the skirts that brushed against my legs.

"You walk perfectly in step. You must be a wonderful dancer," she said as if to encourage me to break an embarrassing silence.

And after a few moments, during which she must have felt the quivering of my tense nerves, she asked, a little sarcastically and with the superiority of a confident woman, "What's the matter? You're shivering."

"Yes, I'm cold."

"Then why not put on your overcoat?"

Her voice was lined with silk.

I put on my coat, a veritable straitjacket, and found myself better protected against the warmth that flowed from her body into mine. The sound of her little feet, keeping time with my footsteps, drew our nervous systems so closely together that I felt almost as if we were a four-footed animal.

In the course of that fateful walk a grafting occurred of the kind which gardeners call "ablactation," which is brought about by bringing two boughs into the closest possible contact.

From that day I was no longer my own master. She had inoculated me with her blood; our nerves were electrically charged; her egg cells yearned to be fertilized by my sperm; her soul craved to be united with my intellect; and my spirit longed to empty itself unrestrainedly into this beautiful vessel.

Had all this happened unconsciously? It was hard to say.

Once more back in my room, I asked myself what I

should do. Run away, forget, try to make my fortune abroad? The idea flashed through my mind to go to Paris, the center of civilization. Once there, I would bury myself in the libraries, be lost in the museums. In Paris I should produce my work.

No sooner had I conceived this plan than I took the necessary steps to carry it out. After a month had elapsed I was in a position to pay my farewell visits.

An unexpected but opportune incident served conveniently as the pretext I needed to cloak my flight. Selma—the Finnish lady I had long since banished from my mind— was having her banns published. I was therefore absolutely compelled to seek forgetfulness and healing for my poor, wounded heart in distant countries. It was as good an excuse as any I could think of. My departure was delayed for a few weeks in deference to the entreaties of my friends who were dreading the autumn storms: I had told them I was going by steamer to Havre.

Furthermore, my sister's wedding was to take place early in October. It began to seem as if my project was going to be postponed forever.

During this time I received frequent invitations from the Baroness. The cousin had returned to her parents, and the three of us generally spent the evenings together. The Baron, unconsciously influenced by the strong will of his wife, seemed more favorably disposed toward me. Moreover, my impending departure had reassured him completely, and he treated me with his former friendliness.

One evening the Baroness' mother was entertaining a small circle of intimate friends. The Baroness, stretched out listlessly on the sofa, suddenly put her head on her mother's lap and loudly confessed her intense admiration for a well-known actor. Did she want to torture me, to see the effect such a confession would have on me? I don't know. But the old lady, tenderly stroking her daughter's hair, looked at me and said, "If ever you write a novel, let me draw your attention to this specimen of the pas-

sionate woman. She's unique. She's never happy unless she
is in love with someone besides her husband."

"It's quite true what Mamma says," agreed the Baroness,
"and just at present I'm madly in love with that actor.
He's irresistible, divine!"

"She's mad," smiled the Baron, wincing but trying to
appear unconcerned.

A passionate woman! The words sank into my heart,
for, jesting apart, those words spoken by an old woman, and
that old woman her own mother, must have contained
more than a grain of truth.

My departure was imminent. On the eve of my leaving
I invited the Baron and his wife to a bachelor's dinner in
my attic. To hide the meanness of the furniture, my little
home was wearing its Sunday clothes and had the appearance of a sacred temple. My damaged wicker sofa
was pushed against the wall between the two window recesses, one of which was filled by my writing table and
the improvised garden, the other by my bookshelves.
An imitation tiger skin was thrown over it and held in
place by invisible tacks.

Taking up the left wall was my large bed-sofa with its
gaudy tick cover. Above it on the side wall hung a vividly
colored map of the world. On the righthand side stood
my chest of drawers with its swing glass, both in the Empire style and decorated with brass ornaments; a wardrobe
with a plaster-of-Paris bust and a washstand, for the moment banished behind the window curtains; the walls decorated with framed sketches—all in all, a gay and varied
show that gave the impression of something old-fashioned.

A porcelain chandelier looking like leaves and flowers—
a type often seen in churches and which I had picked up
in a junk shop—was suspended from the ceiling. The cracks
were skillfully concealed by a wreath of artificial ivy I
had found some little time ago at my sister's. Beneath the
three-armed chandelier stood the dining table. A basket
filled with roses, which glowed red among the dark foliage,

was placed on the white damask tablecloth, and the roses, reaching up to and mingling with the drooping ivy shoots, gave the whole the effect of a flower show. Round the basket that held the roses stood an array of wine glasses, red, green, and opal, which I had bought cheaply at a sale, for each of them had a flaw. The same thing applied to the dinner service: plates, salt cellars, and sugar bowl of Chinese, Japanese, and Swedish porcelain.

I had but a dozen cold dishes to offer to my friends, most of them chosen more with an eye to their decorative value than because they were good to eat, for the meal was to consist principally of oysters. My landlady had good-naturedly lent me the indispensable articles for the banquet, an unprecedented event in my attic. . . . At last everything was satisfactorily arranged, and I could not help admiring the setting: these mingled touches betrayed on a small scale the inspiration of a poet, the research of a scientist, the good taste of an artist, the gourmet's fondness for good food, and the love of flowers, which concealed in their delicate shadows a hint of the love of women. If the table had not been laid for three, one might have guessed that it was to be an intimate feast for two, the first delights of a love adventure, instead of the feast of reconciliation that it actually was. My room had not seen a female visitor since that unbearable woman who must have been inflicted on me for my sins. Her boots had left ineradicable traces on the woodwork of my sofa. The looking glass on the chest of drawers had reflected no female figure since then. And now a woman of blameless life, a mother, a lady of education and refinement, was coming to consecrate this place which had seen so much work, misery, and pain. And it is indeed a sacred festival, said I rhapsodically to myself, since I am prepared to sacrifice my heart, my peace, perhaps my life, to ensure the happiness of my friends.

Everything was ready when I heard footsteps on the fourth-floor landing. I hastily lit the candles, for the last time straightened the basket containing the roses, and a moment later my guests, exhausted with having climbed four flights of stairs, stood panting before my door.

I opened. The Baroness, dazzled by the lights, clapped her hands as if she were admiring a successful stage setting.

"Bravo!" she exclaimed. "You are a first-class stage director."

"Yes, I occasionally write plays to develop patience and—"

I took off her cloak, bade her welcome, and made her sit down on the sofa. But she could not keep still. With the curiosity of a woman who has never been in a bachelor's flat but has gone straight from her father's house to her husband's bed, she began to examine the room. She seized my penholder, fingered the blotter, searched about as if she were determined to discover a secret. Strolling to my bookshelves, she glanced curiously at the backs of the volumes. In passing the looking glass she stopped for a few seconds to arrange her hair and push the end of a piece of lace into the opening of her blouse. She examined the furniture piece by piece, and smelled the flowers, all the time uttering little cries of delight.

When she had finished her voyage of discovery around my room, she asked me, naïvely, without any *arrière-pensée*, and looking about for a piece of furniture which appeared to be missing, "But where do you sleep?"

"On the sofa."

"Oh, how wonderful a bachelor's life must be!"

And the dreams of her girlhood awoke in her brain.

"It's often very dull," I replied.

"Dull to be one's own master, have one's own home, be free from all supervision! Oh, what I wouldn't give to be independent! Matrimony is abominable! Isn't it, darling?" She turned to the Baron, who had been listening to her good-naturedly.

"Yes, it *is* dull," he agreed, smiling.

Dinner was ready and the banquet began.

The first glass of wine made us feel merry, but all of a sudden, remembering the occasion for our unceremonious meeting, a feeling of sadness mingled with our enjoyment. We began to talk of the pleasant days we had spent together. We re-experienced all the little adventures of our trips and picnics. And our eyes shone, our hearts beat more quickly, we pressed hands and clinked glasses with one another. The hours passed rapidly, and we realized with growing distress that the moment of parting was approaching. At a sign from his wife, the Baron produced an opal ring from his pocket and held it out to me.

"Here, my dear fellow," he said, "take this little keepsake as a token of our gratitude for the friendship you have shown us. May fate give you your heart's desire! This is my sincerest wish, for I love you as a brother and respect you as a man of honor! A pleasant journey! We will not say 'farewell' but *'au revoir.'*"

As a man of honor? Had he guessed my motive? Read my conscience? Not at all! . . . For in well-chosen words, anxious to explain his little speech, he burst out into a string of abuse of poor Selma; he accused her of having broken her word, of having sold herself to a man who . . . well, to a man whom she did not love, a man who owed his happiness merely to my extraordinary decency.

My extraordinary decency! I felt ashamed but was carried away by the sincerity of this simple heart, which judged a little too hastily perhaps. I suddenly felt very unhappy, inconsolably unhappy, but I kept up the pretense.

The Baroness, deceived by my clever acting, misled by my assumed indifference, believed me to be in earnest, and with motherly tenderness tried to comfort me.

"Have done with her!" she urged; "forget all about her. There are plenty of girls, far better and much more honest than she is. Don't fret; she's not worth crying for, since she couldn't even wait for you. Besides, I may tell you now—I've heard things about her. . . ."

And with a pleasure she was quite unable to conceal, she proceeded to disgust me still further with my supposed idol.

"Just think," she exclaimed, "she practically proposed to an officer of good family, and she made herself out to be 30 percent younger than she is. She's nothing but a common flirt, take my word for it."

A disapproving gesture from the Baron made her realize her blunder. She pressed my hand and apologized, looking at me with eyes so wistful and tender that I felt as if I should die.

The Baron, a little intoxicated, made sentimental speeches, took me into his confidence, overwhelmed me with brotherly love, besieged me with endless toasts that lost themselves in the outer reaches of the ether. His puffy face beamed benevolently. He looked at me with his caressing, melancholy eyes. Their glance dissipated every shadow of doubt about the sincerity of his friendship I might have entertained. Surely he was nothing but a big, good-natured child, of unquestionable integrity; and I made a vow to behave honorably towards him, even if it should kill me.

We rose from the table to say goodby, perhaps forever. The Baroness burst out sobbing and hid her face on her husband's shoulder.

"I must be mad," she exclaimed, "to be so fond of this dear boy. His going away always breaks my heart!"

And with an outburst of affection, at once pure and impure, interested and disinterested, passionate and full of angelic tenderness, she put her arms around my neck and kissed me in her husband's presence. Then she made the sign of the cross over me and turned to go.

My old charwoman, who was waiting on the threshold, wiped her eyes, and we all shed tears. It was a solemn moment, never to be forgotten. The sacrifice had been made.

I went to bed at one o'clock in the morning, but I was

unable to sleep; fear of missing the steamer kept me awake.

Worn out by the farewell parties which had been following one on top of the other for a week, my nerves unhinged from too much drinking, groggy from idleness, overwrought by the excitement of the evening, I tossed and turned until the day broke. Knowing that my will power was temporarily enfeebled, and loathing railway journeys because, according to what I've been told, the shaking and jolting is injurious to the spine, I had elected to travel by steamer. Also in the back of my mind was the thought that this would prevent any attempt on my part to draw back. The boat was to start at six o'clock in the morning, and the cab called for me at five. I started on my way alone.

It was a windy October morning, foggy and cold. The branches of the trees were covered with hoarfrost. When I arrived on the North Bridge, I imagined for a second that I was the victim of an hallucination. There was the Baron, walking in the same direction as my cab. Contrary to our agreement, he had risen early and had come to see me off. Deeply touched by this unexpected proof of friendship, I felt altogether unworthy of his affection, full of remorse for ever having thought evil of him.

We arrived at the dock. He accompanied me on board, examined my cabin, introduced himself to the captain, and recommended me to his special attention. He behaved like an older brother, a devoted friend, and we said goodby to each other, deeply moved.

"Take care of yourself, old boy," he said. "You don't look too well."

I really felt out of sorts, but I pulled myself together until the mooring ropes were cast adrift.

Then a sudden terror of this long and senseless journey seized me, a frantic desire to throw myself into the water and swim to the shore. But I had not the strength to yield to any impulse and I remained standing on deck, unde-

cided what to do, waving my handkerchief in response
to my friend's goodbyes until he vanished, blotted out by
the vessels riding at anchor in the roads.

The boat was a heavily loaded cargo steamer with but
one cabin on the main deck. I went to my berth, stretched
myself on the mattress and pulled the blankets over me,
determined to sleep through the first twenty-four hours so
as to circumvent any attempt at escape on my part. I
must have been unconscious for half an hour when I suddenly started from my sleep as if I had received an electric
shock, a very ordinary result of drinking too much and
sleeping too little.

In a second the whole dreary reality flashed into my
mind. I went on deck to exercise my stiff limbs. I watched
the barren brown shores receding before my eyes, the
leafless trees, the yellowish-gray meadows. In the hollows
of the rocks snow was already piling up. The water looked
gray with sepia-colored spots. The sky was leaden and
full of gloom. The dirty deck, the uncouth sailors—everything contributed to deepen my depression. I felt an unspeakable longing for human companionship, but there did
not appear to be a single passenger—not one! I climbed
on the bridge to look for the captain. I found him a bear
of the worst description, absolutely unapproachable. I was
a prisoner for ten days, solitary, cast away among people
without understanding, without feeling. Sheer torture was
all I could look forward to.

I resumed my walk on deck, up and down, in all direc-
tions, as if that would increase the speed of the boat. My
burning brain worked under high pressure; a thousand
ideas flashed into my mind in a second; the suppressed
memories rose, jostling and chasing each other. A pain
like toothache began to torment me, but in my confusion
I could neither describe nor locate it. The further the
steamer advanced into the open sea, the greater became
the strain. I felt as if the umbilical cord that bound me to
the country of my birth, to my family, to her, was tearing

asunder. Deserted by everybody, tossing on the high seas between heaven and earth, I seemed to be losing all foothold, and in my loneliness I felt afraid of everything and everybody. It was doubtless a sign of constitutional weakness, for I remembered that as a boy I had cried bitter tears on a pleasure trip at the sudden thought of leaving my mother. I was twelve years old then, but physically I was developed far in advance of my years. The reason, in my opinion, was that I had been born prematurely, or perhaps that attempts at abortion had been made—an all too common occurrence in large families. At any rate, I felt sure that this was the cause of the despondency that invariably overcame me when I was about to make a change in my surroundings. Now, in tearing myself away from my familiar environment, I was tormented with dread of the future, the unknown country, the ship's crew. Oversensitive, like every prematurely born child whose exposed nerves are waiting for the still bleeding skin; defenseless like a crab that, having cast its shell, seeks protection underneath the stones and feels every change of the sinking barometer, I wandered about, trying to find a soul stronger than mine, take hold of a firm hand, feel the warmth of a human presence, look into a friendly eye. Like a squirrel in its cage I ran around the upper deck, picturing to myself the ten days of suffering that awaited me. I remembered that I had been on board for only an hour! A long hour, more like a day of agony . . . and not a glimmer of hope at the end of this accursed journey! I tried to reason with myself, and all the time rebelled against reason.

Who compelled me to go? Who had a right to blame me if I returned? . . . Nobody! And yet! . . . Shame, the fear of making myself a laughingstock, honor! No! No! I must abandon all hope. Moreover, the boat would not call anywhere on her way to Havre. Forward, then, and courage!

But courage depends on strength of body and mind, and

at the moment I lacked both. Haunted by my dreary thoughts I turned toward the lower deck, for by now I knew the upper deck down to its smallest details, and the sight of its rails, rigging, and tackling bored me like a book that one knows by heart. As I opened the glass door, I almost tumbled over a person seeking shelter from the wind behind the cabin. It was an old lady, dressed in black, with gray hair and a careworn face.

She gazed at me attentively with sympathetic eyes. I walked up to her and spoke to her. She answered me in French, and we soon became acquainted.

After the exchange of a few commonplaces, we confided to each other the purpose of our journeys. She was not traveling for pleasure. The widow of a timber merchant, she had been staying with a relative in Stockholm and was now on her way to visit her insane son, confined in a lunatic asylum at Havre. Her account was so simple and yet so heart-rending that it affected me strongly, and it is likely that her story, impressing itself on the cells of my already overwrought brain, led up to what followed.

All of a sudden the lady ceased talking, and gazing at me with a look of dismay, exclaimed sympathetically—

"Are you ill?"

"I?"

"Yes, you look ill. You should try to get some sleep."

"To tell you the truth, I never closed my eyes last night. I'm overtired. I've been suffering from sleeplessness for some time. Nothing seems to be able to give me the rest I need."

"Let me try. Go to bed at once. I will give you something that will put you to sleep on your feet."

She rose, pushed me gently before her, and persuaded me to go to bed. Then she disappeared for a moment, returned with a small flask, and gave me a spoonful of sleeping medicine.

"Now you're sure to sleep."

I thanked her, and she carefully covered me with the

blankets. How well she understood what she was about! She radiated warmth, that warmth a hungry baby seeks at the breast of its mother. Under the gentle touch of her hands I grew calm, and two minutes later I began to sink into a coma. I seemed to have become an infant again. I saw my mother busying herself around my bed and caring for me. Gradually her fading features mingled and became one with the finely chiseled face of the Baroness and the sympathetic face of the dear nurse who had just left me. In the care of these dream women, who hovered around my bed, I faded away like a paling color, went out like a candle, lost consciousness.

When I awoke I did not remember any dream, but a fixed idea haunted me as if it had been suggested to me during my sleep: I must see the Baroness again or else go out of my mind.

Shivering with cold, I sprang from my bed, which was damp and wet from the salt-laden wind, penetrating through every chink and cranny. When I stepped out of my cabin the sky was a pale-gray lead plate. On deck the great waves washed the tackling, watered the planks, and splashed my face with creamy white foam.

I looked at my watch and calculated the distance the steamer must have traveled while I slept. In my opinion we were now in the archipelago of Nörrköping. All hope of return was therefore dead. Everything was strange to me—the scattered islands in the bay, the rugged coast, the shape of the cottages dotted along the shore, and the cut of the sails on the fishing smacks. Amid these unfamiliar surroundings I felt even more homesick. A sullen wrath choked me; I felt a wild despair in finding myself packed on this cargo boat in spite of myself, in deference to a higher power, in the imperious name of honor!

By the time my wrath had exhausted itself, my strength had also come to an end. Leaning against the rail, I let the spray lash my burning face, while my eyes greedily devoured the coastline, eager to discover a ray of hope.

And again and again the idea of swimming ashore returned to me.

For a long time I stood gazing at the swiftly receding outlines of the coast. I grew calmer, rays of a tranquil happiness illuminated my soul, and for no apparent reason my brain began to work less feverishly. Pictures of beautiful summer days, memories of my first youth came into my mind, although I was at a loss to understand why I should suddenly think of them. The boat was rounding a promontory. The roofs of red houses with white garlands rose above the fir trees, a flagpole poked through the cluster of gardens, a bridge, a chapel, a church steeple, a graveyard. . . . Was it a dream? A delusion?

No, it was the quiet seaside place where I had spent many summers in my student days. Up there was the tiny house where I had passed a night, last spring, with her and him, after we had spent the day sailing on the sea and wandering through the woods. It was there—there—on the top of that hill, under the ash trees, on the balcony, where I had seen her delicate face, illuminated by the sunshine of her golden hair, and crowned by the little Japanese hat with the blue veil, while her small gloved hand had beckoned me to come to dinner. . . . She was there now, I could see her plainly, she was waving her handkerchief to me. . . . I could hear her melodious voice. . . . But . . . what was happening? The boat was slowing down, the engine stopped . . . the pilot cutter came to meet us . . . in an instant . . . a flash of thought—a single, obsessing thought, struck me like an electric shock. Like a tiger I bounded up the stairs leading to the bridge—I stood before the captain.

"Have me put ashore at once—or I shall go mad!"

The captain looked at me sharply, scrutinized me, and without vouchsafing a reply, as dismayed as if he had looked into the face of an escaped lunatic, he called to the second officer and said without any further hesitation,

"Have this gentleman and his luggage put ashore. He's sick."

Within five minutes I was on board the pilot cutter, which was rowed with such vigor that I was on land in no time at all.

I possess a remarkable gift: I can become blind and deaf when it suits me. I was walking along the road leading to the hotel without having heard or seen anything injurious to my vanity; neither a glance from the pilots betraying that they guessed my secret nor a disparaging remark from the man who was carrying my luggage. After arriving at the hotel, I asked for a room, ordered an absinthe, lighted a cigar, and began to reflect.

Was I mad or wasn't I? Had the danger really been so great that an immediate landing had been necessary?

In my state of mind I was incapable of forming an opinion, for a madman, according to the doctors, is not conscious of his mental disorder, and the logic of his ideas proves nothing against their irregularity. Like a scientist I examined similar occurrences that had happened to me before. When I was still a boy at college, my nervous excitability, aggravated by very painful events, the suicide of a friend, a delirious love affair, and fear of the future, had increased to such an extent that everything filled me with apprehension, even in broad daylight. I was afraid to stay in a room by myself; I was haunted by my own specter; and my friends took turns spending the night with me, while the candles burned and the fire crackled in the stove.

Another time, in an attack of wild despair following all sorts of misfortunes, I ran cross-country, wandered through the woods, climbed to the top of a pine tree, sat astride a branch and made a speech to the branches below me, endeavoring to drown out their soughing voices, imagining that I was a speaker addressing a hostile and threatening crowd. That had happened not so very far from here on an island, where I had spent many summers, the headland of which was plainly visible from where I stood. Remembering that incident with all its ridiculous details, I could not help admitting to myself that I was subject at times to mental aberrations.

What was I to do now? Should I communicate with my friends before the rumor of my attack reached the town? But the disgrace and shame of having to acknowledge that I was on a level with the incompetents! The thought was unbearable.

Lie, then! Double back without being able to throw the pursuers off the scent. It went against the grain. Tormented by doubts, hesitating between different plans of escape from this maze, I longed to run away in order to be spared the terrible cross-examination that awaited me. I wanted to hide myself in a hole in the woods like a wild animal that feels it is soon going to die.

With that idea in mind, I went slowly through the narrow streets. I climbed over huge rocks, soaked and slippery from the autumnal rains, crossed a stubble field, reached the little house where I once had lived. The shutters were tightly closed; the wild vine covering the walls up to the roof was stripped of its leaves, and the green latticework was plainly visible.

As I stood again upon that sacred spot—sacred to my heart because it had seen the first blossoming of our friendship—the sense of my loss that for a time had been forced into the background reasserted itself. Leaning against one of the supports of the wooden balcony, I wept like a lost child.

I remembered having read in the *Thousand and One Nights* that lovers fall ill with unsatisfied longing and that their cure depends entirely on the possession of the beloved one. Snatches of Swedish folksongs came into my mind, about young maidens who, in despair of ever being united to the object of their affections, waste away and bid their mothers prepare their deathbeds for them. I thought of Heine, the old skeptic, who sings of the tribe of the Asra, "who die when they love." There could have been no doubt of the genuineness of my passion, for I had gone back to childhood, obsessed by one thought, one picture, one single, overpowering sensation, prostrating me and rendering me unable to do anything but sigh and moan.

To distract my thoughts, I let my eyes travel over the glorious landscape spread out at my feet. Bristling with fir trees and an occasional pine tree, the thousands of islands seemed to swim in the enormous bay, gradually decreasing in size and transforming themselves into reefs, cliffs and sandbanks until the huge archipelago terminated at the gray-green line of the Baltic, where the breakers dashed against the steep bulwarks of the remotest cliffs.

The shadows of the drifting clouds fell in colored strips on the surface of the water, passing from dark brown through all the shades of bottle-green and Prussian blue to the snowy white of the crested waves. Behind a fortress situated on a steep cliff rose a column of black smoke, ascending without a break from an invisible chimney, to be blown down again by the wind onto the foaming waves.

All of a sudden the dark hull of the cargo boat I had just left came into view. The sight wrung my heart, for the steamer seemed like a witness to my disgrace. Like a shying horse I bolted and fled into the wood.

Underneath the pointed arches of the fir trees, with the wind whistling through the needles, my anguish increased. Here we had been walking together when the spring sunshine lay on the first green, when the firs put forth their purple blossoms that exhale a perfume like that of the wild strawberry, when the juniper scattered its yellow pollen into the wind, when the anemones pushed their white heads through the dead leaves under the hazel bushes. Her little feet had pressed the soft, brown moss, spread out like a rug, as she sang her Finnish songs in a silvery voice. Guided by the clear light of remembrance, I found again the two gigantic trees, grown together in an unending embrace. The two trunks were bending to the violent gusts of the wind and rubbing against each other with a grating noise. From here she had taken a little footpath to gather a water lily that grew in a swamp. With the zeal of a setter I tried to discover the trace of her pretty foot, the imprint of which, however light, I felt sure I could not miss. With bent shoulders and eyes glued to the ground, I searched the path without finding anything. The ground was covered with the footprints of the deer, and I might just as well have tried to follow the trail of a wood nymph as discover the spot the dainty shoe of the adored woman had trod. Nothing but mudholes, cow dung, fungi, toadstools, puffballs decaying and decayed, and the broken stalks of flowers. Arrived at the edge of the swamp, which was filled with black water, I found a certain fleeting comfort in the thought that this mudpuddle had once reflected the sweetest face in all the world. In vain I looked for the spot where the water lilies grew; it was covered by dead leaves, blown down by the wind from the birch trees. I retraced my footsteps and plunged into the heart of the forest. The rustling of the wind in the branches deepened with the growing size of the trees.

In the very depth of despair I sobbed aloud, the tears raining down my cheeks. Like a wild stag I trampled on the fungi and toadstools, tore up the young plants, dashed myself against the trees. What did I want? I didn't know myself. My pulses throbbed, an inexpressible longing to see her again came over me. She whom I loved too deeply to want to possess had taken possession of my whole being. And now that everything was at an end, I longed to die. Life without her was impossible.

But with the cunning of a madman, I decided to get some satisfaction out of my death by contracting pneumonia, or a similar fatal disease, which would keep me in bed for weeks. I could see her again and could kiss her hand in saying goodby forever.

Comforted by this sudden thought, I turned my steps

toward the coast; it was not difficult to find it; all I had to do was follow the roar of the breakers that led me across the wood.

The coast was precipitous and the water deep—everything as it should be. With a care and an orderliness that scarcely accorded with my dire intentions, I undressed myself, hid my clothes in a group of alder trees, and pushed my watch into a hole in the rock. The wind was cold; at this time of year, in October, the temperature of the water was barely above the freezing point. I took a run over the rocks and threw myself headlong into the water, aiming at a cleft between two gigantic waves. I felt as if I had fallen into red-hot lava. But I rose quickly to the surface, dragging up with me pieces of seaweed I had glimpsed at the bottom—the tiny vesicles were scratching my legs. I swam out into the open sea, breasting the huge waves, greeted by the laughter of the seagulls and the cawing of the crows. When my strength began to fail, I turned and swam back to the cliff. Now the moment of greatest importance had arrived. According to all instructions given to bathers, the real danger consists in remaining naked too long out of the water. I sat down on the rock that was most fully exposed to the wind and allowed the October gale to lash my bare back. I felt my skin shrink. Spontaneously my muscles pulled in tight, my chest contracted, as if the instinct of self-preservation would protect the vital organs at any price. But I was unable to sit still, and seizing the branch of an alder tree, I climbed up into it. The tree swayed with the convulsive, uncontrollable movements of my muscles, but by holding on I succeeded in remaining in the same place for some time. The icy air scorched my thighs like a red-hot iron. At last I was convinced that I had had enough and hastily dressed myself. Night was falling now. When I re-entered the woods it was quite dark. Terror seized me, I hit my head against the lower branches of the trees, and had to feel my way along. Suddenly, under the influence of my frantic fear, my senses became so acute that I could tell the variety of the trees surrounding me solely by the rustling of their branches. What depth there was in the bass of the firs, with their firm and closely set needles forming gigantic guitars. The tall and more pliable stems of the pines gave a higher note, their sibilant fife resembling the hissing of a thousand snakes. The dry soughing of the branches of the birch trees recalled memories of my childhood, burning sorrows mingling with my first sensual pleasures. The rustling of the dead leaves clinging to the branches of the oaks sounded like the rustling of paper. The muttering of the junipers was almost like the whispering voices of women telling each other secrets. There was a dull crunch from the alder tree as the wind tore off one of its branches. I could have distinguished a pine cone from the cone of a fir tree by the sound it made in falling. I detected nearby mushrooms purely by my sense of smell, and the nerves of my big toe seemed to feel whether it trod on soil, club moss, or maidenhair.

Guided by the acuteness of my sensations, I came to the enclosure of the graveyard and climbed over the stile. I felt a momentary pleasure in the sound of the weeping willows lashing the tombstones which they overhung. At last, stiff with cold, shaking at every unexpected noise, I reached the village, where the feeble light from the houses guided me to the hotel.

As soon as I had arrived in my room I sent off a telegram to the Baron, informing him of my sudden illness and enforced landing. Then I drew up for him a full statement of my mental condition, mentioning my former attacks, and asking him to keep the matter quiet. I gave him to understand that my illness had as its immediate cause the conduct of my unfaithful love, whose publicly announced engagement had robbed me of all hope.

I went to bed exhausted, certain I had contracted a serious illness. Then I rang for the servant and asked her to send for a doctor. On her reply that no doctor was avail-

able, I begged her to send for a clergyman so that I could
make my last wishes known to him.

And from that moment I was prepared to die or to
experience the outbreak of insanity.

The clergyman appeared almost immediately. He was a
man about thirty, and looked like a farmhand in Sunday
clothes. Red-haired and freckled, a half-vacant look in his
eyes, he did not inspire me with sympathy. For a long
time I could find no words, I did not know what to confess
to this man who had neither education, the wisdom of
age, nor a knowledge of the human heart. He stood stiffly
in the center of the room, as self-conscious as a farmboy
in front of his city cousin, until I motioned him to take a
chair.

Then he began his cross-examination.

"You have sent for me, sir? There is something weighing
on you, isn't there?"

"Yes."

"There is no happiness but in Jesus."

Although I was aspiring to quite another sort of happiness, I did not contradict him, and the evangelist rambled
on, uninterruptedly, monotonously. The old phrases of the
catechism lulled me gently to sleep, and the presence of a
human being linked through moral guidance to my soul
gave me comfort and strength.

But the young preacher, suddenly doubting my sincerity,
interrupted his discourse with a question: "Do you hold
the true faith?"

"No," I replied, "but don't let that stop you. Your
words are doing me good. . . ."

And he returned to his work, the monotonous sound of
his voice, the radiations from his eyes, the warmth that
emanated from his body, affected me like a magnetic fluid.
In half an hour's time I was fast asleep.

When I awoke, the mesmerist had gone. The servant
girl brought me some kind of drug or opium with strict in-
junctions from the druggist to be careful, as the bottle con-

tained enough poison to kill a man. As soon as she had turned her back, I naturally drank the whole contents of the flask at a gulp. Then firmly determined to die, I buried myself under the blankets. Sleep was not long in coming.

When I opened my eyes on the following morning I was not in the least surprised to find my room flooded by brilliant sunshine: my sleep had been visited by vivid and brightly colored dreams.

"I dream, therefore I exist," I said to myself. I felt my body all over so as to discern the degree of fever, or the presence of any signs of pneumonia. But in spite of my determination to bring about a crisis, my condition was fairly normal. My brain, although feeling a little heavy, functioned easily, no longer under the high pressure of the previous day, and twelve hours' sleep had fully restored the vigor which, thanks to physical exercises of all descriptions, practiced since my early youth, I usually enjoyed. . . .

A telegram was handed me. My friends were informing me that they would arrive by the two o'clock boat.

I was overwhelmed with shame. What was I to say? What attitude should I adopt? . . . I pondered. . . .

My reawakened manhood rebelled against humiliating resolutions. After a hasty review of the circumstances, I decided to remain at the hotel until I had completely recovered and continue my journey by the next steamer. In this way honor would be saved, and the visit from my friends would be but one more leavetaking—the very last.

When I remembered what had occurred on the previous day, I hated myself. That I, a freethinker, a skeptic, should have committed such absurdities! And that clergyman's visit! How was I to explain that? It was true, I had only sent for him in his official capacity, and as far as I was concerned, he had served only as a hypnotist! But to outsiders it was bound to look like a conversion. Monstrous confessions would very likely be hinted at, a criminal's last statement on his deathbed. What a pretty topic for the villagers who stood in close touch with the city! What a treat for the old gossips!

The only way to save the situation was to leave the country without a moment's delay. Like a castaway, I spent the morning walking up and down on the veranda, watching the barometer, studying the timetables. Time passed fairly rapidly. The steamer appeared at the mouth of the estuary before I had made up my mind whether to walk to the dock or remain at the hotel. Having no desire to be stared at by an inquisitive crowd, I finally went to my room. A few minutes later I heard the voice of the Baroness: she was making inquiries of the landlady about my health. I went out to meet her, and she almost kissed me before the eyes of all the bystanders. With a heart full to overflowing, she deplored my illness, which she regarded as the result of overwork, and advised me to return to town and put off my journey until the spring.

This was one of her good days. In her closely fitting fur coat with its long, fine hairs, she looked just like a llama. The sea breezes had brought the blood to her cheeks, and in her eyes, magnified by the excitement of her visit, I could read an expression of infinite tenderness. In vain I begged her not to alarm herself on my account and assured her that I had almost fully recovered. She thought I looked as if I had one foot in the grave, declared me unfit for work, and treated me like a child. And how perfectly she played the part of a mother! The tone of her voice was a caress; she playfully used terms of endearment; she wrapped her shawl around me. At the table she spread my napkin over my knees, poured out some wine for me, looked after me in every way. I wondered why she did not devote all this attention to her child rather than to the man who was all the time striving to hide his passion, which threatened to defy all control. In this guise of a sick child, it seemed to me that I was like the wolf who, after having devoured the grandmother, lies down on her bed waiting to gobble up Little Red Ridinghood.

I blushed before the unsophisticated and loyal husband who overwhelmed me with kindness and asked for no explanations. And yet I was not at fault. I obstinately hardened my heart, and received all the attentions the Baroness showered on me with an almost insulting indifference.

At dessert, when the time for the return journey had come, the Baron proposed that I should return with them. He offered me a room in his house which, he said, was waiting to receive me. I am glad to say that my answer was a decided refusal. Playing with this kind of fire terrified me and I was firm in my decision. I would stay here for a week to recover entirely and then return to my old attic in town.

In spite of all their objections, I persisted. Strange, as soon as I pulled myself together and acted like a man of decision, the Baroness became almost hostile to me. The more I vacillated and humored her whims, the fonder she seemed of me, the more she praised my wisdom, my amiability. She dominated and bewildered me; but as soon as I opposed her seriously, she turned her back on me and treated me with dislike, almost with rudeness.

While we were discussing the Baron's proposal to live under one roof, she drew a glowing picture of such an arrangement, dwelling on the pleasantness of being able to see one another at any time without a previous invitation.

"But, my dear Baroness," I objected, "what would people say if you were to take a bachelor into your home?"

"What does it matter what people say?"

"But your mother, your aunt? Moreover, my man's pride rebels against such a measure, permissible at best only in the case of a minor."

"Bother your man's pride! Do you think it manly to drown without making a sound?"

"Yes, madame, the one thing a man must do is show himself to be strong."

She grew angry and refused to admit that there was any real difference between the sexes. Her woman's logic confused me. I turned to the Baron, whose answering smile showed plainly what a small opinion he had of female reasoning.

About six o'clock the steamer weighed anchor and bore my friends away. I returned to the hotel alone.

It was a splendid evening. The sun had set in an orange-colored sky, white stripes were lying on the deep blue water, a coppery moon was rising behind the fir trees.

I was sitting at a table in the dining room, lost in thoughts, alternately mournful and serene, and did not notice the landlady until she stood close by me.

"The lady who's just left is your sister, isn't she?" she asked.

"Not at all."

"Isn't she? You resemble one another remarkably! I'd have sworn you were brother and sister."

I was not in the mood to continue such a conversation, but it left me in a ferment of thoughts.

Was it possible that my constant preoccupation with the Baroness during the last few days had left her imprint on my features? Could one really suppose that her facial expressions had been duplicated in mine during the six months' union of our souls? Had the instinctive desire to please one another at any price been the cause of an unconscious selection of gestures and expressions, suppressing the less pleasing in favor of the more seductive? It was not at all unthinkable that a mingling of our souls had taken place and that we no longer belonged to ourselves. Destiny, or rather instinct, played its awful part. The stone had been set rolling, overthrowing and destroying everything that barred its way: honor, reason, happiness, loyalty, wisdom, virtue!

And this guilelessness! Proposing to receive under her

roof an ardent young man, at the age when the passions are boiling most furiously. Was she a hussy in disguise, or had love obscured her reason? A hussy! No, a thousand times no! I appreciated her candid ways, her gaiety, her sincerity, her motherly tenderness. That she was eccentric, uneven in temperament, she had herself acknowledged in speaking of her faults—but vicious? No! Even the little tricks she occasionally resorted to in order to cheer me up were much more the tricks of a mature woman who amuses herself by teasing and bewildering a timid youth and then laughs at his confusion, than those of a coquette whose object it is to excite a man's passions.

But I felt I had to exorcise the newly wakened demon, and in order to continue to mislead my friends I sat down at the writing table and scribbled a letter on the old familiar theme of my unhappy love affairs. I added two impassioned poems entitled "To Her"—poems that could be understood in two ways. It was open to the Baroness to be annoyed. Letter and poems remained unanswered. Perhaps the trick had grown threadbare, perhaps the subject was no longer interesting.

The calm and tranquil days that followed hastened my recovery. The surrounding landscape seemed to have adopted the favorite colors of the adored woman. The woods, in which I had spent hours of purgatory, now smiled on me. Never in my morning rambles did I find as much as even the shadow of a painful memory lurking in its deep recesses where I had fought with all the demons of the human heart. Her visit and the certainty that I should see her again had given me back life and reason.

Knowing from experience that nobody who returns unexpectedly is quite welcome, it was not without misgivings that I called on the Baroness as soon as I was back in town.

In the front garden everything proclaimed winter: the trees were bare; the garden seats had been removed; there were gaps in the fence where the gates had been; the withered leaves were dancing on the paths; the cellar holes were stuffed with straw.

I found it difficult to breathe in the close atmosphere of the drawing room, heated by tiled stoves. Built against the walls, the large white stoves looked like sheets hanging from the ceiling. The double windows hung on their hinges; every chink was pasted over with paper; the space between the inner and outer windows was filled with cotton meant to look like snow, giving the large room the appearance of a death chamber. In imagination I endeavored to strip it of its manor-like furniture and recall its former aspect of an austere middle-class home: bare walls, a white pinewood floor, and at opposite ends of the black dining-room table, without a tablecloth and with eight legs that made it resemble a spider, the severe faces of my father and stepmother.

The Baroness received me cordially, but her melancholy face betrayed grief. Both uncle and father-in-law were there, playing cards with the Baron in an adjoining room. I shook hands with the players and then returned with the Baroness to the drawing room. She sat down in an armchair underneath the lamp and took up some crochet work. Taciturn, morose, not at all pretty, she left the conversation entirely to me, and since she made no replies, it soon degenerated into a monologue. I watched her from my chimney corner as she sat with drooping head, bending over her work. Profoundly mysterious, lost in thought, she seemed at times oblivious of my presence. I wondered whether I had called at an inconvenient time or whether my return to town had really created the unfavorable impression I had half-anticipated. All at once my eyes, traveling around the room, were arrested by a display of her ankles underneath the tablecloth. I beheld her finely shaped calf clothed in a white stocking; a gaily embroidered garter belted that charming muscle that turns a man's head because it stimulates his imagination and tempts him to reconstruct the rest of the body. Her arched foot with its high instep was dressed in a Cinderella slipper.

At the time I took it for an accident, but later on I learned that a woman is always conscious of being looked at when she exhibits more than her ankles. Fascinated by the sight, I changed the conversation and skillfully maneuvered it to the subject of my supposed love affair.

She drew herself up, turned towards me, and glanced at me sharply.

"You can at least pride yourself on being a faithful lover."

My eyes remained riveted on the spot underneath the tablecloth where the snow-white stocking shone below the cherry-colored ribbon. With an effort I pulled myself together. We looked at each other; her pupils shone large in the lamplight.

"Unfortunately, I can," I replied dryly.

The sound of the falling cards and the exclamations of the players accompanied this brief exchange.

A painful silence ensued. She resumed her crochet work and with a quick movement allowed the skirts to drop over her ankles. The spell was broken. My eyes were gazing at a listless woman badly dressed. Before another quarter of an hour had gone by I took my leave, pleading that I did not feel well.

As soon as I arrived in my attic I brought out my play,* which I had resolved to rewrite. Hard work would help me to get over this hopeless love, which otherwise was bound to end in a crime from which instinct, cowardice, and upbringing made me shrink. And once more I decided to break off these fatal relations.

An unexpected incident came to my assistance. Two days later the cataloguing of a library belonging to a collector who lived at some distance from the town was offered to me.

And thus I came to pitch my tent in a spacious room,

---

* *Master Olof.*—ED.

lined with books up to the ceiling, of an old manor ho~~~
dating from the seventeenth century. Sitting here, I co~~~
let my imagination travel through all the epochs of ~~~
country's history. The whole of Swedish literature was re~~~
resented, from the old prints of the fifteenth century~~~
the latest publications. I gave myself up to my wor~~~
eager to find forgetfulness—and I succeeded. A week ha~~~
elapsed and I had never once missed my friends. On Sat~~~
urday, the day on which the Baroness generally was "a~~~
home," an orderly brought me an invitation from the
Baron, full of friendly rebuke for having kept away from
them so long. I was half-pleased, half-sorry to find myself
able to send an amiable refusal in reply, regretting that
my time was no longer my own.

When a second week had gone by, another orderly, in
full dress, brought me another communication. This time
it came from the Baroness. It was a rather curt request to
call and see her husband, who, she said, was laid up with
a cold. She begged me to let them have news of me. It
was impossible to make further excuses. I went immediately.

The Baroness did not look well, and the slightly indis-
posed Baron was having a boring time in his bed in the
bedroom. The sight of this Holy of Holies, which had been
hidden from my eyes up to now, aroused my instinctive
aversion to married life in a common room where husband
and wife exposed themselves on the thousand occasions
that demand privacy. The giant bed that the Baron occupied brazenly proclaimed the intimacy of their union.
The heap of pillows piled up by the side of the sick
man boldly marked the wife's place. The dressing table,
the washstands, the towels, everything struck me as being
unclean, and I had to blind myself to overcome my disgust.

After a few words at the foot end of the bed, the Baroness invited me to take a glass of liqueur in the drawing
room, and, as if she had guessed them, she spoke my

ughts as soon as we were alone. In short, disjointed
ntences she poured out her heart to me.

"Isn't it wretched?"

"What?"

"You know well enough what I mean. . . . A woman's
xistence: without any aim in life, without a future, without an occupation. It's killing me!"

"But your child, Baroness! It will soon be time to begin
her education. . . . And she may have brothers and sisters. . . ."

"I don't want any more children! Do you think I am in
the world for the sole purpose of being a nurse?"

"Not a nurse, but a mother in the highest meaning of
the word, equal to her task."

"Mother or housekeeper! No, thank you! One can hire a
housekeeper! It's easier. And besides, what do you expect
me to do with myself? I have two maids, excellent substitutes. No! I want to live. . . ."

"Go on the stage?"

"Yes!"

"But that's out of the question!"

"I know that only too well! And it bores me, stupefies
me . . . drives me crazy!"

"What about a literary career? It's not in such bad repute as the stage."

"Drama is for me the highest of all arts. Come what
may, I shall never cease to regret the fact that I have
missed my vocation. And, my God, what did I get in exchange? . . . What a disappointment!"

The Baron called to us and we returned to his bedside.

"What was she talking about?" he asked me.

"We were talking about the theater," I replied.

"She's crazy!"

"Not as crazy as you think," retorted the Baroness and
left the room, slamming the door.

"She doesn't sleep at night," began the husband, growing confidential.

"No?"

"She plays the piano, she lies on the sofa, or else she chooses the wee small hours to do her accounts. For heaven's sake, my dear young sage, tell me what I'm to do to put an end to her crazy ideas!"

"Perhaps if she had a large family?" I ventured.

He pulled a face, then tried to look unconcerned.

"She was very ill after her first baby was born . . . and the doctor has warned her . . . and moreover, children cost so much. . . . You understand?"

I understood, and I took care not to refer to the subject again. I was too young at the time to know that it is the sick women who order the doctor what to prescribe for them.

Presently the Baroness returned with her little girl and began to put her to bed in her small iron cot. But the little one refused to be undressed and began to scream. After a few futile attempts to calm her, her mother threatened her with the rod.

I cannot bear to see a child being punished without losing my temper. I remember on one such occasion raising my hand against my own father. Allowing my anger to get the better of me and doing nothing to conceal it, I stepped between them.

"Really," I said, "do you think a child cries without a reason?"

"She's naughty."

"Then there's some cause for it. Perhaps she's sleepy, and our presence and the light irritate her."

Taken aback, and perhaps realizing she had acted like a shrew, she agreed with me; and with that I departed.

This glimpse of her home life cured me of my love for some weeks. I must confess that the scene with the rod contributed more than anything else to the hateful impression I retained of that evening.

8

The autumn dragged on monotonously and Christmas drew near. The arrival of a newly married couple from Finland, friends of the Baroness, brought a little more life into our relationship, which had lost much of its charm. Thanks to the Baroness, I received numerous invitations and presented myself in evening dress at suppers, dinners, and occasionally even at a dance. While moving in this, her world, which in my opinion lacked dignity, I could not help noticing that the Baroness, under cover of an exaggerated candor, paid a great deal of attention to the young men, watching me furtively all the while, however, to see the effect of her conduct on me. Irritated and disgusted by her brazen flirtations, which I considered bad form, I responded by a callous indifference. It hurt me that the woman whom I adored should behave like a vulgar coquette.

She always seemed to be enjoying herself immensely and prolonged the parties till the small hours of the morning. I became more and more convinced that she was a woman filled with unsatisfied desires and bored with her home life, that her longing for an artistic career was dictated by a petty vanity, a desire to be seen and enjoy herself. Vivacious, restless, exuberant, she possessed the art of attracting attention. She was always the center of a crowd, more through her skill in gathering people around her than because of any natural magnetism. Her great vitality, her nervous excitability, compelled the most refractory to listen to her, to pay homage to her, and I noticed that as soon as her nervous energy was exhausted the charm was broken and she was left sitting alone and unnoticed in a quiet corner. Ambitious, yearning for power, perhaps heartless, she took care that the men paid her every attention and neglected the women. Doubtless she had made up her mind to see me at her feet, doting, vanquished, sighing. One day, after an evening of triumph, she told one of her girl friends that I was madly in love with her.

When I called at her friend's house a short time afterward, I stupidly remarked that I had hoped to meet the Baroness.

"Oh, indeed!" laughed the lady of the house. "You haven't come to see me, then! How unkind of you!"

"Well, I haven't. To tell you the truth, I'm here by appointment."

"A rendezvous?"

"You may call it that, if you like. Anyhow, you'll give me credit for having put in a prompt appearance!"

The meeting had indeed been arranged by the Baroness: I had but carried out her instructions in calling. She had compromised me to save her own skin.

I paid her back by spoiling a number of parties for her; my absence robbed her of the enjoyment she got from contemplating my sufferings. But I had to pay a heavy penalty! Watching the houses to which I knew her to be invited, I plunged the dagger into my heart, trembling with jealous rage whenever I saw her in the arms of a partner, gliding past the windows in her blue silk dress, with her sunny curls rising and falling in the quick movements of the dance, with her charming figure turning and spinning on the tiniest feet in the world.

9

We had rounded the stormy cape of the year; spring was in the offing. We had passed the time at big parties, and in little get-togethers with just the three of us boring ourselves to death. There had been separations and reconciliations, skirmishes and armistices, bickerings and outbursts of devotion and friendship. I had gone away and I had come back.

March was near, a fateful month in the countries of the north. Animal heat rages and the destinies of lovers are fulfilled: vows are broken; the ties of honor, of family, of friendship count for nothing.

The Baron was on duty early in the month and invited me to spend a day with him at the guardhouse. I accepted his invitation. A son of the people, raised in a middle-class home, cannot but be impressed by the insignia of the highest power in the land. At the side of my friend I walked along the passage, continually saluted by passing officers. I listened to the rattling of the swords, the "Who goes there?" of the sentinels, the beating of the drums. We arrived at the guardroom. The military decorations of the room stirred my imagination; the portraits of the great generals filled me with reverence; the colors taken at Lutzen and Leipzig, the new flags, the bust of the reigning king, the helmets, the resplendent cuirasses, the charts of battles, all these roused in me that feeling of uneasiness that the lower classes feel in contemplating the attributes of the ruling powers.

And in his impressive surroundings the captain grew so imposing that, standing by his side, I was ready to call on him for help in case of danger.

As we entered the Baron's office a lieutenant rose, saluted, and stood at attention, and I felt myself at least superior to the hierarchy of lieutenants, the perennial rivals of authors in the favor of the ladies and feared enemies of the sons of the common people.

A soldier brought us a bowl of punch, and we lighted our cigars. The Baron, anxious to amuse me, showed me the Golden Book of the regiment, an artistic collection of sketches, water paintings, and drawings, all of them representing distinguished officers who had during the last twenty years belonged to the Royal Guards; portraits of the men who had been the envy and admiration of my school friends, whom they had aped when they played "changing of the guard." It tickled my lower-class instincts to see all those favorites of fortune caricatured in this book, and counting on the applause of the democratic Baron, I indulged in little sallies at the expense of those disarmed rivals. But the boundary line of the Baron's democratic sympathies differed from mine, and he resented my sallies. Caste prevailed; he turned the leaves more quickly and did not stop until he came to a large drawing representing the insurrection of 1868.

"Look at this!" he said with a sarcastic smile. "How we charged into that mob!"

"Did you take part in it?"

"Didn't I! I was on duty that day, and my orders were to protect the stand opposite the monument the mob was attacking. A stone hit my helmet. I was passing out the cartridges when a royal messenger on horseback arrived and stopped my little band from firing, which meant I had to stand there as a target for the stones thrown by the crowd. That's all I ever got for my democratic sympathies with the rabble!"

And after a pause he continued, laughing and trying to catch my eye—"You remember the occasion?"

"Perfectly," I said. "I was walking in the procession of the students." But I did not mention the fact that I was one of that special mob he had been so anxious to fire on. My sense of justice had been outraged because that particular stand had been reserved for a favored few and denied to the people at a public festival. I had been on the side of the attacking party, and I remembered vividly how I had flung stones at the soldiers.

The moment I heard him pronounce the words "mob" and "rabble" with aristocratic disdain, I understood the apparently unreasonable discomfort I felt upon entering the enemy fortress, and the sudden change that had come over my friend's features at my sarcasms depressed me. The hatred of race, the hatred of caste, tradition, rose be-

tween us like an insurmountable barrier, and as I regarded
him sitting there, the sword between his knees—a sword of
honor, the hilt of which was ornamented with the name
and crown of the royal giver—I felt strongly that our friendship was but an artificial one, the work of a woman who
constituted the only link between us. The haughty tone of
his voice, the expression of his face, seemed more and
more in harmony with his surroundings and took him
farther and farther away from me. To bridge the gulf
separating us, I changed the conversation and inquired
after his wife and little daughter. Instantly his brow
cleared, his features relaxed and resumed their normal
expression of good nature. Seeing him look at me with the
benevolent eyes of the ogre caressing Tom Thumb, I made
bold to pull three hairs out of the giant's beard.

"Cousin Matilda is expected at Easter, isn't she?" I
asked.

"She is."

"I shall make love to her."

He emptied his glass. "You can try," he said, smiling
scornfully but still like a good-natured giant.

"What do you mean? Has somebody else claimed her?"

"Not that I know of! But . . . I think I may say that—
. . . Well, you can always try!"

And with a tone of deepest conviction, "But it won't do
you a damn bit of good, old boy!"

This blunt warning struck me as an insult, and in reaction to it I began to conceive an audacious plan. I would
defy this all too insolent cavalier, and rid myself of a sinful
love by a happy combination: I would transfer my affections to another woman, which would simultaneously give
satisfaction to the Baroness, whose legitimate feelings had
been hurt.

It had grown dark. I rose to go home. The captain
accompanied me past the sentinels, and we shook hands
at the barrier gate, which he slammed after me. It sounded
like a challenge.

Spring had come. The snow had melted, the streets were free from ice. Half-starved children were selling little bunches of liverwort in the streets. The windows of the flower shops glowed with azaleas, rhododendron and early roses; radishes and cauliflower from Algeria were on display as the first delicacies of spring. Under the North Bridge the sun with its golden wands was setting fire to the lapping waves. At the docks the steamers were being newly rigged and painted in sea-green and scarlet cinnabar. People who had become dry and brittle during the long dark winter began to soak up the sun and spring to life. And the animal in man felt the goad of desire prick its flesh. How unlucky are the weak ones when the pairing off begins and love gives free rein to the long-repressed passions!

10

The pretty little she-devil had arrived and was staying with the Baroness.

I paid her a great deal of attention. She had apparently been informed of my designs and amused herself with me. We had been playing a duet, and she had pressed her right breast against my left arm. The Baroness noticed it and was annoyed. The Baron glared at me with jealous rage. At one moment he was jealous of his wife, at the next he accused me of flirting with the cousin. Whenever he left his wife to whisper in a corner to Matilda, I would start a conversation with the neglected Baroness. He would lose his temper and interrupt our conversation with an irrelevant question. I would answer him with a sarcastic smile. Sometimes I ignored him completely.

11

A family dinner at the Baron's. The mother of the Baroness was present. She had grown fond of me and, worried and anxious like all old women, suspected that something was going on behind the scenes.

Following an impulse of motherly love, dreading some unknown danger, she seized my hands and said, "I'm sure that you're a man of honor. I don't know what's going on in this house. But promise me that you will watch over my daughter, my only child, and if ever anything should happen—which must not happen—promise that you will come to me and tell me everything."

"I promise," I answered, and kissed her hand in the Russian fashion; she had been married to a Russian for many years and had been left a widow not very long ago.

And I shall keep my promise!

12

We were dancing on the edge of a volcano. The Baroness had grown frighteningly pale, emaciated, plain. The Baron was jealous, rude, and insolent toward me. If I stayed away for a day or two, he sent for me, received mo with open arms, and tried to explain everything by a misunderstanding, while in reality we understood each other only too well.

Lord knows what was going on in this house! One evening the charming Matilda had retired into her bedroom to try on a ball dress. The Baron quietly disappeared soon after, leaving me alone with his wife. After half an hour had gone by, I asked what had become of her husband.

"He's playing lady's maid to Matilda," she replied.

Clear enough. But she immediately regretted her words

and added, "There's no harm in it; they're related. One shouldn't be too ready to think evil!"

Then she changed her tone.

"Are you jealous?"

"Are you?"

"Perhaps I shall be by and by."

"God grant that you will be soon! It's the wish of a true friend."

The Baron returned, and with him the girl dressed in a pale green evening dress, cut very low.

I pretended to be dazzled by her appearance and, screening my eyes with both my hands, exclaimed, "You know, it's dangerous to look at you, Matilda."

"Yes. Isn't she lovely?" asked the Baroness in a strange voice.

After a short time the Baron and Bébé withdrew, and for the second time we were left by ourselves.

"Why are you so unkind to me these days?" she asked, with tears in her voice, gazing at me wistfully with the eyes of a whipped dog.

"I? . . . I had no idea that . . ."

"You've changed towards me. I wonder why. . . . If I'm to blame in any way . . ."

She pushed her chair closer to mine, looked at me with luminous eyes, trembled and . . . I got to my feet.

"The Baron's absence is really extraordinary, don't you think? This confidence on his part is humiliating!"

"What do you mean?"

"It's not right of him to leave his wife alone with a young man and shut himself up with a girl. . . ."

"You're right, it's an insult to me. . . . But what about your behavior?"

"Never mind my behavior! I can't stand this. I despise you for holding yourself so cheaply. What are those two doing in there?"

"He's helping Matilda with her dress!" she answered

with an innocent face and a mischievous smile. "What do you expect me to do?"

"A man doesn't help a woman dress unless something's going on between them."

"She's a child, he says, and regards him as a father."

"I'd never allow my children to play 'papa and mama,' much less grown-up people."

The Baroness rose, went out of the room and returned with her husband.

We spent the rest of the evening making experiments with animal magnetism. I made a few passes over her forehead, and she acknowledged that it calmed her nerves. But all of a sudden, just as she was going into a trance, she shook herself, started to her feet, and looked at me with troubled eyes.

"Let me go!" she exclaimed. "I won't! You're bewitching me!"

"It's your turn now to try your magnetic powers," I said, and I submitted to the treatment.

She made the same passes I had made. My eyes began to close. There was deep silence on the other side of the piano. My glances strayed to the legs and the lyre-shaped pedal of the instrument and . . . Did I imagine it? I sprang up from my chair. At the same moment the Baron appeared from behind the piano and offered me a glass of punch.

The four of us raised our glasses. The Baron looked at his wife. "Why not drink to your reconciliation with Matilda?" he suggested.

"Your health, little witch!" exclaimed the Baroness with a smile. Turning to me she added, "You'd never guess it, but you are the reason we quarreled!"

For a moment I did not know how to reply. I asked her to explain her words.

"No, no! no explanation!" they answered in chorus.

"That's a pity," I replied. "In my opinion we've been playing 'hide-and-seek' far too long."

The rest of the evening passed amid general constraint.

"You are the reason," I repeated to myself on my way home, searching my conscience.

What was the meaning of all this? Was it nothing but the childish whim of her imaginative mind? Two women quarreling over a man! They must be jealous, then. Was the Baroness so foolish that she would give herself away in such a manner? Hardly. But then what? There must be something at the bottom of it.

"What *is* going on in this house?" I asked myself, brooding over the strange scene that had startled me in the evening, the very improbability of which made me hesitate to believe that I had seen anything really wrong.

This senseless jealousy, the apprehension of the old mother, the Baroness' excitability stimulated by the spring air, all this confused my mind; it all seethed and fermented in my brain. After spending a sleepless night thinking about it, I resolved a second time not to see her again and thus avoid the threatening calamity.

With this intention I arose in the morning and wrote her a sensible, candid, and respectful letter. In carefully chosen language I protested against an abuse of friendship. Making myself sufficiently clear, I asked for forgiveness of my sins, blamed myself for having caused ill-feeling between relatives, and the devil knows what else I said!

The result was that the Baroness met me as if by accident, as I was leaving the library at my usual time. She stopped me on the North Bridge and led me aside to one of the paths in Charles XII Square. Almost with tears in her eyes she entreated me to come back, not to ask for explanations, but just to be one of them again as in the old days.

She was incredibly charming this morning. But I loved her too dearly to compromise her.

"Don't stand here. You're ruining your reputation," I said, watching the passers-by, whose curious glances embarrassed us. "Go home at once, or else I will!"

She looked at me with eyes so full of helplessness that I longed to kneel down before her, kiss her feet, and ask her forgiveness.

But instead I turned my back on her and hastily disappeared down a side street.

After dinner I went home to my attic, glowing with the satisfaction of having done my duty, but with a broken heart. Those sad, helpless eyes!

A short siesta gave me back my determination. I rose and looked at the almanac. It was the thirteenth of March.

"Beware the Ides of March!" Those famous words from *Julius Caesar* sounded in my ears as the servant entered bringing me a note from the Baron.

He begged me to spend the evening with him, saying that his wife was not well and that Matilda was going out.

I had not the strength to refuse.

The Baroness, more dead than alive, met me in the drawing room, pressed my hand against her heart, and thanked me warmly for having resolved not to rob her of a friend, a brother, for the sake of a mere nothing, a misunderstanding.

"I really think she's going out of her mind," laughed the Baron, releasing me from her hands.

"I *am* mad, I know, mad with joy that our friend has come back to us after he had decided to leave us forever."

And she burst into tears!

"She's been suffering a great deal," said the Baron, disconcerted by this truly heart-rending scene.

And, indeed, she looked as if she had a high fever. A dark fire burned in her eyes, which seemed to take up half of the little face; her cheeks were of a greenish pallor. The sight of her hurt me. Her frail body was shaken by fits of coughing, as if she had consumption.

Her uncle and father-in-law arrived unexpectedly. The fuel in the great stove was replenished, and we sat down before the fire without lighting the lamps, to enjoy the cozy hour of the gathering twilight.

She took a seat by my side, while the three men began to talk politics.

I saw her eyes shine in the dusk. I felt the warmth streaming from her body, probably the result of the attack of hysteria she had just had.

Her skirts brushed against my trousers. She leaned over to say something meant for my ears alone and smuggled a whispered question to me—"Do you believe in love?"

"No!"

My "no" struck her like a blow, for I had at the same time jumped up and changed my seat.

She must be mad, a nymphomaniac, I thought; and afraid of a scandalous scene, I suggested that we should have the lamps lighted.

During supper, uncle and father-in-law discussed Cousin Matilda to their heart's content, praising her domesticity, her skill in needlework. The Baron, who had poured several glasses of punch down his throat, now burst out into extravagant eulogies and deplored with alcoholic tears the unkind treatment to which the "dear child" was subjected at home. Nevertheless, apparently in the very depth of sympathetic sorrow, he pulled out his watch and prepared to leave us, as if he suddenly remembered a duty he had to perform.

"You must excuse me, gentlemen," he said, "but I promised Bébé to meet her and see her home. Don't let me disturb you. I shall be back in an hour."

The old Baron, his father, tried unsuccessfully to detain him. His artful son insisted on keeping his word and slipped away, after having extracted a promise from me to await his return.

We remained at table for another quarter of an hour and then went into the drawing room. The two old gentlemen soon left us and retired to the uncle's room, which the nephew had fitted up for him a little while ago.

I cursed fate for having caught me in a trap that I had done my utmost to avoid. I steeled my throbbing heart, I raised my head as a cock raises his comb, I bristled like a watchdog, I determined to crush at the outset any attempt to create a scene, tearful or amorous.

Leaning against the tile stove I smoked my cigar, silent, cold, and stiff, waiting to see what would happen.

The Baroness was the first to speak.

"Why do you hate me?"

"I don't hate you."

"Remember how you treated me only this morning!"

"Please don't speak of it!"

The unaccustomed and apparently unmotivated rudeness of my replies was a strategical error. She saw through me and changed her tactics.

"You wanted to run away from me," she continued. "Shall I tell you why I suddenly went to Mariafred?"

After a two-second silence I said, "Probably for the same reason I decided to go to Paris."

"Then . . . it's clear," she said.

"And now?"

I expected a scene. But she remained calm and regarded me mournfully. I had to break the silence, which was fraught with more danger than words.

"Now that you know my secret," I said, "let me give you a word of warning. If you want me to come here again now and then, you mustn't ever lose your head. You see, I love you to exaltation. I could live contentedly at your side without any other wish than to look at you. If you should ever forget your duty, if you should betray by as much as a look the secret that lies locked in our hearts, then I shall confess everything to your husband, regardless of the consequences!"

Carried away by my words, she raised her eyes.

"I swear it to you! How strong and good you are! How I admire you! But I'm ashamed. I want to surpass your honesty. I want to . . . Shall I tell Gustav everything?"

"If you like. But then we shall never see each other again. After all, it's not his business. The feelings in my

heart are not wrong, and even if he knew everything, could
he kill my love? No! The fact that I love the woman of my
choice is my own affair as long as I don't infringe the
rights of another. However, do as you please. I am prepared for anything!"

"No, no! He must know nothing; and since he does what
he wants, goes where he wants—"

"There I don't agree with you! It's not the same thing.
If he chooses to degrade himself, so much the worse for
him. But that's no reason why—oh, no!"

The ecstasy was over. We had come back to earth.

"No!" I repeated. "But you have to admit that it's beautiful, new, almost unique. To love, to tell one another of it.
Period. Nothing else!"

"It's as beautiful as a novel," she cried, clapping her
hands like a child.

"But it doesn't generally happen like that in the weekly
serials."

"How good it is to remain honorable!"

"Causes the least trouble!"

"And we shall always meet as before, without fear."

"And without reproach."

"And no more misunderstandings! But are you sure that
Matilda is nothing—"

The door opened. Height of banality! The two old gentlemen crossed the drawing room carrying a dark lantern.

"Notice how life is a medley of the ridiculous and the
sublime!" I said to her. "Notice how reality differs from
fiction. I wouldn't dare to draw a scene like this in a novel
or a drama. It would fall absolutely flat. Just think—a confession of love without kisses, rhetoric, or the bending of
knees, and terminated by the appearance of two old men
throwing the light of a dark lantern on the lovers! And yet
there's the secret of Shakespeare's greatness, who shows
us Julius Caesar in nightgown and slippers, starting from
his sleep at night, frightened by childish dreams."

The bell rang. It was the Baron and pretty Matilda. As

he had a guilty conscience, he overwhelmed us with amiability. And I, eager to show myself in my new part, told him a barefaced lie.

"I've been quarreling with the Baroness for the last hour!"

He looked at us suspiciously, and scenting the air like a hound, seemed to catch the wrong scent I had planted.

As for myself, I withdrew.

13

What unparalleled childishness it is to believe in a purely chaste love! The secret that we shared was already the source of danger. It was like a child conceived in secrecy. It took shape after the union of our souls and strove to see the light.

More than ever before we longed to meet and compare notes. We yearned to live again through the last year, in which we had been playing hide-and-seek. We resorted to all kinds of trickery. I introduced the Baroness to my sister, who, having married the headmaster of a school, a man with an old, aristocratic name, in a way belonged to her set.

Our meetings were harmless enough to begin with, but we grew more ardent and our passions demanded an outlet.

In the first days following our mutual confessions, she gave me a packet of letters, written partly before, partly after the thirteenth of March, the date of our confessions. I should never have been allowed to read these letters into which she had poured all her sorrow, all her love.

14

Monday

My dear Friend,

I am longing to see you, today as always. I want to thank you for listening to me yesterday without that sarcastic smile with which it is now your rule to regard me! Why do you have to smile that way? If you only knew how it irritates me! I turn to you trustfully, at a moment when I am in dire need of your friendship, and you cover your face with a mask. Why? Is it necessary that you should disguise your feelings? You have yourself admitted in one of your letters that it is a mask. I hope it is, I can see it is, and yet it hurts me, for it makes me think that I have acted stupidly again . . . and I wonder: What is he thinking of me? I am jealous of your friendship; I am afraid that you will despise me. Tell me that it will never happen! You must be good and loyal to me. You must forget that I am a woman—don't I only too often forget it myself! I was not angry with you for what you said yesterday, but it surprised and pained me.

Do you really believe me capable of wanting to excite my husband's jealousy for the sake of taking a mean revenge? Think of the danger to which I should expose myself if I attempted to win him back through jealousy! What should I gain? His anger would fall upon your head, and we should forever be separated! And what would become of me without your company, which is dearer to me than life!

I love you with a sister's tenderness, not with the whims of a coquette. . . . It is true that I have known moments when I longed, when it would have been heaven, to take your darling little head into my hands, to look deep into your dear eyes, so full of wisdom; and I am sure I should have kissed you on your smooth, adorable forehead, but never in your life would you have received a purer kiss. It's just part of

my affectionate nature, and if you were a woman I
should love you just as much, provided that I could
respect a woman as highly as I respect you.

Your opinion of Matilda makes me very happy. One
has to be a woman to be pleased about such a thing.
But imagine how I felt when I saw her winning all
the victories! But I'm partly to blame, too. I encouraged this flirtation because I considered it no more
serious than a child's game. Feeling sure of his affection, I allowed my husband perfect liberty. The consequences have shown how completely wrong I
was. . . .

Wednesday

He is in love with her and has told me so. It's gone
so far, I have to laugh at the whole thing. Think:
after seeing you to the door, he came back to me,
took my hands, looked me in the eyes—I trembled,
for my conscience was not clear—and said entreat-
ingly: "Don't be angry with me, Marie! But . . . let
me go to Matilda's room tonight. I'm terribly in love
with her!"

What was I to do? Should I cry or laugh? And he
confessed this to me, to me who am tormented by
remorse, forced to love you from afar, hopelessly! Oh,
these stupid, senseless ideas of honor! Let him indulge
his passion! I still have you! You are my love, and my
desires as a woman are not so dangerous that they can
make me forget my duties as a wife and mother. But
notice the conflicting double nature of my feelings.
. . . I love you both, and I could never live without
him, the brave, honest friend of my heart . . . nor
from now on without you either!

Friday

At last you have lifted the veil that for so long has
hidden the secret of my heart. And you don't despise
me! Merciful God! You even love me. You have
spoken the words which you had determined to leave
forever unspoken. You love me! And I am a guilty

woman, a criminal, because I love you in return. May God forgive me! For I still love him too and can never leave him.

How strange it is! . . . To be loved! Loved by him and by you! I feel so happy, so calm, that my love cannot possibly be sinful! Surely I should feel remorse if it were—or am I so hardened?

How ashamed I am of myself! It was I who had to speak the first word of love. My husband is here, he holds out his arms for me, and I go over and kiss him. Am I sincere? Yes! Why did he not take care of me while there was yet time?

It's all like a story. How will it end? Will the heroine die? Will the hero marry another? Will they go their separate ways? And will the denouement be satisfactory from a moral point of view?

If I were with you at this moment, I should kiss your brow with the same devotion with which the religious believer kisses the crucifix, and I should put far behind me all the baseness, all the cheapness that I see in what I have done. . . .

15

Was this hypocrisy or did I deceive myself? Did these semireligious ecstasies spring from nothing but hidden desires and passions? No, not passions only. The desire to perpetuate the life one has been given has become more complicated than that, and even among the lower animals psychic characteristics are transmitted through sexual love. Therefore, love affects both body and soul, and one is nothing without the other. If it were but passion, why should she prefer a delicate, nervous, sickly youth like me to a giant like him? If it were only the love of the soul, why this longing to kiss me, why this admiration for my small feet, my well-shaped hands and nails, my high forehead, my abundant hair? Or were those hallucinations caused by the intoxication of her senses, excited by her

husband's excesses? Or did she feel instinctively that an
ardent youth like me would make her far more happy
than that inert mass she called her husband? She was no
longer jealous of his body; therefore, she had ceased looking upon him as a lover. But she was jealous of all of me,
and therefore she was in love with me!

16

One day when visiting my sister, the Baroness was
seized with an attack of hysterics. She threw herself on the
sofa and burst into tears, infuriated with the disgraceful
conduct of her husband, who was spending the evening
with Cousin Bébé at a regimental ball.

Losing control of herself, she threw her arms around me
and kissed me on the forehead. I returned kiss for kiss.
She called me by endearing names. We were being
chained together, and I desired her madly.

In the course of the evening I recited Longfellow's "Ex-
celsior" to her. Genuinely moved by this impressive poem,
I fixed my eyes on her, and as if she were hypnotized, her
face reflected every shade of feeling expressed on my own.
She had the appearance of a madwoman, a visionary.

After supper her maid called for her in a cab to take her
home. I meant to come no farther with her than the street
but she insisted on my getting into the cab, and in spite of
my protestations she ordered her maid to sit on the box
beside the driver. As soon as we were alone we kissed each
other without a word. I felt her delicate body thrill and
yield completely under my kisses. But I shrank from viola-
tion—why should I disarrange the branches on a family
tree?—and left her at her door, unhurt, ashamed of herself
and, perhaps, also a little angry.

I no longer had any doubts; I saw clearly. She was trying to seduce me. It was she who had given the first kiss,
she who had taken the initiative in everything. From this

moment I was going to play the part of the seducer, for I was no Joseph in spite of my stiff-necked attitude on questions of honor.

17

On the following day we had arranged to meet at the National Museum.

I adored her as I saw her coming up the marble staircase, under the gilded ceiling, as I watched her little feet tripping over the flags of variegated stucco, her aristocratic figure clothed in a black velvet costume trimmed with military braid. I hurried to meet her and, like a page, bent my knees before her. Her beauty, which had blossomed under my kisses, was striking. The rich blood in her veins shone through her transparent cheeks. This statue of a young old maid had quickened under my caresses and grown warm at the fire of life. Pygmalion had breathed on the marble and held a goddess in his arms.

We sat down before a statue of Psyche, which Sweden had acquired in the Thirty Years' War. I kissed her cheeks, her eyes, her lips, and she received my kisses with a rapturous smile. I improvised the part of a seducer, employing all the sophisms of the orator, all the arts of the poet.

"I entreat you," I said, "abandon your desecrated marriage. Get out of that polluted bedroom. Don't consent any longer to live this *ménage à trois*—or you'll force me to despise you. Return to your mother, devote yourself to art; in a year you will be able to appear before the footlights. Then you will be free to live your own life."

She added fuel to the fire by kissing me. The flames flared up as I warmed to my subject. I overwhelmed her with words, the object of which was to extract a promise from her to tell her husband everything, whatever the consequences might be for us.

"But suppose things end badly?" she interposed.

"And what if we do lose everything? I could no longer love you if I can no longer respect both of us. Are you a coward? Do you think you can win the reward without sacrificing something? Be as noble as you are beautiful; dare the fatal leap, even at the risk of perishing! Let everything be lost save our honor! A few more days like this and I shall have seduced you, you can be sure of that. My love is like lightning that will strike you! I love you as the sun loves the dew—to drink it. So on to the scaffold! Sacrifice your head but keep your hands clean! Don't imagine that I could ever lower myself to sharing you with somebody else! Never! All or nothing!"

She feigned resistance, but in reality she threw a grain of powder into the open flames. She complained of her husband and by her remarks gave me a glimpse into her bedroom, the very thought of which made my blood boil.

He, the numbskull, poor as myself, without prospects, indulged in the luxury of two mistresses, while I, the man of talent, the aristocrat of the future, sighed and writhed under the torture of my unsatisfied longings.

But all of a sudden she veered round and tried to calm my excited nerves by reminding me of our agreement to be brother and sister.

"Too dangerous. Leave that game to others. Stupid old maid's talk. Let us be man and woman, lover and beloved! That's the honest way. I adore you! I adore everything belonging to you, body and soul, your golden hair and your honest heart, the smallest feet that ever wore shoes in Sweden, your candor, your eyes lost in the darkness of a cab, your bewitching smile, your white stocking and your cherry-colored garter. . . ."

"What?"

"Yes, my lovely princess, I've seen them! And now I want to kiss your throat just there where the roundness of your breasts begins! I promise to smother you with kisses, strangle you between my arms. My love for you fills me with the strength of a god. Did you think I was a weakling? My sickness was imaginary, or, rather, assumed. Beware of the sick lion! Don't come near his den or he'll kill you with caresses! Off with these indecent masks! I want you, and I'll have you! I've wanted you from the first moment I set eyes on you! That was only a fairy tale—the story of Selma the Finlander—a fabrication! A lie! And so is the friendship of our dear Baron! He loathes me, the man of the middle classes, the provincial, the déclassé, as I loathe him, the aristocrat!"

She seemed quite unexcited by this avalanche of revelations. There was nothing new in it; we had known this all along without putting it into words.

And we separated with the firm resolution not to meet again until she had told her husband everything.

18

I spent the evening at home, anxious and uneasy, waiting for telegrams from the battlefield. To distract my thoughts I emptied a sack containing old books and papers on the floor and sat down among this litter to examine and classify it. But I found it impossible to concentrate my thoughts. I stretched myself out at full length, resting the back of my head on my hands and, my eyes fixed with a hypnotic stare on the candles burning in the old chandelier, I lost myself in a reverie. I was longing for her kisses and laying my plans for her seduction. As she was sensitive and strange, I felt that the utmost delicacy would be necessary, that I must allow matters to arrange themselves, that a single clumsy movement would spoil everything.

I lighted a cigarette and imagined that I was lying in a meadow. It amused me to view my little room from below. Everything seemed new to me. The sofa, the scene of many erotic conquests, brought me back to my voluptuous dreams of love, which however were quickly paralyzed by the fear that everything would be ruined because of my idiotic principles.

Analyzing the thought that had checked my ardor, I discovered in it a great deal of cowardice; some fear of the consequences; a bit of sympathy with the man who stood in danger of being betrayed; a few drops of disgust for the indecent promiscuity; a portion of genuine respect for the woman I could not bear to see degrading herself; a measure of pity for the daughter; a mere grain of compassion for the mother of my beloved, in case of a scandal; and in the depths of my miserable heart a vague presentiment of the difficulty I should find later on if ever I should wish to sever our connection.

"No," I said to myself, "all or nothing! She must be mine alone and forever!"

While I was thus musing, there came a discreet tapping at my door, and almost simultaneously a lovely head appeared in the opening, flooding my attic with sunshine. A roguish smile drew me away from my papers into the arms of my beloved. After a hailstorm of kisses on her lips, fresh with the cold outside, I asked, "Well, what has he decided to do?"

"Nothing! I haven't told him yet!"

"Then you are lost! Stay away from me, you unfortunate woman!"

And keeping firm hold of her, I took off her close-fitting fur coat—a foretaste of the inevitable undressing scene—removed her beaded hat, and drew her to the fire. Then she found words.

"I hadn't the courage. . . . I wanted to see you once again before the catastrophe, for God knows, he may decide to divorce me . . . !"

I closed her lips with mine, pushed a little table to her seat, and brought from my cupboard a bottle of good wine and two glasses. By the side of them I set a basket with roses and two lighted candles, arranging everything in the manner of an altar. For a footstool I gave her a thick, priceless old edition of Hans Sachs's poems, bound in calf, furnished with gold locks, and ornamented with a portrait of Luther—a book I had taken home from the Royal Library.

I poured out some wine. I gathered a rose and fastened it in the golden thicket of her hair. I moistened my lips on the glass raised to drink to her health, to our love. I knelt down before her and worshiped her.

"How beautiful you are!"

For the first time she saw me as a true lover. She was delighted. She took my head between her hands, kissed it, and ruffled with her fingers the tangled strands of my unruly hair.

Her beauty filled me with respect. I looked at her as one looks at an awe-inspiring altar piece. For her part, she was enchanted to see me without the hated mask. My words intoxicated her, and she was filled with delirious joy when she found that my love for her was at once tender, respectful, and full of fire.

I kissed her shoes, blackening my lips. I embraced her knees without touching the hem of her dress. I loved her just as she was, fully dressed, chaste as an angel, as if she had been born clothed, with wings outside her dress.

Suddenly the tears came into my eyes, I could not have said why.

"Are you crying?" she asked. "What's the matter?"

"I don't know. I'm too happy, that's all."

"You, capable of tears! You, the man of stone!"

"Me! You don't know how often I've cried!"

Being a woman of experience right to her pretty fingertips, she imagined that she possessed the remedy for my secret sorrow.

She rose from the sofa and pretended to be interested in the papers scattered about on the floor.

"You seemed to be stretched out on the grass when I came in," she said, smiling archly. "It's fun to make hay in the middle of the winter, isn't it?"

She sat down on a pile of papers. I threw myself down beside her. Another hailstorm of kisses. The idol was tottering, ready to fall. Gradually I drew her closer to me, holding her captive with my lips, so as not to give her time to escape the fire in my eyes and the glow of my lips. I embraced her, and we stretched out—on the grass!—like lovers, yielding to our passion like angels, fully dressed, without the ultimate union. We rose up content, happy, without remorse, like angels who have not fallen.

Love is inventive! We had sinned without sinning, yielded without surrendering. Ah, the charming generosity of a woman of experience! Merciful to the young apprentice, she finds her pleasure in giving, not in receiving.

Suddenly she recovered her senses, remembered the claims of reality, and prepared to go.

"Until tomorrow?"

"Until tomorrow!"

19

She had confessed everything to him. Now she thought herself guilty, for he had wept. He had wept scalding tears! Was he a big baby or a sly dog? Probably both. Love and delusion are inseparable, and it is indeed difficult to know ourselves as we really are.

But he was not angry with us and was not against our seeing each other and being intimate—provided that we remain chaste!

"He is more noble and generous than we are," she said in her letter. "He still loves both of us!"

What a milksop! He consented to receive in his house a man who had overwhelmed his wife with kisses. He believed us to be so sexless that we could continue to live like brother and sister.

It was an insult to my manhood, and I responded with a definite and lasting goodby!

20

I stayed at home, a prey to the bitterest disappointment. I had tasted the apple and it had been snatched from me. My imperious love had repented; she was suffering from remorse; she heaped reproaches on me—she, the temptress! A sickening thought flashed through my mind. Had I been too shy? Did she want to break with me because I had been too timid? Since the thought of the act from which I had shrunk had not seemed to disturb her, her passion must be stronger than mine. But come back to me once more, my beauty, and I will teach you better.

At ten o'clock I received a letter from the Baron, in which he said that his wife was, it seemed, seriously ill.

My reply was a request to be left in peace. "I have been long enough the cause of unpleasantness between you; forget me, as I will forget you."

Towards noon a second letter arrived:

> Let us once more revive our old friendship. I have always respected you, and, in spite of your error, I am convinced that you have behaved like a man of honor. Let us bury the past. Come back to me as a brother, and the matter will be forgotten. Everything will be as before.

The pathetic simplicity, the perfect confidence of the man touched me. In reply I mentioned my misgivings, pleaded with him not to play with fire, begged him to leave me alone.

At three o'clock in the afternoon I received a last communication. The Baroness was dying; the doctor had just left her; she had asked for me. The Baron entreated me not to refuse her request, and I went. Poor me!

I entered. The room stank of chloroform. The Baron received me with tears in his eyes.

"Now what's the matter?" I asked with the coolness of a doctor.

"I don't know. But she nearly died."

"And the doctor, what did he say?"

"Nothing. On his way out he shook his head and said it was not a case for him."

"Did he give her a prescription?"

"No. Nothing."

He took me into the dining room, which had been transformed into a sickroom. She was lying on a couch, stiff, haggard, her hair falling over her shoulders, her eyes glowing like red-hot coals. She moved her hand, and her husband put it into mine. Then he withdrew to the drawing room and left us by ourselves. I was still cool and unmoved, scarcely trusting my eyes. I was suspicious of the whole spectacle.

"Do you know that I nearly died?"

"Yes."

"And you don't feel sorry?"

"Oh, yes!"

"You are not moved; no look of sympathy, no word of commiseration."

"You have your husband!"

"Hasn't he himself brought us together?"

"What are you suffering from?"

"I'm very ill. I shall have to consult a gynecologist."

"Indeed."

"I'm afraid! It's terrible! If you knew how I have suffered! . . . Put your hand on my head. . . . It feels so good. . . . Can't you smile? . . . Your smile fills me with new life! . . ."

"The Baron—"

"You want to leave us? Abandon me?"

"What can I do for you?"

She began to cry.

"You surely can't want me to play the lover here," I

said curtly, "with just a wall between us and your child and your husband?"

"You are a monster! A man without a heart! A—"

"Goodby, Baroness!"

I went. The Baron conducted me through the drawing room, but not quickly enough to prevent me from catching sight of a woman's skirt disappearing through one of the other doors. It reminded me of a bedroom farce.

The Baron closed the door behind me with a bang that echoed through the staircase and gave me the impression I had been kicked out.

No doubt about it. I had been the witness to some highly melodramatic double-dealing. This mysterious illness, what was it? Hysteria? No. In German, *Mutterwut*, a passion for children. Or, more freely translated, an irresistible desire to be pregnant—being in heat—a feeling that may be repressed for years by the forces of shame and convention, but sooner or later it breaks out.

She had always lived in a state of semicelibacy, always on guard against pregnancy, always unsatisfied after the unfinished embrace, and so she was driven into the arms of a lover by these starved passions. And now at the very moment when she thought that her lover had been conquered and was incontestably hers, he had slipped through her fingers, and he, too, in his turn had left her unsatisfied.

When I had finished my analysis I had come to the conclusion that their deceit and dishonesty had driven both husband and wife to seek happiness with others who promised them full satisfaction. The disappointment at my flight had brought the Baroness back into the arms of her husband, who had received a fresh stimulus to fulfill his duties as a husband, which seemed more attractive to him after his wife had been warmed up for him by the Lover.

They were reconciled, and the story was over.

Exit the devil.

Curtain.

21

No, not quite.

She visited me again in my room and I drew from her a full confession, brutal in its frankness.

In the first year of her marriage she had known nothing of the ecstasies of love. After her baby was born, her husband grew indifferent to her, and as he did not want another child, he adopted certain half measures in their relations.

"Then he has never made you happy, this man with the shoulders of a giant?"

"Hardly ever. . . . Once in a while maybe . . . not very often."

"And now?"

She blushed.

"The doctor has advised him to give himself completely."

She sank back on the sofa and hid her face in her hands.

Excited by these intimate confessions, I attacked her gently. She offered no resistance, she trembled and breathed heavily, but at the psychological moment she felt remorse and repulsed me.

Strange enigma that was beginning to irritate me!

What did she want from me? Everything! But she shrank from the real crime, the illegitimate child.

I took her in my arms and overwhelmed her with hot kisses. She freed herself and left me, still pure and whole, but, I thought, a shade less disappointed than the last time.

And now what? Confess to the husband? That had already been done.

Give him all the details? Why bother? There were no details to give.

22

She continued to visit me.

And whenever she came she sat down on the sofa, saying she was so tired.

One day, tired and ashamed of always playing timid, furious at my humiliation, probably suspected of being impotent, I raped her—if "raped" is the right word—and rose to my feet after it was over, arrogant and happy, bursting with pride and self-satisfaction, as if I had paid off a debt to a woman.

But she got up looking rather miserable and down at the mouth. "That's the end of the proud Baroness," she sighed.

She began to worry about the possible consequences. Her downcast eyes betrayed the disappointment that is always felt after sex-by-chance, sex rushed through without the necessary calm.

"Is that all?"

She walked out with slow steps. I watched her from my window until she turned the corner and I sighed too, "Is that all?"

The son of the people had carried off the alabaster beauty, the commoner had won the aristocrat, the swineherd had mated with the princess! But at what a price!

A storm was brewing. All sorts of rumors circulated in the town. The fair fame of the Baroness was compromised.

Her mother asked me to call on her. I went.

"Is it true that you are in love with my daughter?"

"Absolutely true."

"And are you not ashamed?"

"I glory in it."

"She has told me that she loves you."

"I was aware of that. . . . I am sorry for you. I regret the possible consequences, but what am I to do? No doubt it's a deplorable business, but we are not guilty, neither she nor I. When we discovered our danger, we warned the Baron. Wasn't that acting correctly?"

"I'm not complaining of your conduct now, but I must protect the honor of my daughter, of her child, of the family! Surely you don't want to ruin us?"

The poor old woman cried bitterly. She had put all her eggs in one basket: the aristocratic alliance of her daughter, which was to rehabilitate her own family. I felt sorry for her.

"Tell me what to do," I said, "and I'll be glad to do it."

"Leave this place, go away from here."

"All right, but on one condition."

"And that is?"

"That you will ask Miss Matilda to return to her family."

"Is that an accusation?"

"More than that, a denunciation. For I believe I'm right in saying that her presence at the Baron's house is not likely to encourage the success of the marriage."

"I agree with you. Oh, that evil girl! I shall tell her what I think of her! But you, you will leave tomorrow?"

"Tonight, if you like."

At this stage the Baroness appeared without warning and interrupted our conversation.

"You must stay! I insist you stay!" she said imperatively. "Matilda should be the one to go!"

"Why?" asked her mother in amazement.

"Because I have decided to get a divorce. Gustav has treated me like an abandoned woman before Matilda's stepfather. I shall prove to them that they're mistaken."

What a heart-rending scene! No surgical operation is as painful as the cutting of family ties. All passions are let loose, all the dirty linen is brought out from the hidden corners of the soul.

The Baroness drew me aside and repeated to me the contents of a letter from her husband to Matilda: abuse of us, and an assurance of his undying love for the girl in terms that proved he had deceived us from the very beginning.

The stone was now as big as a rock, rolling on to crush both the innocent and the guilty.

23

The parties began to haggle, and there seemed to be no hope of a settlement.

Fresh misfortunes occurred. The bank did not pay the ordinary yearly dividend. The Baron was on the verge of ruin. The threatening poverty was made the pretext for the divorce, since the Baron could no longer maintain his family. For appearances' sake he asked his colonel whether his wife's proposed theatrical career would in any way interfere with his own. The colonel gave him to understand that if his wife went on the stage, he would have to leave the service. Which provided a splendid opportunity for lashing out at aristocratic prejudices. During all this time the Baroness, under medical treatment for uterine abscess, continued to live at her husband's house although she had left his bed and board. She was always in pain, irritable and despondent, and I found it impossible to rouse her from her deep depression. My strenuous efforts to inspire her with some of my youthful confidence were wasted. In vain I drew for her glowing pictures of the career of an artist, the independent life in a home of her own, a home like mine, where she would enjoy freedom of body and soul. She listened to me without replying; the stream of my words seemed to galvanize her like a magnetic current, but without penetrating to her consciousness.

A divorce agreement between the two parties had been arrived at at last. It was decided that after all legal formalities had been complied with, the Baroness should proceed to Copenhagen, where an uncle of hers was living.

The Swedish consul at Copenhagen would communicate with her on her supposed flight from her husband's house, and she would inform him of her wish to have her marriage annulled. After that she would be free to return to Stockholm and to make her own plans for the future. Her dowry would remain in the possession of her husband, as well as all the furniture, with the exception of a very few things. The Baron would have custody of their child unless the latter contracted a second marriage, but the Baroness would have the right to see her child whenever she wished.

The financial question gave rise to a violent scene. To save the remnants of a fortune which had almost disappeared, the father of the Baroness had made a will in which he left everything to his daughter. Her scheming mother had obtained possession of the inheritance and was paying her son-in-law a certain percentage. Since such a procedure was illegal, the Baron insisted that the will should now come into force. The old mother-in-law, furious at the reduction of her income, denounced her son-in-law to her brother, Matilda's father, and exposed the Baron as the girl's lover. The storm burst. The colonel threatened to cashier the Baron; a lawsuit was impending.

Now the Baroness left no stone unturned to save the father of her child. And to clear him I was made the scapegoat.

I was prevailed upon to write a letter to Matilda's father in which I took the sins of everybody and the responsibility for all the mischief on my own shoulders, called God to witness that the Baron and the girl were innocent, and asked the offended father to forgive me for all the crimes that I, and I alone, had committed and for which I, and I alone, should suffer.

It was a noble and courageous deed, and the Baroness loved me for it in the way that a woman loves a man who has allowed her to trample on his honor, his self-respect, his good name.

So in spite of my resolution not to get mixed up in these unsavory family matters, I had been forced to these hateful measures.

The mother-in-law paid me many visits and, always appealing to my love for her daughter, tried to incite me against the Baron, but in vain. I took my orders from no one but the Baroness. Moreover, on this point I sided with the father. As he was taking charge of the child, the dowry belonged to him, whether it was worth anything or not.

Ah, April! Springtime of love! The beloved woman on the sickbed; intolerable meetings at which the two families washed their dirty linen, with which I certainly never had the least desire to come into contact; tears; rudeness; quarrels that brought to light everything base that had been hidden under the veneer of propriety and a good upbringing. That's what comes of sticking one's nose in a hornet's nest!

Naturally our love suffered. Finding one's mistress always exhausted from quarrels, her cheeks red with anger and irritation, and with nothing but legal terms on her lips, hardly served as an aphrodisiac.

Again and again I attempted to instil into her my thoughts of consolation and hope, even though they were often anything but spontaneous, for my nerves were exhausted. She accepted everything, sucked my brain dry, consumed my heart. In exchange, she looked upon me as a garbage can into which she threw all her rubbish, all her grief, all her toubles, all her cares.

In this hell I lived my life, dragged on my misery, worked for a bare sufficiency. When she came to see me in the evening she sulked if I went on with my work; and it was not until I had wasted a couple of hours with tears and kisses that I succeeded in convincing her of my love.

Love to her meant continuous adoration, slavish attentiveness, unceasing sacrifice.

I was crushed down by my heavy responsibility. I could see the moment not very far off when misery, or the birth of a child, would force me into a premature marriage. She had claimed but three thousand crowns for one year to cover the costs of her artistic training. I had no faith in her dramatic career. Her pronunciation was still marked by a frightening Finnish accent, and her features were too irregular for the stage. To keep her from brooding I made her recite poetry and set myself as her teacher. But she was too much occupied with her disappointments, and when after a rehearsal she had to admit that her progress was very small, she was completely inconsolable.

How dreary our love was! Her continual fear of pregnancy and my lack of experience with the means of avoiding this danger combined to make a prolonged torture of our love, which should have been a source of strength and energy to enable us to endure these oppressive circumstances. Joy was no sooner born than it was slain; her fear would affect me too; and we would part, frustrated, disappointed, robbed of the greatest happiness life has to give. What a caricature of real love!

There were moments when I missed the whores, but my monogamic nature hated a change of partners. Anyway, however unsatisfactory our embraces may have been, they provided a deeper spiritual joy perhaps, and my unextinguished passion served as a guarantee for the continuance of our love.

24

The first of May. All the necessary documents had been signed. Her departure was fixed for the day after tomorrow. She came to me and threw her arms around me.

As we had never discussed marriage, I did not quite understand what she meant. We sat in my little attic, sad and thoughtful. Everything was permitted to us now, so that temptations were less. She accused me of indifference and I proved the contrary to her. Then she accused me of sensuality: she wanted adoration, incense, hymns of praise.

She had hysterics and complained that I no longer loved her. Already!

After an hour of flattery and blandishments she grew calmer, but she was not really herself until she had reduced me to tears of despair. Then she made a fuss over me. The more humble I was, the more I knelt before her, small and miserable, the more she loved me. She hated strength and manliness in me. To win her love I had to pretend to be wretched and unhappy so that she could pose as superior to me, play "little mother" and console me.

We had supper in my room. She laid the table and prepared the meal. After supper I claimed the rights of a lover. The sofa was transformed into a bed, and I undressed her.

It was love resurrected, for a young girl lay trembling in my arms, and brutality was transformed into tenderness. The animal had no part in this union of souls! But if one could only say where the spiritual ends and the animal begins!

Reassured by her doctor on the question of her condition, she gave herself to me wholeheartedly. She was radiant with joy, content and happy. Her beauty shone out. Her eyes sparkled. My poor attic had become a temple, a sumptuous palace. I lighted the broken chandelier, my reading lamp, all the candles to illuminate our happiness, our love joy, the only thing which makes our miserable lives endurable.

For it is these moments of ecstasy and rapture that accompany us on our thorny pilgrimage through life; the memory of these fleeting pleasures, condemned only by those who are envious, give us the strength to live and to outlive our former selves. They constitute the real love.

"Don't speak ill of love," I said to her. "Worship nature in all her forces. Honor that god who forces us to be happy in spite of ourselves!"

She had no reply, for she was happy. Her yearning was stilled. Her face was flushed. The ardor of our embraces had driven the warm blood through her beating heart into her cheeks; her eyes, moist with voluptuous joy, reflected the flame of the candle. The rainbow tints of her veins appeared more vivid, like the plumage of birds in spring-time. She looked like a girl of sixteen, so delicate, so pure were her contours. The dainty head with its masses of golden hair, half-buried in the pillow, might have been a child's. Her tiny body, more fragile than thin, was lying half-veiled by her batiste chemise—reminiscent of a Greek chiton—gathered at her waist into a thousand creases, hiding her thighs but exposing her knees where those beautiful muscles and ligaments meet in a confusion of lines that reminded me of mother-of-pearl. And the lace-work at the top climbed up over her breasts like a lattice through which two small kittens were sticking their little pink noses. And her shoulders emerging from the top of the chemise were like handgrips carved in ivory to fit snugly in my hands.

She reclined on my sofa, like a goddess, watching me worship her, stretching herself lazily, rubbing her eyes, and casting furtive glances at me half shamefaced, half provoking.

How chaste in her abandonment is the beloved woman when she surrenders herself to the caresses of her lover! And though her superior mentally, man is only happy when he has won the woman who is his equal. My former flirtations, my sexual intercourse with women of a lower class appeared to me to be recidivism, a crime against the race. The white skin, the faultless hands, the perfectly formed feet with nails as white and regular as piano keys —were they signs of degeneration? Were they not rather on a par with the glossy skin of the wild beast, its slim, sinewy legs that show hardly any muscle? The beauty of a woman lies in the sum total of qualities that are worthy of being perpetuated in harmony with the man who best appreciates them. This woman had been pushed aside by her husband; therefore she no longer belonged to him, for she had ceased to please him. He could no longer see any beauty in her, and it was left to me to make this flower blossom into rare loveliness, perceptible only to the Chosen Man with eyes to see.

What a guiltless pleasure to possess one's beloved! Like the well-being that comes with the fulfillment of a duty! And this is called a sin! Oh, what a heavenly sin, what a blessed desecration, what a divine guilt!

Almost midnight. From the barracks close by came the "Who goes there?" of the relieving guards. It was time to part.

I accompanied my beloved on her way home, and as we were walking along side by side I tried to kindle in her the fire of my enthusiasm, my new hopes. I startled her with the plans that her kisses had ripened in me. She came closer as if to find strength in contact with me, and I gave her back tenfold what I had received from her. When we had arrived at the high railings she noticed that she had forgotten her key. How annoying! But, bent on showing her my mettle by invading the lion's den, I climbed the railings, dashed across the courtyard and knocked at the front door, prepared for a stormy reception from the Baron. My throbbing heart was thrilled by the thought of fighting my rival before her eyes. The favored lover was transformed into a hero! Fortunately, it was only a maid who came to open the door, and we said our most intimate goodnights to each other, quite calmly, with the maid, who had not taken the trouble to respond to our "Good evening," looking on in contemptuous silence.

25

From now on she felt sure of my love and abused it.
She came up to my place and could not find words

enough to praise her husband. Deeply affected by Matilda's banishment, he had succumbed to his wife's pressure and made her a promise to save appearances by accompanying her to the station. If both he and I were to see her off, her departure would not have the appearance of flight. Moreover, the Baron, no longer angry with me, had offered to receive me at his house and, in order to put a stop to the rumors, show himself during the next few days about the town in my company.

I appreciated the generosity of this big child with the honest heart, and out of consideration for him I demurred.

"We're not going to disgrace him like that. Never!"

"Remember that it is a question of my child's honor."

"But, darling, what about *his* honor?"

She laughed at the idea, looked upon me as eccentric.

"But that beats everything! You're making me a byword, you're degrading us all!" I exclaimed. "It's folly! It's unworthy."

She began to cry. After she had sobbed for an hour and overwhelmed me with reproaches, I succumbed to that irresistible weapon, her tears, and consented to do her bidding. But I grumbled at my tyrant and cursed those falling crystal drops that increased tenfold the power of her glances.

She was stronger than both her husband and myself. She was leading us by the nose into disgrace! Why did she want this reconciliation? Was she afraid of a duel to the death between me and the Baron, with dreadful disclosures afterwards?

My God, what a punishment she had inflicted on me by compelling me to revisit this dreary house! But, cruelly egotistical, she had no sympathy with another's anxiety. Imagine, I had been compelled to promise her, on my oath, to deny the whole story of the illicit relationship that existed between the Baron and her cousin in order to stop all slander. I went to this last meeting with slow steps and a sinking heart. There lay the garden with its cherry trees

and narcissus in full bloom. The arbor where her marvelous beauty had bewitched me was bursting into leaf. The
turned-up flowerbeds looked like black shrouds spread out
on the lawn. I pictured the forsaken little girl wandering
about there alone, looked after by some maidservant sewing away at her work, indifferent to her. I pictured her
growing up, awakening to the facts of life, and being told
one day that her mother had deserted her.

I mounted the stairs of the fatal house, which was built
against a sand quarry, and called up the memories of my
childhood. Friendship, family, love, all had been soiled,
and in spite of our efforts a sin against marriage had
stained the threshold of this house.

Who was to blame?

The Baroness opened the door and secretly kissed me
behind it before we went into the drawing room. I could
not suppress a momentary feeling of loathing and pushed
her aside. It reminded me of the backstairs flirtations of
servants. Behind the door! Without pride, without dignity!
What in damnation was I to think of a woman like that?

She pretended that I was reluctant to enter the drawing
room and asked me in a loud voice to come in at the very
moment when, embarrassed by the humiliating situation in
which I found myself, I hesitated and was on the point of
retracing my footsteps. A lightning flash from her eyes, and
my hesitation was reduced to ashes. Paralyzed by her
complete self-assurance, I gave in.

Everything in the drawing room pointed to the breaking up of the household. Underlinen, dresses, petticoats
were scattered all over the furniture. On the piano lay the
lace-trimmed chemises I knew so well. On the writing desk
was a heap of stockings and underpants, the delight of my
dreams a short time ago but now nauseating to look at.
She went on picking and counting and folding, brazenly,
shamelessly.

"Did I corrupt her in so short a time?" I asked myself,

gazing at this exhibition of a respectable woman's most
intimate garments.

She examined one piece after another, and put in one
pile everything which could be mended yet once more. A
pair of panties with worn tapes was put in the pile—non-
chalantly, unconcernedly.

I was as pained as if I were at an execution, while she
merely listened absent-mindedly to my futile conversation.
I was waiting for the Baron, who had locked himself into
the dining room to write letters.

At last the door opened. My emotions made a sudden
turnabout when I saw that it was only the little girl who
had come in, puzzled to know the reason of all this
turmoil. She ran up to me, accompanied by her mother's
spaniel, and as usual held up her forehead to be kissed. I
blushed, I got angry, and turned to the Baroness.

"You might at least have spared me this!"

But she did not understand.

"Mamma is going away, darling, but she'll soon be back
and bring you lots of toys."

The little dog begged for a caress—he, too!

A little later the Baron appeared.

He walked up to me, broken, crushed, and pressed my
hand, unable to utter a word. I honored his evident grief
by a respectful silence, and he withdrew again.

Dusk was beginning to gather in the corners of the
room. The maid lighted the lamps without seeming to
notice my presence. Supper was announced. I wanted to
go. But the Baron added his pressing invitation to that of
the Baroness, and in so touching and sincere a manner that
I accepted and stayed.

And we sat down to supper, the three of us, as in the
old days. It was a solemn and unforgettable moment. The
talk wandered here and there until the question "Who is
to blame?" brought tears to our eyes. "Who is to blame?"
Nobody, destiny, a series of incidents paltry in themselves,
a number of forces. We shook hands, clinked our glasses

together, and spoke of our undying friendship exactly as in
the days gone by. The Baroness alone kept up her spirits.
She made the program for the following day: the meeting
at the railway station, the walks through the town, and
we agreed to everything.

At last I rose to go. The Baron accompanied us into the
drawing room. There he laid the hand of the Baroness into
mine and said with choking voice—"Be her friend. My part
is over. Take care of her, guard her from the wickedness
of the world, cultivate her talent. You're better able to do
it than I, a poor soldier. God protect you!"

He left us. The door closed behind him and we were
alone.

Was he sincere at that moment? I thought so at the
time, and I should like to think so still. He was of a sentimental nature and fond of us in his way. Doubtless, the
thought of seeing the mother of his child in the hands of
an enemy would have been painful to him.

It is possible that later on, under adverse influence, he
boasted of having fooled us. But such a thing would really
have been foreign to his character at this time. Besides,
after the event no one likes to admit having been duped.

26

It was six o'clock at night. I was pacing the large hall of
the Central Station. The train for Copenhagen was due to
leave at six-fifteen, and neither the Baron nor the Baroness
had appeared.

I felt like a spectator at the last act of a gruesome
melodrama; I was longing wildly for the end. Another
quarter of an hour and there would be peace. My nerves,
disordered by these successive crises, clamored for rest,
and the coming night would restore some of the nervous
fiber I had used up and squandered for the love of a
woman.

Finally she arrived—in a cab drawn by a wreck of a horse and driven virtually into the ground by the cabbie.

Always careless and always too late!

She rushed toward me like a lunatic.

"The traitor! He's broken his word! He's not coming!" she exclaimed so loudly that she attracted the attention of the passers-by.

It was certainly unfortunate, but I could not help respecting him for it. "Good for him! He's quite right."

"Hurry and buy a ticket for Copenhagen! Or else I'll stay here!"

"No. Be sensible. If I went with you it would look like a kidnaping. All Stockholm would talk about it tomorrow."

"I don't care. . . . Hurry!"

"No, I won't!"

But I could not help pitying her at the moment, and the situation was becoming unbearable. A quarrel, a lover's quarrel was inevitable.

She knew it instinctively, and seizing my hands, she implored me with her eyes. The ice melted. The sorceress won. I wavered. I succumbed.

"But only as far as Katrineholm!"

"As you wish."

Her luggage was being checked at the baggage room.

Everything was lost, including honor, and I had before me the prospect of an agonizing journey.

The train moved out of the station. We were alone in a first-class compartment. The Baron's nonappearance depressed us. It was a contingency we had not prepared for, a bad omen. An uneasy silence reigned in the carriage. One of us had to break it. She spoke first.

"Axel, you don't love me any more!"

"Perhaps not," I replied, worn out by a month of troubles.

"And I have sacrificed everything to you!"

"Sacrificed everything? To your love, perhaps, but not to me. And haven't I sacrificed my life to you? You're

angry with Gustav but you're venting your anger on me.
At least be reasonable."

All she did was cry.

What a wedding trip! I steeled my nerves, put on my
armor. I made myself insensitive, hard, impenetrable.

"Spare your emotions. From today you must use your
common sense. Weep, weep until you're dry, but then lift
up your head. You're behaving like a silly goose, and I've
worshiped you as a queen, as a ruler, because I thought
myself the weaker. Don't make me despise you. Don't
ever try to blame me alone for what's happened. I admired
Gustav's intelligence last night. He has realized that the
big events in life have always more than one cause. Who
is to blame? You? I? He? She? The threatening ruin, your
passion for the stage, the abscess in your womb, the inheritance from your thrice-married grandfather? Or your
mother's hatred of bearing children, which certainly contributed to your instability? The idleness of your husband,
whose profession left him too much leisure? My instincts?
The instincts of the man who has risen from the lower
classes? My accidental meeting with your Finnish friend
who brought us together? An endless number of motives,
only a few of which are known to us. Don't debase yourself before the mob who will unanimously condemn you
tomorrow. Don't believe, like those poor in spirit, that you
can solve such an intricate problem by ignoring both the
unfaithful wife and the seducer. Besides, have I really
seduced you? Be candid with yourself, with me, while
we're here alone without witnesses."

But she would not be candid. She could not: if she
could, she wouldn't be a woman. She knew herself to be
an accomplice; she was tortured by remorse. She had but
one thought: to ease her conscience by throwing the whole
blame on me.

I let her have her way and wrapped myself in an em-
bittered silence. Night fell. I opened the window and
leaned against the door, gazing at the quickly passing

black firs and the pale moon rising behind them. Then a lake passed, surrounded by birch trees; a brook bordered by alders; cornfields, meadows, and then firs again, a long stretch of them. A mad desire to throw myself out of the carriage seized me; a desire to escape from this prison where I was watched by an enemy, kept spellbound by a witch. But the anxiety for her future oppressed me like a nightmare. I felt responsible for this woman who seemed like a stranger to me, for her unborn children, for the support of her mother, her aunt, her whole family, and so on forever and forever.

And now I shall have to make it my business to see to it that she is a success on the stage; I shall have to bear all her sorrows, her disappointments, her failures, so that one day she can throw me in the dirt like a squeezed-out lemon—me, my whole life, my brain, the marrow of my spine, my lifeblood; all in exchange for the love I gave her, and which she accepted and called "sacrificing herself to me." Delusions of love! Hypnotic powers of sex!

She sat without moving until ten o'clock, sulking. One more hour and we should have to say goodby.

All at once, with a word of apology, she put her two feet on the cushioned seat, pretending to be worn out with fatigue. Her languid glances, her tears had left me unmoved. I had kept my head and my strength of purpose in spite of her sophistries. Now everything collapsed. I beheld her adorable boots, a tiny piece of her stocking.

Down on your knees, Samson! Put your head in her lap, press your cheeks against her knees, ask her to forgive you for the cruel words with which you have lashed her— and which she didn't even understand! Slave! Coward! You lie in the dust before a stocking, you, who thought yourself strong enough to shake the world! And she, she only loves you when you lower yourself. She buys you for a minute's worth of the spasms of love—dirt cheap, for she has nothing to lose in tapping you of an ounce of your most precious fluid!

The engine whistled. The train glided into the station. She kissed me with motherly affection, made the sign of the cross on my forehead—although she was a Protestant—commended me to the Lord, begged me to take care of myself and not to worry.

The train steamed out into the night, choking me with its smoke.

I breathed—at long last—the cool evening air, and enjoyed my freedom. Alas! but for a moment. No sooner had I arrived at the village inn than I broke down, desolate at the thought of being without her. I loved her, yes, I loved her, loved her, just as I had seen her at the moment of parting; for that moment recalled to me the first sweet days of our friendship when she was the lovely, womanly, tender mother who spoiled and caressed me as if I had been a little child.

But all the same I loved her sexually, desired to possess her. My heart burned with a desire to feel her heart burning with desire! Was there something abnormal in this instinct of mine? Am I the creature of one of nature's whims, a freak? Are my feelings perverse, since I find gratification in possessing my mother? Is this an unconscious incest of the heart? . . .

I asked for writing material and wrote her a letter in which I told her that I would pray to God for her happiness.

Her last embrace, you see, had led me back to God, and under the influence of her parting kiss, still lingering in my mustache, I forsook the new faith that presages the progress of humanity.

The first stage in the downfall of a man had been reached. The others would follow irrevocably—steps leading to utter degradation, to the verge of insanity.

PART TWO

1

The day after our departure the whole town knew that Baroness X had eloped with one of the employees of the Royal Library.

Exactly what we could so well have foreseen and feared. And I wanted to protect her reputation! Everything had been forgotten in a moment of weakness.

She had ruined everything, and there was nothing for me to do but bear the consequences and try to minimize the unfortunate effects the story would have on her artistic career, all the more unfortunate in that there was only one theater where she could possibly make her debut, and loose morals were scarcely a recommendation at the Royal Theater.

The morning after my return I sought to provide myself with an alibi by going, on some pretext or other, to call on the chief librarian, who was at home with a minor ailment. After that I promenaded the main streets and reported to work at the usual hour. In the evening I went to the Press Club and deliberately spread the news that the Baroness was getting a divorce, and added that the only reason for the action was the Baroness' determination to go on the stage and that no other significance was to be attached to it. I also insisted that husband and wife were on the best of terms and that their separation was due entirely to social prejudices.

If I had only known what harm I was doing myself

by spreading these rumors and proclaiming her inno-
ence. . . .

No, no, I still would have done the same thing.

The papers scrambled eagerly for the latest smart society scandal, and the public scoffed at the mention of an
irresistible love of art, always a more or less doubtful
phenomenon, but especially so when actresses are concerned. The women readers in particular were skeptical,
and the forsaken child remained an ugly fact that nothing
could explain away.

In the meanwhile I received a letter from Copenhagen.
One long cry of despair. Her conscience was tormenting
her, she was dying to see her abandoned child, and her
relatives were giving her all sorts of trouble. They had, in
league with the Baron, she thought, spirited away some
documents that were absolutely essential to the divorce
proceedings.

I refused to go to her, and furious with the Baron, I
sent him an indignant note. He replied with a few arrogant
words, and this brought about a breach between us.

One telegram, two telegrams, and peace was restored.
The document turned up and the divorce proceedings
moved ahead.

To make her feel better I spent my evenings writing
down detailed instructions on how she was to behave,
told her to work, study acting, go to the theaters. To give
her an extra job I suggested that she should write up her
reports on the theater and I would try to place them in
one of our best papers.

No answer. I had every reason to think that my helpful
advice had been taken the wrong way by this intractable
woman.

A week went by, a week of anxiety, troubles, work. And
then early one morning while I was still in bed I received
a letter postmarked Copenhagen. She was calm and in
good spirits; she seemed unable to hide a certain pride on
account of the quarrel between the Baron and myself.

(She was in a fair position to form an opinion, since she had received the respective letters from both of us.) She found the "duel" not without style and admired my pluck. "It is a pity," she concluded her letter, "that two men like you and the Baron should not be friends." Then she gave me a detailed account of what she was doing to while away the time. She was evidently enjoying herself. She had made her way into second-rate artistic circles, something I did not like. She described an evening spent at some club in the company of a number of young men who paid her a great deal of attention. She had made the conquest of a musician, a youth who had sacrificed his family to his art. "What a strange similarity between our two cases!" she remarked. Then followed a detailed biography of the interesting martyr and an admonition not to be jealous.

"What was she trying to say?" I wondered, taken aback by the half-sarcastic, half-sympathetic tone of her letter, which appeared to be written between two entertainments.

Was it possible that this coldly voluptuous madonna was one of those women who are born frivolous and wanton? A coquette, a cocotte?

I sat down at once and dashed off a furious scolding in which I etched her portrait for her. I called her Madame Bovary. I begged her to stop dancing on the edge of the precipice.

In reply, "as a proof of her absolute faith in me," she sent me the letters that the young enthusiast had written to her. Love letters! The same old use of the term "friendship," the inexplicable sympathy of the souls, and the whole list of the trite and, to us both, so familiar words: "brother and sister," "little mother," "playmates," and so on, covers under which lovers are accustomed to hide in order to abandon themselves ultimately to playing the beast with two backs.

What was I to think? Was she sick? Was she an unconscious criminal who remembered nothing of the terrible experience of the last two months when the hearts of three men were on fire for her? And I who had been used as a decoy, a stalking-horse, and a scapegoat, I was ruining my career in order to clear the way for her to enter the irregular life of an actress.

A new torture! To see the woman whom I adored slipping into the gutter.

But then my soul was filled with unspeakable compassion, and sensing the fate that awaited this perverse woman, I swore to myself that I would help her, do everything in my power to shield her from a fatal catastrophe.

Jealous! That vulgar word invented by a woman in order to mislead the man she has deceived or means to deceive. The hoodwinked husband shows his anger, and the word jealous is flung in his face. Jealous husband equals betrayed husband. And there are women who look upon jealousy as synonymous with impotence, so that the betrayed husband can only shut his eyes, powerless in the face of such accusations.

She returned after a fortnight, pretty, fresh, in high spirits, and full of bright memories, for she had thoroughly enjoyed herself. She was wearing a new dress with touches of brilliant coloring, which struck me as vulgar. I was puzzled. She who used to dress so simply, so quietly, with such exquisite taste, was becoming positively garish.

Our meeting was colder than either of us had expected. There was a constrained silence at first, followed by a sudden outburst.

The flatteries of her new friends had turned her head. She gave herself airs, teased me, made fun of me. She spread her gorgeous dress over my shabby sofa and resorted to her old tricks. For a moment I forgot all resentment in a passionate kiss. Nevertheless, a slight feeling of anger remained at the bottom of my heart and found vent in a torrent of reproaches. Subdued by my violent impetuosity, which contrasted so strangely with her own indolent nature, she took refuge in tears.

"How can you be so absurd as to imagine that I was flirting with that young man?" she sobbed. "I promise you never to write to him again, although I'm sure he'll think it rude of me."

Rude! One of her favorite catchwords. A man pays her attention—in other words, makes advances to her—and she listens politely for fear of being rude. What a sly bitch!

Unfortunately, she was wearing a brand-new pair of the loveliest little shoes, and I was lying at her feet. Damnation! She was wearing black silk stockings, her leg was a little fuller than it had been, and the whiteness of her knees shone forth through this black veil of mourning. Those black legs moving in a cloud of skirts were the devil's temptations. . . . Tired of her constant fear of pregnancy, I lied to her. I told her that after much diligent research in the library I had learned how to cheat nature. I suggested certain preventive techniques to her and alleged that I had an organic defect which made me, if not sterile, at least less dangerous. I repeated my assurances until I finished by believing them myself, and in the end she gave me a clear stage to do as I wanted and made me responsible for all consequences.

She had moved in with her mother and aunt on the third floor of a house on one of the main thoroughfares. As she threatened to visit me in my own room if they prevented me from seeing her, I was allowed to call. But the thought of the supervision of these two old women, whom I knew to be watching us through the keyhole all the time, was not very stimulating.

It was becoming clearer every day how much the Baroness had lost. Once a respected married woman, mistress of an aristocratic establishment, she had returned to the conditions of her childhood. She was under the control of her mother, almost a prisoner in one room, kept by two old women who were themselves needy. The mother never lost an opportunity to remind her of her careful upbringing and how she had been educated to take an honorable social position, and the daughter remembered the happy time when her prince had come to rescue her from her mother's prison. Bitter words were spoken on both sides, tears and insults were all too frequent, and I had to pay for them when I called in the evening . . . to visit a prisoner under the eyes of a warden and witness.

Having had enough of that, we tried to meet in one of the city parks. But that was going from bad to worse: we were the objects of the contemptuous glances of everyone who passed by. The spring sun that exposed our misery and wretchedness became hateful to us. We missed the darkness; we longed for winter that could hide our shame; but summer was upon us with its long duskless nights.

Our former friends dropped us one after the other. Even my sister, intimidated by the now universal gossip, grew suspicious and distant when the ex-baroness at a little supper party tried to keep up her spirits by taking too much wine, became intoxicated, proposed a toast, smoked cigarettes, and generally behaved in a way that excited the disgust of the women and the contempt of the men.

"That woman's a common prostitute!" said a respectable married man and father of a family to my brother-in-law, and the latter took the first chance to repeat the remark to me.

When on the following Sunday evening we arrived at my sister's house, where we had been invited to supper, the servant informed us to our consternation that her master and mistress were out. The height of humiliation! We spent the evening in my room, a prey to anger and despair, talking about suicide. I pulled down the blinds to shut out the daylight, and we sat together in misery waiting for night and darkness before I could walk her back home again. But the summer sun did not set until late, and at eight o'clock we both felt hungry. I had no money, and neither did she. There was nothing to eat or drink in the cupboard. These moments were some of the most wretched moments of my life and gave me a foretaste of misery to come. Reproaches, cold kisses, floods of tears, remorse, disgust.

I tried to persuade her to go home and have supper with her mother but she was afraid of the daylight, and moreover, she did not dare return so early when she had lied to her mother that she had been invited out to dinner. She had eaten nothing since two o'clock, and the melancholy prospect of going to bed supperless aroused the wild-beast hunger in her. She had grown up in a wealthy home and had been used to every kind of luxury. She had no idea what poverty meant, and consequently she was completely unstrung. I, who had been familiar with hunger from childhood, suffered torture to see her in such a situation. I ransacked my cupboard but could find nothing. I searched the drawers of my writing table, and there among all sorts of keepsakes, faded flowers, old love letters, discolored ribbons, I found two pieces of candy that I had kept in remembrance of a funeral. I offered them to her just as they were, wrapped in black paper and tinfoil. A distressing banquet indeed, these candies in their mourning dress!

Depressed, humiliated, apprehensive, I raged and thundered furiously against all respectable women who closed their doors on us, drove us out. "Why such hostility and contempt? Have we committed a crime? No! It's just a question of a straightforward divorce, strictly according to the law."

"We have been behaving too correctly," she said, trying to comfort herself. "People are hypocrites. They tolerate open, shameless adultery but condemn divorce. A high standard of morality indeed!"

We were agreed on that, but the facts remained. The crime continued to hang over our bowed heads as we waited for the blow to fall.

I felt like a boy who has robbed a bird's nest. The

mother had flown away, the little one lay on the ground, chirping plaintively, deprived of the warmth of the mother's wings.

And the father? He was left desolate in the plundered nest. I pictured him of a Sunday evening, an evening like this when the family assembles around the fireplace, alone in the drawing room with the silenced piano; alone in the dining room eating his solitary dinner; alone in bed. . . .

"Oh, no, nothing of the kind!" she interrupted my musings. "You'd be much more likely to find him lounging on the comfortable sofa at Matilda's brother-in-law's stuffed and bloated after a big meal, squeezing the hand of my poor, dear, libeled little cousin, reveling in the outrageous stories told of his wife's ill conduct—his wife, who refused to become a member of his harem! And both of them, surrounded and upheld by the sympathy and applause of this hypocritical world, are eager to throw the first stone at us."

Her words set me thinking, and after a while I ventured the thought that the Baron had led us by the nose, that he had schemed to rid himself of a troublesome wife, so as to be able to marry again, and that he had illegally managed to secure her dowry.

She became indignant at once. "Don't say anything against him! It was all my fault!"

"Why can't I say anything against him? What is he—a saint?"

One might almost have thought so, for whenever I attacked him she took his part.

Was it the freemasonry of caste that made her stand up for him? Or were there secrets in their intimate life together that made her fear his enmity? I have never been able to solve this riddle, nor discover the reason for her loyalty to him, which no disloyalty on his part could shake.

At long last the sun set and we parted. I slept the sleep of the famished. I dreamed that I had a millstone around

my neck while making incredible efforts to wing my way
toward heaven.

2

Bad luck plagued us. We sent inquiries to the director
of the theater about a possible time for the Baroness' debut. He replied that as the director he could not possibly
negotiate with a woman who had deserted her family. We
tried everything and everything failed. After a year of
separation her resources would dry up and she would be
left to beg in the streets. And poor me, an underpaid
clerk, I would have to lend her a helping hand.

To find out what the situation really was she decided to
call on one of her old friends, the great tragedienne*
whom she used to meet at parties and who had lain like a
bitch at the feet of the "blonde baroness" and called her
"my little elf."

The great tragedienne, a first-class adulteress whose
hands were black with sin while her husband was still
alive, received the decent sinner with insulting remarks
and closed the door in her face! Perfect!

Nothing left to do but take vengeance, no matter how.
"All right," I said, "that does it! Why not become a

* The great tragedienne was evidently Elise Hwasser (1831–
94), leading actress at the Royal Theater in Stockholm from
1850 to 1888. Among her many roles, the following may suggest her range: Jane Eyre in the Birch-Pfeiffer adaptation of the
Brontë novel (1854)—Siri von Essen by appearing in this
role would be challenging comparison with her; Desdemona
opposite the American Negro actor Ira Aldridge (1857); Queen
Anne in Scribe's *A Glass of Water* (1860); Clara in Goethe's
Egmont (1866), and Hermione in *A Winter's Tale* (1871). She
went on to interpret some of Ibsen's leading roles: Lady Inger
in *Lady Inger of Østraat* (1877); Lona Hessel in *Pillars of
Society* (1877); Nora in *A Doll's House* (1880)—one of her
infrequent failures; and Mrs. Alving in *Ghosts* (1883).—ED.

playwright? Write some plays and get them produced on that very same stage. Why step down when you can step up? You can walk all over that actress. In one leap you'll be way on top of her. Expose to all the world this lying, hypocritical, vice-ridden society that opens its drawing rooms to whores and closes them to a woman separated from her husband. Now, there's a great subject for a play!"

But she was one of those weak, docile souls who cannot fight back.

"No, no revenge!"

Really desiring revenge, but cowardly, she left it up to God to do the dirty work and leave her free of any responsibility, which she shoved off on that scarecrow.

But I didn't give up that easily, and finally we got a lucky break. A publisher asked me to edit an illustrated book for children.

"It's perfect for you," I said to the Baroness. "Just put the text in shape. There's a hundred crowns in it for you."

I provided her with all the material she needed, and I let her think that she had done all the work. And she got the hundred crowns. But what I didn't have to do before she got them! The publisher demanded that my name appear on the cover of this picture book. My name! and I was supposed to be an aspiring playwright. It was literary prostitution. And my enemies who had predicted I could not be a writer now had something to talk about.

Next I got her to write an article for a morning paper, which she managed to do in a middling sort of way. The article was printed but the paper didn't pay anything.

I ran around and dug up a ten-crown note that I gave the authoress as if—pious deceit—it came from the newspaper office.

Poor Marie, former baroness! How happy it made her to give her small income to her desperate mother, who had been forced by the collapse of her finances to rent out furnished rooms.

The old ladies now began to look upon me as their rescuer, and from their desks they drew out copies of translations that all the theaters had refused, which they now entrusted to me, thinking I had fabulous powers of dealing with directors. I was finally buried under useless odd jobs that brought chaos into my own work and only succeeded in drowning me in the blackest misery.

My small savings dwindled as a result of·the time I had lost at work and the daily wear and tear on my nerves. To retrench I had to cut down on my meals, and I returned to my old habit of going to bed without supper.

Encouraged by the few pennies that had come her way, Marie started to write a play in five acts. I seemed to have sown in her soul the unproductive seed of my poetic aspirations, and in this virgin soil it germinated and grew while I remained sterile, like a flower that scatters its seed and withers. My soul was lacerated, sick to death. The influence of that little female brain, so different from the brain of a man, disturbed and disordered the mechanism of my thoughts. I was at a loss to understand why I thought so highly of her literary gifts, why I kept on urging her to write, for with the exception of her letters to me, which sometimes showed a unique quality but frequently were quite commonplace, I had no proof that she could write at all. She had become my living poem; she had taken the place of my vanished talent. Her personality was grafted on mine and was dominating it. I existed only through her. I, the mother-root, led an underground life, nourishing this tree that was growing sunwards and promising wonderful blossoms. I delighted in its marvelous beauty, never dreaming that the day would come when the offshoot would separate from the exhausted trunk to bloom and dazzle independently, proud of its borrowed splendor.

The first act of her play was finished. I read it. In my hallucinated condition I found it perfect; I proclaimed my sincere admiration and heartily congratulated the author. Marie was amazed herself at the talent she possessed, and I painted a rosy picture of her future as an author. But there was a sudden change of plans. Marie's mother reminded us that she had a friend, a woman interested in painting, owner of an estate, very rich, and what was most important, an intimate friend of the foremost actor at the Royal Theater and his wife, both of whom were bitter rivals of the great tragedienne.

Under the moral protection of the wealthy woman the husband-and-wife team proposed to provide for Marie's studies up to the time of her debut. To make the necessary arrangements Marie was invited to spend two weeks at the friend's estate, where she would meet the famous actor and his wife, who—what luck!—had gotten very definite and very promising news from the director of the theater. This canceled out what we had heard before, which, it turned out, was all made up, a fabrication of Marie's mother, who had tried to discourage Marie from going on the stage.

Now she was saved, and I for my part could sleep once again and catch my breath and catch up on work.

She stayed away two weeks. To judge from her few letters she enjoyed herself. She tried out for her friends, who said she had an extraordinary talent for the stage.

When she returned she rented a room in the country from a farmer's wife, who provided her with food. That meant she was free from her old wardens and could meet me every Saturday and Sunday without witnesses. Life granted us a smile or two in spite of the depression we found ourselves in after the recently granted divorce. And out in the country the pressure of social conventions was lessened, and the bright sun of summer chased away the shadows in our hearts.

3

Her appearance under the patronage of two famous actors was announced in the autumn and put a stop to all

gossip. I did not like the part chosen for her, a small character part in an old-fashioned play. But her teacher
counted on the sympathy of the audience and the effect of
a good scene, in which she refused a marquis who saw in
her only a rare ornament for his drawing room, and took
him down a peg or two by declaring that in her eyes the
noble heart of the poor young man was infinitely more
precious than the title and all the wealth of the marquis.

As I was dismissed from my post as her teacher, I was
able to devote all my time and attention to my scientific
studies and the writing of a paper destined for some academy. This was necessary in order to prove myself a man of
letters and earn a permanent post at the library. With
ardent zeal I gave myself up to ethnographical research in
connection with the Far East. It acted like opium on my
brain, which was exhausted by the struggles, cares, and
agonies I had undergone. Inspired by the ambition to show
myself worthy of my beloved, whose future appeared in
the rosiest hues, I achieved wonders of industry. I shut
myself up in the vaults of the Royal Castle from morning
till night, enduring the damp and icy atmosphere without
a complaint, defying hunger and poverty.

4

Just as Marie was to make her stage debut,* her little
daughter died of a tubercular brain disease. Another
month of tears, reproaches, and remorse followed.

* When Siri von Essen (1850–1912), the woman who became
Strindberg's first wife, decided to go on the stage, she had to
start with the fundamentals, for she had had no training as an
actress and she had a noticeable Finnish accent. Theater people
advised her to study abroad, preferably in Paris, but this was
beyond her means. To get a position at the Royal Theater in
Stockholm it was necessary for a novice actress to spend one
season giving three "debut" performances, on the basis of which
she would, hopefully, be offered a contract. Siri studied acting

"It is a judgment on you," declared the child's grandmother, glad to thrust the poisoned dagger into the heart of the daughter-in-law, whom she had begun to hate because she had brought dishonor on her name.

Marie was broken-hearted, and spent day and night at the bedside of the dying child under the roof of her former husband, chaperoned by her former mother-in-law. The father was overcome with grief at the death of his only child, and bowed down with sorrow, he longed to meet again the friend of former days, the witness of the past. One evening, a few days after the little girl's funeral, my landlady informed me that the Baron had called and had left a message to the effect that he hoped to see me at his house.

Considering the unusual circumstances that had led up to the breach, I wanted anything but a reconciliation. I sent him a polite refusal.

A quarter of an hour had hardly elapsed when Marie herself appeared, dressed in deep mourning, full of tears, and begged me to comply with the pleas of the inconsolable Baron.

I found this mission in abominable taste. I scolded her sharply and pointed out to her how ambiguous and un-

---

and rehearsed her first roles with Betty Almlöf, the wife of the popular actor Knut Almlöf of the Royal Theater. She also studied speech with Bertha Tammelin and stage movement with Signe Hebbe. Her debut, planned for early January 1877, had to be postponed a couple of weeks, on account of the death of her child on January 13. On January 27 she made her official debut, appearing as Camille in *En teaterpjes* (*A Stage Play*), an adaptation of Louis Leroy's *Les plumes de paon*. She acquitted herself well and the critics liked her. On April 13 she played Jane Eyre in an adaptation of the novel made by Birch-Pfeiffer. The illness of her mother no doubt affected Siri's performance, which was adequate but not much more. Her mother died on May 29. In June Siri signed a contract with the Royal Theater for the year July 1, 1877 to July 1, 1878, at a salary of 2100 crowns plus three crowns for each performance she gave. —ED.

justifiable in the eyes of the world such a situation would
be. She upbraided me with my prejudices, implored me,
appealed to my generous disposition, and ended by making me agree to the indelicate proposal.

I had sworn never again to enter that old house, the
scene of the tragedy. But the Baron had moved. He had
taken rooms not far from me and very close to Marie. I
was glad to be spared another visit to the old place, and
accompanied the divorced wife on her visit to her former
husband.

The mourning, the evident grief, the grave and gloomy
appearance of the house all combined to rob our meeting
of any trace of strangeness or embarrassment. The habit of
seeing these two people together was a bar to any feeling
of jealousy on my part, and the tactful and cordial bearing
of the Baron helped to reassure me completely.

We dined together, we drank and played cards just as
in the old days.

On the following day we met in my room; on a third
evening at Marie's, who was now living in a house belonging to an old lady. We fell into our former habits and
Marie was happy to see us together. It comforted her, and
since we had ourselves under perfect control, nobody was
offended or aggrieved. The Baron looked upon us as being
secretly engaged; his love for Marie seemed to be dead.
Sometimes he even talked of his unhappy love affair, for
Matilda was carefully watched by her father and out of
his reach. . . . Marie teased and comforted him alternately, and he made no secret, now, of his true feelings.

At parting their intimacy was more marked and aroused
in me a certain amount of disgust, if not jealousy.

One day Marie told me that she had been to see the
Baron and stayed to have dinner with him on the grounds
that she had urgent business with him in connection with
her daughter's estate, which the Baron inherited.

I objected to this lack of taste. I told her that her
conduct might even be called indecent. She burst out

laughing, teasingly reminded me of my former railings against prejudice, and in the end I joined in her laughter. It was ridiculous, it was crazy, but it was smart, it was sophisticated to set oneself above the crowd, and it was beautiful to see virtue triumphant.

After that, she visited the Baron whenever she pleased, and I even believed that to amuse him she rehearsed her role in the play before him.

Up to now we had had no quarrels, for any jealousy I might have felt disappeared as soon as I got used to the state of things, and I never quite lost the old illusion that they were husband and wife. But one evening Marie came to see me alone. On helping her take off her cloak, she spent more than the usual amount of time rearranging her dress. Well-versed in female behavior, I sensed that something was wrong. She sat down on the sofa opposite the looking glass, talking volubly all the time. Her conversation struck me as forced; she cast furtive glances at her reflection and tried to smooth her hair when she thought I wasn't looking.

A horrible thought flashed into my mind. Unable to control my agitation, I exclaimed, "Where have you been?"

"With Gustav."

"What did you do there?"

She started, but quickly controlling herself, she replied, "I was studying my part."

"That's a lie!"

She was indignant. She accused me of being absurdly jealous and deluged me with explanations. I wavered. As we were invited out that evening, I had to postpone all further investigation.

Thinking of this incident today and after careful consideration, I would swear that she—to put it mildly—committed bigamy in those days. But at that time I was completely charmed by her wiles and let myself be deceived.

What had happened? . . . Probably this—

She had dined alone with the Baron. They had had

coffee and liqueur. She was seized with that after-dinner lassitude. The Baron advised her to lie down on the sofa and rest awhile, a proposal which did not displease her . . . The rest followed as a matter of course. Solitude, complete confidence, old memories exerted their influence on the former man and wife, who did not feel any shyness in each other's presence. He, living in celibacy, was tempted, aroused, and the thing happened. Why deny themselves a pleasure that would hurt no one—as long as a certain person did not find out about it? She was her own mistress, since she had never taken money from her lover; and as for breaking a promise—what is that to a woman! Perhaps she regretted the loss of a male who was better adapted to her needs. Perhaps, now that her curiosity was satisfied, she yearned again, as she compared them, for the stronger man; for in erotic conflicts the sensitive and delicate lover, however ardent, is always beaten by the athlete. In a word, it was more than probable that she, his longtime bedmate, who had dressed and undressed herself a thousand times in the presence of this man who knew every tiny secret of her body, was not averse to treating him to a sweet dessert after this intimate dinner for two, especially as she was free from responsibility and her woman's heart pitied the lonely man. And, on my word of honor, if I had been in his shoes as the humiliated (if not exactly deceived) husband, if I had been the one who had been pushed aside by a rival and had later found my rival's mistress in my power, I swear by all the gods both old and new that she would not, for all the devils in hell, have gone from my bedroom unmolested.

But since the beloved lips never tired of using the sublime words "honor," "decency," "morality," I refused to harbor any such suspicions. Why?

Because a woman will always get the better of her lover, if he is a man of honor. He flatters himself that he is the only one because he wants to be the only one, and the wish is father to the thought.

I recall now a remark made to me by someone who lived across the street from the Baron. For no apparent reason he alluded to the Baron as "farming on the share system." I was not aware of it then, but the insinuation was quite deliberate. That was twelve years ago. Now, why has that phrase stuck in my mind among all the thousands I have heard and forgotten since then?

Today Marie's loyalty seems to me in the highest degree improbable, incredible, impossible.

It was also a significant fact that the Baron, when we were alone together, always manifested a lively interest in prostitutes; and one evening, after dining with him at a restaurant, he went so far as to ask me for certain addresses. Simply a trick to hoodwink me, of course!

Another thing that struck me was his attitude towards Marie. He treated her with a somewhat disdainful courtesy. She behaved like a cocotte towards him, while her passion for me during our moments together seemed to be more and more on the wane.

5

At last Marie made her debut before the footlights. She was a success for many and complex reasons. In the first place, everybody was curious to see a baroness on the stage. Secondly, the middle classes were sympathetic because they delighted in the blow dealt to social prejudices by this divorce; the bachelors, the sexless, the enemies of matrimonial slavery, lavished flowers on her; not to mention the friends and relations of the great actor who were interested in her because he had been her teacher and was bringing her out.

After the performance the Baron asked both of us and the old lady with whom Marie was living to supper.

Everybody was nearly drunk with excitement over the success. Marie displeased me with her overelegant coiffure and the red make-up still on her cheeks and the black penciling still on her eyebrows. She was no longer the virginal mother with whom I had fallen in love, but an ordinary actress with insolent gestures and vulgar manners. She boasted, cut in on everybody's conversation, and behaved in general like an unbearably conceited person.

In her imagination she had scaled the highest summits of art, and she dismissed all my remarks, my suggestions, with a shrug of her shoulders or a condescending, "My dear, you wouldn't understand."

The Baron looked like some sort of unhappy lover. But for my presence he would have kissed her. Under the influence of an incredible quantity of Madeira, he opened his heart to us and regretted that art, divine art, should claim so many cruel sacrifices.

The press—many palms had been greased—confirmed her success, and a contract with the theater seemed likely.

Two photographers fought for the honor of being permitted to photograph the debutante. A successful little magazine sold the portrait of the new star, together with her biography.

What struck me most in looking at these new portraits was the fact that not one of them resembled the old one in my possession. Was it possible that her character and the expression of her face could have changed in so short a time, in a year? Or was she a different woman when she reflected the love, the tenderness, the compassion that my eyes radiated as soon as I looked at her? The expression of her face on these portraits was vulgar, hard, and insolent; every feature expressed a cruel coquetry, a challenge. One pose in particular disgusted me. She was represented leaning over the back of a low chair in such a manner that the beholder could see her bosom, which was only partly hidden by a fan resting against the upper part of her dress. Her eyes seemed riveted on the eyes of an invisible person, not myself, for my love, coupled with respect and tenderness, never caressed her with the shameless lubricity that one employs to warm up a streetwalker. The photograph reminded me of those obscene pictures which are furtively offered to passers-by at the doors of low dives under cover of night.

When she offered me this portrait I refused to accept it.

"What!" she exclaimed in a piteous voice, which for a moment revealed her carefully concealed want of true refinement, "you refuse my photograph? You don't love me any more!"

When a woman says to her lover, "You don't love me any more," she has already ceased to love him. From this moment on, I knew that her love was growing cold.

She realized that her feeble soul had drawn from me the courage, the boldness necessary to arrive at her goal, and now she wanted to be rid of the troublesome creditor. She had been stealing my thoughts while she seemed to scorn them with her contemptuous, "You know nothing about it, my dear!"

This uncultured woman, whose only accomplishment was her fluent French, whose education had been neglected, who had been brought up in the country, who knew nothing of literature or the stage, to whom I had given the first lessons in the correct pronunciation of Swedish, whom I had initiated into the mysteries of metrics and prosody, treated me as if I were an incompetent idiot.

For her second role, which was due to come up soon, I suggested a wonderful melodramatic part, one of the greatest in the repertory.* She rejected it. Sometime later she told me which role *she* had chosen; it was the same one I had suggested!* . . . I analyzed the part for her, I drew her costumes, pointed out the places where she

* *Jane Eyre.* (See footnote on pages 171–72.)—ED.

could produce the most dramatic effects, advised her how to handle her exits, and emphasized the dominant features in the character she was portraying.

Then began a silent battle between the Baron and me. He, theatrical director of the Royal Guards, coach for the amateur actors in his garrison, set himself up as an expert in the dramatic arts, and Marie fell for his so-called ideas, accepted him as her teacher and rejected my instruction. And what a marvelous subjective esthetic he espoused as the epitome of truth and naturalness! The most banal, the simplest, the most vulgar stage behavior he advocated on the ground that it was natural.

I'll go along with him in principle as far as modern comedy is concerned, in which the characters are involved in all the thousand trivialities of everyday life. But that sort of acting is impossible and insufferable in an English melodrama, for example. Grand passions cannot be expressed like witticisms in a drawing-room conversation.

But apparently the difference was too subtle to be grasped by a mediocre mind, which draws general conclusions from a single fact. If it works in one case, the rule will fit all cases! . . .

The day before her performance Marie honored me by showing me her costume. In spite of my protests, my solemn pleadings, she had chosen some dust-gray material that made her look like a corpse.

Her only answer to my objections was to snap at me with this truly feminine argument: "I'll have you know that Madame X, the great tragedienne, gave a magnificent performance in exactly the same kind of dress!"

"Of course she did. But Madame X is not a blonde like you. What suits a blonde doesn't suit a brunette."

She didn't understand this and became angry with me.

I warned her to expect a fiasco, and her second role did indeed prove to be a failure.

The tears, reproaches, even insults that followed!

As misfortune would have it, a week later her rival appeared in the same part to celebrate some jubilee or other, and she was honored with a transparency bearing her name and picture, cartloads of flowers, and huge wreaths set up on the stage.

Of course, Marie was furious with me and made me responsible for her failure, simply because I had prophesied it. Her failure and disappointment brought her still nearer to the Baron; it drew them together with the sympathy that always unites inferior characters.

I, the man of letters, the playwright, the dramatic critic, at home in all the literatures through my work and position at the library, in correspondence with the finest intellects of the world—I was cast aside like a worn-out garment, treated like an idiot, considered of no more importance than a footman or a dog.

But although her second appearance had been a failure, she was engaged at a salary of 2400 crowns per annum! However, her ascent to the great heights of the dramatic art was over before it got started. Classed among the second-rate actresses, she would be cast for small parts, society women, mere dressed-up dolls, and spend her days at the dressmaker's. Three, four, sometimes five different dresses on one and the same evening would swallow up her insufficient pay.

What bitter disappointments, what heart-rending scenes, as she watched her parts grow smaller and smaller, until they consisted of a few sentences only. Her room had the appearance of a dressmaker's workshop, littered with dress materials, patterns and millinery. The former mother, the great lady who had left the drawing rooms she despised and renounced dress and fashion to devote her life to the lofty ideals of art, had become a bungling seamstress who worked at her sewing machine till midnight so that she might play before an indifferent bourgeoisie for a few minutes the part of a great lady.

Passing time behind the scenes during rehearsals, when she stood in the wings for hours waiting for the cue that would bring her before the footlights to say two or three words, developed in her a taste for gossip, for idle talk and off-color stories. It killed all honest striving to rise above her condition; the soul was shorn of its wings and fluttered toward the earth, toward the gutter.

The decline continued. She continued to deteriorate, and after her dresses had been remodeled again and again for lack of money to buy new ones, she was deprived of even her small parts and degraded to walk-ons.

Poverty was staring her in the face, and her mother, ceaselessly prophesying misfortune like a modern Cassandra, made her life miserable, and society, well acquainted with her sensational divorce and the premature death of her little girl, cried out against the unfaithful wife and unnatural mother. It was but a question of time before the manager of the theater would not be able to shield her against the hostility of the audience. The great actor, her teacher, disowned her and admitted his mistake in believing in her talent.

So much ado, so much unhappiness, to humor a woman who did not know her own mind.

And still matters grew worse, for Marie's mother suddenly died of heart disease. Of course, the public placed the blame on the troubles her ruined daughter had caused her.

Again my honor was involved. I worked myself into a lather against the injustice of the world and made a desperate effort to save her from the gutter. I proposed the foundation of a weekly paper for the discussion of the drama, music, literature, and art, and she, thankful now for any helping hand held out to her, gratefully accepted my proposal. In this paper she was to make her debut as a critic and writer of *feuilletons*, and so gradually make a name for herself among publishers. She put two hundred crowns in the enterprise. I undertook the editorial work and proofreading. Since I was well aware of my complete incapacity as a business manager, I left her to attend to the sale and advertisements, the proceeds of which she would split with the manager of her theater, who was also the proprietor of a newsstand. The important thing was to publish the first number at the time advertised. Everything was ready, but at the last moment we lacked the necessary funds and credit.

Alas! I had put my fate into the hands of a woman! On publication day she remained calmly in bed and slept till noon.

Convinced that everything was well, I went to town, but everywhere on my way I was greeted with sarcastic smiles.

"Well, where can we get the wonderful paper?"

"Everywhere!"

"Or nowhere!"

I went into a newspaper shop.

"We haven't received it yet," said the clerk.

I rushed to the printing office. It had not left the press yet.

A complete failure! We had an angry scene. Her innate carelessness and ignorance of the publishing trade exonerated her to some extent. She had completely relied on her friend, the theatrical manager.

The two hundred crowns were gone. My time, my reputation, and untold hours of work, all were wasted.

And the only thought I had was: we were irrevocably lost.

I proposed that she should die with me. After all, what was to become of us? She was now quite destitute and I had not the strength to save her again.

"Let us die," I said to her. "We're just living corpses, walking around, obstructing traffic."

She refused.

"You're a coward, my proud Marie, a coward! And you're cruel. Forcing me to watch you sink so low while the whole world laughs and sneers."

I went to my tavern, got drunk, and slept it off.

I went to see her early on the following morning. The

alcohol seemed to have made me more clear-sighted. For the first time I really noticed the change in her. Her room was untidy, her dress slovenly, her beloved little feet were thrust into a pair of old slippers, the stockings hung in wrinkles around her ankles.

Such squalor!

Her vocabulary had become enriched by some ugly theatrical slang. Her gestures were vulgar, her eyes filled with hate, her tongue poisonous.

She remained stooping over her work, without looking at me, as if she were working out some malicious plan.

Suddenly, without raising her head, she said hoarsely, "Do you know, Axel, what a woman is justified in expecting from the man she's living with?"

Thunderstruck, unwilling to trust my ears, I faltered. "No . . . what?"

"What does a woman expect from her lover?"

"Love!"

"And what else?"

"Money!"

The vulgar word made it unnecessary for her to go on, and I left her, convinced that I had guessed correctly.

"Whore! Whore!" I spat the word, stumbling through the drab, autumnal streets. We had reached the last stage. . . . Payment for pleasures received! Her profession admitted without shame!

If she had only been in dire need, without a cent to her name. But she had just inherited her mother's property, some furniture, and the shares of stock which, although they were not very secure, represented a few thousand crowns. And besides that, she still regularly collected her salary from the theater.

It was all quite inexplicable to me. . . . Until I thought of Miss B——, her landlady and close friend. And what a brutal thought that was.

She was about thirty-five years old and looked suspiciously like a procuress—disgustingly so. No one knew what she lived on. Always in financial straits but always dressed in grand and extravagant clothes when she appeared on the streets, she would worm her way into families in order to borrow eventually some petty sums of money, while she constantly complained about her wretched existence. A very shady character, who loathed me: She knew I saw through her.

I recalled an episode that had occurred some months before that I had then thought was of no consequence. Miss B— had extracted a promise of a loan of one thousand crowns from a Finnish lady who was a friend of Marie's. But the promise remained just that, a promise. At the suggestion of Miss B— and to protect the badly bruised reputation of her Finnish friend, Marie promised to raise the money. And somehow she did. Then Marie found herself harshly criticized by the Finnish lady, who demanded an explanation. Miss B— declared herself absolutely innocent and thrust all the blame on Marie. It was then I expressed my suspicions concerning this mysterious woman, and my revulsion, and advised Marie to have nothing to do with anyone whose transactions smacked of extortion.

But what excuses she offered for her false friend! . . . Later she changed the whole story, said it was based on a misunderstanding; and finally she reduced the whole incident to a figment of my "depressing imagination."

Now, wasn't it possible that the adventuress had insinuated the disgusting idea of "presenting me with the bill"? Almost certainly, for a phrase like that wasn't in Marie's line and she had a hard time getting it out. At least, I wanted to believe that, hoped that it was true. If she had merely asked me for the money she had invested in the paper, the money that had been lost through her fault—that would have been simple female mathematics. Or if she had insisted on an immediate marriage—but she was opposed to that. No, there could be no doubt about it: it was a question of paying for love—the orgasms, the countless kisses, the rumpled petticoats. It was payment for all this that she demanded. . . . And suppose I sent her my bill—for my hourly wages, for the wear and tear on my nerves and my brain, expenses incurred in the use of my blood, my name, my reputation—a statement of my sufferings, a receipt for my closed career!

Oh, no, it was her privilege to keep the books, and I didn't raise any objections.

I spent my evening at a restaurant, wandered through the streets, and pondered the problem of degradation. Why is it so painful to watch a person sink? Because there is something unnatural in it, for nature demands personal progress, evolution, and every backward step means the dissipation of force. The same argument applies to the life of the community, where everybody strives to work his way upward to a position of material riches or public honor. Comes the tragic feeling which seizes us in seeing a man ruined, tragic as autumn, sickness, death. This woman, who had not yet reached her thirtieth year, had been young, beautiful, frank, honest, amiable, strong, and well-bred. In two short years I had seen her fall so low so quickly.

For a moment I tried to blame myself. The thought that the fault was mine would have been a comfort to me. But try as I would, I did not succeed. Had I not taught her the cult of the beautiful, the love of high ideals and noble acts? And all the while she adopted the vulgarities of her theatrical friends, I had improved, I had acquired the manners and language of fashionable society, the self-possession that is considered the hallmark of good breeding. I had become chaste in love, anxious to spare modesty and not to offend against beauty and seemliness, for only in that way can we forget the brutality of an act that to my mind is much more spiritual than physical.

I was rough sometimes, when necessary, but never vulgar. I killed outright, didn't play cat and mouse. I called a spade a spade, but never hinted and insinuated; my clever remarks were my own, arising by chance, prompted by a given situation, but I never tried to dazzle with the witticisms of musical comedies or comic papers.

I loved cleanliness, purity, beauty in my daily surroundings. I would rather have refused an invitation than appear in an unstarched shirt. I never received her in dressing gown and slippers. I may not have been able to offer her more than bread and butter and a glass of beer, but I always served them on a clean tablecloth.

It was not I who had set her a bad example. It was obvious she did not love me any more. She did not want to please me any longer. She belonged to her audience. She painted herself and dressed herself for the public. She belonged to them and not to me, and with that she had become a common woman who could present her bill for a specified number of nights of pleasure. . . .

During the next few days I shut myself up in my library. I mourned for my love—my splendid, mad, divine love. All was over, and the battlefield on which the struggle had raged was silent and still. Two dead and so many wounded to satisfy a woman who was not worth a pair of old shoes! If her passion had at least been roused by the longing for motherhood, if she had been driven by the unconscious desires of the young woman who offers herself—just for the sake of offering herself. But she detested children. In her eyes motherhood was humiliating. Unnatural and perverse woman that she was, she debased the maternal instinct to a purely sensual pleasure. She was driving her family to extinction because she realized she was a degenerate species in the process of dissolution; and in order to conceal her inmost desire to be eradicated and annihilated she uttered those grand phrases about our duty to live for higher ends, for the good of humanity at large.

I loathed her, I tried to forget her. I paced up and down before the rows of bookshelves, unable to rid myself of the accursed nightmare which haunted me. I had no desire for her, or for her company. She disgusted me. And yet a deep compassion, an almost paternal tenderness made me feel responsible for her future. If I left her—? Left to her own devices she would go under, either as the mistress of her former husband or mistress of all the world.

I was powerless to lift her up, powerless to struggle out of the morass into which we had fallen. I resigned myself to remain tied to her, even if I had to witness and share in her downward course. She was dragging me down with her—life had become a burden to me, I had lost all enthusiasm for my work. The instinct of self-preservation, hope, was dead. I wanted nothing, desired nothing. I became terribly shy; I frequently turned away from the door of my restaurant and, foregoing dinner, returned home, threw myself on my sofa, and buried myself under the blanket. There I lay, like a wild beast with its death wound, rigid, with an empty brain, unable to think or sleep, waiting for the end.

One day, however, I was sitting in a back room of my restaurant, a private room where lovers meet and threadbare coats hide themselves, both afraid of the daylight. All at once a well-known voice woke me from my reverie: A man wished me a good afternoon.

He was an unsuccessful architect, a relic of our late bohemia, which was now scattered to the four winds.

"So you are still alive!" he said, sitting down opposite me.

"Just barely. What about you?"

"So-so . . . off to Paris tomorrow. . . . Some fool left me ten thousand crowns."

"Lucky dog!"

"Unfortunately, I have to devour it all by myself. . . ."

"That's not so unfortunate. I've got a good set of teeth and a remarkable imagination. Just what you need to help you dispose of your unexpected fortune."

"Really? Would you care to come? . . ."

"I'd leave instantly."

"Is it a bargain, then?"

"It's a bargain."

"Tomorrow night, by the six o'clock train, to Paris!"

"And afterwards? . . ."

"A bullet through the head!"

"The devil! Where did you get that idea?"

"From the way you look. Everything about you shouts suicide."

"What a haruspex! Well, pack up—and off to Paris!"

When I saw Marie that night I told her the good news. She listened with every appearance of pleasure, wished me a pleasant time, and repeated again and again that it would do me a world of good, would refresh me mentally. In short, she seemed well pleased and overwhelmed me with motherly affection, which touched me deeply. We spent the evening together, morbidly nostalgic, talking of the days that had gone by. We made no plans, for we had lost faith in the future. Then we parted. . . . Forever? . . . The question was not raised. We silently agreed to let chance reunite us or not.

6

The journey really rejuvenated me. It stirred up the memories of my early youth and I felt a mad joy surging in my heart. I wanted to forget the last two years of misery, and not for one single moment did I feel inclined to speak of Marie. The whole tragedy of the divorce was like excrement, something to spit on and casually turn one's back on. I could not help smiling up my sleeve at times, like a fugitive who is firmly resolved not to be taken again. I felt like a debtor escaping his creditors by fleeing to a distant country.

For two weeks I reveled in the Paris theaters, museums, and libraries. I received no letters from Marie, and was beginning to hope that she had got over our separation and that everything was for the best in the best of all possible worlds.

But after a while I grew tired of wandering about and began to lose interest in things. I stayed in my room and read the papers, oppressed by vague apprehensions, by an inexplicable uneasiness.

The vision of the white woman, the fata morgana of the virginal mother, began to haunt me and disturb my peace. The picture of the shameless actress was wiped out of my memory. I remembered only the Baroness, young, beautiful, her fragile body transfigured and clothed with the beauty of the Promised Land dreamed of by ascetics.

I was indulging in those painful but lovely dreams when I received a letter from Marie. She informed me in words that broke my heart that she was about to become a mother, and implored me to save her from dishonor.

Without a moment's hesitation I packed my portmanteau. I left Paris by the first train for Stockholm. I was going to make her my wife.

I had no doubt about the paternity of the expected baby. For a year and a half I had enjoyed the embraces of Marie without thought of consequences. I looked upon the result of our irregular relations as a blessing, as an end of our sufferings, but also as a fact that burdened us with a heavy responsibility which might spell ruin. At the same time, however, it was the starting point for a new adventure, a new experience. Moreover, I always had a very high conception of married life; I considered it the only possible form under which two persons of opposite sex could live together. Life together held no terror for me. My love received a fresh stimulus from the fact that Marie was about to become a mother. She arose purified, ennobled, from the mire of our illicit relationship.

On my arrival at Stockholm she received me very ungraciously and accused me of having tricked her. Forced to discuss the delicate subject, I explained to her that though a constriction in the urethra does diminish the chances of conception, it does not entirely eliminate them. On several occasions in the past we had been frightened by false alarms. What had now happened should not have come as a surprise to us.

She hated matrimony. Her objectionable friend had impressed upon her that a married woman is a slave who works for her husband gratuitously. I detest slaves, and therefore proposed a modern arrangement in keeping with our views.

I suggested that we should take three rooms, one for her, one for myself, and a common room. We should neither do our own housekeeping nor have any servants in the house. Dinner should be sent in from a neighboring restaurant, breakfast and supper be prepared in the kitchen by a daily servant. In this way expenses were easily calculated and the causes for unpleasantness reduced to a minimum. Furthermore—and to avoid the embarrassment of being accused of having wasted my wife's fortune—I suggested a marriage agreement. The dowry, which in Sweden and Norway it is ignominious for a man to accept, provides in the more civilized countries a contribution made by the wife to give her the illusion that she is not living entirely off her husband. To keep both parties happy, the Germans and the Danes have adopted this scheme: The wife brings her furniture with her to the marriage so that the husband maintains the impression that he is staying with his wife, while she continues to feel at home and to think that she is supporting her husband.

Marie had recently inherited her mother's furniture, articles without any intrinsic value, their only claim to distinction being a certain sentimental merit of old association and an air of antiquity. She proposed that she should furnish the rooms, arguing that it would be absurd to buy furniture for three rooms when she had enough for six. I willingly agreed to her proposal.

There remained only one more point, the main one, the expected baby.

We were agreed on the necessity of keeping its birth a secret, and we decided to place it in a foster home in town until such time as we could adopt it.

The wedding was fixed for the 31st of December. During the remaining two months I made every effort to find a respectable means of supporting a family.

For this purpose, and knowing that Marie would soon be compelled to renounce her work at the theater, I renewed my literary efforts. I worked with such ease that at the end of the first month I was able to offer for publication a volume of short stories,* which was accepted without difficulty.

Fortune favored me. I was appointed assistant librarian with a salary of twelve hundred crowns, and when the collections were transferred from the old building to the new one I received a bonus of six hundred crowns. This was good fortune indeed, and taken together with other favorable omens led me to think that a relentless fate had tired of persecuting me.

The foremost magazine in Finland offered me a staff post as reviewer at fifty crowns per article. The official *Posttidningen*, published by the Swedish Academy, gave me the much-coveted order to write the art reviews for thirty-five crowns the column. Besides all this I was given the job of proofreading a new edition of classic works and seeing them through the press.

All this good fortune came to me in those two months, the most fateful months of my whole life.

My short stories appeared almost immediately and were a great success. I was hailed as a master of this particular genre. The book was regarded as marking an epoch in

* *Från Fjärdingen och Svartbäcken (Town and Gown)*, sketches of student life in Uppsala, published by Albert Bonnier in 1877.—ED.

Swedish literature, because it was the first to introduce modern realism.

It was unspeakable happiness to me to lay at the feet of my poor adored Marie a name which, apart from the titles of a royal secretary and assistant librarian, was beginning to be known, with every prospect of a brilliant future. Someday I should be able to give her a fresh start, to reopen her theatrical career, which for the moment had been interrupted by perhaps undeserved misfortune.

Fortune was smiling at us with a tear in her eye. . . .

The banns were published. I packed my belongings and said goodby to my attic, the witness of many joys and sorrows. I marched into that prison that none dread—we perhaps less than others, since we had foreseen all dangers, removed all stumbling blocks.

And yet. . . .

PART THREE

1

What inexpressible happiness it is to be married! To be always near the beloved one, safe from the prying eyes of a fatuous world. To have regained the home of one's childhood with its sheltering love, found a safe port after the storm, acquired a nest for the little ones.

Surrounded by nothing but objects that belonged to her, mementos and relics of her parents' house, I felt as if I were a shoot grafted on her trunk. The oil paintings of her ancestors deluded me into thinking that I had been adopted by her family, since her ancestors would also be the ancestors of my children. I received everything from her hand. She made me wear her father's watch and chain. My dinner was served on her mother's china. She poured on me a continuous stream of trifling presents, relics of old times, that had belonged to famous warriors celebrated by the poets of her country—a fact that impressed a commoner like me not a little. She was the benefactress, the generous giver of all these gifts, and I entirely forgot that it was I who had reclaimed her, lifted her out of the mire, made her the wife of a man with brilliant prospects; forgot that she had been an unknown actress, a divorced wife with a bad reputation, a woman whom very probably I had saved from the worst.

But what a happy life we led! We realized the dream of freedom in marriage. No double bed, no common bedroom, no common dressing room. Nothing unseemly degraded the sanctity of our union. Marriage as we understood and realized it was a splendid institution. With separate rooms we always had reason and opportunity to exchange tender goodnights, repeated again and again; we had the joy of wishing each other good morning, of asking how we had slept; and we preserved the pleasure of stolen visits, always preceded by polite and courteous requests for permission, quite different from the more or less graciously endured rapes of the conventional marriage bed. And I got through an amazing amount of work, staying at home by the side of my beloved wife, who was sewing tiny garments for the expected baby. What a lot of time I had wasted in rendezvous and idleness in the days gone by!

After a month of absolute intimacy Marie was laid up with a premature confinement. We had a tiny daughter, hardly able to draw breath. Without a moment's delay the baby was taken charge of by a nurse whom we knew to be a decent woman, and two days later it passed away as it had come, without pain, from sheer want of vitality, just after it had received private baptism.*

The mother received the news with regret, but it was regret not unmingled with relief. A burden of infinite cares and worries had fallen off her shoulders, for she knew well enough that social prejudice would not have permitted her to keep the prematurely born infant under our own roof.

After this incident we firmly made up our minds on one point: no more children! We dreamed of a life together, a life of perfect comradeship, of a man and a woman, not a life of celibacy but a life in which each was free to pursue his own goal in life. Since she had learned not to take any more chances with me, we decided to make use of the simplest and safest precautions.

Now that every obstacle had been removed, every threatening danger overcome, we began to breathe freely

* Siri von Essen and Strindberg were married December 30, 1877. A child was born to Siri on January 21, 1878, and died the same day.—ED.

and reconsider our position. Since I was ostracized by my
relations, no meddlesome member of my family threatened
the peace of our home, and since the only relative of my
wife's who lived in town was her aunt, we were spared
the frequent calls and visits which so often give rise
to serious troubles and trials in the first months of married life.

Six weeks later I discovered that two intruders had insinuated themselves into my wife's confidence.

One of them was a dog, a cocker spaniel, a blear-eyed
little monster, which greeted me with deafening yelping
and barking every time I entered the house, as if I were
a stranger. I always disliked dogs, those protectors of
cowards who lack the courage to fight an assailant themselves, but I particularly disliked this dog because it was
a leftover from her first marriage, a constant reminder of
her former husband.

The first time I protested and ordered it to lie down, my
wife reproached me gently and made excuses for the little
beast. It had belonged, she said, to her little girl who had
died. And she never imagined that I could be quite so
cruel! And so on, and so on. . . .

One day I found traces of the little monster on the
drawing-room carpet. I punished it, and she called me a
hangman who ill-treated dumb creatures.

"What did you expect me to do, my dear? Talk to it?
We don't speak the same language."

She began to cry and sobbingly confessed that she
could not help being afraid of such a cruel man. . . .

The monster continued to dirty the drawing-room
carpet.

So I put myself in charge of educating the dog, persuading my wife that dogs become very obedient and that a
little perseverance does wonders in training an animal.

She lost her temper, and for the first time reminded me
that the carpet belonged to her.

"Take it away, then; I never agreed to live in a pigsty."

The carpet remained where it was, but the dog was watched more carefully. My remonstrances had had some effect.

Nevertheless, fresh catastrophes occurred.

In order to keep down our expenditures and save the trouble and expense of a kitchen fire, we decided to have a cold supper in the evening. Entering the kitchen accidentally on one occasion, I was amazed to find a roaring fire and the maid engaged in frying veal cutlets.

"Who are these cutlets for?"

"For the dog, sir."

My wife joined us.

"My dear girl—"

"Excuse me, I paid for them!"

"And what if you did! I have to be content with a cold supper! I eat worse than your dog. And I pay, too."

She paid for them! Fine, fine!

Henceforth the cocker spaniel was looked upon as a martyr. Marie and a girl friend, a brand-new friend, adopted the habit of worshiping the beast, which they had decorated with a blue ribbon, behind locked doors. And the dear friend heaved a sigh at the thought of so much human malice incarnate in my detestable person.

An irrepressible hatred for this interloper who was everywhere in my way took possession of me. My wife made a bed for it with down pillows and some soft blankets, which obstructed my way whenever I wanted to say good morning or goodnight to her. And every Saturday, the day I looked forward to through a week of toil, counting on a pleasant evening with her alone when we could talk undisturbed of the past and plan for the future, she spent three hours with her friend in the kitchen, the maid made up a blazing fire, the whole place was turned upside down —and why? Because Saturday was the monster's day for a bath.

"Don't you think you are treating me heartlessly?"

"How dare you call her heartless?" exclaimed the friend.

"A gentler soul never breathed. Why, she doesn't even shrink from sacrificing the happiness of her marriage for a poor forsaken animal!"

Some little time after, I sat down to a dinner that was beyond description.

For some time past the food that was sent in daily from a neighboring restaurant had been getting worse and worse, but my darling, with her irresistible sweetness, had made me believe that it was I who had grown more fastidious. I believed her—she never tired of telling me that she was the soul of frankness and honesty.

The fatal dinner was served. There was nothing on my dish but bones and sinews.

"What on earth is this?" I asked the maid.

"I am sorry, sir," she replied, "but I had orders to reserve the best pieces for the dog."

Beware of the woman who has been caught in the act! Her wrath will fall on your head with fourfold strength.

She sat as if struck by lightning, unmasked, shown up as a liar, a cheat even, for she had always insisted that she was paying for the dog's food out of her own pocket. Her pallor and silence made me feel sorry for her. I blushed for her. Hating to see her humiliated, I behaved like a generous conqueror. I tried to console her. I playfully patted her cheek and told her not to get upset over such a trifle.

But generosity was not one of her virtues. She burst into a torrent of angry words. My origins were all too evident; I had no education, no manners, since I rebuked her before a servant, a stupid girl who had misunderstood her instructions. There was no doubt that I, and I alone, was to blame. Hysterics followed, she grew more and more violent, jumped up from her chair, threw herself on the sofa, raved like a maniac, sobbed and screamed that she was dying.

I was not taken in by her histrionics and I watched her unmoved.

"What a fuss over a cur!"

But she continued to scream and I began to worry. A terrible cough shook her body, which since her confinement had grown even more fragile. Finally I was taken in and sent for the doctor.

He came, examined her heart, felt her pulse, and surlily turned to go. I stopped him on the threshold.

"Well?"

"H'm! nothing at all," he answered, putting on his overcoat.

"Nothing? . . . But . . . ?"

"Nothing whatever. You know how women are. . . . Good day!"

If I had only known then what I know now—the secret for curing attacks of hysteria, whether severe or slight. But the only thing that occurred to me at the time was to kiss her eyes and ask her pardon. And that was what I did. She pressed me to her heart, called me her good little boy who should take care of her because she was very delicate, very weak, and would die one day if her little boy did not stop making such awful scenes.

To make her quite happy I took her dog on my knees and scratched its back, and for the next half hour I was rewarded with looks full of the tenderest affection and gratitude.

From that day the dog dirtied the place without shame or restraint as if possessed by the spirit of revenge. But I controlled my temper.

I waited for a favorable opportunity, for the happy chance that would deliver me from the torture of an unclean home. . . .

And the moment arrived. On returning to dinner one day, I found my wife in tears. She was in great distress. Dinner was not ready. The maid was looking for the lost dog.

Hardly able to conceal my joy, I made every effort to comfort my inconsolable wife. But she could not understand the simple fact that I could sympathize with her in spite of my inward satisfaction in finding the enemy gone. She saw through me and exclaimed, "You're delighted, I know you are. You enjoy your friends' misfortunes, that's how mean you are, fundamentally mean. It shows that you don't love me any more."

"Darling, I love you as much as ever, believe me. But I detest your dog."

"If you love me, you must love my dog too!"

"If I didn't love you, I'd have slapped you before now!"

The effect of my words was startling. To strike a woman! Imagine, striking a woman! She was carried away by the thought. The idea came into her head that I had turned out her dog, poisoned it.

We went to every police station, we paid a visit to the dog butcher, and in the end the disturber of our peace and happiness was recovered. My wife and her friend, regarding me as a poisoner, or at any rate a potential poisoner, celebrated its recovery with great rejoicings.

Henceforth the monster was kept a prisoner in my wife's bedroom. That charming retreat of love, furnished with exquisite taste, was turned into a dog kennel.

Our apartment already too small, became uninhabitable. I ventured to remark about it, but my wife replied that her room was her own to do with as she liked.

Then I started on a merciless crusade. I left her strictly alone until she was on edge with desire and ready to offer me invitations.

"Why do you never come to say good morning to me now?"

"Because I can't get near you."

She sulked. I sulked too. For another fortnight I lived in celibacy. Then, tired out, she found herself compelled to come to my room and beg for what she wanted from me. She hated me all the more for this.

Finally she gave in and decided to have the troublesome interloper destroyed. But instead of having it done forthwith, she invited her friend to assist her in the enactment of a farewell farce, entitled "The Last Moments of the Condemned." She went to the length of begging me on her knees to embrace the dirty animal as proof that I harbored no ill will, arguing that dogs might possibly have an immortal soul and that we might meet again in another world.

The result was that I gave the dog its life and freedom, and was rewarded with a flood of gratitude.

At times I fancied that I was confined in a lunatic asylum. But alas, when one is in love, one cannot be particular.

This scene, "The Last Moments of the Condemned," was renewed every six months during the next six years.

You, young men, who read this plain tale of a man, a woman, and a dog, offer me your deepest compassion, sympathize with me, for my sufferings lasted three times three hundred and sixty-five days of twenty-four hours each. Admire me for staying alive. But if it is true that I am crazy—as my wife maintains—blame no one but me, who lacked the courage to poison that dirty dog once and for all.

2

Let us turn for a moment to Marie's friend—an old maid of about forty years, secretive, full of ideals and principles with which I had lost all sympathy long ago.

She was my wife's consoler. In her arms she wept over my dislike of her dog. She was a ready listener to Marie's abuse of matrimony and the slavery and serfdom of women.

She was rather reserved and careful not to interfere in our household. Anyhow I noticed nothing, for I was completely preoccupied with my work. But I had an idea that she was in the habit of borrowing small sums from my wife. I said nothing until one day I saw her carrying off some of the table silver with the intention of pawning it for her own benefit.

I said a word or two about it to Marie and explained that even under the dotal system this sort of comradeship was very unwise. She never dreamed of helping me, her husband and best friend, in this way, although I was in difficulties and worried by debts.

"Since you listen to such proposals from strangers," I said to her, "why not lend me your shares? I could raise money on them."

She objected, arguing that the shares had fallen so low as to be practically valueless and consequently unsaleable. Moreover, it was against her principles to transact business with her husband.

"But you don't object to a stranger, who can give you no security whatever, who lives on a pension of seventy-five crowns per annum! No, that's all right! Don't you think it just a little strange to refuse to help your husband, who is trying to make a career so he'll be able to take care of you when you have spent your own money, not to mention the fact that your interests are identical?"

She yielded. A loan of about three thousand five hundred crowns was arranged, with the doubtful shares left as security.

From this day on, she looked upon herself as my patroness and told everybody who cared to listen that she had set me on my career by sacrificing her dowry. The fact that I was a well-known writer before I had ever set eyes on her was quite forgotten. But it was bliss to me to look up to her, to be indebted to her for everything: my life, my happiness, my future!

In our marriage contract I had insisted on settling all her property on herself, partly because her financial affairs were in chaos. The Baron owed her money, but instead of paying her in cash, he had guaranteed a loan she had raised. In spite of all my precautions I was requested by the bank on the morning after our wedding to guarantee the sum. My objection was so much wasted breath. The bank did not look upon my wife as responsible, since by her second marriage she had again legally become a minor,* and to my great indignation I was compelled to sign the guarantee, to put my signature in place of the Baron's.

In my perfect simplicity I had no idea of what I was doing. But I was naïve, innocent, stupid. I thought I was doing what every man of the world would have done in my place.

3

One evening while I was closeted in my room with a friend, the Baron called. It was his first call since our wedding. My predecessor's visit seemed to me in bad taste, to say the least; but since he did not mind meeting me, I pretended to be pleased to see him. When I accompanied my friend to the door, however, I did not think it necessary to introduce him. Later on, my wife reproached me for the omission and called me unmannerly. I replied that she, as well as the Baron, for that matter, were the most tactless people one could imagine.

A violent quarrel ensued in which she called me a boor. One word led to another, and certain pictures were mentioned that had once belonged to the Baron but were now decorating my walls. I begged her to send them back to him.

"You cannot return presents without hurting the giver,"

* As part of the feminist breathrough, and due largely to the discussion stirred up by Fredrika Bremer's novel *Hertha* (1856), a law was enacted in 1858 decreeing that unmarried women attained majority at the age of twenty-five. In 1876 when Siri von Essen divorced Baron Wrangel, she would have been twenty-six and would thus have enjoyed a certain legal freedom that would be denied her when she remarried and became once again responsible to her husband.—ED.

she exclaimed. "He doesn't dream of returning the presents you gave him but keeps them as a proof of friendship and trust."

The pretty word "trust" flabbergasted me. My eye fell on a piece of furniture that awakened unpleasant memories.

"Where does this desk come from?"

"I got that from Mamma."

True enough, but she omitted to add that it had passed through her first husband's house.

What a strange lack of delicacy, what bad taste, how utterly heedless of my honor! Was it done intentionally to lower me in the eyes of my fellow men? Had I fallen into a trap set by a termagant?

I surrendered unconditionally without struggling against her infernal logic, convinced that her aristocratic upbringing ought in all doubtful cases to guide me where my own views did not suffice. She had an answer for everything. The Baron had never bought a single piece of furniture. Everything belonged to her—and since the Baron did not scruple to keep *my* wife's furniture, I need not scruple to accept all articles that belonged to my own wife.

The last phrase, "Since the Baron did not scruple to keep *my* wife's furniture," satisfied me more than anything else. And since the pictures hanging in my drawing room were proofs of a noble trust and testified to the ideal character of our relationship, they remained where they were; I even carried simplicity to the length of telling all inquisitive callers who was the donor of those landscapes.

I never dreamed in those days that it was I, the commoner, who possessed tact and delicacy—instincts that are frequently found among the lower classes but are just as frequently lacking in men and women of the aristocracy, where boorishness is too often concealed under a thin veneer. . . . If only I had known to what manner of woman I had entrusted my fate! . . . But at the time I was still completely ignorant of that!

4

As soon as Marie had got over her confinement, which compelled her to live quietly for a time, she was seized with a craving for excitement.

Under the pretext of studying her art, she visited the theaters and went to public entertainments while I stayed at home and worked. Protected by the title of a married woman, she was received in circles that had been closed to the divorcee. She was anxious that I should accompany her because my continued absence created a bad impression. But I felt it was no concern of mine. Referring to the personal-freedom clause in our verbal contract, I gave her complete liberty to come and go wherever she wanted.

But still everyone asked, "Where's your husband? We never see him."

"Good," said I, "they'll soon hear him!"

Before long "spouse" became a kind of nickname for me, and my wife began to look down on me.

During the solitary hours I spent at home I worked on an ethnographical study that was to qualify me for promotion at the library. I was in touch with all the learned authorities in Paris, Berlin, Petersburg, Irkutsk, and Peking, and, seated at my desk, I held in my hands the threads of a perfect net of connections all over the Old World. Marie reproached me for this. She would have preferred to see me writing plays, and she got angry with me. I suggested that she await the results and not condemn my work prematurely. But she would have none of these Chinese researches that brought in no money. A new Xanthippe, she severely tried my Socratic patience by insisting that I was frittering away her money—always *her* money —on nonsense.

My existence at this time was a strange mixture of the bitter and the sweet, and one of my daily worries was

Marie's theatrical career. In March it was rumored that the company at the Royal Theater would be reduced at the end of May when contracts came up for renewal. This, in addition to the usual daily grievances, gave rise to fresh floods of tears during the next three months. Every day the house was filled with all the unemployed actors from the Royal Theater. My spirit, grown aristocratic through the knowledge I had acquired and the development of my talent, rebelled against the presence of this rabble—lacking culture, without refinement, unbearably vain and intolerably boring, imagining that the banalities they expressed in backstage slang were new and original.

Nauseated by these parties, I begged to be excused in the future. I urged her to cut herself off from these pestilential boors whose failure could only infect us and rob us of the strength and backbone we had to have.

"Aristocrat!" she sneered.

"Aristocrat if you like, darling, but I'm an aristocrat because I aspire to the heights—the heights of talent, of course, and not the molehills of the titled aristocracy. But certainly this doesn't keep me from feeling also all the pain and misery of the disinherited."

When I ask myself today how I could have lived for years chained to a woman who nagged and pestered me and who, with the help of her friends and her dog, pillaged and plundered me, I believe the answer lies in the small demands I made and in my ascetic philosophy that taught me not to expect too much of people. But above all it was my love for her. I loved her so much that I bored her with my attentions, and more than once she let me know that the way I clung to her irritated her. But when she caressed me, when I laid my burning head in her lap, when her fingers played with my lion's mane, everything was forgotten, everything was forgiven. This was happiness itself, and like a fool I stammered out the confession that life without her would be unthinkable, that my whole existence hung on the thread she held in her hand. Marie came to think of herself as a higher being. Since I had lowered myself before her, she treated me like a child, babbling over me and calling me pet names.

She knew I was caught and she did not hesitate to use her power.

When summer came she moved into the country and took her maid with her. Moreover, she persuaded her friend to come and live as a boarder in the summer home, for she was afraid of being lonely during the week, when my work kept me at the library—all this against my will, for we had little money and I was afraid her friend could not pay. Marie said I was being "horrid" and reproached me with speaking ill of everybody. So I gave in—to avoid another scene and a forced celibacy. I gave in—as always, unfortunately.

After a whole week as a bachelor I welcomed Saturday as a red-letter day. With a jubilant heart I caught an early train, and then set out for a three-mile walk under the scorching sun, carrying bottles and other provisions for Sunday. My blood danced in my veins, my pulse throbbed at the thought of seeing Marie in a few moments. She would run to me with outstretched arms, her hair flying in the breeze, her face pink and rosy from the sweet, healthful country air. And having had nothing to eat since my morning coffee, I felt my mouth watering at the thought of a delicious, carefully prepared Sunday dinner. At last I glimpsed the cottage through the spruce trees near the shore. At the same time I saw Marie and her friend, in light summer dresses, stealing away to the bathhouse. I shouted to them with all the power in my lungs. They were within earshot; they could not help hearing me. But they only hastened their footsteps, as if they were running away from me, and disappeared into the bathhouse.

What was that supposed to mean?

The maid, hearing me pace up and down in the house,

came in, confused and embarrassed, obviously expecting some unpleasant questions.

"Where are the ladies?"

"Gone to bathe, sir."

"When will dinner be ready?"

"Not before four o'clock, sir. The ladies have only just got up, and I have been busy helping the young lady to dress."

"Did you hear me call?"

"Yes, sir."

So they had really run away from me, driven by an uneasy conscience, and I, hungry and tired, would have to wait hours for my dinner.

What a reception after a week of hard work and longing! The thought that she had run away from me like a truant schoolgirl hurt more than anything.

When she returned to the house, she found me curled up on the sofa in a very bad mood, naturally. She kissed me as if nothing had happened, trying to prevent the storm from breaking. But this time she had no control over my disposition. An empty stomach has no ears and a heavy heart is not eased by false kisses.

"Are you upset?"

"My nerves are. Don't rub them the wrong way."

"Don't talk to me as if I were your cook!"

"I don't want you to be my cook, but don't prevent the cook we have from doing her work!"

"You forget that Amelia has a perfect right to the services of our maid. She's paying to stay here."

"Didn't you hear me calling?"

"No!"

A deliberate lie. I felt my heart would break.

Dinner—my Sunday dinner—was one long torture. And afterwards, wailing and crying, Marie inveighed against matrimony, holy matrimony, the only true happiness in the world, crying on the shoulder of her friend and covering her filthy little dog with insane kisses.

Cruel, false, deceitful—oh, such a beautiful and tender heart!

And so it continued with infinite variations during the whole summer. I spent my Sundays with two idiots and a dog. They tried to make me believe that the domestic unpleasantnesses were due to my nerves and urged me to see a doctor.

I had intended to take my wife sailing on Sunday mornings. But she never got up before lunch. She would spend the time primping and making herself pretty, and I would have to go sailing alone until dinnertime; after that it was too late.

What a dear tender heart! She could riddle me with pinpricks and then cry bitterly one morning because the gardener was killing a rabbit for dinner, and in bed that night she confessed to me that she had been praying that the poor little creature would not suffer too much under the ax.

A psychiatrist has recently stated that an exaggerated love for animals combined with a hard-hearted indifference to the sufferings of one's fellow creatures is a symptom of "moral insanity."

What is one to make of a woman who could pray for a rabbit and at the same time torment her husband with a smile on her lips?

On our last Sunday in the country she took me aside, flattered my generosity, appealed to my kind heart, and begged me to cancel Amelia's debt to us, pleading her limited means.

I consented without even discussing the matter, without telling her that I had anticipated the suggestion, foreseen the little stratagem, and known that it was inevitable. But she, always armed to the teeth, even when nothing was said against her, had to have the last word.

"Anyway, if I had to, I could pay for her myself!"

No doubt. But could she have paid for the annoyance and trouble caused by her friend?

But husband and wife must not fall out over trifles, now must they?

5

At the beginning of the new year the old country was shaken by a general crisis,* and the bank that had loaned money on Marie's shares failed. I was notified that my loan would be called in and that I would have to make good with hard cash. That was a blow. But, fortunately, after endless difficulties the creditors agreed to give me a year's respite.

That was a terrible year, the worst of them all.

As soon as things calmed down a bit, I looked around for ways to stay afloat.

In addition to my work at the library I started a novel on modern life, filled newspapers and magazines with articles, and at the same time finished my scientific paper. Marie, whose contract was about to expire, was rehired for another year out of pity, but her salary was reduced to fourteen hundred crowns. Now I was better off than she, for she had lost her capital in the crash.

This put her in a terrible mood and she took it out on me. Her independence meant more to her than anything else. In order to get back on equal footing with me, she attempted to raise a loan, but these attempts proved abortive and only led to her blaming me for everything. By acting thoughtlessly she did me more harm than good in her efforts to save herself and lighten my load. I appreciated her good intentions but I could not help criticizing her methods.

* Heavy investments in railroads, which did not pay off for some time, brought about a financial crisis in Sweden. As a result of this, in January 1879, a year after his marriage to Siri, Strindberg went bankrupt. As security for a bank loan he had borrowed from Siri railroad bonds issued by one of the companies that failed.—ED.

Always nagging and peevish, she began to reveal certain deceitful and treacherous sides to her nature, and fresh events cast a glaring light on disturbing aspects of her emotional life.

A masquerade ball was given at the theater and I made her promise not to go dressed as a man. She gave me her solemn oath, for I had been very insistent—for reasons that I could not explain. The next day I learned that she had not only gone dressed in white tie and tails but that she had gone to supper later on with some of her male friends.

Her lying was bad enough, but I was especially upset by the thought of that supper party.

"So what?" she said when I remarked on her behavior. "I'm a free woman, aren't I?"

"No," I said, "you're a married woman. You bear my name and we are responsible to each other. If you hurt your own reputation, mine also suffers—mine more than yours."

"I see. That means I'm not free?"

"Nobody can be absolutely free in society. Everybody's life is tied to the lives of other people. For example, what would you have said if I had invited some women friends to supper?"

She insisted she was free to do as she liked; that she was at liberty, if she felt so inclined, to ruin my reputation —free to do anything and everything. She was an aborigine. Freedom to her meant freedom to act as a tyrant and to trample into the dust the honor and happiness of her fellow creatures.

This scene, which developed into a row and ended in an hysterical crying spell, was soon followed by another, which was all the more disturbing inasmuch as I was not sufficiently initiated into the secrets of sexual life. Its abnormalities seemed frightful and awful, like all things that one cannot immediately account for.

One evening, when the maid was busy in the room

next to mine, making up Marie's bed for the night, I heard half-suppressed screams and smothered laughter as if someone were being tickled. I felt a strange fear, an inexplicable apprehension that threatened to find release in an outburst of anger. I threw open the door and caught Marie with her hands buried in the wide-open waist of the maid's dress and with her libidinous lips glued to the maid's pearl-white breast.

"What do you think you're doing, you poor fools! Are you crazy?" I thundered at her.

"What do you mean? We're only playing!" Marie replied impudently. "It's none of your business."

"Yes, it *is* my business! Come here!"

And face to face I explained what was wrong with her behavior.

But she accused me of having "a dirty mind" and said I was perverted to see vice in the most innocent of games.

Watch out for a woman caught red-handed! This one emptied a whole chamberpot of abuse on my head.

In the course of our discussion I reminded her of the unreasonable attachment she had confessed to have for her cousin, the pretty Matilda. But with the most innocent voice in the world she replied that she herself had been amazed at her inclination, as she had "never thought it possible for one woman to be so madly attracted to another woman."

This naïve confession reassured me. I remembered that one evening at my brother-in-law's Marie had quite openly spoken of her passionate love for her cousin, without blushing, without being conscious that there was anything at all unusual in her conduct.

But I was still angry. Choosing my words carefully, I suggested that she beware of little pranks that, though they might be harmless to begin with, could lead to unfortunate results.

She made some inane reply, called me—as usual—a fool (she always treated me as the most naïve and ignorant person in the world), and finished off by saying that I had been telling her a pack of lies.

What was the use of explaining to her that in the law books such offenses were punishable crimes? What was the use of trying to convince her that medical books termed such intimacies perversions?

No, I was the perverted one, because I knew all about such things! Nothing could persuade her to stop her innocent games.

She was one of those unconscious criminals who might better be confined in female reformatories than kept at home.

6

Towards the end of the spring she introduced a new friend into the house. This was one of her pretty theatrical colleagues, a woman of about thirty. Like Marie she too was threatened with the loss of her job, and consequently I felt sorry for her—sorry to see this beautiful woman, recently idolized by all, reduced to such straits for no apparent reason, unless it was because the theater had hired the daughter of the great tragedienne. A triumph always requires hecatombs of victims.

Nevertheless, I disliked her. She was aggressive and always gave me the impression of a woman on the prowl. She flattered me, tried to enchant me, no doubt in order to divert my attention, because she understood that I could see right through her.

Occasionally there were jealous scenes between the old friend and the new one. They insulted each other to their hearts' content, but I chose not to lend them my ears. . . .

Before the summer was over it became obvious that Marie was pregnant again. We estimated that her confinement would take place in February. It struck us like a bolt from the blue. It was now necessary to get the wind into our sails and to make port before time ran out on us.

My novel was published in November.* It was an enormous success. The money poured in and we were saved!

Famous, renowned, hailed as a writer with a unique talent, declared a master of the novel, I could breathe easily again after a year—no, many years—of worry and trouble, and we could look forward to the birth of the child with indescribable joy. In anticipation, we christened it and even bought Christmas presents for it. My wife was happy and proud of her condition, and our close friends fell into the habit of asking how "the little chap" was—just as if he had already arrived.

Having won enough fame and honor for myself, I now resolved to rehabilitate Marie and save her threatened career as an actress. To achieve this I wrote a play in four acts and submitted it to the Royal Theater. It contained a sympathetic role in which Marie had every chance to reconquer the public.†

On the very day the baby was born I heard that the play had been accepted and that she had been cast in the principal role.

Everything was for the best in this best of all possible worlds; the broken tie between me and my family was firmly reknit by the birth of the baby.‡

The good time, the springtime of my life had arrived. There was bread in the house, and even a few bottles of

---

* *The Red Room*, a *roman à clef* about the intellectual and bohemian life in Stockholm, was published in 1879 and immediately established Strindberg's reputation as a master of the realistic novel. There were four printings of the novel in 1879 and 1880, 1550 copies in each printing, for which Strindberg received a total of 2000 crowns.—ED.

† The play was *The Secret of the Guild*. The part of Margaret, somewhat like Gretchen in *Faust*, was written with Siri von Essen in mind.—ED.

‡ Karin Strindberg, the first child in the marriage to survive infancy, was born February 26, 1880.—ED.

wine. The beloved and adored mother was enjoying herself again and had regained all her former beauty. The indifference and neglect with which she had treated her first baby were transformed into the tenderest care for the newborn infant. Summer had come again, and I was able to ask for a few months' leave to travel and to live out in the woods with my family on one of the green islands of the Stockholm skerries.

And I was beginning to reap the harvest of my scientific researches. An article of mine was honored by being read before the *Académie des Inscriptions et Belles-Lettres* of the *Institut de France*. I was elected a member of several foreign scientific societies, and the medal of the Russian Geographical Society was conferred on me.*

Having at the age of thirty won an excellent position in the literary and scientific world and with a brilliant future before me, I found the greatest happiness in laying my trophies at Marie's feet. . . . But she was angry with me because I had upset our equilibrium. I had to make myself smaller and smaller to spare her the humiliation of belonging to a man who was superior to her. Like the good-natured giant in the fable, I allowed her to pull my beard, but she wanted to presume on my good nature. She liked to belittle me in front of the servants and visiting friends, especially her women friends. She gave herself airs, grew swelled-headed (I helped inflate her) and the more I lowered myself the more she trampled on me. I deliberately fostered in her the delusion that I had her to thank

* In April 1879 Strindberg was elected a member of *La Société des Etudes japonais, chinoises, tartares et indo-chinoises.* His article "Relations de la Suède avec la Chine" was read before the *Académie des Inscriptions et Belles-Lettres* on January 6, 1879. In the same year, for his discovery of an eighteenth-century map of Siberia, drawn by a Johan Renat, Strindberg was awarded the silver medal of the Russian Geographic Society. Also in the same year, Strindberg published a study of Strahlenburg's map of Asia in the journal of the Swedish Society for Anthropology and Geography.—ED.

for my fame, which she did not understand and which she apparently disparaged. I took positive delight in making myself out to be her inferior. I was happy to be no more than the husband of a charming woman, and eventually she came to believe that she possessed my genius. This applied to everything in our life, large and small. For instance, being an excellent swimmer myself, I taught her to swim. In order to encourage her, I pretended to be afraid, and she would love to ridicule me by telling people about her own derring-do. I enjoyed it enormously.

But the days passed. In my adoration of the mother-woman I didn't concern myself too much about the fact that I was tied to a woman of thirty. The critical age set in, however, the beginning of a period full of dangers and pitfalls. I could see indications, perhaps not fraught with disaster for the moment, but which nevertheless carried in them the seeds of discord.

After her confinement physical antagonism was added to temperamental incompatibility. Sexual intercourse became disgusting. When her passion was aroused, she was transformed into a shameless coquette. She took malicious delight in making me jealous; at other times she would abandon herself to an alarming extent, possibly under the pressure of her wild cravings and desires.

One morning we went out in a sailboat, accompanied by a young fisherman. I took charge of tiller and mainsail; the boy attended to the foresail. My wife was sitting near him. The wind dropped and silence reigned in the boat. All at once I noticed that the young fisherman, from under his cap, was sending rather lascivious looks in the direction of my wife's feet. . . . Her feet? . . . Perhaps she was showing him her legs also. I could not tell from where I sat. I watched her. Her concupiscent eyes devoured the boy's body. In order to remind her of my presence I made a sudden gesture, as if I were waking from a dream. She pulled herself together with an effort, and, her eyes resting on the tops of his high boots, she clumsily extricated herself from an awkward position by remarking, "I wonder whether boots like those are expensive?"

Now, what was I supposed to think of such a stupid remark, I'd like to know.

To divert her mind from the voluptuous current of her thoughts I suggested, under some pretext or other, that we change places.

I tried to forget this sad and irritating scene, tried to persuade myself that I had been mistaken, although similar scenes were stored up in my memory, recollections of her burning eyes outlining my body beneath my clothes.

A week later my suspicions were reawakened by an incident that once and for all destroyed my hopes of having made a mother out of this perverse woman.

One of my friends spent a weekend with us. He began to make up to Marie. She rewarded his courtesy by flirting outrageously with him. It grew late, we said goodnight to each other, separated, and Marie pretended to go to bed.

Half an hour later I heard voices on the balcony. I stepped out quickly and caught my wife and friend sitting together sharing a bottle of brandy. I controlled myself quite well, but the following morning I showered her with reproaches for making me look ridiculous in front of other people.

She laughed, called me a man of prejudices, said I had a "fantastic and dirty mind"—in fact, paraded her whole repertory of futile arguments before me.

I lost my temper; she performed her hysterical scene and played it so well I finally asked her to forgive me for *my mistakes!* My mistakes, of course, for had I not reprimanded her for what any decent person would regard as improper behavior!

Her final words finished me.

"Darling, you don't think I could bear to go through the horrible business of a divorce a second time?"

And brooding over all these unpleasant events, I escaped into sleep, the happy refuge of the duped husband.

What is a coquette really? . . . A woman who makes advances. Coquetry is nothing but making advances. That's all.

And jealousy? . . . The fear of losing one's most precious possession. . . . And the jealous husband? . . . A ridiculous figure, for the ridiculous reason that he cannot make up his mind to lose his most precious possession.

7

I had one success after another. All our debts were paid. Money poured in. But although a great proportion of my income went into the household fund, we were always short of money. Marie, who kept the household accounts and handled the cash, was always clamoring for more. And that made for more violent scenes.

Her contract with the theater was not renewed. Her dramatic career was definitely over. It goes without saying that I had to bear the consequences. It was all my fault! . . . If only she had never married me! . . . The part I had written for her was forgotten; as a matter of fact, she had completely ruined it by acting it without the slightest conception of the part's subtleties.

It was at about this time that, thanks to a play by a celebrated Norwegian male bluestocking, everyone started to meddle in that chitchat called "the woman question," and all feeble minds were obsessed by a perfect mania for finding oppressed women everywhere. Since I refused to be taken in by this nonsense, I was stamped for the rest of my life as a "woman hater."

A few plain home truths from me on the occasion of our

next quarrel threw Marie into a violent fit of hysterics in her grand style. This was just after the greatest discovery of the nineteenth century for the treatment of neurotic ailments. The cure was as simple as all great truths.

When the screams of my patient were at their loudest and most violent, I seized a water bottle and thundered the magic words, "Get up, or I shall pour this water over you!"

She stopped screaming at once—and my Adored One shot at me a look full of admiration, amazement, gratitude, and deadly hatred.

For a moment I was frightened, but the awakened male in me would not retreat so quickly.

Again I lifted the water bottle and shouted, "Stop your silliness or I'll drown you!"

She got to her feet, but only to call me wretch, skunk, coward, milksop—perfect evidence that my cure had been completely effective.

Husbands, duped or otherwise, believe me, for I am your sincere friend. I present to you this dear secret that may once and for all rid us of the grand hysterics. Remember it—it might come in handy.

From that day my departure from this world was irrevocably settled, jotted down in a woman's notebook. My Adored One began to detest me. I knew too much of female cunning; there was no room for me in this world. The female sex had decided on my physical and mental destruction, and my own wife, as the avenging Fury, had accepted the awful and difficult mission of torturing me to death.

She began her task by introducing her friend into the house as a tenant, persuading her to rent a furnished room in our apartment—this, in spite of my most violent opposition. Marie even went to the length of suggesting that she take her meals with us, a proposition I fought tooth and nail. But notwithstanding my protest and all my precautions, I constantly felt the skirts of the beautiful intruder brushing against me wherever I went into the house. I could almost fancy myself a bigamist. The evenings I wanted to spend with my wife I spent with myself, for she remained invisible, closeted in her friend's room, where they enjoyed themselves at my expense, smoking my cigarettes and drinking my liquor. I began to detest the woman quite earnestly, and since I could not hide my feelings—at any rate not sufficiently—I often brought Marie's wrath on my head for having been found wanting in courtesy towards the "poor child."

Not satisfied with having estranged Marie from husband and child—the baby was boarded out with a neighbor, a forty-five-year-old shrew—the fair friend demoralized my cook. They got drunk together on my beer.

I found the maid fast asleep at the stove, the food ruined. Their incredible consumption of beer rose to almost five hundred bottles a month.

The fair friend was nothing more than a man-eater and I was her prey.

One day Marie showed me a cloak she said she wanted to buy. I liked neither the color nor the cut and advised her to choose another. The friend, who happened to be present, kept it for herself and I forgot all about it. Two weeks later I received a bill for a cloak bought by my wife. This meant that Marie, who must have known what was going on, had lent herself to a trick well known to the theatrical demimonde.

As usual, I became the target of her wrath when I asked her to break off all connections with this adventuress. . . .

And things went from bad to worse.

Sometime later Marie, posing as the submissive wife, trying to work on my feelings, calling for understanding, begged me quite humbly to let her accompany the "poor child," as a reference, on a visit to an old friend of the "poor child's" late father's whom she intended to ask for a loan. The request struck me as very strange. I suspected a deadly trap when I began to think about her friend's bad reputation: she was rumored to have affairs with old men. I implored Marie for the sake of our innocent child to open her eyes, to rouse herself from her trance before she fell into the abyss. . . . Her only reply was a repetition of her old phrase: "Your evil imagination . . ." Worse and worse.

At a luncheon that the Beautiful Intruder arranged for the purpose of beguiling a renowned actor into making her a proposal of marriage, a fresh revelation awaited me, a revelation that roused me from my stupor.

The champagne flowed freely and the ladies got drunk as usual. Marie was reclining in an armchair, and in her lap sat her friend, whom she was kissing on the lips as unembarrassed as you please. Interested in this strange spectacle, the famous actor called to one of his friends, and pointing at the couple as if bringing an accusation, exclaimed, "What did I tell you! Do you see?"

Doubtless he was alluding to certain rumors that were being spread around, and there was a hidden meaning in the laughing words.

What was I to do?

As soon as we arrived home, I implored Marie to shake off this infatuation and, at least for the sake of our child, stop doing things that gave her a reputation for licentiousness. She openly admitted she enjoyed kissing pretty women; her friend was not the only one of her colleagues whom she treated in this way. At the theater, in the dressing rooms, she bestowed the same favor on others, and she had no intention of denying herself this pleasure, this innocent fun, which only in my "perverted imagination" could seem vicious.

It was impossible to make her see what she was doing. There was only one remedy left: make her pregnant again and reawaken the motherly instincts in her.—She was wildly indignant and furious, but her condition kept her at home for some months.*

After her confinement she changed her tune. Either fear of the consequences of her perverted passions made her play the coquette, or else her female instincts had been reawakened. Anyway, from then on, she flirted passionately with the men; but she did it too openly to make me really jealous.

Without a job, with nothing to occupy her time, full of whims, despotic, she was bent on making war with me to the knife.

Imagine, one day she tried to prove to me that it was cheaper to keep three maids than two! I was fed up with the stupid arguments of a lunatic, so I simply picked her up and threw her out of the room.

She swore vengeance. She hired a third maid, who was absolutely superfluous in the house, and then no work was done at all. To the accompaniment of the melody of three girls quarreling all day long, the house went to rack and ruin. They sat in the kitchen getting soused on beer and feeding their lovers at my expense.

To complete the picture of my matrimonial bliss, one of my children fell ill, and this brought two more servants into the house, making a total of five, plus two doctors. By the end of the month I was five hundred crowns in debt. I redoubled my energies to meet expenses, but the strain on my nerves was beginning to tell.

On top of all this misery, she was forever reproaching me with having squandered her more than doubtful dowry. She forced me to pay an allowance to her aunt in Copenhagen, who now, in turn, accused me of having wasted her "fortune." She drove me crazy with her incredibly silly arguments and explained that Matilda's mother on her death-

* A third child, Greta, was born to Siri and Strindberg on June 9, 1881.—ED.

bed had distinctly declared that Marie was to share the inheritance with her, the aunt. I couldn't make head or tail of it. One fact remained: I had to support this lazy, useless, greedy aunt, since the "fortune" never existed except as a mirage. Nevertheless I gave way in the matter. I even agreed to guarantee a sum of money, raised by an older friend, Mysterious Adventuress Number One. I went along with it all, since my adored wife had hit on the idea of selling me her favors. For the privilege of kissing and embracing her, I admitted everything. I admitted having wasted her dowry, squandered her aunt's "fortune," ruined her theatrical career by marrying her, even having undermined her health.

From then on, I saw the progressive triumph of legal prostitution, introduced under the protection of holy matrimony.

She carefully treasured up all my admissions and worked them into a legend that the scandal papers greedily snapped up later and that was assiduously spread by all those of her friends whom, one after the other, I had turned out.

My ruin had become an insane obsession with her. At the end of the year I found that I had given her twelve thousand crowns for household expenses, and yet I was compelled to ask my publishers for an advance.

If I complained about her extravagance, she would riposte, "Well, then, don't make babies. Don't make your wife miserable! Oh, when I think of the high position I had, and what I gave up to marry you!"

But I had an answer for that.

"As Baroness, my dear, your husband gave you three thousand crowns and debts. I've given you three times as much!"

She said nothing; she just let me hunger for her. So when night came I admitted everything she wanted me to. Yes, yes, three thousand is three times as much as ten thousand! Yes, yes, I am a blackguard, a miser, a *bel ami,* who had risen at the expense of his adored wife, adored more especially in her low-cut nightgown!

To get rid of her venom she wrote the first chapter of a novel, the subject of which was the exploitation of a woman slave by a crafty husband, whereas through my writings there always glided the white wraith of a lovely golden-haired woman, a madonna, a little mother, and I was forever chanting her praises, creating a glorious myth around the figure of the wondrous woman who by God's grace had been sent to brighten the thorny path of a struggling writer. . . . And in the meantime her damned face emerged from the pens of the critics encircled with a completely unmerited nimbus; for the critics never tired of glorifying the "good genius" of the pessimistic novelist.

And the more I suffered under the perversities of my maenad, the more eagerly I strove to weave a crown of light for her sacred head. And the more the brutal reality overwhelmed me, the more there flamed up in my mind mirages of my goddess. . . . Ah, Love!

8

There were times when I was forced to believe that my wife hated me and wanted to get rid of me in order to marry a third man.

Sometimes a strange look in her face made me suspect her of having a lover, and her coldness toward me strengthened my suspicions.

One day my smoldering jealousy burst abruptly into fierce flames, our marriage was shaken to its very foundations, and hell opened wide at our feet.

"I'm sick," she suddenly declared. She was suffering from some vague disease of the spine or the back—she was uncertain which.

I sent for the children's doctor, an old college friend of mine. He diagnosed rheumatic knots on the muscles of the back and prescribed a course of massage. I had no objection to make, for there seemed to be no doubt of the reality of the disease. As I had no idea of the intimate nature of the massage treatment, I remained completely absorbed in my literary work and paid no attention whatever to the progress of the cure. Moreover, my wife did not appear to be dangerously ill, for she came and went as usual, visited the theaters, never refused an invitation, and was always the last to leave a party.

One evening at a small gathering of friends, someone suddenly began to bewail the dearth of lady doctors in our modern society. He said it must be very unpleasant for a woman to undress before a stranger, and, turning to Marie, he asked, "Right? Isn't it very unpleasant?"

"Oh! a doctor doesn't count."

That was the first I suspected what these massage séances really were. Simply by seeing the expression of sensuality on Marie's face, an expression that had puzzled me for some time, a terrible suspicion gripped my heart.

She undressed before this immoral bachelor, notorious as an out-and-out voluptuary and libertine.

And I had been completely ignorant of it! . . .

When we were alone, I asked her for an explanation. Unconcernedly she described the treatment.

She kept her underskirts on, but everything else was rolled down and her whole back was naked.

"And you're not embarrassed?"

"Why should I be embarrassed?"

"You always pretend to be embarrassed in front of me."

Two days later the doctor called to see one of the children. From my room I caught snatches of a more than strange conversation between him and my wife. They were laughing and exchanging words mumbled with their hands over their mouths. . . .

Presently they entered my room, the smiles still on their lips. Plunged in dark thoughts, I tried fumblingly to strike up a conversation that by and by drifted to the subject of women patients.

"You understand women's complaints, don't you, old boy?" I said.

Marie stared at me. She looked like a fury. There was so much hatred blazing in her eyes that I felt a cold shiver down my back.

When the doctor had left, she turned on me, raging.

"Whore!" I spat the word in her face.

It escaped my lips against my will, a flash of insight breaking through. Immediately the insult came home to me and struck me in the heart, and when my eyes fell on the children, I knelt down and apologized, on my knees and in tears.

But she played the fury. Two hours of pleading would not soften her. To make amends for the great injustice I had done her, and to some extent also influenced by her raging hatred, I conceived the idea of arranging for her a pleasure trip to Finland in the shape of a theatrical tour, extending over several weeks.

I started negotiations with theatrical managers, succeeded in coming to terms, and raised the money.

She sailed and piled up victories in her homeland and laurel wreaths from her relatives.

In the meantime I was left alone with the children in the country, where I fell ill, and believing myself to be near death, I sent telegrams asking her to return home. The trip would not interfere with her business, since she had fulfilled all her engagements.

When she returned and found me walking around and healthy, she accused me of having brought her back on false pretenses, telegraphed lies, merely to take her away from the pleasant time she was having with her relatives. . . .

Soon after her return I noticed a new turn in her unpredictable behavior that filled me with increased uneasiness.

Contrary to her former habits, she gave herself to me unreservedly.

"How can it be that all her fear of becoming pregnant has vanished?" I asked myself without feeling like asking her point-blank about it.

On the next morning and the days that followed she talked of nothing but the pleasant time she had spent in Finland, and carried away for the moment by her memories, she told me that she had met an engineer on the steamer, an enlightened, modern man who had convinced her that there was no such thing as sin in the world, and that circumstances and destiny alone were responsible for all happenings.

"Certainly, my dear. But for all that, our actions continue to have consequences. I admit that there is no such thing as sin because there is no personal God; nevertheless, we are responsible to those we wrong. There may be no sin in the world, but crime exists as long as there is a law in force. The theological conception of sin may be abrogated, but vengeance, or rather retribution, remains a fact of life and can be used against whomever has hurt us."

She had grown somber but pretended not to understand me. At last she said, "Only the wicked revenge themselves."

"Agreed. But with so many wicked people in the world, who can be sure that he is dealing with a man broadminded enough not to retaliate?"

"But it's still fate that controls our actions."

"True. But fate also guides the dagger of the avenger."

At the end of the month she had a miscarriage.

That was sufficient proof of her infidelity, I thought. And from that moment suspicion grew slowly into certainty and filled my heart with bitterness.

She did her utmost to persuade me that I was "mad"! To listen to her, my suspicions were but the figments of an overworked brain.

And once again I accepted her forgiveness for my errors.

To mark our reconciliation I wrote a play containing a splendid part for her, a part it was impossible to ruin. On the seventeenth of August I handed her the play together with the deed of gift that conferred on her all the rights. She could do with it what she liked as long as she herself played the part I had written for her. It was the result of two months' strenuous work. She accepted it without a word of thanks as a routine sacrifice laid on the altar of Her Majesty the quondam Queen of the Stage.

In the meantime the housekeeping went from bad to worse. I was unable to interfere, for she regarded every opinion expressed by me, every suggestion of a change made by me, as an insult and a humiliation. I had to remain passive, powerless in face of the wanton extravagance of the servants, who wasted the food and neglected the children.

Added to our economic misery were the domestic quarrels. When she returned from her trip to Finland, paid for out of my personal account, she had two hundred crowns in her pocket, the financial result of her tour. Since she was in charge of the cash, I made a mental note of the sum, and when she asked me for money long before the usual date, surprised by the unexpected demand, I asked her what she had done with her money. She had lent it to her friend, she said, and citing the law, she argued that she was free to dispose of all monies she herself had earned.*

"What about me?" I replied. "Having charge of the household money doesn't mean stealing from it."

"It's different for the wife!"

"For the oppressed woman, you mean? For the female slave who tolerates a man giving her everything she needs? There you have the logical consequences of that nonsense called 'woman's emancipation.'"

Everything Emile Augier forecast in *Les Fourchambault*

* A law passed by the Swedish Parliament in 1874 gave married women the right to dispose of their own earnings as they saw fit.—ED.

about the system of marriage settlements has been fulfilled. The husband has become the slave. And you know there are plenty of men who allow themselves to be deceived to such an extent that they dig their own graves! Real sweet fools!

While the misery of my married life slowly unreeled, like a ribbon off a spool, I took advantage of my literary reputation to tilt at foolish prejudices and attack antiquated superstitions. In a volume of satires,* I threw a handful of pebbles at the principal charlatans of the metropolis, not forgetting the sexless women.

I was at once branded a libeler; Marie wasn't wasting any time. To keep herself in the clear she made friends with the enemy. Day and night she played the respectable woman and complained to all and sundry of the bitter misery of being tied to a scandalmonger! And she ignored the fact that behind the pamphleteer was an important novelist and playwright.

Like a holy martyr, she remained unperturbed by the dismal prospects of her unfortunate children. They would have to bear the consequences of the dishonorable actions of a father who had squandered their mother's dowry, ruined her theatrical career, and, to top it all, mistreated her. About the same time an item appeared in one of the papers stating that I was insane, and a brochure, written to order and paid for in cash, spread abroad the martyrdom of Marie and her friends. Not one of the absurdities that her dirty little female brain had hatched was forgotten.

She had won the game.

And as she saw me crumple before the blows of my enemies, she assumed the role of the pious mother weeping

---

* *Det nya riket* (The New Kingdom), published in 1882. It is often considered the best political and social satire in the Swedish language.—But when it first appeared it turned many of Strindberg's admirers against him. They accused him of being a muckraker. From this time on Strindberg found himself increasingly isolated in Sweden.—ED.

over the prodigal son, and captivating all the world, except me, she drew all my friends over to her side, false ones and true ones alike. Isolated, in the power of a vampire, I abandoned all attempt at defense. Could I raise my hand against the mother of my little angels, against my Adored One?

Never!

I succumbed. She bathed me in kindness—in public. At home she had nothing for me but contempt and insults.

I was exhausted by overwork and misery. Headaches, nervous irritability, stomach pains. . . . The doctor diagnosed catarrh of the stomach.

That was a rather unexpected result of mental strain.

It was curious—very curious—that the illness did not break out until after I had decided to go abroad, which I figured was the only means of escaping from the net woven around me by those countless friends who were everlastingly commiserating with my wife. The symptoms of this mysterious malady first showed themselves on the day after a visit to a friend's laboratory, from which I had taken a bottle of cyanide that would put me out of my misery if I needed it. This bottle I had locked up in one of my wife's cupboards.

Paralyzed and depressed, I was lying on the sofa, watching my children at play, thinking of the good old days that lay behind me, preparing myself for death and determined to leave nothing in writing that could throw light on the cause of my death or my sinister suspicions.

I was ready to make my exit, disappear from sight, killed by the woman whom I forgave with my last breath.

The last bit of juice had been squeezed out of me. Marie was watching me out of the corners of her eyes, perhaps wondering how much longer I should linger on this earth before I left her to enjoy in peace the income that the collected works of the famous writer would yield her and the stipend that the government would undoubtedly grant her for the education of the children. . . .

She was a success in my play, so huge a success that the critics called her a great tragedienne. She almost burst with pride and she was allowed to choose whatever she wanted for her next part. The result was a complete fiasco.* And now that she could no longer deny the fact that it was I who had made her, that it was I she had to thank for her laurels, the strength of her debtor's hatred increased. She made the rounds to all the various theatrical managers but could find no engagement and finally forced me to reopen negotiations with Finland. I was willing to leave my country, my friends, my publisher, to settle in the midst of her friends—who were my enemies. But the Finns wouldn't take her. Her career was over.

During all this time she led the life of an idle woman free from all duties as mother and wife, and when my health did not permit me to accompany her to the artistic circles that she frequented, she went alone. Sometimes she did not come home until early in the morning, often intoxicated and making enough noise to wake the whole house. And my gorge would rise as I heard her vomiting in the night nursery, where she slept.

What is a man to do in a case of this sort? Denounce his own wife? Impossible! Divorce her? No! I looked upon the family as an organism, a plant, a whole of which I was an integral part. I could not exist independently of it; without the mother, life seemed impossible to me, even if I had the custody of the children. My heart's blood transmitted through my wife's uterus flowed through the veins

* *Herr Bengts hustru* (Sir Bengt's Wife), Strindberg's first play on the subject of love and marriage, was performed on November 25, 1882, at the New Theater (not the Royal Theater) with Siri Strindberg in the title role. The critics were disappointed in the play, a rather tame work coming from the notorious satirist, and suggested that Siri had saved the play from being a failure. Siri next appeared in J. J. Wecksell's *Daniel Hjort* (first performed 1864), a popular history play in the Shakespearean manner, set in Finland. In the 1882 revival with Siri playing the lead it was not well received.—ED.

of their small bodies. The whole was like a system of arteries intimately connected and interdependent. If a single one were cut, my life would ebb away with the blood that was sucked up by the sand. For this reason the infidelity of the wife is a terrible crime. One cannot help sympathizing with the "Kill her!" of a well-known author[*] who shows us a father stricken to death because he has come to doubt the legitimacy of his offspring, deceived and betrayed by a mother without conscience.

Marie, on the other hand, having identified herself with the crazy endeavors to increase women's rights and liberties, fully endorsed the new doctrine that the woman who deceives her husband is not guilty since she is not his property.

I could not degrade myself to spy on her, nor did I want proof, for that would have meant death to me. I wanted to deceive myself and live in a world of my own that I could beautify at will.

But I was deeply wounded. I knew that the family tree had been spoiled and blighted; I knew that the children who would bear my name and be supported by my earnings were not mine. Nevertheless I loved them, for they had come into my life to be my future existence. Deprived of the hope to live again in my children, I floated in space like a phantom that breathes through aerial roots.

Marie seemed to lose patience because I lingered so long. If she treated me with the tender love of a mother before witnesses, she constantly nipped at me in secret, like the little acrobat's father in the wings. She tried to hasten my end by cruelty. She invented a new torture. Justifying her conduct with my temporary weakness, she treated me as if I were impotent. One day, proudly boasting of her physical strength, she threatened to strike me. She rushed at me, but I seized her by the wrists and forced her down on the sofa.

---

[*] Alexander Dumas *fils* in *L'Homme-Femme*, 1872.—ED.

"Admit that I am the stronger in spite of my weakness!"

She would not admit it. She merely looked nonplussed and furious at having made a mistake. She left the room sulking.

In our mutual struggle she had all the advantages of the woman and the actress. Think of me, dear reader, a man doomed to ceaseless hard labor and forced to hold my own against an idle woman who spent all her time spinning intrigues. Eventually the man in this unequal struggle is certain to be caught in a net closing in on him from all sides.

Besides, when she accused me to other people of being impotent by way of excusing her own sins and crimes, did not honor, modesty, sympathy compel me to say nothing about a certain physical defect in her, the result of her first confinement and aggravated by the three following, known as rupture of the perineum? Would a man who never talked about his marriage secrets to strangers hit on the idea of broadcasting his wife's defects?

Impotent! It was I who constantly sought her favors, passionately, desperately; and to satisfy this passion what disgusting concessions did I not have to make! She had no reason to complain about me. But a bitch by nature, she had to run around and taste everything, even if it meant destroying her own happiness and that of her children.

"In love," said Napoleon, that excellent judge of women, "one only wins by running away." But how could a carefully guarded prisoner escape? And as for a man sentenced to death. . . .

My brain recovered after a rest, and I conceived a plan of escape from this stronghold, guarded by a termagant and the friends whom she had so successfully duped. I used cunning. I wrote a letter to the doctor in which I expressed my fear of going insane and hinted that a trip abroad might help prevent it. The doctor fell in with my suggestion, and I at once informed Marie of his opinion, against which there was no appeal.

"The doctor has ordered it!"—her very formula when she had successfully dictated to the doctor the treatment she wished him to prescribe for her.

She grew pale when she heard the news.

"I don't want to leave my country!"

"Your country? . . . Finland's your country! And as far as I know, there is nothing in Sweden that you could possibly miss. You have no relations here, no friends, no career."

"I can't possibly go. . . ."

"Why?"

She hesitated: "Because I'm afraid of you! I don't want to be left alone with you!"

"You afraid of a lamb that you lead by the nose? Cut it out! What's the real reason?"

"You're a devil, a lousy devil, and I won't stay with you unprotected!"

She must have a lover. Or else she was afraid I'd outlive her if her crimes were discovered.

I frightened her! I who crouched at her feet like a dog, who kneeled in the mud to worship her white feet, I whose lion's mane she had clipped, leaving only a few horse's bangs! I who had a turned-up mustache and turned-down collar in order to fight better against her redoubtable lovers!—I frightened her!

Her fear of me increased my fear all the more and stimulated my suspicions.

"This woman has a lover whom she hates to leave, or else she is afraid of retribution," I said to myself.

After endless discussions she wheedled a promise out of me to stay away no longer than a year.

I promised.

The will to live returned and I eagerly finished a volume of poems that was to be published in the winter following my departure.

Summer in my heart, I sang with fresh inspiration. I sang of my Adored One as she appeared to me on the day of our first meeting, a blue veil fluttering from her straw hat, a blue veil that became the flag I hoisted to the top of the mast when I sailed into stormy seas.*

One evening I read this poem to a friend. Marie listened, utterly rapt. When I had finished she burst into tears, put her arms around me, and kissed me on the forehead.

A consummate actress, she played before my friend the part of the loving wife. And the idiot regarded me from that day as a jealous nut whom heaven had blessed with the sweetest of wives.

"She loves you, old boy," my friend assured me again and again! And four years later he reminded me of this scene as a convincing proof of her fidelity.

"I swear to you, at that moment she was sincere," he reiterated.

"Sincere in her remorse, perhaps! . . . As I sang the praises of this wanton, this whore, she was transformed into a madonna! . . . Of course, of course!"

Don't you believe it, mister!

9

At last her friends cleared out of the house.

The last one, the pretty one, had disappeared in the company of a well-known scientist who had returned from an expedition with four decorations and an assured future. Without a penny to her name the fair lady who had lived in my house free, seized the opportunity, leeched on to the poor boy, who had been living a celibate life for a whole year, seduced him one black night in a cab, where for some reason or other she found herself with him, and forced him into marrying her by making a scandalous scene

* This poem, "Sailing" ("Segling"), appeared in Strindberg's *Poems in Verse and Prose*, published in 1883.—ED.

in a third house to which they had both been invited. As soon as she felt sure of her position, she dropped her mask, and at a party where she got drunk and forgot herself she called Marie a degenerate. A colleague, who happened to hear the remark, thought it his duty to tell me at once.

Marie, with a few words, proved that the accusation was ridiculous, and in the future my door was closed to the lady, although this meant the loss of my old scientist friend forever.

Although I was not sufficiently curious to go more deeply into the meaning of the word "degenerate," it left its sting in my bleeding flesh. New insults, uttered by the same impure lips, referred to the suspicious life Marie had led during her tour in Finland. My old suspicions arose with fresh vigor. Her miscarriage, our conversation on fatalism, the way she let me carry on in our most intimate moments—all these things strengthened my intention to leave the country.

Having seen what use she could make of a sick poet, Marie transformed herself into a sister of mercy, a nurse, and, if required, an insane-asylum orderly.

She wove a martyr's crown for her own head, acted with absolute independence behind my back and, as I discovered later on, went so far as to borrow money from my friends in my name. At the same time, valuable pieces of furniture disappeared from our house and were carted to Adventuress Number One to be sold by the latter.

All this aroused my attention, and for the first time I put this question to myself: "Could Marie have secret expenses for things I didn't know about? Was this the cause for those secret sales? The cause of the enormous housekeeping expenditures? And if this was the cause, what was the object?"

I was now enjoying the income of a government minister, more than that of a Swedish general, and yet I led a miserable life and felt as if my feet were chained to an iron ball. But we lived very simply. We ate like petit bourgeois;

the food was cooked so badly that it was at times inedible. We drank like workingmen, ale and schnapps; our cognac was of the worst kind—we even had a reputation for the poor cognac we served. I smoked nothing but a pipe, never had any recreation except about once a month when I spent an evening with the boys to rouse myself.

Only once, when I was beside myself with anger, did I decide to look into the matter. I asked an experienced lady for advice. She laughed when I asked her whether our household expenses were not rather high; she told me that we must be mad.

I had every reason therefore to believe in extraordinary and secret expenditures. But the object? Relations? Friends? Lovers? Nobody cares to enlighten a husband; everybody for some strange reason is in league with the adulteress.

After endless preparations the date of our departure was fixed. But now a new difficulty arose, a difficulty that I had long foreseen and that was accompanied by a whole series of tearful scenes. The spaniel was still alive and kicking. How much annoyance it had caused me already! Especially as so much attention was devoted to him that the children were habitually neglected.

However, the day dawned when to my inexpressible joy Marie's idol and my evil genius, the old, diseased, half-rotten, stinking dog was to end its days. Marie herself, I was convinced of it, now desired its death, and only the thought of the innocent pleasure that its disappearance would give me led her to postpone the "dog question" again and again and invent fresh annoyances to make me pay through the nose for the forthcoming days of bliss.

But at last she arranged a farewell feast, staged heart-rending scenes, had a chicken killed, of which I was served the bones since I was in such poor health, and then she went to town, taking the monster with her.

After two days' absence she announced her return in a few cold words. What else could a "murderer" expect?

Drunk with happiness, freed of six years' bitterness, I went to the dock to meet her, expecting to find her alone. She received me as if I were a poisoner, huge tears in her eyes, and when I approached to kiss her, she pushed me away. Carrying in her arms a large parcel of extraordinary shape, she walked on slowly, as if she were marching behind a hearse, in a slow rhythm as if to the strains of some unheard funeral march.

The parcel held the corpse! My God! the funeral ceremony had been reserved for me, the last blow of fate! I had to get a man to make the coffin and two men to dig a grave, and I was compelled to be present at a distance for the obsequies of the murdered innocent. It was most touching, most enlightening! Marie sank into a mood of somber piety and prayed to God for the victim and its slayer. Amid the laughter of the onlookers she placed a cross on the grave, the cross of the Savior who had—at last—delivered me from a monster, innocent in itself but terrible as embodiment and instrument of the malice of a woman who lacked the courage to openly persecute her husband.

After a few days of profound mourning, during which she refused to kiss me she couldn't possibly kiss a poisoner!—we left for Paris.

PART FOUR

1

My main destination was Paris, where I hoped to meet old friends who were familiar with my eccentricities, acquaintances who knew all about my impulses, my whims, my paradoxes, my recklessness, and were consequently in a position to gauge accurately the present state of my mind. In addition to this, some of the foremost Scandinavian writers had just taken up permanent residence in Paris, and I meant to claim their protection in order to defy Marie's sinister schemes, which aimed at nothing less than having me committed to a lunatic asylum.

During the whole journey she continued to be hostile and, when there was no one around, treated me as altogether beneath contempt. She was always lost in thought, absent-minded, indifferent. In vain I took her sightseeing in the towns where we were forced to spend the nights; she took no interest in anything, saw nothing, hardly listened to me. My attentions bored her; she seemed to be fretting for something. But for what? Not for the country where she had suffered, where she did not have a single friend! But for a lover, perhaps?

During the whole time she behaved like the most impractical and ignorant of women. She displayed none of the qualities of the organizer and manager, of which she had boasted so much. She insisted on staying at the most expensive hotels, and for the sake of one night she often had all the furniture rearranged, she demanded to see the hotel proprietor for a badly served cup of tea, she stormed up

and down the halls and made everyone angry at us. Insisting on lying in bed until noontime, Marie managed to
have us miss the best trains; through her carelessness
our luggage went astray; and when we left a hotel she
would generously hand out one mark in tips.

"You're a weasel, afraid of what they might say," she
said in reply to one of my remonstrances.

"And you're an ill-bred, slovenly, slatternly mess!"

It was a charming pleasure trip.

As soon as we had arrived in Paris and settled down
among my friends, who were proof against her spells, she
found that I had got the better of her and felt like a wild
animal caught in a trap. She was furious because one of
the most renowned Norwegian authors* received me
warmly and overwhelmed me with kindness. She promptly
detested him, for she sensed in him a friend who might
someday raise his voice in my favor.

One evening at a dinner for artists and writers he proposed my health, calling me the chief representative of
modern Swedish literature. Marie, poor martyred wife of
the "notorious pamphleteer and libeler" was present. The
applause and bravos of the diners, who drank to my
health, depressed her to a degree that aroused my pity,
and when the speaker tried to make me promise to stay for
at least two years in France, I could no longer resist the
sad and sorrowful expression in her eyes. To comfort her,
to give her some kind of support, I replied that I never
took an important decision without consulting my wife.
My reward was a grateful look and the sympathy of all the
women present.

But my friend remained obdurate. He urged me to pro-
long my stay, and with a fine flourish of oratory asked all
those present to support his proposition. All raised their
glasses in response.

My friend's obstinacy still seems inexplicable to me, al-

* Bjørnstjerne Bjørnson.—ED.

though I quite well understood at the time that a secret struggle was being fought between my wife and him, the reason for which I could not guess. Maybe he was better informed than I and had penetrated my secrets with his clear sightedness and instinct, since he was himself married to a woman of strange morals.

Mysteries hitherto unrevealed!

Marie did not feel at home in Paris, where her husband's worth and genius were generally acknowledged, and after three months' stay she hated the beautiful city. She was indefatigable in warning me of "the false friends who would one day bring me misfortune."

Then she found herself pregnant again, and once more hell opened before me.

But this time I had no reason to doubt that I was the father. I could pinpoint the date, and certain things reminded me of the precise moment of conception and the circumstances surrounding it.

We folded our tents and made our way to Switzerland, the French-speaking part, and no sooner had we installed ourselves in a pension, which we did to avoid all quarrels on the subject of housekeeping, than she began making up for lost time. Being alone now and without friends, I was again in her power.

From the very beginning she posed as the keeper of a harmless lunatic. She got to know the doctor, warned the proprietor and proprietress, and informed the waitresses, the servants, the other guests. I was shut off from association with intelligent people of my own kind who might understand me. At meals she revenged herself for the silence to which she had been condemned in Paris. She missed no opportunity of joining in the conversation and literally inundated us with a never-ending stream of the foolish twaddle I had rebuked her for a thousand times. And since the uncultured, commonplace crowd among whom we lived always very politely agreed with her, all I had to do was be silent and, *voilà*, she was completely convinced of her superiority.

However, she looked fragile, as if some sorrow were gnawing at her, and she treated me with dislike and contempt.

Everything I loved, she detested. She sniffed at the Alps because I admired them; she scorned the beautiful walks; she avoided being alone with me; she made a practice of anticipating my wishes so as to thwart them; she said Yes whenever I said No, and vice versa. She hated me to the point of absolute loathing.

Alone and solitary in a strange country, I had to seek her company. When we stopped talking for fear of quarreling, I had to be content with merely seeing her at my side, with feeling that I was not quite isolated.

When her pregnancy was a fact I no longer felt it necessary to be quite so careful in our most intimate relations. Since there was no excuse for turning me away, she thought of ways of stimulating me and provoking me, but when she saw my happiness and contentment after our uninhibited lovemaking, she was angry for having given me that wholesome joy.

It was too much of a good thing. My nervous symptoms were the result of sexual abstinence, first, last, and always! But simultaneously my stomach catarrh grew worse. I was so ill that I could take nothing but beef tea; I lay awake at night with terrible cramps and tortured by an unbearable thirst that I tried to relieve by drinking cold milk.

Trained by long study, my well-developed brain was thrown into confusion by contact with an inferior brain, and every attempt to bring it into tune with my wife's gave me spasms. I tried to get to know people, talk to them. But they treated me with the forbearance a sane person usually shows to a lunatic. For three months I hardly opened my lips, and at the end of that time I noticed with horror that I had almost lost my voice and, from sheer want of practice, no longer had any control of the spoken word.

As compensation, I began a brisk correspondence with my friends in Sweden. But their guarded language, their deep sympathy, their well-meant advice, plainly betrayed the opinion they had formed of my mental condition.

Marie triumphed. I was on the verge of getting soft in the head, and the first symptoms of a persecution mania showed themselves.

Mania? Did I say "mania"? But I *was* being persecuted, and consequently it was altogether logical that I thought I was being persecuted!

It was as if I were becoming a child again. Extremely feeble, I lay for hours on the sofa, my head in her lap, my arms around her waist, like Michelangelo's *Pietà*. I pressed my forehead against her bosom, she called me her child, and I chimed in, "Your child, yes." I forgot my sex in the arms of the mother who was no longer female but sexless. Sometimes she regarded me with the eyes of the conqueror, sometimes she looked at me kindly, seized with the sudden tenderness the hangman is said to feel sometimes for his victim. She was like the female spider that devours her mate immediately after having been impregnated.

While I suffered thus, Marie led a very strange life. She always remained in bed till about one o'clock. After the noon meal she went to town, frequently without any definite purpose, and did not return until supper, sometimes even later. When I was asked where my wife was, I would reply, "In town!," and the inquirer would smile furtively and walk away.

I never suspected her. I never thought of playing the spy.

After supper she remained in the drawing room, talking to strangers.

At night she often treated the maid to cognac, and I

could hear their low voices, but I could never bring myself to the degradation of listening at her door. . . .

Why not? Because there are some things one doesn't do.

Why not? Because of ideas inculcated on me by my up-bringing and a manly set of scruples.

Three months passed. Then the fact suddenly struck me that our expenditures were enormous. Now that we were living in a pension, it was easy to check them.

We paid twelve francs a day at our pension—that is, three hundred and sixty francs a month—and I had given Marie a thousand francs a month. That meant six hundred francs a month had disappeared in incidental expenses.

I asked her to account for her extravagance.

"The money went for unexpected expenses!" she exclaimed furiously.

"What! three hundred and sixty francs for budgeted expenses, and you spent six hundred francs for incidentals? Do you think I'm a fool?"

"I don't deny you've given me a thousand francs, but you spend most of it on yourself!"

I began to calculate.

"Have I? Let's see! Tobacco (very inferior quality), and cigars at one penny each: ten francs. Postage: ten francs. . . . What else?"

"Your fencing lessons!"

"I've only had one. Three francs!"

"Riding!"

"Two hours. Five francs."

"Books!"

"Books? Ten francs . . . altogether thirty-eight francs. Let us say one hundred francs. That leaves five hundred francs for incidental expenses. . . . Pretty hard to swallow!"

"Do you mean to say I'm robbing you? You—you cad!"

What could I say? Nothing at all! . . . I was a cad, and on the following day all her friends in Sweden were informed of the progress of my insanity.

And gradually the myth grew and developed. The salient characteristics of my personality became more and more unmistakable as time went on, and instead of the harmless poet, a fabulous figure was sketched, blackened, touched up until it closely resembled a criminal.

I attempted to escape to Italy where I felt sure of meeting artists and men after my own heart, but the attempt was a failure and we returned to the shores of the Lake of Geneva to await Marie's confinement. When the child was a few days old, Marie the martyr, the oppressed wife, the slave without rights, implored me to have it baptized.* She knew very well that in my controversial writings I had fought the superstition of Christianity tooth and nail and could not possibly practice the rituals of its Church.

Although she was not in the least religious herself and had not set a foot inside a church for the last ten years or been to communion for goodness knows how long, and although the only beings she prayed for were dogs, chickens, and rabbits, the thought of this baptism, which she meant to elaborate into a great festival, completely obsessed her. I had no doubt that she was motivated by the thought of my dislike of all these ceremonies that I considered insincere and that were opposed to all my convictions.

But she implored me with tears in her eyes, appealed to my kind and generous nature, and in the end I yielded to her importunity—on condition, however, that I was not expected to be present at the ceremony. She kissed my hand, thanked me effusively for what she called a mark of my affection for her, and assured me that her baby's baptism was a matter of conscience to her, a very vital matter.

The baptism took place. After her return from church, she ridiculed the "farce" in the presence of many witnesses, posed as a freethinker, made fun of the ceremonial, and even boasted that she knew nothing whatever of the faith into which her son had just been received.

* A fourth child (the third to survive infancy) was born to Siri and Strindberg on April 3, 1884.—ED.

Having had her way, she could afford to laugh at the whole business. The "vital matter" transformed itself into a victory over me, a victory that served to strengthen the hands of my adversaries.

Once again I had humiliated myself, laid myself open to attack, in order to humor the caprice of a power-mad woman.

But my cup was not yet full. A Scandinavian lady appeared on the scene, full of that nonsense called woman's emancipation. When she and Marie became friends, what chance did I stand?

She brought with her the pitiable book of a castrated writer who, rejected and disavowed by all parties, became a traitor to his own sex by embracing the cause of all the bluestockings in the civilized world. After having read *Man and Woman* by Emile de Girardin, I, for my part, could foresee all the results of this women's movement.

To depose man and put woman in his place and return to the matriarchy, to dethrone the true lord of the world who created civilization, spread the blessings of culture, who fathered all the great thoughts, the arts, the professions, all that is great and beautiful in the world, and crown woman who, with few exceptions and those, insignificant ones, has not shared in the great work of civilization, was in my mind a direct challenge to my sex. The very thought of having to witness the recognition and apotheosis of these intelligences of the Bronze Age, these anthropoids, these semi-apes, this pack of pestilent animals, roused my manhood. And a strange fact worth nothing was that I was cured of my illness, cured through my intense repugnance to an enemy, who, though intellectually inferior, was more than a match because she totally lacked any moral code.

I take this very seriously, since in a tribal war the less honorable, the more degenerate comes out on top. Man's prospects of winning the battle are very dubious, considering his inborn respect for woman—to say nothing of the privileges he bestows on her by being the breadwinner and giving her leisure time to prepare her battle plans. I armed myself for this new war and planned a book that in my mind would be a gauntlet flung right in the face of the emancipated women, those fools who demanded freedom at the price of man's bondage.

Spring approached and we changed our pension. Our new abode was a kind of purgatory where I was continually watched by twenty-five women who furnished me with necessary copy for my polemic against these poachers on men's rights.

In three months' time the book was ready for publication. It was a collection of stories* of matrimonial life, with an introduction in which I voiced a great number of disagreeable home truths along this line:

Woman is not a slave by any stretch of the imagination, for she and her children are supported by her husband's work. She is not oppressed, for nature has ordained that she should live under the protection of her husband while she fulfills her mission in life as a mother. Woman is not man's equal in the realm of intellect, and man is not her equal when it comes to bearing children. She is not essential to the great work of civilization, since man understands its tasks and purposes better than she does. Evolution teaches us that the greater the difference between the sexes, the stronger and more fit will be the resulting offspring. Consequently "masculinism" in woman, the equality of the sexes, is a retrogression and an utter absurdity, the last dream of romantic and idealistic socialism.†

* *Married* (*Giftas*) was published in the fall of 1884.—ED.

† Strindberg lost his socialist and democratic sympathies during 1886–87, mainly because of the controversy surrounding his position on woman's emancipation. The young advanced thinkers of the time usually believed in both democracy and feminism. When Strindberg came out strongly against feminism and Ibsenism many of his admirers deserted him. Then the aristocratic

Woman, man's necessary appendage, the spiritual crea-
tion of man, has no right to the privileges of her husband,
since she constitutes "the other half" only by virtue of her
numbers; comparatively, she is merely the sixth part of a
sixth. She should not, therefore, invade the labor market,
and man for his part must be responsible for the support of
his wife and family. And the fact should be stressed that
every time a woman wrests a job from a man, there is
inevitably one more old maid or prostitute.

One can estimate the rage of the "masculinists" and the
formidableness of their party when one realizes that they
could demand the confiscation of my book and bring a
lawsuit against me.

But for all their cleverness, they did not succeed in
bringing off their stratagem of masking their attack by
charging me with blaspheming against religion, for the
nonsense spouted by the sexless had already been raised
to the rank of religion.*

Under those circumstances, Marie said she was absolutely opposed to my going back to Sweden, since my
resources would not permit me to take my whole family.
What really upset her was that I might escape from her
strict guardianship and, worse still, that my appearance in
court, before the public, would give the lie to the rumors

---

side of his nature came to the fore. He had already abandoned
his socialist views—for the time being—when he first read
Nietzsche in the summer of 1888.—ED.

* In his short story "The Wages of Virtue" in *Married* Strindberg referred to Holy Communion as "a shameless hoax acted
out with Högstedt's Piccardo wine at 65 öre a bottle and
Lettström's cornmeal oblates at one crown per pound, which
the priest represents as being the flesh and blood of the rabble-
rouser Jesus of Nazareth who was executed 1800 years ago."
Under pressure from Queen Sophie, the Swedish Government
in 1884 brought charges of blasphemy against Strindberg's publisher. Strindberg returned to Stockholm to stand trial with his
publisher. After deliberating four hours the jury brought in a
verdict of not guilty.—ED.

concerning my mental condition that she had so sedulously disseminated.

She pleaded illness, without being able to say exactly what was the matter, and stayed in bed. Nevertheless I decided to appear personally in court and left for Sweden.

The letters that I wrote to her during the following sad weeks, while I was threatened with two years' penal servitude, were full of love, love rekindled by distance and a forced celibacy. My overwrought brain cast glamor over her fragile form, wove a resplendent halo around her sweet face, while abstinence and longing clothed her with the white garments of the guardian angel. Everything that was base, ugly, evil disappeared; the madonna of my first love dream reappeared. It went so far that I admitted to an old journalist friend "that the influence of a good woman had made me more humble and pure-minded." Did this confession make the rounds of the Scandinavian papers? You may be sure it did!

And did she, the infamous wife, laugh when she read it? Well, at any rate, the public got its money's worth.

Marie's replies to my love letters bore witness to the keen interest she took in the financial side of the question. But as the ovations I received in the theater, in the street, and in court increased, she changed her attitude, called the judges stupid, and regretted that she was not a member of the jury.

She met my ardent declarations of love with watchful reserve, refused to admit anything, and confined herself to the repetition of the words "agree and understand one another," and blamed my failure to understand her for the catastrophes of our marriage. And I could swear that she herself never understood a single word of the language of her learned author.

Anyway, among her letters there was one that reawakened my old suspicions. So I let her know that if I was fortunate enough to escape the meshes of the law, I would like to settle down in some foreign country.

This upset her. She rebuked me, threatened me with the loss of her love, appealed to my pity, groveled on the ground, evoked the memory of my mother, and confessed that the thought of never again seeing her country (by which she did *not* mean Finland!) sent cold shudders down her spine and would kill her.

Now, why cold shudders at that thought?

To this day I still don't know.

Finally I was acquitted by the jury. A banquet was given in my honor, and—oh, sublime irony!—Marie's health was drunk "because she had persuaded me to appear personally before my judges."

That was superb!

As soon as possible I returned to Geneva, where my family had lived during my absence. To my great surprise Marie, whom I had believed to be ill and in bed, met me at the station. She looked well and happy but seemed a trifle absent-minded.

I soon recovered my spirits, and the evening and night which followed fully compensated me for all the harassments I had endured during the past weeks.

On the following day I discovered that we were living in a boardinghouse patronized mainly by students and prostitutes. While listening to their jokes, it came home to me with a bang that Marie had found pleasure in drinking and playing cards with these shady characters. The vulgar tone and the shocking intimacies pained me. Marie posed to the students as the little mother (her old game), and she had become the bosom friend of the most objectionable of the women, whom she introduced to me—a slut who came down to dinner roaring drunk.

And in this brothel my children had lived for six weeks! And they didn't notice a thing, had not the slightest prejudice. And her illness—simulated—had not prevented her from taking part in the dubious amusements of this disreputable company.

She dismissed all my remonstrances and made it clear

what she thought of me. I was jealous, conservative, snobbish! . . . And again we went at each other full tilt!

2

A new bone of contention appeared on the scene: the question of the education of the children. The nurse, an uneducated country girl as stupid as they come, was made their governess and, in collusion with the mother, committed the most outrageous follies. The two women, extremely lazy both of them, liked to stay in bed until late in the morning. Consequently, the children were obliged to stay in bed also, no matter how wide awake they were. If they insisted on getting up, they were punished. As soon as I became aware of this state of things, I interfered. Without a word of warning I sounded reveille in the nursery and was greeted with shouts of delight as a liberator. My wife invoked the principle of personal freedom—which according to her meant obstructing the freedom of others. I ignored her.

The monomania of weak and inferior brains that desire to equalize what can never be equal raised havoc in my family. My elder daughter, a precocious child, had for years been allowed to play with my illustrated books and had besides enjoyed many of the privileges usually enjoyed by the firstborn. Because I would not extend the same privileges to the younger one, who had no idea of how to handle an expensive book, I was accused of being unfair.

"There ought to be no difference whatever," she said.

"No difference? Not even in the quality of clothes and shoes?"

There was no direct reply, but a contemptuous "stupid fool" shortly made up for the omission.

"To every one according to merit and ability! This for the elder, that for the younger one!"

But she refused to understand my meaning and stubbornly maintained that I was an *unjust* father who "hated" my younger daughter.

To tell the truth, I was more attached to the elder one because she awakened in me memories of the first happy days of my life, and also because she was old enough to understand things; and I may also have been influenced by the fact that the younger one was born at a time when I had grave doubts of my wife's fidelity.

The mother's "justice," I may say, evidenced itself in complete indifference to the children. She was always either out or asleep. She was a stranger to them, and they became more and more devoted to me because I sympathized with them. This aroused her jealousy, and in order to conciliate her I made a practice of letting her distribute the toys and candies I bought for them, hoping that in this way she might keep their affection.

The children were a very important part of life to me, and in my darkest moments, when I was almost broken by my isolation, contact with them bound me afresh to life and their mother. For the sake of the children the thought of divorcing my wife was unthinkable—an ominous fact, as far as I was concerned, for I was becoming more and more her abject slave.

3

The result of my attack on the strongholds of the feminists soon made itself felt. The Swiss press attacked me in such a manner that my life in Switzerland became unbearable. The sale of my books was prohibited, and I fled, hunted from town to town, to France.

But my former Paris friends had deserted me. They had become my wife's allies, and surrounded and hemmed in like a wild beast, I again changed the arena. Almost without means I at last found neutral territory in a colony of artists in the neighborhood of Paris. But I had run into a trap, and I remained caught for ten miserable months, among the worst in my life.

The society I found myself in consisted of young Scandinavian artists, recruited from professions as various as they were strange. But, worse still, there were numerous female artists—women utterly free from prejudices, completely emancipated and wildly enamored of hermaphroditic literature that convinced them that they were the equals of man. They tried to conceal their sex as far as possible by adopting certain masculine manners and habits. They smoked, drank, played billiards . . . and made love to each other.

The crowning touch!

As an alternative to utter isolation, I made friends with two of those monstrous women. One of them was a so-called literary woman, the other a dauber.* The writer

---

* The two "monstrous women" were Sofie Holten and Marie David. The former, the daughter of a Danish clergyman, was about twenty-seven years old at this time. As a painter, she is known only for her portrait of Strindberg, made in 1885. Marie David, only twenty, was the illegitimate daughter of a married woman whom the Danish critic Georg Brandes fell in love with in the 1860s. Marie liked to believe that Brandes was her real father, but he denied this; and there was no physical resemblance. Marie's mother was a very free-thinking woman who refused to abide by the rules and conventions of Christian society. She finally left her husband, taking her two youngest children with her (her husband obviously did not regard them as his) and settled in Naples, where she later became converted to Catholicism and died of tuberculosis. It was said that Marie acquired her taste for liquor when she was a mere child and her mother lay ill. All the evidence supports Strindberg in his description of her as a virtual alcoholic. And all accounts agree that she had a weak character. She eventually returned to Copenhagen and was well on her way to becoming a derelict when her relatives took charge of her and sent her to a home in the country. Then, in 1891, when Siri was being divorced from Strindberg, Marie moved in with her. Strindberg tried to get the church council handling the divorce to take the children away from Siri on the ground that the presence of Marie David created a sexually perverse atmosphere unfit for children. Marie

called on me first, as is customary when one happens to be a well-known author. My wife was jealous at once. She was anxious to win for herself this new ally of mine, who seemed sufficiently enlightened to appreciate my arguments against the half-women.

But certain events happened that made my henceforth notorious mania break out irrepressibly.

The hotel boasted of an album that contained caricatures of all the well-known Scandinavians, sketched by Scandinavian artists. My portrait was among them, adorned with a horn slyly formed out of one of my locks of hair.

The artist was one of our most intimate friends. I concluded that my wife's infidelity was an open secret; everybody knew it—everybody except myself. I asked the owner of the album for an explanation.

Marie had taken care to inform him of my mental condition soon after our arrival, and he swore that the decoration on my forehead existed in my imagination only, that there was no trace of it in the sketch, and that I had worked myself into a passion for no reason whatever. I had to be content with this explanation until I could obtain more reliable information.

One evening Marie and I were sipping our coffee in the hotel garden in the company of an old friend who had just arrived from Sweden. It was still broad daylight, and from where I sat I could watch every expression on Marie's face. The old man gave us all the latest news, and in pass-

---

sued Strindberg for libel and for assault and battery—Strindberg had once pushed her off his porch. The court found in her favor on both counts, and Strindberg was fined 498.80 crowns and threatened with imprisonment. During the years that Marie lived with Siri and the children in Finland, subsequent to the divorce, her income was eked out by money sent by one of her Danish relatives under the guise of dividends and interest from Marie's non-existent fortune. Like her mother, Marie became a convert to Catholicism, and, also like her mother, died of tuberculosis —in a cloister.—ED.

ing, he mentioned the name of the doctor who had treated my wife by giving her massages. She did not let the name pass without comment but interrupted him with a scornful, "Really! Don't tell me you know the doctor?"

"Oh yes, he's a very popular man. . . . I mean to say he enjoys a certain reputation—"

"As a Casanova," I interposed.

Marie's cheeks grew pale. A cynical smile drew up the corners of her mouth so that her teeth showed. And the conversation dragged on amid a general sense of embarrassment.

When I was left alone with my friend, I begged him to tell me frankly what he knew of those rumors that were giving me so much uneasiness. He swore a solemn oath that he knew nothing and had heard no such rumors. Finally, after persistent urging, I drew from him the following enigmatical words of comfort: "Moreover, my dear fellow, if you suspect one man, you may be sure that there are several."

That was all. But from this day on, Marie, who had till then been so fond of telling stories about the doctor and uttering his name in public that it seemed as if she were trying to get accustomed to talking about him without blushing under some compulsion that got the better of her scruples, never again alluded to him.

This disclosure acted on me like a brutal spur and I took the trouble to search my memory for similar evidence. I suddenly remembered a play that had appeared at the time of my trial for blasphemy. It shed light—dim light, I admit, but yet sufficient for me to find the channel that led to the source of those rumors.

It was a play by the famous Norwegian bluestocking, the promoter of the equality mania, and I had read it without in the least connecting it with my own case. I saw how perfectly it fit, however, once I granted the most awful assumption about my wife's reputation.

In brief, this was the story of the play:*

A photographer (the realism of my *romans à clef* had won me this designation) had married a girl of doubtful morality who had formerly been the mistress of a rich man. Secret funds she received from her former lover kept her home going and enabled her to learn her husband's profession. While she worked, her lazy husband loafed and spent his time in the cafés, drinking with boon companions.

Thus the facts had been disguised and artfully confused with the consent of the publisher, who knew well enough that Marie was a translator, but who did not know that I edited her translations gratis and paid her the entire proceeds of her work.

Matters did not improve when the unfortunate photographer discovered that his daughter, whom he idolized, had come into the world prematurely and was not his child at all, that he had been duped by his wife when she had prevailed on him to marry her.

To complete his degradation the deceived husband accepted a large sum from the old lover in lieu of damages.

In this I saw an allusion to Marie's loan that the Baron had guaranteed; it was the same guarantee that I had been compelled to countersign on our wedding day.

But I couldn't see any likeness between the illegitimate birth of the child in the play and my own case, for my little daughter was not born until two years after our marriage.

But wait a minute! . . . What about the child who died? . . . I was on the right track! . . . The poor little dead baby! . . . She whose coming had been the cause of my marriage that otherwise might never have taken place.

A not altogether sound inference but nevertheless an inference that could be drawn. Everything fitted in. Marie

* Ibsen's *The Wild Duck,* which was published in November 1884.—ED.

had visited the Baron after the divorce, he was on friendly terms with us, the walls of my home were decorated with his pictures, there was the loan, and the rest of it.

I was determined to do something about this and prepared a big scene for the afternoon. I intended to suggest that Marie should draw up an indictment, or rather a defense, that would clear us both, for both of us had been attacked by the masculinists' straw man, who doubtless had been bribed into undertaking this honorable job.

When Marie entered my room, I received her in the most friendly manner.

"What's the matter now?" she asked.

"A very serious thing that concerns us both equally."

I told her the story of the play, and added that the actor who played the part of the photographer had felt called upon to make up to resemble me.

She reflected, silently turning over thoughts, a prey to very evident excitement.

Then I began the defense.

"If it is true, tell me, and I'll forgive you. If the little one who died was indeed Gustav's baby, well—you were free at the time, only vague promises bound you to me, and you had never accepted anything from me. As for the hero of the play, he behaved in my opinion like a high-minded man; he was incapable of ruining the future prospects of his wife and daughter. The money he accepted for support of the child was nothing but a quite legitimate compensation for an injury done to him."

She listened with great attention. Her little philistine soul nibbled at the bait without, however, swallowing it. To judge from the calm that smoothed her conscience-stricken features, my assertion that she had had a right to dispose of her body as long as she had never taken money from me pleased her. And she agreed that the deceived husband was indeed high-minded. "A noble heart," she maintained. Still without the confession I was leading her toward, I approached the end of my prepared scene. I showed her the way out of the difficulty; I appealed to her for advice as to the best means of rehabilitating ourselves, suggested that we should publish our "defense" in the shape of a novel, and so cleanse ourselves before the world and our children from all those infamies. . . .

I talked for an hour. She sat at my writing table, playing nervously with my penholder without making a sound, except for a few short exclamations.

I went out, took a walk, played a game of billiards, and when I returned I found her still sitting in the same place, motionless, like a statue. I had been gone two hours.

She roused herself when she heard my footsteps.

"You were setting a trap for me!" she said.

"Not at all! Do you think I want to lose the mother of my children forever?"

"I consider you capable of anything. You want to be rid of me. You made an attempt some time ago when you introduced me to Mr. Y. . . ." She mentioned a name that had never before come up in this connection. "That's it! Mr. Y, who was supposed to seduce me so you could catch me in the act as an adulteress."

"What! Who told you that?"

"Helga!"

"Helga?"

She was Marie's last "friend" before we left Sweden. A lesbian's revenge!

"And you believed her?"

"Of course I did. . . . But I fooled you both, him and you!"

"You mean you betrayed me with a third party?"

"I didn't say that!"

"But you just confessed it! If you fooled both of us, you must have betrayed me! That's only logical!"

She tried to get out of this by demanding proof of *me*. Proof! . . .

But the revelation of so much treachery floored me. It surpassed the lowest depths of degradation of which I held a human heart capable. I bowed my head, I fell on my knees, I whined for mercy.

"How could you believe that woman! You believed that I wanted to be rid of you! I who have never been anything to you but a true friend, a faithful husband, I who can't live without you! You complained of my jealousy . . . while I regarded all women who run after me, trying to make love to me, as evil spirits. You believed her! . . . You believed in her!"

She was moved to compassion. All at once, yielding to a prompting to tell the truth, she confessed that she had never really believed it.

"But still you have deceived me. . . . Admit it, I'll forgive you. Deliver me from the terrible, black thoughts that torment me!"

Admit. . . .

She admitted nothing but merely confined herself to calling Mr. Y a scoundrel.

A scoundrel—my most intimate, my closest friend!

I wanted to die. Life was unbearable. . . .

During dinner she was more than kind to me. As soon as I had gone to bed, she came into my room and, sitting on the edge of my bed, stroked my hands, kissed my eyes, and at last, shaken to the very foundation of her soul, burst into uncontrollable weeping.

"Don't cry, darling. Tell me what's the matter. Let me comfort you! . . ."

She stammered unintelligible, disconnected words about my generous heart, my kindness, my forbearance, the great compassion that extended even to the worst of sinners.

What a preposterous anomaly! I accuse her of adultery, she caresses me and deluges me with praise!

But the fire had been kindled and the flames could not be extinguished.

She had deceived me!

I had to know with whom.

The following week was one of the darkest of my whole life.

I fought a desperate fight against all principles, inborn, inherited, or acquired through education, in order to obtain proof. I resolved to open Marie's letters and make sure how I stood with her. And yet, although I allowed her to open all the letters that came for me during my absence, I recoiled from tampering with that sacred law, that tacitly agreed upon and most fragile of social ordinances, the inviolability of private correspondence.

But for all that, I could not resist the temptation. A day dawned when the sacred law was forgotten. There was the letter, broken open by my trembling fingers, trembling as if they were unfolding the death warrant of my honor.

It was a letter from the adventuress, friend Number One. In mocking and contemptuous words she wrote of my insanity and concluded with a prayer to the good God that He might soon deliver "her dear Marie" from her martyrdom by extinguishing the last glimmer of my reason. After I copied the worst passages, I resealed the envelope, laid it aside, ready to hand it to my wife with the evening mail. When the time came I gave it to her and sat down by her side to watch her while she read it.

When she came to the part where the writer prayed for my death—at the top of the second page—she burst into laughter, shrill, cruel laughter.

So my Adored One saw no other way out of her difficulties than my death! It was her only hope of escape from the consequences of her indiscretions. When I was gone, she would cash in my life insurance, receive the pension due the widow of a famous writer, then either marry again or remain a gay widow all her life. . . . My Adored One! . . .

Moriturus sum, and I resolved to hasten the catastrophe by drowning myself in absinthe, my only source of happiness, and in billiards, balm to my burning brain.

Meanwhile, a fresh complication confronted me, worse,

if possible, than any of the previous ones. The authoress who had pretended to be in love with me made a conquest of Marie, and Marie became so devoted to her that people began to talk. Simultaneously, the jealousy of the authoress' former "inseparable" was aroused, which did not exactly lessen the ugly rumors.

One evening in bed, hot and excited from our embraces, Marie asked me whether I was in love with her friend. . . .

"Don't be crazy! She's disgusting—a lush! You're joking."

"I'm mad about her!" she replied. "Strange, isn't it? . . . I'm afraid to be alone with her!"

"Why?"

"I don't know! She's so delicious. . . . A wonderful body . . ."

"Really? . . ."

The following week we invited some of our Paris friends, artists without moral scruples or prejudices, and their wives.

The men came, but alone. The wives sent apologies so transparent that they amounted to insults.

Dinner degenerated into a perfect orgy. The scandalous conduct of the men nauseated me.

They treated Marie's two friends as if they were prostitutes, and when everyone was more or less intoxicated I saw my wife letting herself be kissed repeatedly by a lieutenant.

I waved my billiard cue above their heads and demanded an explanation.

"He's a childhood friend, a relative! Don't make yourself ridiculous, my poor darling," she riposted. "Besides, it's an old Russian custom to kiss in public, and we Finns are Russian subjects."

"Rubbish!" exclaimed one of the guests. "Those two relatives! Never on your life!"

I nearly committed murder. I—

The thought of leaving my children without father and mother arrested my arm.

When I was alone with Marie, I let her have it.

"Whore!"

"Why?"

"Because you let yourself be treated like one."

"Don't tell me you're jealous?"

"That's right. I'm jealous. Jealous of my honor, the dignity of my family, the reputation of my wife, the future of my children! Because of your disgusting conduct we're ostracized by all decent women. Letting yourself be kissed like that in public by a stranger! You know what you are? A slut. You don't see, don't hear, don't understand what you're doing! You're completely lacking a sense of duty! If you don't change for the better, darling, I'll have you put in a cage. And to begin with, I forbid you to have anything more to do with those two women!"

"It's all your fault! You egged me on!"

"I wanted to see how far you would go! A trap to catch you red-handed."

"See how far I would go! I know what you suspect about me and my friends, but do you have any proof?"

"Proof, no! But I've heard your cynical confessions. And didn't one of your friends admit that in her own country she would fall into the hands of the law?"

"I thought you denied the existence of vice!"

"I don't care how your friends amuse themselves so long as their games don't interfere with the welfare of my family. However, from the moment that their 'peculiarities,' if you prefer this word, threaten to injure us, they are, as far as we are concerned, criminal acts. True, as a philosopher, I don't admit the existence of vice but only of physical and moral defects. And when this unnatural 'vice' was discussed only recently in the French Parliament, all the French physicians of note were of the opinion that it was not the province of the law to interfere in these matters, except in cases where citizens incurred some harm."

I might as well have preached to a stone wall. How could I hope to make this woman, who acknowledged no other law than her animal instincts, grasp a philosophical distinction!

To be quite sure of the facts, I wrote to a friend in Paris and asked him to tell me the plain truth.

In his reply, which was very candid, he told me that my wife's perverse tendencies were no secret in Scandinavia and that the two Danish women were well-known lesbians in Paris, where they frequented the lesbian hangouts.

In debt at our hotel and without money, we were unable to move. Fortunately, the two Danish ladies got into trouble with the peasants after seducing a very beautiful girl and were compelled to leave town. But since we had known them for eight months, an abrupt termination of our friendship was impossible. Moreover, they belonged to good families, were well educated, and they had been my comrades in time of trouble, and I resolved to grant them a retreat with honors. A farewell banquet was therefore arranged in the studio of one of the young artists.

At dessert, when every one was more or less floating on wine, Marie, overcome by her feelings, rose to sing a romanza she had set to the well-known song in *Mignon*. In it she bade farewell to her friend.

She sang with fire and genuine feeling, her almond-shaped eyes were full of tears and glowed softly in the reflection of the candlelight. She opened her heart so that even I was touched and charmed. There was a naïveté, an ingenuousness in this woman's love song to a woman, so pathetic that it kept all unchaste thoughts at bay. Strange, but she didn't look at all like a man-woman. No, she was the loving, tender woman, mysterious, unfathomable.

And you should have seen the object of her tenderness! A red-haired woman, with masculine features, a hooked nose, a massive chin, yellow eyes, cheeks bloated from drinking, a flat chest, crooked fingers—a truly hideous woman. A farmhand would not have looked at her.

When she had finished her song, Marie sat down by the side of this freak. The latter rose, took Marie's head in her two hands and, instead of kissing her, sucked her lips and filled her mouth with them. That at least was pure and unadulterated sensuality, I said to myself, and saying "skål" to her, I drank with the redheaded monster till she was dead drunk.

She stumbled to her knees, looked at me with large, bewildered eyes, and, her body piled up against the wall, she went on hiccoughing and laughing idiotically. I had never before seen such ugliness in human shape. From that moment on, my thoughts about women's emancipation remained fixed and firm.

The banquet ended with a row in the street. The painter's girl climbed up on a road sign and, between vomitings, howled like a wolf. The next morning the two Danes left.

Marie passed through a terrible crisis and I was genuinely sorry for her. Her longing for her friend, her sufferings were unmistakable—a genuine instance of unhappy love. She went for solitary walks in the woods, sang love songs, visited the favorite haunts of her friends, exhibited every symptom of a wounded heart. I began to entertain fears for her sanity. She was unhappy and I could do nothing to console her. She avoided my caresses, pushed me aside when I tried to kiss her, and my heart was full of hatred for the woman who had robbed me of my wife's love.

Perfectly unconscious of herself, even more so than usual, Marie made no secret of the identity of the person for whom she was mourning. She talked of nothing but her love and her sorrow. It was incredible!

The friends carried on a brisk correspondence in the meanwhile, and one day, beside myself because of the celibacy they had forced upon me, I seized one of the letters. It was a genuine love letter. "My darling, my little puss, my clever, delicate, tender, noble-hearted Marie; that coarse husband of yours is but a stupid brute . . . ," and so on. The letter further suggested that she should leave me, proposed ways of escape. . . .

That did it! I stood up against my rival and on that same evening—God have mercy—Marie and I fought in the moonlight. She bit my hands, I dragged her to the river to drown her like a cat—when suddenly I saw a vision of my children, which brought me to my senses.

I resolved to put an end to myself, but before doing so I determined to write the story of my life.

The first part of the book was finished when the news spread through the village that the Danish ladies had engaged rooms for the summer.

I instantly had the trunks packed and we left for German Switzerland.

4

Lovely Aargau! Sweet Arcady, where the postmaster tends the flocks, where the colonel drives the only cab, where the young girls are virgins when they marry, and the young men shoot at targets and play the drum. Utopia! Land of golden beer and smoked sausage; birthplace of the game of ninepins, the House of Hapsburg, William Tell, rustic merrymakings and naïve songs straight from the heart, the land of pastors' wives and vicarage idylls!

Peace returned to our troubled hearts. I recovered, and Marie, weary of strife, wrapped herself in undisguised indolence. We used backgammon as a safety valve, and our conversations, so fraught with danger, were replaced by the rolling of dice. I drank good, wholesome beer instead of blood-warming wine and nerve-shattering absinthe.

The influence of our environment soon made itself felt. I was amazed to find that such serene calm could follow the storms we had weathered, that the resiliency of the mind could withstand so many shocks, that we could forget the past, that I could fancy myself the happiest husband of the most faithful of wives.

Marie, deprived of all society and friends, uncomplainingly devoted herself to her children. After a month had elapsed the little ones were dressed in clothes that she had cut out and made with her own hands. She was never impatient with them and allowed them to absorb her completely.

For the first time now I noticed a certain lassitude in her. Her love of pleasure was less pronounced; approaching middle age announced itself. How grieved she was when she lost her first tooth! Poor girl! She wept, put her arms around me, and implored me never to cease loving her. She was now thirty-seven. Her hair had grown thinner, her bosom had sunk like the waves of the sea after a storm, the stairs tired her little feet, her lungs no longer worked with the old pressure.

And I, although I had not yet reached my prime, although my virility was increasing and my health blooming, I loved her more than ever at the thought that now she would belong entirely to me and our children. She was finally mine. Shielded from temptations, surrounded by my tender care, she would grow old in the fulfillment of her duties toward her children. . . .

Her return to a more normal state of mind manifested itself in many pathetic ways. Realizing her hazardous position as the wife of a man thirty-eight years young, she did me the honor of being jealous of me. She was more particular about the details of her dress and her make-up, took care of herself during the day so that she might be fresh and able to please me in the evening.

But she need have had no fear; I was monogamous by temperament, reliably monogamous. And far from abusing the situation, I did my utmost to spare her the cruel pangs of jealousy by giving her proof after proof of my renewed love.

5

In the autumn I made up my mind to take a tour through French Switzerland. I intended to be away for three weeks, and never to stay longer than a day at any one place.

Marie, still obsessed with the idea of my shattered health, tried to dissuade me from such an exhausting trip.

"I am sure it will kill you," she repeated over and over again.

"We shall see!"

The trip was a point of honor with me, an attempt to win her back completely, to rewaken in her the love of the virile man.

I returned after incredible hardships, strong, brown and healthy.

She greeted me with a look of admiration, a challenge in her eyes, quickly followed, however, by a look of unpleasant disappointment.

I, on the other hand, hard up after three weeks' absence and abstinence, treated her as a man treats a mistress, a wife from whom he has been parted all too long. I put my arm around her waist and seized her like a conqueror, in spite of the fact that I had just finished a forty-hour journey without a break. Upset, afraid of revealing her true feelings, tortured by the fear that she would find the woman-tamer in her husband, she did not know what to say, what face to make.

When my excitement had abated a little, I noticed that she looked different than when I had left. I looked at her carefully. Her missing tooth had been replaced, and that made her look much younger. Certain details of her dress betrayed a wish to please, a polished coquetry. It aroused my attention. I soon discovered the reason in the presence of a young girl of about fourteen, with whom she was exceedingly friendly. They kissed one another, went for walks together, bathed together. . . .

There was nothing left for me to do but to take her away at once. We took rooms in a German pension on the shores of the Vierwaldstätter See.

Marie lapsed into her former ways.

A young lieutenant was staying in the pension. She made up to him, played ninepins with him, and took long, melancholy walks in the garden while I worked.

One day at dinner I noticed that they exchanged tender glances, although no words were spoken. They seemed to caress one another with their eyes. I resolved to put them to the test at once, and, suddenly thrusting my head between them, I looked straight into my wife's face. She tried to throw me off the scent by letting her eyes glide along the young man's temples until they rested on the wall where there was a huge poster advertising beer. Confused, making no sense at all, she hit upon the remark, "Is that a new brewery?"

"Yes, it is. . . . But don't think you're fooling me for one moment," I retorted.

She bent her neck as if I had pulled in the reins, sat silent, consternated.

Two days later in the evening, on the pretext of fatigue, she kissed me goodnight and left the room. I too went to bed and, after reading for a little while, fell asleep.

I awoke with a start. Someone was playing the piano in the drawing room. A voice was singing—Marie's voice.

I arose and called the children's nurse.

"Go and tell your mistress to go to bed at once," I said. "Tell her that if she refuses I shall come down myself with my cane and teach her decent behavior, even if I have to thrash her in public."

Marie came upstairs at once. She seemed ashamed, and with an air of injured innocence she asked me why I had sent such an extraordinary message. Why would I not allow her to stay in the drawing room, since there were other ladies present?

"That's not what riles me. I don't care if you stay in the drawing room. What I object to is your sly way of getting rid of me whenever you want to be there by yourself."

"If you insist, very well, I'll go to bed."

This innocence, this sudden submission! . . . What had happened?

Winter had arrived in good earnest. There was an abundance of snow, the sky was leaden, everybody had left. We were the last guests in the modest hotel, and because of the cold we took our meals in the large public dining room of the restaurant.

One morning at breakfast, a strong thickset, handsome man, a butler or valet to judge by appearances, sat down at one of the tables and ordered a glass of wine.

In her usual free and easy manner, Marie carefully looked him over, measured his body with her eyes, and drifted into a reverie. The man went away, confused and flattered by her attention.

"My, what a handsome man," she remarked, turning to the host.

"He used to be my porter."

"Really, now. Unusually good-looking for his class! The way he carried himself, I mean. Yes, very handsome!"

And she went into details, praising his manly good looks in terms that amazed the hotel proprietor.

On the following morning the dashing ex-porter was already in his place when we entered. Dressed in his Sunday best, hair and beard trimmed, he appeared to be fully aware of his conquest. He bowed; my wife acknowledged his bow with a graceful bending of her head; he squared his shoulders and gave himself the airs of a Napoleon.

He returned on the third day, determined to break the ice. He started a polite and gallant conversation of the sort one might have on back porches, all the while addressing himself directly to my wife without wasting any time over the usual trick of first ingratiating himself with the husband.

It was incredible!

But the plain fact was that Marie, flattered by the attention, allowed herself to be drawn into this dear conversation in the presence of her husband and children.

Once more I tried to open her eyes, begged her to be more careful of her reputation. And once again all I got for my efforts was her usual retort about my "nasty mind."

A second Apollo came to the rescue. He was the village tobacconist, a fat man, at whose shop Marie was in the habit of making small purchases. More shrewd than the porter, he tried to make friends with me first; he was of a more enterprising nature. At the first meeting he stared impudently at Marie and loudly exclaimed to our host, "My God, what a good-looking family."

Marie's heart caught fire, and the village beau returned night after night.

One evening he was drunk and more insolent than usual. He approached Marie while we were playing backgammon, leaned over her, and asked her to explain the rules of the game to him. I answered as civilly as I could under the circumstances, and the worthy man returned to his seat. Marie, more tender-hearted than I, felt obligated to make amends for my rudeness. She turned to him with the first question that came to her mind. "Do you play billiards?" she said.

"No, madame. That is, I play badly. . . ."

He rose again, approached a step or two, and offered me a cigarette. I declined.

Then he turned to Marie. "Perhaps you, madame?"

Fortunately for her, for the tobacconist, and for my family, she too declined. But she almost purred as she did it.

How could this man offer a respectable lady a cigarette in a restaurant and in the presence of her husband? Was I a jealous fool? Or was my wife's conduct so scandalous that she excited the desire of the nearest man, whoever he might be?

We had a scene in our room, I regarded her as a sleepwalker whom I had to awaken before the worst happened. She was walking straight to her doom without being in the least aware of it. I drew up a table of contents of her sins, old and new, and minutely analyzed her conduct.

Without a word, pale-faced, sunken-eyed, she listened until I had finished. Then she rose and went downstairs to bed. But this time—for the first time in my life—I fell so low as to spy on her movements. I crept downstairs, slipped unhesitatingly to her bedroom door, and put my eye against the keyhole. The rich glow of the lamp fell on the children's nurse, who sat opposite the door right in my field of vision. Marie was pacing the room excitedly, vehemently denouncing my unfounded suspicions, carrying on as if she were the accused conducting her defense. She repeated every remark I had made about her as if she wanted to rid herself of them by spitting on them.

"And I'm innocent! Absolutely innocent! . . . Oh, but let me tell you, it wasn't that I haven't had opportunities to do something wild and crazy. . . ."

She produced two glasses and a bottle of beer, and they drank together. They sat down side by side and Marie virtually undressed the maid with her eyes. Closer and closer she moved to the girl, put her head on the well-developed breast of this new "friend," slipped her arm around her waist and begged to be kissed. . . .

Poor Marie! Poor, unhappy woman, seeking comfort far from me, who alone could set her mind at rest and give her peace. All of a sudden she drew herself up, listened, and pointed toward the door.

"Someone's there!"

I slipped away.

When I returned to my observation post, I noticed that Marie was half undressed, exposing her shoulders to the gaze of the girl, who, however, didn't seem especially interested. Then she resumed her defense.

"It's absolutely certain he's crazy! I shouldn't be surprised if he tried to poison me. . . . I suffer unbearable pains in my stomach. . . . But no. . . . I wouldn't dare believe that. . . . Perhaps I ought to fly to Finland. . . . What do you think? . . . Only it would kill him, he loves the children so much. . . ."

What was this, if not the harping of a sick conscience? . . . Stung with remorse, she was terror-stricken and sought refuge on the bosom of a woman! She was a perverted child, an unfaithful wife, a criminal—but, above all, an unhappy, tortured woman.

I lay awake all night, a prey to my tormenting thoughts. At two o'clock in the morning I heard her moaning in her sleep, moaning in a terrifying way. Full of pity, I knocked on the wall to dispel the ghosts that haunted her. It was not the first time.

She thanked me on the following morning for having helped her. I petted her, begged her to tell me, her best friend, everything.

"Tell you what? . . . I have nothing to tell."

I would have forgiven her for whatever crime she had confessed to me at that moment. I felt so sorry for her. I loved her with such an infinite love, in spite of, or perhaps because of, all the misery she had wrought. She was an unhappy, unfortunate human being. But instead of delivering me once and for all from the terrible doubts and suspicions that haunted me, she resisted me savagely. She was herself so far gone as to believe that I was insane. The instinct for self-preservation had forced her to build up a melodramatic story that bore some resemblance to the facts and behind which she could shield herself from the attacks of her anguished conscience.

6

After the New Year we made our way toward Germany. We halted on the shores of the Boden See.

In Germany, the land of militarism, where the patriarchal system is still in full force, Marie felt completely lost. No one would listen to her silly talk about alleged women's rights. Here young girls had just been forbidden to attend the university; here the dowry of a woman who marries an officer of the army has to be deposited with the War Office as the inalienable property of the family; here all government appointments are reserved for the man, the breadwinner of the family.*

Marie struggled and fought as if she were caught in an ambush. On her first attempt to hoodwink me she was severely taken to task by the women in the group. For the first time I found the fair sex entirely on my side, and poor little Marie had to lick the dust. Friendly chats with the officers braced me. Their manner and behavior influenced mine in accordance with the law of adaptation, and after ten years of spiritual emasculation my manhood reasserted itself.

I let my hair grow as it liked and combed away the bangs on which Marie had insisted. My voice, which had grown thin and reedy from everlastingly baby-talking to an hysterical woman, regained its former resonance. The

* By contrast, in Sweden women had been given in 1845 equal rights of inheritance with men, in 1846 the right to engage in business on their own, in the 1850s the right to enter public service, in 1863 the right to vote in local elections, in 1870 the right to enter the university to study medicine and to practice it, and in 1873 the right to take any academic examination. See also the footnotes to pages 204 and 229.—ED.

hollows in my cheeks filled out, and although I was now beginning my fortieth year, my whole physique gained in strength and vigor.

I was on friendly terms with all the women in the house and soon fell into the habit of taking a very active part in the conversation, while Marie, poor, unpopular Marie, had to play second fiddle.

She began to be afraid of me. One morning, for the first time in the six years of our marriage, she appeared fully dressed in my bedroom before I was up. I could not understand this sudden change. We had a stormy scene, during which she let it out of the bag that she was jealous of the girl who came into my room every morning to light the fire in my stove.

"And I detest your new ways!" she exclaimed. "I hate this so-called manliness and I loathe you when you put on airs!"

Well, I knew that it had always been the page, the lapdog, the weakling, "her child" that she loved. The married woman never loves the man in her husband, however much she may admire it elsewhere.

I became more and more popular with the women. I sought their society. My whole nature was expanding in the friendly warmth that radiated from women, real women who inspired respectful love, the unconscious surrender of the man by which he pays tribute to the womanly woman.

But at about that time we began discussing our return home to Sweden. My old suspicions rose up anew. I shrank from the renewal of old relations with former friends, some of whom might quite conceivably have been my wife's lovers. To put an end to my doubts, I determined to cross-examine her minutely. I had already sent letters to friends in Sweden inquiring about the truth of the sly rumors that were being spread about my wife's unfaithfulness, but, as was to be expected, I was unable to elicit a candid statement.

Everybody pitied the "mother," only the "mother." Who cared whether the "father" would be destroyed by ridicule?

In my investigation of the possibilities open to me, I hit upon the idea of making use of the resources of the new science of psychology and mind-reading. I introduced it into our evening amusements, as if it were a game, employing the manipulations of Bishof* and his colleagues. Marie was on her guard. She charged me with being a spiritualist; sarcastically called me a superstitious free-thinker; overwhelmed me with abusive words, and badly chosen ones, at that—in fact, used every means in her power to divert me from these practices, which she realized boded her no good.

I pretended to give in and dropped hypnotism, but only to attack her face to face when she was least prepared.

The opportunity came one evening when we were sitting alone in the dining room, facing each other. I gradually led the conversation to gymnastics. I succeeded in interesting her so much that she was carried along and, compelled either by my will power or the association of ideas I had aroused in her mind, she mentioned massage. This suggested the pain caused by the treatment, and remembering her own experience with her doctor she exclaimed, "Oh yes, massaging, hurts—really. I can still feel the pain now when I think of—"

That was enough. She bowed her head to hide her pallor. Her lips moved as if she were trying to say something different. Her eyelids flickered. A terrible silence followed, which I prolonged as much as possible. This was the train of thought that I had set in motion and steered, full steam ahead, in the intended direction. In vain she tried to put on the brake. The abyss lay before her; she

---

* Bishop (not Bishof), a mesmerist and mind-reader, enjoyed a vogue in Sweden in 1884, holding séances in the homes of the aristocracy and even at the summer palace, where the King and the court participated.—ED.

could not stop the engine. With a superhuman effort she broke from the grip of my eyes and rushed out of the room.

The blow had struck home.

She returned a few minutes later, her face looking more calm and reposed. Under pretense of demonstrating to me the beneficial effect of massage, she came behind my chair and stroked my forehead. Unfortunately for her, the little scene was acted before a mirror. A furtive glance, and I could see a pale ghost, with wild and terrified eyes that scrutinized my features—and our searching glances met.

Contrary to her habit, she came and sat on my knee, put her arms round me lovingly, and murmured that she was so tired she felt dizzy.

"You must have been a bad girl today. Why else would you be petting me like this?"

She hid her face on my chest, kissed me and went out of the room, bidding me goodnight.

All right, I know perfectly well that this isn't the sort of evidence to satisfy a jury, but it was enough for me, who knew her so well.

All the more, since only a short time ago my brother-in-law had thrown that masseur out of his house because of the way he had behaved with my sister.

7

Not for anything in the world would I return to my own country, where I would inevitably find myself involved in degrading situations. I would be compelled to associate daily with men suspected of being my wife's lovers. To escape the ridicule that the duped husband is invariably subject to, I fled to Vienna.

Alone in my hotel, I was haunted by the vision of my former beloved. Utterly unable to work, I began to write to her—two letters every day, which were like so many love letters. The strange town affected me like a tomb. I moved through the throng like a phantom. But soon my imagination began to fill this solitude with people. I invented a romantic story for the sole reason of introducing Marie into this dreary desert. The inert matter of the buildings, the dead people sprang to life. I pictured her as a famous singer, and to lend my dream a semblance of reality and make of the fine city a more convincing background for her, I made the acquaintance of the director of the conservatory of music. I, the blasé man who detested the theater, went to the opera or to a concert every night. Everything interested me intensely because I reported everything to her. No sooner had I arrived at my hotel than I sat down and gave her a minute description of how Miss So-and-so sang her big aria tonight, and I drew comparisons that were invariably in her favor.

If I went to the art galleries, I saw her in every room. I spent an hour before the Venus of Guido Reni in the Belvedere because she was so like my Adored One. And in the end my longing for her body grew so irresistible that I packed my bags and returned home as fast as the express could carry me. I was bewitched; there was no means of escape from her.

Beautiful homecoming!

My love letters seemed to have rekindled Marie's love. I ran up the little garden path to meet her. I covered her face with passionate kisses, and taking her head between my hands, I said, "You really can work magic, you little witch, can't you?"

"What? Don't tell me your journey was an attempt to get away?"

"Yes, an attempt! But you are stronger than I. . . . I surrender!"

On my writing table stood a bouquet of red roses.

"You do love me a little, you little monster, don't you?"

She was as shy as a young girl—she blushed. . . . It was all over with me—my honor, my efforts to break the chains that bound me and that I longed for all too much when I was free from them.

A whole month of springtime in our hearts. We chirruped like starlings, kissed, hugged, embraced each other endlessly, played and sang duets at the piano, played backgammon—the most beautiful days of the last five years seemed pale in comparison. Spring in our autumn! Did we never think that winter could not be far behind?

8

I was fast again in her toils, kicking and floundering. Convinced that the love philter she had given me to drink had drugged and intoxicated me, she relapsed into her former indifference. She neglected her appearance and no longer took the trouble to look her best, although I remonstrated with her, for I realized that the result of all this would be a growing coldness. Even her preference for her own sex reappeared, more dangerous and more pitiable, for now she cast her glances at minors.

One evening we had invited the commandant and his fourteen-year-old daughter, our hostess and her daughter, who was a girl of fifteen, and a third girl of about the same age to a quiet little party with music and dancing.

Toward midnight—to this day I tremble when I think of it—I saw that Marie, who had been drinking freely, had gathered the young girls around her and, devouring them with lascivious eyes, was kissing them on the lips in the way that lesbians do.

From a dark corner of the room the commandant was watching her every move hardly able to control himself. In a flash I saw the prison, penal servitude, the unavoidable scandal that we could never live down, and I threw myself into the group of young girls and broke it up by asking the girls to join in the dancing. . . .

When we were left alone I took Marie to task. We argued and stormed till daylight. Having had more liquor than was good for her, she lost her head and confessed terrible things I had never even suspected before.

Beside myself with anger, I repeated all my indictments, all my suspicions, and burst out with a new one, which struck me as quite superfluous when I thought about it afterwards.

"And this mysterious illness, these awful headaches—"

"Why, you miserable—! Are you accusing me of giving you sy—?"

I insist I had never thought of that. I had only intended to mention the symptoms of cyanide poisoning that I had observed in myself. But now all of a sudden something from the past flashed into my mind, something that at the time had seemed so improbable that it had left no permanent trace in my memory. . . .

Now my suspicions were sharpened when I remembered a certain phrase in an anonymous letter I had received a short time after Marie's divorce—"the whore of Södertälje"!

What did it mean? I had made inquiries but got no results. Was I on the track of something new?

When the Baron, Marie's first husband, met her in Södertälje, she was practically engaged to a young lieutenant, a man who was known to be not altogether healthy. Poor Gustav must have played the part of the unsuspecting friend in need. . . . And that would account for the warm gratitude she felt for him even after the divorce, when she had confessed to me that *he had delivered her from dangers.* . . . What dangers she had never mentioned.

But "the whore of Södertälje"? . . . How? . . . I thought of the retired life which the young couple led, without friends, without parties, without invitations to society—they had been ostracized by their own class.

Could it be that Marie's mother, formerly a governess

from the lower classes who had tricked a Finnish baron, Marie's father, into a marriage with her; who had fled to Sweden to escape from pressing debts; could it be that she, the widow who so cleverly concealed her poverty, had sunk so far as to sell her own daughter when they were living in Södertälje?

The old woman, still a coquette at the age of sixty, had always inspired in me mingled feelings of compassion and dislike. Stingy, pleasure-loving, with the manner of an adventuress, a veritable "man-eater," she regarded every man as an object to be exploited. She had made me support her sister, just as she had previously deceived her first son-in-law, the Baron, with a tall tale about a dowry, and then swindled her creditors to create the dowry.

Poor Marie! Her remorse, her unrest, her dark moods were rooted in that shady past. In putting old events by the side of new ones I had the key to the quarrels between mother and daughter, brutal quarrels, frequently verging on physical violence; and I could understand a hitherto incomprehensible confession that slipped out of Marie once when she said she would love to put her foot on her mother's throat!

Had her game been to silence the old woman? Probably. For the latter had threatened to ruin our lives by confessing "everything."

There could have been no doubt of Marie's dislike for her mother, to whom the Baron frequently referred as "that skunk," an invective that he never explained to me except by hinting that she had taught her daughter every trick there was for catching a husband.

All of this strengthened my determination to leave her. I had to! There was no alternative. And I left for Copenhagen to make every possible inquiry into the past of this woman to whom I had given my name and with whom I would always be associated in the future.

9

In meeting my countrymen after several years' absence, I found that they had formed very definite opinions of me. The tireless efforts of Marie and her friends had won them over and deluded them. She was a holy martyr; I was a madman, *le cocu imaginaire*.

To discuss it—! It was like beating my head against a stone wall. People listened to what I had to say with a furtive smile and stared at me as if I were a strange animal. No information was given me. I was deserted by everyone, especially by the envious ones who secretly yearned for my ruin so that they might rise over my fallen body. So I returned to my prison, where Marie met me with evident misgivings. I learned more from the expression on her face than I had learned during the whole of my sad journey.

For two months I champed at the bit. Then I fled for the fourth time, in the height of summer, this time to Switzerland. But the chain that held me was not an iron chain that I might have been able to snap but a rubber cable that stretched without breaking. The stronger the tension, the more violently was I pulled back to the starting point. Once more I returned, and now I was rewarded with her open contempt, for she was sure that my next attempt to free myself would be my death, and my death was her only hope.

That was when I fell ill, severely ill, so that I believed myself to be dying. I made up my mind to write the whole story of what I had been through. I could see plainly now that I had been in the power of a vampire, and I made up my mind to live long enough to cleanse myself of the filth with which that woman had sullied me. I wanted to live long enough to revenge myself when I had gathered from every possible source the proofs of her infidelity.

10

I hated her now with a hatred more fatal than indifference because it was the other side of love. It grew there in hiding to such an extent that I am tempted to formulate an axiom: I hated her because I loved her. It was on a Sunday, while we were dining in the summer arbor, that the electric force that had gathered during the last ten years discharged itself. I don't know what caused it. No matter! I struck her, for the first time in my life. I slapped her face repeatedly, and when she tried to defend herself I seized her wrists and forced her on her knees. She uttered a terrified scream. The temporary satisfaction I had felt at my action gave way to dismay. The children, frightened to death, cried out with fear. It was the worst moment of my miserable life! It is a crime, a most unnatural crime, to strike a woman, a mother! And in the presence of her children. . . . It seemed to me that the sun ought to hide its face. . . . I felt sick to death.

And yet there was peace in my soul, like the calm after a storm, a satisfaction such as is only derived from duty done. I regretted my action but I felt no remorse. It was merely a matter of cause and effect.

In the evening I saw her walking in the moonlit garden. I joined her; I kissed her. She did not repulse me; she burst into tears. We walked for a few minutes, then she accompanied me to my room and stayed with me, making love until midnight.

Strange marriage! In the afternoon I struck her; at night we held each other in our arms.

Strange woman who kisses her executioner with hot and willing lips!

Why had I not known it before? If I had struck her ten years ago I should now have been the happiest of husbands.

There's a piece of advice!

Remember it, fellow members of the league of deceived husbands!

But in the meantime she began planning her revenge. A few days after this incident she came into my room, began telling me a long, rambling story, and after endless digressions gave me to understand that she had once, only once, been raped. It had happened, she said, while on her theatrical tour in Finland.

My analysis had been corroborated!

Humbly she implored me not to think that it had happened more than once, not to think she had had many lovers.

That meant many times many lovers.

"Then it is true. You have deceived me, and in order to hoodwink the world you've spread this myth of my insanity. To hide your crime more completely you meant to torture me to death. You're the worst sort of scoundrel. I know that for a fact now. We've got to get a divorce!"

She threw herself at my feet, weeping bitterly, begging me to forgive her.

"Yes, all right, all right. I forgive you, but we've got to be divorced."

11

On the following day she was very quiet. On the second day she had regained her former self-possession. On the third day after the catastrophe she behaved in every respect like an innocent woman.

"Now that I have shown myself to be so generous and noble as to admit everything, I have nothing to reproach myself with."

She was more than innocent: she was a martyr who treated me with insulting condescension.

Unconscious of the consequences of her crime, she did

not understand my dilemma. If I continued to live with her, I would become a public laughingstock; if I left her, I would have nothing to live for. My life was ruined.

Ten years of martyrdom settled for with a few slaps in the face and a day of tears. It wasn't fair.

For the last time I slipped out of my home, secretly, for I had not the heart to say goodby to my children.

On a beautiful Sunday afternoon I went on board a steamer bound for Constance, having firmly decided to visit friends in France, where I would immediately set down the story of this woman, the true representative of the age of the unsexed.

At the very last moment Marie appeared on the dock, tear-stained, excited, feverish, yet pretty enough to drive me mad. But I remained cold, callous, silent, and received her treacherous kiss without returning it.

"Can't you at least say we're still friends?"

"No. Enemies for the short time I have left."

We parted.

The steamer pulled away. I watched her walking along the wharf, trying to draw me back with the magic of those eyes that had held me under their spell for so many years. She ran back and forth like a lost little dog, that awful bitch! And I waited for the moment when she would throw herself into the water. I would jump after her and we would drown together, joined in one last embrace. But she turned away and disappeared down a little side street, leaving me with a last impression of her bewitching face, her silhouette, her delicate little feet that I had allowed to trample on my throat for ten years without a cry or a murmur, except in one of my books, but even there I had misled the public by concealing the real crimes of this monster, she who had always been eulogized by her poet.

To steel my heart against grief and regret I went at once into the saloon. I sat down to dinner, but an aching lump in my throat compelled me to rise, and I went back up on deck.

I caught sight of the green hill gliding past, the green hill on which stood the white cottage with the green shutters. My little ones abided there, in that plundered nest, without protection, without means to live. . . .

An icy pang shot through my heart. I felt like the cocoon of the silkworm when the great steam engine slowly reels off the shining thread. At every stroke of the piston I grew thinner, and as the thread lengthened, the cold that chilled my heart increased.

It was death that was approaching.

I was like an embryo prematurely detached from the umbilical cord. What an indivisible living organism the family is! I had thought so at that first divorce from which I had recoiled with pangs of conscience that nearly killed me. But she, the adulteress, the murderess, she had not recoiled! . . .

At Constance I caught the train for Basel. What a wretched Sunday afternoon! If there were a God, I would beg him to preserve even my bitterest foes from such agony.

Now it was the locomotive that reeled up my intestines, my brain lobes, my nerves and arteries, all my insides, so that by the time I arrived at Basel I was a skeleton.

At Basel I was overwhelmed with an irresistible desire to revisit all those places in Switzerland we had visited together, to gladden my sad heart with memories of happy hours spent with Marie and the children.

I stayed for a week in Geneva and some days at Ouchy, haunted by my misery from hotel to hotel, without peace or rest, like a lost soul, like the Wandering Jew. I spent my nights in tears, conjuring up the little figures of my beloved children—I visited the places they had visited—I fed "their" seagulls on the Lake of Geneva—a restless ghost, a wretched phantom.

Every morning I expected a letter from Marie, but no letter came. She was too clever to furnish her enemy with written evidence. I wrote to her several times a day, love letters, forgiving her for all her crimes—but I never mailed them.

Truly I say to you, my judges, that if I could have collapsed into insanity it would have happened in those hours of keenest agony and bitterest sorrow.

Utterly exhausted, I gave my imagination free rein and wondered whether Marie's confession had not been a ruse to get rid of me and begin life all over again with someone else, her mysterious lover, the unknown stranger, or worst of all, the Danish lesbians! I saw my children in the hands of a stepfather or the clutches of a stepmother who would grow fat on the proceeds of my collected works and who would counterfeit the story of my life, seen through the eyes of that hermaphrodite who had robbed me of my wife. The instinct of self-preservation stirred within me; I conceived a cunning plan. Since it was impossible for me to work if I was not in the bosom of my family, I decided to return to them and stay with them until I had written a novel, and all the while I would be taking the most careful notes on Marie's crimes. In this way she would become the unconscious tool of my revenge, which I could throw away when I had finished the job.

With this end in view I sent her a telegram, businesslike, free from all sentimentality. I informed her that my petition for a divorce had been refused, pretended that I required a power of attorney from her, and suggested an interview at Romanshorn, on this side of the Boden See.

When I had sent the telegram, I felt relieved. On the following day I took the train and arrived on time at the appointed place. The week of suffering was a thing of the past. My heart was beating normally, my eyes shone with added luster. I drew a deep breath at the sight of the hills on the opposite shore where my children lived. The steamer approached the dock, but I couldn't see Marie. Presently I caught sight of her on the pontoon bridge, her face woebegone, ten years older. The sight of

her, suddenly grown old, wrung my heart. She walked
with dragging footsteps, her eyelids were red with weeping, her cheeks hollow, her chin drooping!

At that moment all feeling of hatred and disgust was
swamped by pity. I felt a strong temptation to take her
into my arms, but I pulled myself together, drew myself
up, and assumed the devil-may-care expression of a young-
blood who had come to some rendezvous. When I
looked at her more closely I noticed in her a strange resemblance to her Danish friend. The likeness was really
extraordinary; she had the same expression, the same pose,
the same gestures, the same way of wearing her hair.
Had the lesbian played me this last trick? Had Marie come
to me straight from the arms of her "friend"?

The memory of two incidents from the beginning of the
summer strengthened my suspicions. One day I had surprised her as she was asking a hotel proprietor in the
neighborhood if there were any rooms available in his
pension.

For whom? For what?

And then hadn't she asked me if I'd mind very much if
she went over to this pension to play a little piano in the
evenings?

Although these little details didn't constitute proof, they
did put me on my guard, and as I accompanied Marie to
the hotel I rehearsed the role I was about to play.

Depressed and ill, as she said she was, she was still cool
and self-possessed. She questioned me very closely and in-
telligently on divorce proceedings, and when she found
that I exhibited no trace of grief or emotion, she dropped
her woebegone aspect and began to treat me haughtily.

During the interview she reminded me so much of her
friend that I was tempted to ask for news of the lady. I
was especially struck by a very tragic pose, a favorite one
of her friend's, a pose which was accompanied by a certain gesture of the hand that rested on the table . . .

hah! I served her a strong wine. She drank it down in gulps and pretty soon she was staggering.

I took the opportunity to ask after the little ones. She burst into tears. She said she had been through a terrible week, with the children asking for their father from morning till night, and she didn't see how she could get along without me.

My wedding ring was no longer on my ring finger. Suddenly she noticed its absence and became terribly upset.

"Your wedding ring?" she asked.

"I sold it in Geneva. I used the money to pay a girl—to restore the balance for a while."

She grew pale.

"Then we are quits. Then—shall we make a fresh start?"

"I see. . . . So that's your idea of justice? You committed an act that had tragic consequences for the whole family. You've made me doubt the legitimacy of my children, and in that way you're guilty of having tampered with the lineage of a family. You've ruined the lives of four people: your three children of doubtful paternity and your husband, whom you have made a public laughingstock as a cuckold. Now, what are the consequences of *my* act?"

She wept. I suggested that the divorce proceedings should go on while she remained in the house as my mistress. And I would adopt the children.

"Wouldn't that be the free love you've always been dreaming of? You who have always cursed matrimony."

She reflected for a moment. My proposal didn't please her.

"Come on! Don't I remember you saying you'd like to be a governess in the house of a widower. Here's the widower for you!"

"Give me time. . . . I have to think about it. . . . But in the meantime, do you intend to come back and live with us?"

"If you ask me to."

"Any time. Just walk in."

And for the sixth time I returned to my family, my hearth and home, but this time firmly resolved to use the respite to finish my story and equip myself with detailed information about this mysterious affair. . . .

12

That's the end of the story, my Adored One. I have got my revenge. Now we're quits. . . .

September 1887–March 1888

ANCHOR BOOKS

BIOGRAPHY, AUTOBIOGRAPHY AND LETTERS

ANDRADE, E. N. da C. Rutherford and the Nature of the Atom, S35
—— Sir Isaac Newton, S42
BEETHOVEN, LUDWIG VAN Beethoven: Letters, Journals and Conversations, trans. & ed. Hamburger, A206
BENDIX, REINHARD Max Weber: An Intellectual Portrait, A281
CASALIS, GEORGES Portrait of Karl Barth, A422
COLETTE My Mother's House *and* The Vagabond, A62
DE BEER, SIR GAVIN Charles Darwin, N41
DICKINSON, EMILY Selected Poems and Letters of Emily Dickinson, ed. Linscott, A192
ESSLIN, MARTIN Brecht: The Man and His Work, A245
FULLER, MARGARET Margaret Fuller: American Romantic—A Selection from Her Writings and Correspondence, ed. Miller, A356
GATHERU, R. MUGO Child of Two Worlds, A468
GEIRINGER, KARL Brahms: His Life and Work, A245
—— Haydn, A361
GRAVES, ROBERT Good-Bye to All That, A123
GREVILLE, CHARLES CAVENDISH FULKE The Great World: Portraits and Scenes from Greville's Memoirs, ed. Kronenberger, A409
JONES, ERNEST The Life and Work of Sigmund Freud, ed. & abr. in 1 vol. Trilling & Marcus, A340
KENDALL, PAUL MURRAY Richard the Third, A455
LEWIS, W. H. The Sunset of the Splendid Century: The Life and Times of Louis Auguste de Bourbon, Duc du Maine, 1670–1736, A355
MAC DONALD, D. K. C. Faraday, Maxwell and Kelvin, S33
NEALE, J. E. Queen Elizabeth I, A105
NEWMAN, JAMES R. Science and Sensibility, A357
SHATTUCK, ROGER The Banquet Years, A238
TAYLOR, A. E. Socrates, A9

LINGUISTICS AND LANGUAGE

HALL, ROBERT A., JR. Linguistics and Your Language, A201
JESPERSEN, OTTO Growth and Structure of the English Language, A46